THE BACHELOR'S RIDE

e-book ISBN: 9781739681029

Paperback ISBN: 9781739681005

Hardcover ISBN: 9781739681012

A complete catalogue record for this book can be obtained from the British Library on request.

Printed and bound in Great Britain by Icongate, 160 Kemp House, City Road, London EC1V 2NX

THE BACHELOR'S RIDE

KOLAPO AKINOLA

ICONGATE

For Mum & Wumi

PROLOGUE

Lagos, Nigeria, January 2014

I found love; at least I called it love. When you're in love, they say you get butterflies – I felt that with Sisi. Sisi Macauley. We had great chemistry, our goals were aligned, our values mirrored each other's. We were soulmates.

One evening, about eighteen months into our courtship, I arranged a special moment. The cameraman and hired photographer were in key positions at the hotel restaurant.

Right in the heart of Lagos at Victoria Island, we'd walked into a glistening place that wrapped itself in opulence. As we arrived at the entrance, two hotel staff rushed forward, their warm smiles met ours. "You're most welcome, ma. This way, sir." They led us to the reception desk where we were received with gracious hospitality from four receptionists. It was our first time staying at the hotel. Sisi and I could not take our eyes off the stunning architectural details and the charming luxurious lobby, oozing nothing but glitz, beautified with rainbow decor that glamorously danced across it. We marvelled at the exquisite hand-paintings that hung in key places featuring contemporary African artworks.

"Baby, wow," she whispered, pointing to the polished engraved wood at the desk that matched her pale-grey dress.

"What a place," I said.

Her dress hugged her nicely without revealing her hips. I loved the touch of simplicity all over the dress.

Sisi held my hand tighter, her face blazing with excitement. "Baby, this place is beyond stunning."

"Sweet, we're in the right place," I whispered to her.

The check-in was completed in no time.

"Ma, as part of our tradition on Sundays to appreciate our wonderful guests, on behalf of the Guest Relation Management, it's our pleasure and honour to present you with a little gesture as our best-dressed guest of the day." A member of staff, standing alongside four others who lined up around us, in their colourful blazers, handed the gift over to Sisi.

Sisi's eyes were wide open. "Oh, my goodness, this is so beautiful," she said. "Thank you, thank you, thank you so much." Her eyes were brimming with tears already. She reached for my shirt's sleeve, as her tears turned to smiles of someone truly touched.

It was a tiny chocolate cake with a creamy ganache and flower. She smelled the rose and couldn't stop rendering endless praises at the hotel's gesture.

One of the staff gave me a small nod. Another winked at me. I returned the smile in disguise. My heartstrings tugged in anticipation of what was to come. "This is amazing, who would have thought hotels now give special gifts on arrivals," I said, pretentiously, as I joined her to appreciate the staff who could see the happiness shimmering inside me.

She opened the cake box briefly. A diamond ring was safely sealed beneath the cake.

We arrived at the restaurant for dinner, nearly four hours later, with the box in my pocket of course, and Sisi's favourite upcoming artist, a rising star, sang a love song and a saxophonist played her favourite tune. Her mood was upbeat, the air smelled of love.

"Heartbeat *mi*, what's going on? Oh my... Oh my God." Her eyes went big. She covered her mouth, looking startled, and against her palm, she screamed at the sight of her favourite singer.

"She's here for you, baby. For us," I said.

Her eyes were glued to mine. I whipped the cake box out. At the sight of it, she burst into laughter. "Oh... oh... oh my God," she stuttered. "You got me. You got me, baby."

The hotel staff, who were in the know, nearly twenty of them, couldn't stop smiling. One of them in tears!

Joy engulfed me, flowing through my veins. A quiet contentment spread on her beautiful face.

The gorgeous chandelier that hung above our heads, swathed in colourful lights, brightened the space. I got down on one knee with the diamond ring in my hand, as her favourite love song played. "You're everything to me, my love. You complete me. Thank you for coming into my life." I said a few more words and put a spin on it. Sweet notes for a sweetheart. "Will you spend the rest of your life with me? Will you marry me?"

Tears touched her eyes. She screamed, "Yes!" She was the happiest I'd ever seen her.

Friends and family rushed forward from their hidden spots, shouting and screaming and laughing. The joy started with us and rippled through them all. Their phone cameras were directed at our faces. "This is so sweet," someone cried. The little crowd cheered on.

Sisi smiled, as she sniffed back the tears. "I love you, babe. With my whole life. I love you so much, thank you my love."

"I love you too," I told her, as I cupped my hand around her shoulder. "So much."

We wrapped each other up in a hug and with sweet words.

NEXT DAY, we celebrated our engagement. We bumped around the city like tourists, explored the newly created parks and the sprawling Lekki Conservation Centre where a lost city was found in an abundance of glorious nature. We ambled around art galleries, squinting and tutting with authoritative ignorance and drove around a few posh residential estates in Ikoyi and Lekki to see the ongoing construction of the Eko Atlantic projects.

Two weeks after, the wedding preparations started in earnest. I'd flown back to London a few days after the engagement. Sisi remained in Lagos; she lived there.

"I'm happy I can actually start planning our big day," Sisi said, over the phone. "I mean officially. Not like how we've planned without a ring for the past six months."

"Should be fun, babe. Will you prefer we hire a wedding planner?" I asked.

"No *joor*, we can't afford to be wasting money. I know it would ease the stress but there's a joy that comes with planning by oneself. We'll be fine, baby," Sisi said, babbling on excitedly. "Guess what, I've listed some beautiful lighting, some candlesticks and the peach roses for the reception. I'm working on colour themes now. I'll tell you details later."

I laughed, enjoying her enthusiasm. We carried on for

another half an hour. Sisi had ideas from A to Z, every tiny detail to make the day perfect – the sweet decorations list, her favourite cake vendor, our first dance choreography, everything else. The whole nine yards.

"*Heartbeat mi*, one more thing I wanted to tell you. You know our area can be unsafe sometime. I can't risk my precious diamond ring being stolen, *o*, so I've stopped wearing my ring outside. I wear it when I'm indoors or outside this area. Just wanted you to know."

Sisi lived in Isolo in Lagos; the area speaks for itself. "Oh yeah, I didn't even think of that. It's OK to apply caution, babe, if that makes you comfortable," I told her.

"Thanks, babe. I know you have early start tomorrow, and I promise I'll let you off to bed after this one last gist. Guess what? You won't believe what Busola did again. Do you believe a love tank can dry up?" She laughed at her own question.

"Busola and Tosin again," I said. "Oh, hang on, what love tank?"

"It's Busola again, *o*. And her weird excuse."

I've never met these people; these imaginary people who break up every time. I sighed, wondering why Busola's excuse was different this time. "There's something fundamentally wrong between these folks. That's, like, three times already in six months."

"Exactly my point. No worries *jare*. Speak to you tomorrow, sleep well Handsome."

The next day after working hours was no different. We jumped on a call and spent the evening planning, gossiping, laughing and dreaming.

Our wedding will be so joyful, and our marriage envied by many, by God's grace, she texted after we'd ended the long call.

I can't wait to get the official kiss, I replied.

Ha-ha. Just official kiss?

Naughty you. And of course, to start the 'main' official duty. LOL, I can't wait joor. She replied with a wink.

IN THE NEXT TWO WEEKS, we'd fixed and ticked a few things off our lists: the wedding day, reception venue, vendors, and honeymoon destination. Although some of our friends and family were super anxious for our big day to come, we'd not issued official invitation cards. Sisi preferred to send them exactly two months before the wedding; it was an attempt to reduce the crowd, the Lagos crowd notoriously known for gate-crashing. I bought into it.

On Monday evening, now about four weeks after our engagement, we were speaking on the call.

"Toyo, there's something, erm. There's something I want to tell you." Her words were punctuated by heavy breathing, her voice seemingly masked with fear.

"Baby, what's the problem?"

She inhaled a sharp breath followed by a moment of silence. "Can we reduce the bridal train by two people?"

"Why?" I asked.

I heard her take a deep breath. "To keep things small, like we've always wanted."

"No, no. I think there's something else on your mind, baby," I said. "Did you have an argument with one of the guys?"

"Of course, not."

We agreed, as we had before, that ten people would be perfect: five bridesmaids, five groomsmen. And we ended the call shortly after.

On Thursday evening, Sisi texted her usual love-dope lyrics: *Baby mi, I can't live my life without you. Your kind is rare. You're one in a million! You bring beauty to my world, light up my soul. God created you just for me. My love. I can't wait for our forever.*

In the early hours of Saturday morning, two days later, we were on a call.

"Sweetheart, you're quiet, is the wedding planning over-whelming you?" I asked.

There was a little silence, then tension in her voice as she said, "Toyosi, I just want us to... I don't know if... give me a sec."

"Is everything OK, dear?"

She let out a dramatic sign. "If we can..." She continued to ramble.

I sensed a shift, unusual shift. I knew something was wrong. Maybe she was worried about how we'd arrange the dance rehearsal. Maybe she wanted a new wedding reception, a bigger venue. We'd agreed a small, beautiful wedding would be perfect for us. Maybe she wanted us to extend our premarital counselling course. Maybe it had to do with her earlier request that we must return to the UK together after the wedding – no waiting around for visa processing. It could have been anything, but I wasn't prepared for such a slap in the face.

"There's something I want to tell you. I've been subtle about this. I want us to have a break. I want to have a break. I need some time to myself, alone. I've been thinking about this, about us, for a while. I can no longer do this."

It was a bolt from the blue. Her voice took on a slipshod tone. The last two sentences dragged in my ears. I was sure I didn't hear her well.

"What?" I asked. "Sisi, what do you mean you can no—?"

But she hung up.

The thumping in my chest stopped. I was numb. I slammed my eyes shut. Then opened them, hoping I'd found an answer. My heart thumped against my throat. I pressed my thumb in between my eyebrows, squeezing it. *My goodness, what's going on?* But I was speaking to myself. Each word stumbled out. It was barely forty-eight hours after I'd received her lyrical messages. *Were they empty words?* We'd kissed each other over the phone the night before. How could everything be so right then suddenly fall apart? *No, nothing is falling apart. It's a joke. She didn't mean it.* The room blurred. I called her again.

She didn't answer; I was sealed in silence, staring at the phone, willing it to ring.

It didn't.

My head was throbbing, aching. I spent the next two hours wondering if I'd missed something. I searched for the cracks. How could there not have been prescient warnings? The red flags. How could I have missed them? I stared across the room like someone who had just woken from a bad dream. *Oh, no, is this why she'd stopped wearing her engagement ring two weeks after the proposal? Was this the hint about the imaginary people who break up every time?* Oh no! I sat up on the bed, both hands supporting my head, as I recalled the events of the past weeks especially her weird questions. Tons of them flashed through my mind.

"All these London girls that are always desperate for husbands, I don't want them to snatch my man, *o*," she'd said. "Or is there someone longing for your heart?"

I'd suspected foul play to this question, but there was no proof. I took it as a joke. "Only you, baby. Only you. We're engaged, remember," I'd said.

As the events flashed through, I remembered how she wanted to reduce the bridal train by two people. My brain clocked. *Oh my goodness, I'd been naïve.*

I was stung to stillness. So, we were the ones not invited to our own wedding? Silence drenched me. I floundered about for an hour or so. There must be an explanation. I scrolled down my phone, furiously, searching for the British Airways customer service contact.

I booked the next flight and scheduled a return trip for the day after. I would be visiting Lagos for twenty-four hours. Insane, I know. I knelt, said my prayers to God, convinced I had to travel.

We'd always had a long-distance relationship. I was the one doing the travelling. I would normally visit Sisi at least four times a year in Lagos.

Why had she ended everything so suddenly? I had hundreds of questions. I needed to ask them.

THE NEXT DAY, before night fell, I'd arrived in Lagos.

I headed to Isolo. Sat in a taxi, my hands were pinching into my skin. I reassured myself, flipping my thoughts from negative 'what if' scenarios. On getting to Sisi's house, I dialled her mobile with my local line. She picked at first ring. "Hey babe, it's me, I'm downstairs."

Shocked and stunned, she rumbled with her words, "Toyosi, you say you're where?"

"I'm in Lagos, I'm downstairs in front of your gate."

"What... what did you say... you're in Lagos?" Her voice sounded shaking, troubled.

She ended the call and few minutes later, she was outside. When Sisi saw me, she said nothing. She looked like she was trying to remember how to breathe or searching for the right words to say. We greeted each other but it was no different to strangers who'd just met.

"Sisi, what's going on? Please talk to me."

Her eyes didn't meet mine. Her arms were folded tightly across her chest.

"Can we find somewhere quiet where we can talk?" I asked.

She led me to a kiosk, a small shop in front of her house in Adeleke Street. It was a good spot to talk besides the distractions of roadside noise, the never-ending singsong cries of street hawkers, and the chimes of sellers' bells tinkling nearby. We sat. She was still holding back in letting our hands touch. She stirred in her seat, then turned away from me as if she saw a bleeding heart bursting with grief. There was no answer yet to my previous question. If I must get something good out of my visit, I'd better be patient. I ignored her irritated huff.

The honk of Danfo drivers split the stillness.

"You came all the way from London to see me?" She was obviously stunned.

I swallowed to clear the gurgling sound in my throat. "Baby, talk to me. Look at us; take a good look at us. What just happened? What's going on?" The anger I felt from London, how I was going to unleash my temper on her, had melted.

"Toyosi, I cannot talk now. When are you going back?"

"Tomorrow."

"OK. Let's talk in the morning."

"No, Sisi. You're not busy now, are you?" I asked. "Let's talk, please."

She snarled at me. I could sense the temper and agitation in her disposition. "No, I can't. Your flight is in the evening. You're flying with BA as usual, aren't you? We will talk in the morning." She took a sharp look in a different direction, shrugging her shoulders.

My throat was suddenly convulsing with pain. I cleared my throat and swallowed again. Anything to restraint my emotion. Anything to keep my voice calm, and my tone polite. Anything to keep me sane. "How did we get to this point, Sisi? How?"

"What do you want me to say, Toyosi? What do you want

me to say? The same thing I already told you over the phone or something different? I need to think things through. I cannot talk about this tonight." She shuddered.

My lips were set in a grim line; her voice threatened my worst-case scenario. My anger resurfaced. Some words were about to leap from my lips, but I decided to put the devil to shame. I took a deep breath. Decided to quench the wave of queasiness worsening in my gut. "OK, tomorrow morning. We'll talk in the morning. Have a lovely night."

I turned to leave.

"Wait," she said, as she turned to block my exit. "You're staying at V.I, aren't you?"

She took my silence for "yes."

"I'll come with you, we'll talk tonight."

The hum of hope stirred the air. We left for the hotel. Neither of us wanted the taxi driver to know our business so we were quiet for most of the twenty-minute journey; we'd become complete strangers. I could see the driver through his rear-view mirror, stylishly checking for sign of rife, protruding his nose to see if her one-word responses infuriated me.

We made it to the hotel. The same hotel where we got engaged a few weeks ago. We checked in and went to my room; it was time to talk. I wilted in a seat.

"I'm all ears, Sisi."

Silence.

She should be talking now, not chewing the corner of her lower lip.

"Baby, won't you say something?" I asked, but my words floated away in her ears.

She rested her back against the bedframe, her left hand resting on her forehead. Her face heavily stamped with unpleasantness. I gave her a few moments to gather her thoughts.

The silence grew deeper. Her angry eyebrows glaring at nothing.

"At least say something. What's the issue?"

She was clenching and unclenching her fists. "Not tonight, Toyosi, not tonight. Tomorrow morning, we'll talk." The muscles in her face tightened as she punched her pillow and flung it hard to the other side of the bed.

"What's the point of coming if you don't want to talk? Make me understand, what exactly is the point? What's come over you, Sisi?" I didn't realise my voice was so loud.

She arched a sly brow. "Should I take my leave?" It wasn't a question. She was already near the door. Her brows were now bumped together in a scowl.

I modulated my voice, almost in an undertone and controlled the troubled rise and fall of my anxiety. "Sisi, I'm sorry. I'm very sorry. What's going on? Did I offend you? Did I say anything wrong? What happened to us?" I started to prattle on, like a foolish lover boy.

She walked back to her seat, angrily resting her chin in her palm. And took her time. "I hate you, Toyosi. I hate you." Her eyes weren't burning with hatred. I knew she meant the opposite. I wanted her to mean the opposite. "You want me to lose my baby?" Her left hand curled on top of her belly. I could see her stomach through the shades of her pink dress. Her words had punched me in the face. *Is she pregnant? Is she crazy?* I was looking for a clue.

"Which baby?" I asked. We'd never had sex, so it made no sense whatsoever.

"Tomorrow, we'll talk. If you can't wait, I'll take my leave." She raised her eyebrows, as she put her bag onto her shoulder, walking towards the door.

"Talk now if you want to talk or leave." I didn't mean it. I didn't want her to move an inch. She wrestled with the door. I obliged. I'll have to wait for this grand speech tomorrow. The night lasted for a year. At first, for a prolonged period, she sat on a chair, unrested, propping her elbows on her knees, bracing her chin on her fisted hands. And then later, she resumed to the bed. As I'd had no further reply, no words were said to each other. We lay on the bed, our backs turned away from each other. My brain struggled to make sense of her wild question. What was she doing next to me if she was carrying someone else's baby? *Or could this be the result of our foreplay last time?* My brain was as gormless as a calf.

After the tossing and turning all night, I was awake. I shook off whatever had gripped me, then stood up and opened the curtains to see the crack of dawn pressing grey smudges into the sky. Morning finally came. If I'd visited Lagos to see her as usual, we'd have been on our knees by now, holding hands, singing and praying to God and the heavenly angels. We'd have consulted God and the angels apportioning blessings, on the matters of our hearts, our future, our lives. Her voice of loud prayers would have woken the next-door occupants; our songs of hymns would have silenced all mortal flesh. We'd shut the wicked and quenched the furious flames. But it wasn't a usual day; the angels were in heaven.

"Toyosi, you're selfish. You're very selfish." It sounded like a good morning message.

At least she was ready to talk. "What did I do?" I asked calmly.

A tear slid down her face. "It's a woman who carries a baby in her womb. A woman, Toyosi. You don't know what it feels like to imagine the thought of losing a child. You don't know. You want us to get married. When I get pregnant and the scan shows our baby has sickle cell, what are we going to do?"

So that's what she's been worrying about.

I walked closer to sit next to her and held her hands. She

removed them. "Sweet," I said, "you know I don't like to see you cry. Please don't cry. I'm so sorry this is bothering you. I'm so sorry. We're in this together, baby." My emotions swirled.

"You haven't answered my question," she said in a tight voice.

"Sweet, we've spoken about this countless time and agreed. We won't be risking an abortion. We agreed on an IVF, which is OK by me."

"Risk happens, Toyosi. All the time. We will be sleeping together because that's what married couples do. What if I get pregnant and the scan says SS, what are we going to do?"

Sisi was a sickle cell carrier (AS) just like me. We knew this but decided to date, nevertheless. We were on the same page. We had a great connection, and the genotype issue was not enough to stop us. She was twenty-six; I was thirty-two. We agreed on a pre-natal diagnosis at the beginning of our relationship to prevent having a child with sickle cell anaemia. We had checks at six months and a year into our relationship.

"Sweet, in the last eighteen months, we've agreed many times that if we're faced with pregnancy outside of IVF, we'll have the baby. Our faith is bigger than our fear."

She stood up from my side and walked towards a seat at the reading table. "No, I don't do faith, I do common sense," she said.

"Those were your words. *Our faith is bigger than our fear.*"

Silence hung in the air.

Her stifled sobs punched through, again. "Did you say IVF was OK by you?" She turned to face me. Her words were scrambling now. "No, I don't think so. You waited for nearly half a day before you agreed to it. Tell me how you're going to afford it, if it fails repeatedly. Tell me. How do I even know you would not change your mind later? How?"

I could tell from her shrill wobbly voice that the conversation would drag.

"Sweetheart, we'll be fine. I've saved some money already, at least for the first one."

She laughed. "You don't get it, do you?" That mocking laugh again. She displayed her hands towards me with scoffs of disbelief. "Show me your account. Show me, Toyosi. Let me see the money you've saved. If it fails again and again. Can you afford it? No, I don't think so. I can't do this, Toyosi. I can't." She yelled the last two sentences.

"We have options, Sisi. The many options we've spoken about." My voice was flat, a little tremulous, a little supplicating. I wanted it to be louder, anything but flat. I resisted the urge for a minute. "Why are you only thinking about the extreme, the negative?"

She huffed out a breath. "Because a woman carries the child. A woman, Toyosi!" The yelling was unreal. It was followed with moments of wordless chatter.

Whoever was drumming in my head needed to stop and stop fast. My head was spinning. The silence was comforting this time. I managed to find two words. "Why now?" The question had the guileless innocence of a child.

Her eyes spoke loudly what her lips couldn't utter. She turned away from me. "I thought I could, but I can't."

I fought for air. I needed something to ease my bleeding heart so wretched right now. "Baby, let's revisit our options." I took a step closer to face her. "A lot of people are faced with this every day. Love won it for Nkechi and Ade, Tolani and Deji." My voice, the sniffling tone, sounded like I was pleading, but I managed to choke back the tears.

Her face stayed the same. "I'm not Nkechi or Tolani." Her voice was expressionless.

"Sisi," I said, the tone was empathetic, "Sisi, we love each—"

"I've always told you that love is not enough. You always say otherwise. Well, this is just an example of one of those situations love can't handle." She brushed past me to sit on the bed. Profound hint of "Don't even try, it's all over," crept into her voice.

I groaned in misery.

A thought of what I would have said on a normal day flashed through my mind: *Our definition of love must be the same before we can argue whether it is truly enough or not.*

Something like heat was bubbling away under my skin. I tried to hide my frustration, but my body language betrayed me. A table mirror in front of me revealed the exasperation. I clamped my lips that were spreading apart and controlled the worrisome breath sticking to the inside of my throat. I let go of my hand worrying over my beard and the skin mark I was creating beneath my chin. My eyes caught her agitation from the reflection. I turned to face her instantly. "Let's talk about it like people who are truly in love. Let's work something out. Even if you want to quit, that's fine but it shouldn't be sudden and brutal like this."

She looked away. "Sudden or not sudden, a break up is a break up." Her tone was cruel.

I gasped in astonishment. My hands were stacked close to my forehead. My head throbbed. My heart thudded. My lips pursed like I'd been chewing a lemon.

The air began vibrating with anger. The room steaming in indignation, reeling up and down.

"Sisi, are you for real?" The calmness broke. The strained voice broke. Everything gave way. I screamed at her. "Why did you deceive me? Why plan our wedding if you wanted to quit? Why did you wait for eighteen months? Why Sisi? Why did you accept the proposal? Why all the plans for the marriage itself? Our future plans. Everything. Why?"

The bedside lamp rattled as my hand mistakenly landed on it. She hovered the room like a threatening storm, her fingers splayed wide mid-air. Her voice echoed in a thunderous scream. "Love is not enough. Love is not enough, Toyosi. I've told you before and I'm telling you again. Love can never be enough. Love will never be enough. That's why."

The rumble stopped. The whimper stopped. Silence crawled into our space and I could hear her breathing, panting. I looked into her eyes, but there was nothing. My soul spoke but not in words. My heart must have burst because something was stuck in my throat.

The drama continued for a while. I stood there, helpless, defeated, broken.

A few minutes passed. Fresh air cleared the smoke in the room.

"And besides, I'm no longer interested in relocating to London," she said.

At this point, I'd lost all my energy, but I fought on, hoping the relationship could still be salvaged. "Why?" I asked. "You couldn't wait to be with me in London, for us to start our lives together, just two days ago. Sisi. Just two days ago. What changed suddenly?"

She was tight-lipped for a few moments.

"I'm relocating nowhere." Her words were mumbled.

We'd spoken about our relocation plans for nearly two years. Once we got married, she'd join me in London, and I'd advise her on a job route to ease relocation. As an engineering graduate, she'd always dreamt of working in the automative industry and for Toyota in particular. The idea was for her to get a job in the Lagos office and then leverage an internal transfer to London. She loved the idea. I helped with her CV preparation, job application and interviews, and, luckily, she was offered the job. She hadn't worked throughout the duration of our relationship. At one point she seemed depressed, and I'd been very supportive.

"This is not what I want," she said. "Can't you understand?" Her tone was surly. "Sorry, London is not for me. Why should I be the one to leave my life behind, leave everything, everything I've ever known? You may not accept it, but you're very selfish. Toyosi, you're so selfish," she added bluntly, then started railing on the dreariness of London life, anything to make a point. "If you want this to work, pack your bags and move to Lagos."

If relocation was the problem, we could still make things work. I held on to a glimmer of hope. From the moment Sisi got the job, she had become power drunk. Because her actions were camouflaged with love messages each day, I didn't read much into it.

I was two years away from becoming a British citizen. I had a decent job, a well-paid one. Relocating to Nigeria to save a relationship would be too costly. I'd just started a fintech business based in Lagos (secure solution for merchants across Africa to accept payments via websites and mobile devices) which I'd registered for both of us. And I'd hoped that if the business did well within a year, it would perhaps ease the relocation situation.

"If relocation is the problem, Sisi, I'll work something out. For now, I can't."

"You see why I said you're selfish. You only think of yourself. Yourself, Toyosi."

I ignored the scathing tone and swallowed to let off whatever stung on my tongue. It wasn't as if a rock had suddenly lodged in my throat. I needed all the patience in the world.

"Let me figure something out. If this is what you're unhappy about, I'll figure something out." I'd said this in a softer and subtler voice and hoped it was enough.

The drama was subdued. *Thank goodness.* An hour later, the situation had calmed down and we went downstairs for breakfast, but I was not hungry. "I love you, Sisi. With my whole heart," I told her, as we began to eat. "Whatever our decision, let's pray about it."

Sisi wasn't the materialistic type. When she began to question why I didn't send her a monthly allowance as another reason, I was shocked. "All my friends receive monthly allowances from their boyfriends. I sometimes wonder."

I'd sent money to Sisi from time to time, buy her gifts, but I did not send her a scheduled monthly allowance. I never knew someone would expect such. She'd never asked for one either. She insisted that she wouldn't be staying at her family residence after the wedding, and wanted to rent a small apartment in Lagos, if the application took longer than expected. Three months was not unheard of. Even six months. I'd set this as part of my priorities as well as the full wedding cost, too, so I fell short on the monthly allowance.

Breakfast was over. The air smelled of breakup. But I breathed well.

"Like I said, let's pray about this, we need God to direct us," I told her.

Like a replay, she picked up on her earlier points: sickle cell worries, relocation inconveniences, disappointment from unscheduled monthly allowance. And added maybe four or five more. Trivialities that characterised every relationship; those we had pushed behind us a year prior. The conversation dragged on. It was pointless to continue. I knew I'd skidded to an abrupt halt. I looked like I'd hit a rocky patch.

"I'll send your ring," she said, as she walked off.

It felt like someone you'd trusted to take a bullet for you was the one pulling the trigger.

Enough of sucking air through my teeth. Enough of trying

to digest defeat. I dragged myself up and returned to the room as humiliation flattened in my spirit. My heart was shredded. I processed the slap of her words. I couldn't feel my heartbeat, but I took consolation in the knowledge that it was drumming in my chest. I sat there thinking. I had been faithful; I had treated her right. I was sincere. I loved her. I respected her. I held to the "no sex before marriage" rule because it was the right thing to do. Even when we were tempted and came close to tearing ourselves apart, I walked away and took a cold shower. She loved me for having self-control. She loved me for being faithful. She loved me for many reasons. I could not comprehend what was happening no matter how much I went over it.

Later that evening before my flight, I went to see her and tried one last time.

"If I get a job opportunity in Lagos and relocate here, will that help?"

"I don't know." She stirred, as if she was tired of my questions.

"Can we re-do the genotype test? You remember Pelumi's story, her initial test result was wrong because the hospital had mistakenly swapped her result for someone else."

She glanced away. That direction of the window was ever buzzing with street noise. No words were said, no resistance either. The silence of sorrow seized the moment. It was as if the rustling noise of the Okada riders, the hiss of traffic, the clatter of touts trotting the road, the clanging of bells from the street sellers; everything had conspired against me as she delivered a grand message that ended this thing, this simulated ersatz, we'd called love.

"I'm no longer in love, Toyosi." Her words wielded sharp like a knife.

PART 1

ONE

I WAS SITTING ON A BATHTUB. A single drop of water traced its way down my cheek. It must have been from slicing the onions when I prepared the goat meat earlier or the blurred sight causing me pain in my eyes. Even though it had been a reflective evening, I was not expecting my energy to be sapped, my lips to be dried, and my tongue to be a gnawing pain at the roof of my parched lips. Even though I'd drunk a gallon of water, every lungful of air still robbed my body. I had not expected fear to be shooting through me like a piercing arrow.

When will I find someone to banter with all day? Someone who I won't be tired of once night falls? This unsettling worry crumbled my day.

Surrounded by shelves of towels and a vanity tray with colognes, detergents and other toiletries, I smelled the scents of soaps – of shea butter, of coconut milk, of pleasant fragrance. My hands smelled of onions. My head, my heart, my feet – the rest of my body – smelled of fear. I'd been sitting here for over half an hour, peeling away the layers of my thoughts from the failed relationship attempts of recent years. From Bimbo to Rene, from Isabella to Sophia, from Hannah to Ada and Zara. Everything outside of my control. I leaned against the tub, sombre, thoughtful, doubtful and then drew in a deep breath to ease the dread souring my stomach and sucked in more air, but reality kept interrupting and forcing me to pay attention.

There must be a better way to switch off a sense of foreboding. I pulled to my feet, walked to the window and open the blinds for fresh air. In the far distance, at the waterfront where artificial land had emerged from the sea, the soaring Pearls Tower of Eko Atlantic was beaming in its newest glory. And next door, a lovely young couple took their place alongside the family lazing on lounges in their holiday-resort-like backyard, under white gauze curtains that curled in the breeze. Two beautiful kids, a boy and a girl, were tottering around the compound causing chaos with their popcorn. Happiness was written on everyone's forehead. The last thing I'd expected to smell in a toilet, in this lonely position, was love. The couple held hands, giggling and pranking over ice cream, emanating laughter so pure. I blinked faster and felt my chest tighten, my breath suddenly short with desire. I swallowed a bubble of anxiety. It was a stark reminder of what I lacked – love. A prickle crept down my spine. Fear stole the moment, fear and envy. I, too, want to hold someone's hand.

It was 8 p.m. on Tuesday, December 6th. I had a flight to catch from Murtala Muhammed International Airport, Lagos, to London's Heathrow in three hours. While it had been a blessing to see my family after a whole year, I was ready to head back to my bland London life. Two weeks in the hustle and bustle of Lagos had been plenty.

I took a cold shower, rushed out of the bathroom leaving the wallowing thoughts behind. With no further delay, I slipped a T-shirt over my head, wore regular jeans and simple trainers. I had folded my clothes earlier into my suitcase and packed some fresh food items – smoked catfish, crayfish, grounded *egusi* and *ugwu* leaves. Everything loaded in my luggage.

Ready to go.

It's about half an hour's drive to the airport, but with the notorious Lagos traffic, the city's nightmare that hop the road like hog-tied frogs, we allowed an hour. Matthew, my best friend, volunteered to take me. He arrived with a big smile on his face.

"The Mayor of London," he shouted, as he climbed out of his new black Range Sport. "You enter a city, and the colour changes. Bravo bro! Well done for painting Lagos red, I hope you're now set for the post-holiday blues."

He was not someone to take seriously. "Mr. Tender." I hailed him.

His car door remained open, as the song blasting his head flowed through. Matthew lived for music; it is the air he breathes.

"Thanks for all the highlife turn-up," he said, as we shook hands. Oh! The freestyling of Afro-Juju at Ariya Gardens in Lekki, the folks who created harmonised lyrics to praise and hype guests, accompanied with loud cheers that rose to a crescendo. We'd joked and reminisced on the phone earlier, easy banter about the highs and lows of my visit.

I placed a laptop backpack in the front seat. "Oh, yeah. You mean those jazzy horns, guitar melodies! Ah, too much enjoyment. Nothing beats highlife entertainment in this town. Trust me, that craft is already on my to-do list when next I visit."

"I bet it is. With all the babes?"

He knew none of that was true. "I don't mean with no babe," I said, smiling, as I rolled my luggage along and took it to his car boot. "My best highlight, though, was the hometown visit to see my folks, and the joy of hosting friends and family for dinner to celebrate my thirty-fifth birthday, my first birthday celebration in ten years."

"Man, you did well. Thanks for not eating the cake and chicken alone."

I laughed as we took our seats in the car. He moderated the volume of the latest afrobeat jamming on the stereo, loud enough to block our eardrums.

"I hope Starboy Wizkid will not block your eardrum someday."

In his sheer exuberance, he nodded and swayed. "As long as the ladies can still hear me when I talk, that's fine."

We drove out of the compound, waving at the gateman who was returning to his duty post with a cigarette dangling from his mouth. Then Matthew asked, "Is there anything else that would have made your holiday more memorable?"

I knew exactly what he meant. He was teasing me about whether I'd met a potential wife. My need to settle down had been a hot topic of discussion during my visit. I laughed. "No," I told him. "Besides, love isn't something you go out to find. Love finds you."

Matthew was the only person who had *discreetly* asked when I'd be settling down. Everyone else, including my mum, chided me to hurry up and marry.

"Oluwatoyosi," she'd said, calling my name with emphasis in a familiar momentous tone, her nose bridging with wrinkles, "erm, how's my daughter doing in London?"

I'd laughed. "There's no daughter for you yet in London, Mum."

She led me to a seat close by in her living room. She held a small grey vintage brooch in her hand. As she rubbed her thumb over it, slowly tapping her right foot three times on the ground as though she was knocking off the heads of her enemies, I knew some parables were coming. It was a tactic of hers, using parables and proverbs to over-enunciate her messages if the situation demanded serious attention. "Our people say when a king's palace burns down, the re-built palace is more beautiful. You know that the fire that burns a royal palace only enhances its splendour. I know you were hurt in the past but please, *ori ade mi* (*my head crown*), focus on re-building the burnt palace. You know you're not getting any younger." She'd said this calmly, a resolve in her eyes said, "don't let my enemies mock me."

"Thanks, Mum," I'd said, trying to stifle a laugh, "but when I marry, I want it to be for the right reasons. Someone I can spend the rest of my life with. Soon, Mum. Soon."

It was 8:30 p.m. and you could see the taillights snaking their way down the airport road, cars stretching bumper to bumper. The unalloted service lane, to the far right where cars were bound to dance, edging on the rims of potholes, was also blocked. Matthew and I could've talked about anything, but we chatted about our recent dating experiences.

"Why do some folks think only women struggle with dating?" Matthew asked.

"I really wonder too, man," I said, "it certainly isn't true."

"Do they think dating for men is like going to Sainsbury to buy milk?"

"I know, right. Some people think we have the advantage and can simply decide to get married whenever we want. It's as if all a guy needs to do is put on some deodorant, trim his hipster beard, and walk out the front door and anyone he chooses will answer his call. I forgive people who think this way; it's ingrained in our culture, but too far from reality."

We'd made it halfway to the airport. The engines were still humming as the motorists waited for their wheels to turn, in a stretched full-beamed lane charming the highway, weaving lane by lane. A siren was blaring loudly behind us. A horde of men in their starched black-black kit were in charge. The traffic veered to the side, an untarred galloping walkway, as police led the way, but the gridlock soon held even the men with guns. "Find the right babe, bro, take your time," Matthew said, swagging his body to the grooving beat, the voice of WizKid's Jaiye Jaiye pouring from the speakers. "Marriage is not all about a ring or a piece of paper signed in front of friends and family to prove a point."

"I know, man."

"Lover man," he said, laughing into the steering. "Tinder is always an option, bro."

About twenty minutes later, the traffic started to move.

"Take your time, bro," Matthew repeated, "just not too long. You remember the proverbial beekeeper's wise talk, don't you? A swarm in May is worth a load of hay. A swarm in June is worth a silver spoon, but you know what they say about a swarm in July?"

I laughed, wondering when he became Pete Edochie. "Is not worth a fly. Isn't it?"

"Yes, you got my drift. Time is always of the essence."

"Thanks, bro," I said. "Only remember, the race is not for the swift," I reminded him using our favourite punchline. "When the time's right, I'll find the right person."

We arrived at the airport and I bid goodbye to Matthew, promising to keep him abreast of all romantic updates. I went through the security checks and border control and decided to take a short walk around the terminal to kill some time.

When I visit home, I like to buy pieces of African art and African-inspired souvenirs as gifts. I had an hour and thirty minutes before my flight, so there was plenty of time. I spotted the art shop and noticed someone walking towards it from the opposite direction. A fascinating scene unfolded before me as I fixed my gaze, peering straight into the distance.

She had a comely figure, and about 5 foot 9 inches tall. Her outfit was simple yet stylish – a classic scoop-neck shirt with dolman sleeves, perfectly paired with casual jeans and a smart-looking pair of thick glasses. She walked confidently, with a natural elegance. It seemed as though my Lagos holiday wasn't over just yet.

I scrubbed a hand down my face, stared a little and flinched when she saw me. We made eye contact for a split second and I caught a fleeting glimpse of her face before she leisurely entered the store. *This can't be a coincidence.* My thoughts were spiralling out of control, but I managed to keep it together. There was something there, something beautiful.

I delayed going inside the shop for a bit, my heart pumping faster with every passing second. *Brace yourself, Toyosi.* I walked in, having forgotten entirely what I'd come for in the first place. The boutique sold an impressive array of both old and modern pieces. There were no cheap knockoffs here; the art was made by hand and made to last. I looked around and saw a few other customers, one or two lined up in the queue.

I kept a close eye on her as she chatted to one of the sales assistants, waiting for the right time, like a snooper waiting to pry, stylishly rehearsing my opening line in my mind. The two voices in my head were contradicting each other. *Pay her a compliment, make her smile,* but then, *flirt with her.* I toyed with both approaches and decided to be myself; good-humoured it would be.

"Good evening, sir. May I be of assistance?" one of the sales assistants said. "I'll help you find the best of whatever you're looking for."

This was not the right time for distractions, but his statement couldn't have been more apt. I smiled and, with feigned interest, picked up a small brass bowl from a set. "I know the best is here," I said.

"That's right, sir," he agreed. "How many are you looking for today?"

"I'm only looking for one thing."

"What's your preference, sir," he asked. "Clay or bronze?"

"I saw the best one before I walked in," I told him. "Give me a moment to check."

I quickly shrugged off the confused salesman, put down the item and turned around to find the mystery woman – but she had gone. *Oh no!* I panicked a little. *Damn that salesman for throwing me off course.* My heart was heavy with disappointment, but then before I could really register the missed opportunity, I became aware of someone standing behind me. I turned and there she was – Miss Pretty.

Phew.

I pretended to appreciate another item so that I could watch her. She played with her hair, twirled and tucked it behind her ear, fidgeted with her hands, and fiddled with her bag. Our eyes almost met. Her gaze slid to the side. My side. As I was about to approach her and say hello, she looked as though she wanted to say something. I cleared my throat and put down the handcrafted bowl I was admiring and waited for her to approach me.

"Hi," she said. "I'm indecisive. I like both of these sculptures. Which one do you think I should pick?"

She didn't introduce herself, but her body language was warm. People say that women angle their body in the direction of their desires; she was angled towards me. *Remember; keep it good-humoured.*

"Oh, lovely," I said in my best English accent. "Both are lovely. Let me take a closer look. Hmm. These are fine examples of artistry, you know. Rich traditional African sculptures.

Both appeal to emotions: one is subtle, the other, overt. You have good eye for art."

"Thanks." She sounded shy. "That's kind of you. I love sculptures. And Lagos has the best."

"Indeed," I agreed. "Lagos, as a matter of fact, has the best of everything."

"You think?" she asked.

"Yes, I do. From beautiful sculptures like these to the best arts and crafts, and," I said, pausing for effect, "beautiful women of many pedigrees." I smiled.

She laughed. "So, what do you think?" She gestured at the statues.

"Both are handcrafted," I said. "Perfect for a calming scene in a home."

"Thanks. Which do you think?" She put a fist on her cheek.

"This one," I said, holding up one of the statues. I could tell from her bright eyes that we preferred the same statue. "It is simple. You could stand it anywhere – a bookcase, mantelpiece or a shelf. Even staircase ledges. And if you decide to hang it on a wall, you can create your own safari. How about that? It's as elegant as a beautiful stranger."

"I agree," she said. "It's symbolic." She paused. "Did you say beautiful stranger? You're too funny."

"Art tells stories, doesn't it?" I said. "Sometimes, the stories are as beautiful as the people who buy them."

"Hmm, a smooth line. Well, thank you for your help. I hope you have a safe flight."

"It was my pleasure," I said, locking her into eye contact. "You have a safe flight too."

No, not so fast. I need to get your digits.

"I'm assuming we're on the same BA flight to London, yeah?" I asked as she turned to the direction of the payment queue.

"Yep, yep," she said, nodding. "But my final destination is Houston, Texas."

It was time to start counting my blessings.

"Should our seats be next to each other," I said, "we can talk more about the beautiful arts and crafts and the beautiful people who buy them."

She laughed. "That would be a huge coincidence, wouldn't it?"

I saw her hitch her bag onto her shoulder and turn to leave. "Well, it's been lovely talking with you," she said. "Thanks again for your help. Have a safe trip."

"And you. Take care."

She went ahead to make her payment. I chose my own pieces and joined the queue; two others had filed in behind her by that time. After paying, she waved goodbye and left the shop, heading for the departure gate.

I thought about our encounter while I waited in line to pay. She was pretty, a natural beauty. She was well spoken and understatedly elegant. She appeared warm, calm and light-hearted. Her skin was radiant, her complexion tan, so uniquely tan and fresh, as if she was made from a blend of brown sugar, cocoa and gold, as if a pot of honey was added. I recalled how she caught my glance and how I smiled at her. Her smile, oh my goodness. *Carabos! Carabos!* (Sorry, I was speaking in tongues!) What a sweet smile; it could light even the darkest of souls. She had perfect straight white teeth. Her dimples were cuter. And then her sweet voice, so soft and soothing. My heart kept fluttered, skipping beats.

Why is everyone taking so long to pay?

I paid quickly and dashed out of the store. The terminal was crowded; it felt as though half of Lagos had decided to head in the same direction. She was on a call, so I waited for a bit, plugged my headphones into my phone, and thanked my lucky stars for a beautiful day. I decided to tease Matthew, who had told me to tell him the second I found 'her'.

So, I sent him a text: *I think I just did.*

Matthew replied almost instantly: *Is the race now for the swift?*

Ha-ha. It is never for the swift.

She must be very special, Matthew teased.

I think she is.

Matthew called for details, snorting out mockery laughter but I rushed him off, hinting that I was still pursuing her. I could hear him snapping his fingers.

"I hope you're chasing something amazing, and not a white rabbit with a top hat," he said.

"No! No be white rabbit. *Nah*, fox. Get off my phone. I'll call you, mate," I said, ending the call.

She sat on a three-seater bench, keeping a close eye on the flight information. One man in his early thirties sat next to her in the middle seat and they started to make small talk, as if he knew her. I'd positioned myself not far off, waiting for her to raise her eyes. I did not miss the moment. I broadcasted a big smile. She smiled back. Great. I closed the gap and greeted the dude. "Hi," I said, nothing more. Half-smile was more than enough for the man tightening his shoulders. But I wasn't going to sit at the other edge. We hadn't introduced ourselves earlier, so I held out my hand. "Hey. Nice seeing you again. My name is Toyosi."

She took my hand and shook it firmly, her skin smooth and warm. "Hi Toyosi, I'm Tamilore." She seemed to understand her siting position wasn't in my favour. She angled her body fully in my direction, completely away from the short man with pot belly.

"It's ten o'clock," I said glancing at my watch. "We have

nearly an hour before our flight. Would you like to join me in the first-class lounge?" I did not look at the man's face.

Thanks to British Airways frequent flyer's mileage, I was choking with benefits! I hoped she wouldn't think I was being flash. She smiled at me and nodded.

Sorry, dude!

Together we made our way to the lounge and found a comfortable sofa; the perfect spot to relax and talk at ease. Decorated lights hung beautifully across the lounge, radiating a warm welcoming feeling. Fresh fruits beckoned and dangled from a couple of trays. Platters of plantain chips, sausage rolls, bean cakes, meat pies, waffles, pancakes, croissants and cheese begged for our attention. Behind the cherries and mounds of grapes were happy faces, tired faces, curious faces, staring at us. We grabbed some light snacks, soft drinks and wine.

As we took our seat, we clinked glasses with cheers.

"What do you do for a living, Tamilore?" I was perched on the edge of my seat, squeezing the wine glass, rolling it from side to side.

She was seated with one leg tucked underneath her, then she crossed her legs and took some grapes, scrunched her hand into her curly hair and flipped a fraction over her shoulder. "I work in media," she said. "Although, not the mainstream media."

I leaned forward to grab some plantain chips. "Interesting. You mean you don't get involved in the anti-Trump poking and daily chaos?" I teased.

"I'm sure Stephen Colbert and Trevor Noah are doing enough poking already."

"Those folks are brilliant, aren't they? So, what kind of media do you do?"

"Lifestyle," she said, uncrossing her legs. She reached forward for more grapes and wine and crossed her legs back, slowly dangling her shoe from her toes. "I showcase the best of African lifestyle and arts from music to fashion to movies and everything else that promotes Africa."

"Awesome," I said, genuinely impressed.

She smoothed her jeans over her hips and took a sip of her wine. "Oh, thank you. I co-host a seasonal TV show. The shows are usually recorded in advance and televised later, so the job gives some flexibility to juggle my time between home and abroad."

I nodded as she spoke. "You have the coolest job, you know. Really amazing."

I couldn't help but get ahead of myself and think that if she found me interesting, that flexibility could come in handy, given that we live in different countries.

"Thank you. What are you doing in Lagos?"

I set my glass on the wine table and raised my eyes to match hers. "Holiday. I came here to see my family. And for a chance to meet a beautiful stranger."

"You do have good sense of humour." She smiled.

"Do I?" I asked innocently. "Thank you."

I sat back and rested my arms at the side of the fancy sofa.

Meeting people who are passionate about changing the African landscape brings me joy, as it does Tamilore. Her passion for media and arts dominated our conversation. She promoted the dawn of a new era in Africa via her show, which I respected immensely.

"So, what do you do, Toyosi?" she asked.

"I'm a painter," I joked.

She pressed the two chocolate brownie waffles she'd already topped with peanut butter and cream cheese, then she nicely drizzled the toppings with honey and filled her mouth in a small bite. "Painting? Hmm. That's different. Do you enjoy your job?"

I had a taste of the meat pie and rubbed my chin. "I love it. Art is fun. One day, I may be basking in the beauty of a fading sun and the promise of night to come, while the next day I may be painting about the sweet embrace or the dark side of it."

"Hmm. That's poetic," Tamilore said, filling her mouth with the waffles. "How about showcasing the best of Africa's unforgettable sights to the world. You know what I mean?"

I had slow nods. I saw an opportunity. "Indeed," I said. "I could skip between the hippos in Zambia and the wonders of the Nile in Egypt."

"Or Zimbabwe's majestic Victoria Falls and the mountain gorillas of the Rwandan rainforest," she added, blushing.

We continued in this manner for a while, trading observations about the wonders of Africa from Marrakech's tribal drummers and snake charmers to the great migration of the Tanzanian wildebeests and everything else in between. With each word she spoke, it became clearer that I had found someone intellectually stimulating.

"What would you like to paint first?" she asked.

I went for it. "I'd rather paint a stranger I meet on my way." She blushed and draped her legs elegantly. She was enjoying this little game, as was I.

"Are you really a painter?"

"Alas, I am not," I said, holding out my hands in a resigned gesture. "I work for a London-based technology services firm that specialises in financial crime detection. Basically," I explained, "I catch bad people who do bad things."

It was an oversimplification, but it was true. I hunt the bad guys: fraudsters, grifters, money-launderers, con-artists, money mules, and the like.

"I'm a data scientist," I said, but I couldn't resist a little twist. "Bill Gates during the day; Shakespeare at night."

"Really?" she asked. "You're a writer?"

"I am."

"Oh, nice. What do you write about? Do you have anything online I could read?"

I took out my phone, attempting to browse through. "I do have some materials online. May I please have your mobile so I could send you a link?"

She blushed. "Hmm. Smart way of asking for a lady's number, yeah?"

I laughed. "You can't blame a brother for trying."

I gently flipped the phone around. Her lips formed a kiss shape as she said "Ooh". A couple who sat next to us stared, smiled and whispered behind their wine glasses. Tamilore took my phone. It was my lucky day; she gave me her Nigerian number and I sent the link.

She rummaged in her bag, reached for her phone and glanced through the page. "This makes sense now," she said. "You're a painter of words. An artist. Are these fictions?"

"Mostly, I write about real-life experiences, especially love stories." I went on to describe my most recent manuscript, a poetry project.

She pressed her lips together and nodded. "How often do you visit Lagos?"

"I try to visit my family once or twice a year. Of course, if I had other good reasons I might visit more often."

She laughed. "You mean like having a pretty woman in Lagos?"

"I mean like having a pretty woman like *you* who loves art in Lagos," I responded.

She rolled her eyes, playfully, then pulled a string of hair from her face and crossed her legs. We didn't feel like strangers anymore; the bond was natural. It felt like an excellent first date. There was a three-dimensional spark: intellectual, physical and emotional.

A few minutes later, we walked to the departure gate together and I noticed everyone staring at us as if we were a couple.

"Thank you, for being such interesting company," Tamilore said, maintaining eye contact as she smiled.

"The pleasure was mine."

We hugged and wished each other a safe flight.

The plane prepared for take-off at ten past eleven.

"Do you have everything you need, sir?" asked a flight attendant.

Of course, I do, besides one thing. "Yes, thank you." I smiled back.

Enthralled, I stared through the window as the plane began to taxi towards the runway as though the plane was outlining my path to happiness, until the engine roared and the wind buffered on the skyline of Lagos, dipping my eyes into half shadowed, half lighted sky.

Shortly after take-off, I handed a note to a flight attendant and asked if she would pass it to Tamilore. The note read, "Your smile is beautiful. Sleep well."

I wasn't expecting a reply, so I was happy when the flight attendant told me the note had been delivered; that was enough. I asked if Tamilore seemed happy to receive it.

"She asked if you paid the postal cost," the flight attendant said, smiling.

I laughed.

"She seemed surprised but happy."

That was good. I was satisfied.

I fixed my headphone. Lyrics I've heard many times before suddenly started to make perfect sense. Carly Simon's *All I Want is You* did the trick. It was only thirty minutes into a six-hour flight. I made my bed and slept comfortably. I woke up just as we descended into Heathrow and said my morning prayers as the plane landed at twenty past five that morning.

I figured out where Tamilore's connection was so that I could say goodbye. Soon, she showed up, but she was in a hurry to make her connecting flight. We exchanged warm greetings, but we only had a minute or two to ask how the flight had gone.

"I've written a reply to your note, but you're not to read it till we've parted," she said.

We looked into each other's eyes and held the gaze for a few seconds. Then we hugged tightly; it lasted longer than our hug the previous night. It felt warm and right. Then we said goodbye. She pushed the note into my hand and ran to catch her flight.

It read, "Aww, you're sweet. And handsome. Get home safe."

I stood on the same spot, watching her walk quickly through the crowd before disappearing around a corner and waved. The little boy in me waved back at her.

A few messages peeped as I switched on my phone. I glanced at Matthew's: *I can't wait to hear if she's your usual honey-coated chocolate or your dreamy iced-chilled strawberry.* He'd made it up. Dark skin or no dark skin, who cared?

Chocolate forever, man of wisdom lol, I replied.

I went home grinning, but I had no outlet for it; Tamilore wouldn't be returning to Nigeria for two months. I typed what I knew into Google. I was surprised to see that she was a bigger celebrity than she'd let on. Perhaps an attempt to hide her light under a bushel. I began scouring her profile for another contact. I found her email address and wrote to her.

I waited and waited for a reply but got none. One week passed. Nothing.

Few days later, I was back to the life of building fraud detection model. Deadline would have to wait. I stepped out for a short break, floating in the winter air, and dialled her mobile again, but it never rang. I composed another email. And clicked *send*.

Day after day, I longed for hope. I waited till the end of the second week, but she never replied to any of my attempts to contact her. I checked the spam folder and the trash files. Still nothing. I kept digging; perhaps I'd missed something.

It was Saturday morning. I embarked on gold mining on Google, flipping one picture over the next, reading her life stories. On Instagram, I'd unlocked access. My mouth was full of roasted peanuts, humming songs of praise until it suddenly went dry and brittle and stretched wide open. I was not expecting my hope to be shattered in a blink. Two adults were sealed by kisses. 'One and only' hangtag on everything I turned. In that slow and warble state, I dragged myself to Facebook where I'd discovered a link to her abbreviated, nicknamed page. There it was; she was in a relationship. Her personal life was all over, nowhere to hide.

That was the end of another of my attempts to find a bride.

The sunset imbued its last glance. I glimpsed the beautiful sky as it took on shades of orange, and thought about the beauty of sunrise and sunset, the hope that the sun will set to rise again. I lay in bed, said my prayers and once more, I remembered the stranger.

Tamilore Talulu.

PART 2

TWO

Ilaro, Nigeria 1991

THE MOON HAD PERCHED. The shaft of moonlight, so bright an hour ago, was now hung in pure darkness. The air released breeze and rustled peace through the holes of the window. Sounds sailed quietly through the breeze. My eyes were closing under the bedspread.

Out of nowhere, a sound of horror tore through the night, ringing through the walls. We heard a sudden bang, a cry of a woman. I could not have mistaken anyone for Mama Bose's voice. "My world has crumbled," she shouted and screamed in Yoruba with all her might. The numbness of sleep in my eyes faded away. Everyone ran towards the compound.

Fear propelled my feet ahead of Mum. I never knew she was faster in a sprint. She grabbed my shoulder, forcing me to a halt before I stood a chance. Frightened and distraught, she shielded me. "Toyosi, Toyosi, you're not to see this, move back." Her breath quickened as she leaned forward. I caught even the unsaid words in her eyes.

I took a step back, watching those arriving with trembling hands, watering eyes.

Mama Bose fell to the floor, rolling, sobbing, screaming in convulsive gasps. She clapped her hands three times, swung backward on the floor in a wail, the iris colour of her eyes had turned red. The community caught the terrifying bawl in an unbroken stream.

"Ah! *Oluwa!*" said Mama Dewale, the next-door neighbour, running into Mama Bose's compound, tugging anxiously at the flap of her wrapper, tears streaming from her eyes. She cried out in a loud groaning, calling for help from no one in particular. "Blood of Jesus! Blood of Jesus! Blood of Jesus!" Her headscarf was now the robe that held her clothes together. She sank on the untarred floor, oblivious of the wet mud. She was inconsolable.

"Why is this happening to us?" asked Baba Ayo, through chattering teeth, rattling teeth, churning temples of his jaw, almost paralysed with grief.

Mum held Mama Bose in her arms, wiping tears that never run dry. I stood there helplessly watching the horror that befell our community, the horror that never seems to end.

A quiet and calm household an hour ago, was now a scene of tragedy. The community had gathered like a swarm of bees. I could see Mama Bose's Pastor, the celestial leader of a small parish, from four streets away, pacing towards the compound with bare feet, his whitish garment moving in accord to his rushed movements. He screeched to a halt as he arrived at the compound, shaking his head. The news had travelled the minute it broke through the walls. In Yoruba culture and in most African culture, it is as though nearly everyone is related. A community raises a child together. The bond creates a sense of family among people. Everyone is connected. And in times like this, everyone mourns.

"Death, how wicked can you be?" everyone lamented, one after the other. For days and weeks to follow, cry of grief – squeals of women, grunts of men – remained with us.

Our mourning had not yet run its course when horror ripped the community apart again. The plague snatched another life and threatened to snatch more.

Howls of agony got worse at the news of Jacob's death. Pain and sadness bloated with heavy discomfort swept through our community, spreading from one household to another. Our world became brutally cold and codded by the darkness.

Bose and Jacob died within a month of one another, from sickle cell anaemia (SS), shortly before their eighth and tenth birthdays. The pain it caused their parents, the broken-heartedness of their grief, their despair, also struck the community. Their deaths were ignorantly tagged *Abiku* (pre-destined to death). No one knew this was sickle cell anaemia, or the cause, other than some ignorant superstitions of our forefathers. Unlike in the olden days when the elders and royal fathers of the land would have visited the mountainside enclave at the dawn of the night, the riverbanks in the darkness hours, the centre of crossroad with Calabash, the market squares – places shrouded in mysteries – for consultations and prophesies, they simply agreed, men of ignorance, that *Abiku* was nothing but pre-destined.

A few days before Bose's death, I left home after school with some other kids – Jacob, Bamike, Bose, Ayo, Michael and Tope – on a daily search for adventure, miles from home. We walked in the woods and splashed in the stream. We'd just walked past the river that rushed and roared day and night, a place wilderness had collided with jungle, and where we'd caught small tilapias the day before, when Bose started to complain about shortness of breath and fatigue. So, we headed home. Her arms and legs started shaking, frightening shaking, as if she had joint pains. Her eyes were yellow, and her fair skin was losing colour and the glimmer it usually had. She often complained about this, pain in the abdomen, chest, bones, joints and occasionally unexplained numbness, drowsiness and sweaty painful hands and feet; no one knew these were symptoms of sickled, low red blood cells.

It was a routine upon which we had lived our lives. During the day, if there were no parties or activities nearby to attend after school hours, we would go outdoors and play football, or swim in the nearby river, or catch fish, or pluck fresh fruit like pawpaw, cashews, mangoes and oranges. We were born for the outdoors. And at night, everyone would assemble, as if it was a World Cup final match, for the moonlight story. And if it was on a Friday night, that year, we'd sit at the veranda for the one-hour talk show called *Iri ri Aye* – life experiences – transmitted on a radio from the State Capital in Abeokuta.

Growing up in Ilaro, a small town in the western part of Nigeria, was pure bliss. It is hard to forget the amazing communal life and the colourful culture, especially traditional marriages and cultural anniversaries. It was the best childhood experience. It was not a fairy tale experience, but it was an exciting backdrop to some of the more turbulent times.

We arrived back home in good time. You could see the sky filled with beautiful stars. Countless stars. And stargazing was one of my favourite things to do, as if I was witnessing the heavenly dance of falling angels. Bose rested for a little while. She'd been pampered with food and nothing more. She later joined us as we sat on the veranda during the full moon.

"Which story do you want to hear today?" Grandma asked, while arranging us in a circle. The girls were given priority in the front row, the boys at the back.

"The tortoise and the hare story," Bamike said.

"Mama told us that yesterday, how a smart slow tortoise

challenged the proud speedy hare," Michael said. "We want a new story."

"Tell us about the King's Magic Drum or the Lucky Fishermen." Bamike said again.

"Those are boring stories." Bose protested.

"Tell us when day turns into night," Jacob and Ayo echoed at the same time.

One of the epic Grandma stories, it was about the historic event that turned day into night when she was a teenager. She had told us the story a dozen times, but each time was different. She would describe the scorching sun of that day, the events that led up to the historic moment – the colourful traditional marriage ceremony of her cousin at their backyard, the simplicity of it, the relevance of it. Grandma was a lot like William Shakespeare. She didn't write any books or stage plays but she was an excellent storyteller.

"Once upon a time, in the middle of the day, a star and the chilly darkness settled and took over the surface of the earth." Her Yoruba storytelling brilliance was always spot on. "The moon blotted out the sun, so it was reduced to a silvery ring of light."

I looked up to observe the dark silhouettes of clouds moving across the moon. "How did that happen?" I asked Grandma, excited, curious, desperate for the information as if I didn't already know, as if she hadn't told the story many times before.

"Were you scared?" Jacob asked.

"Please tell us more!" Bose said.

"Grandma, what's the moral of today's story?" That was Tope.

"Let Mama finish the story first." Bamike and Micheal this time.

"I will answer all your questions, my children," Grandma continued. "It started so slowly. The moon waxes and wanes.

The sun started to fade. Everybody ran out to see it. Shouting, screaming, excited. Then what was left of the silvery light started to disappear. We didn't know what was happening. Then it was gone. The moon had covered the sun. For about three minutes, there was total darkness. *Osan ti do ru.* Day had turned into night. We were so happy to have experienced it. Our father told us it happens once a lifetime." Grandma went on to highlight the excitement and frightening moments of impact, how her family, the people of Ilaro and its province and the entire world, were stunned in what she'd described as the most memorable event of 1937. And afterwards, she answered all our many questions.

We didn't know what an eclipse was. We couldn't understand how the full-blown solar eclipse plunged daytime into darkness. And this was only one of Grandma's moonlight stories. She had quite a few; there was always something new and refreshing each time. We were told stories about love, compassion, selflessness, forgiveness, hard work. You name it. And every time, either for admonishment or persuasiveness, Grandma would use metaphors and figurative expressions. To emphasise the importance of teamwork, she'd say, "The hand of the child cannot reach the shelf, nor the hand of the adult gets through the neck of the gourd." And if calamity, other than death, befalls, she'd say, "If something that was going to chop off your head only knocked off your cap, you should be grateful."

For a ten-year-old born and bred in Ilaro, it was a perfect life.

Sadly, within a two-month interval, Bose and Jacob were no longer with us. Darkness had engulfed our daytime. The moon had blotted out the sun.

We wished it was an eclipse.

My eyes welled with tears. I sniffed it off, but it never went away during the days and weeks that followed. The same happened to my family too. Each one with his or her dewy-eyed nostalgia and ashen face. In the end, the community still tagged their death as *Abiku*.

A few days after Jacob had passed, I'd observed something different with my mum; her anxiety seemed to grow, and she shuddered convulsively and continuously at almost everything. Her usual calmness was replaced by worries, each day more worrying than the previous. Our daily prayer devotion became more fervent and it was no longer only a morning session. She introduced evening sessions too, which replaced the suspended weekly moonlight tales. We'd sing solemnly and pray fervently until we grew out of breath. And it was compulsory, even if you were knocked out after eating Grandma's mouth-watering soup.

I wasn't at my best either. I'd lost my appetite, my temperature was high, and I was sweating profusely with some abdominal pain and diarrhoea. Mum did the diagnosis and recommended malaria relieving tablets. A few days after, I was back on my feet.

Two months after, our grief had dulled in the way grief does. The long-term school break of three months was approaching. It was Saturday morning and Mum sat in the living room, listening to the headline news on the radio and picking stones from the beans she planned to cook.

"Toyosi, you have to get tested in Lagos during your upcoming vacation," Mum said, with a worried look on her face.

"Get tested?" I asked, in a faint voice. "For what, Mum?"

She snorted. "For sickle cell anaemia."

"What's that?"

"I don't know the details. I'll be double checking with Dr. Kayode on Monday."

"Don't scare me, Mum. Do I have a disease?"

"No, you don't, my son. Nothing to worry about," Mum said, locking me into a long tight embrace. "There's no *Abiku*, but you have to get tested," she added.

"OK. But why can't I get tested here in the hospital where you work?"

"There's no testing facility yet at General Hospital, but Dr. Kayode and his team are currently facilitating the campaign," she said, hugging me tighter.

Mum worked as a nurse, so she knew a bit about the disease but not enough to draw connections to the fallacy of *Abiku*. She had her suspicions and had been trying to find out more from her senior colleagues at work. If her suspicions were right, perhaps it would explain why Bose and Jacob, like many other people, died; maybe there was a way to stop it.

"OK, Mum. I'll get tested in Lagos," I said, slowly, looking into her eyes for relief.

She took me by both arms. "Don't be scared, it will be at your uncle's hospital."

"Testing at Uncle's hospital would be awesome, I can't wait to see Lagos," I told her with a cheery half-smile, as if the news of visiting my uncle's hospital would ease Mum's worries. It did. Her face brightened, no obvious signs of nervousness.

My uncle, Dr Ote, was one of Nigeria's foremost elder statesmen who trained abroad as a medical doctor in the 1950s and owned a private hospital in the heart of Lagos. He'd made it big; I mean *real* big. My Lagos vacation would be at his house, and I was anxiously looking forward to the experience.

As a child, I had great dreams. I was hopeful for a brighter future. I'd lost my dad at an early age, so Mum was the only breadwinner for me and my half-brother.

It was black out. I leaned forward to pick up a lantern, for study time, and sat on a mat on the veranda. The candle I used the day before had burnt down too quickly, and Mum was yet to get a replacement. I preferred the lantern, although the night-flying crawlies often flitted noisily around the bulb and got an unwanted invitation to an endless circular dance.

And if NEPA, the government agency who regulate power across the country, was merciful to us, the front door light would issue an invitation to attract bugs and insects, like a moth to a flame – and a distraction to my studying time.

"Go inside and study," Mum said, flicking away insects around the lantern.

The next day was no different. I burnt the candles at both ends.

***

SCHOOL TERM WAS FINALLY OVER, and I was set for our Lagos holiday.

"What are you looking forward to the most in Lagos?" Mum asked, as she was picking through my clothes for the trip.

"Three things, Mum. Food, food and food."

"You always have plenty food here. Anything else besides food?"

"I want to see the Third Mainland Bridge; I read it's the longest bridge in Africa."

"You're right. It was just completed last year."

"And the beaches. We don't have any here. Rivers are not the same, o," I said.

Mum smiled. "Pray all goes well. You'll be relocating to Lagos soon with everything it has to offer at your fingertips."

"Thanks, Mum," I said, even though I didn't fully understand the conditional prayer.

The next day, we left for Lagos in high spirits. By the time the public transport had arrived at the final bus park in Oshodi, I was asleep. Mum tapped me.

"Wake up, wake up, we're in Lagos. Toyosi, open your eyes. We're in Lagos now."

I woke up to absolute chaos. Our bus was at a standstill. Yellow buses were coming from all directions, crawling in the endless lanes of traffic. Men were hanging around the bus door, greeting each other with a stream of expletives, hurling insults at some of the passengers, and smiling and yelling. Some passengers, too, responded with thundering insults, flung back and forth. Black exhaust smoke swirled thickly around us, fumes belching out. A growl of passing trucks echoed loudly from an overhead bridge, which was about fifty metres away, was ear-splitting. Hawkers and traders blocked our exit while competing for customers; some spoke in street chants; others bantered for attention; some balanced bottled groundnuts, water sachets, sausage rolls and other items on trays on their heads; others strapped newspapers and other items to their chests. Commotion from all directions. Clouds of crowds, sounds and noise erupted as if we were met with cacophony of strange voices, strange world, and yet everyone looked like it was just another normal day.

Mum had told me earlier about Oshodi's notoriety for grid-locks and as a market of legends. "*Oya*, hold my hand, don't leave my hand *o!*" Mum said, as we walked past the session of the gridlock with meat sellers, the butchers in a long row, with their sharp knives knapping on slabs to display the flies, hurling in the air, as though moths were also in display for sale. Still, the flies trailed the mountain of the slaughtered goat meats, rams and cows.

We embarked on one of the yellow buses to Obalende where we took a ten-minute motorbike ride to my uncle's estate at Ikoyi. While on our way to Obalende, I saw the city's slums and men sleeping under bridges. The streets were littered with dirty bins, and mounting heaps of rotten waste; it was a filthy environment attracting mosquitoes and all sorts of bugs. The environment released an unwelcoming odour of rotten eggs, burnt rubber and exhaust fumes. Some men, enduring with great stoicism, rummaged through the waste wreathed with smoke, looking for anything – re-usable items, recycling plastics, bottles, metal straws – anything as a means of survival. Under the busy flyover that highlighted the streets trading complexity, some kids, most of whom in barefoot, were swarming around vehicles. I quickly turned my head away. I wasn't shocked, but the sight of kids begging was distressing.

Finally, the traffic began to ease, and we hit the Gbagada-Oshodi expressway towards the Third Mainland Bridge. It felt like a dream sliding into view. But the commercial drivers were insane. These drivers lurched at full throttle, revved their engines continuously, competed with one another while at great speed, honked insanely, a chorus like kids playing with plastic toys, and played their music loudly enough to pierce your eardrums.

"We're approaching Third Mainland Bridge in less than five minutes," Mum said.

"Really?" I asked enthusiastically. "My Lagos dream is coming true."

"Many of your dreams will come true, including Harvard, someday," she said.

I laughed. Mum smiled. Harvard is just another word for "greatness" in my family. Neither of us knew where it was or what it would take to get there. But it didn't matter.

And soon after, we reached the eight-lane, eleven-kilometre bridge and drove for nearly fifteen minutes. It was a jewel of architecture, an iconic engineering marvel, neatly marked with black and white stripes. The waterfront glistened in the sunset.

The water was blue and beautiful; its tranquillity overwhelmed me. And fresh air came for the first time. If only this feeling could last forever. My eyes roved, observing flashy and not-so-flashy cars, sailing like riverboats. The bridge curved ahead and snaked over the piers. On the other side with four lanes, it was a snail-paced tailback. Two bulletproof cars, wailing sirens, shovelled past and a convoy followed. Some drivers swerved into the lane, attempted to cheat, but soon order was restored by an angry Danfo driver. As I lost the sight of the drama, I returned my eyes to the right, to a floating slum with wooden tents on waters, and not far off, I saw some fishermen at work paddling on canons. The stilts of the lagoon welcomed me to Lagos.

In some measure, the bridge connected the poor and the rich. The high and mighty on one side, the low and powerless on the other. I was overwhelmed by the skyline views of a few skyscrapers not far off, unfolding in front of us, painted orange. Mum pointed and said, "That's Victoria Island where only rich people live." Like in most cities, two distinct classes resided in Lagos: the super-rich and others who wished to be like them.

Our bus drove through the bridge and when we emerged on the other side and continued the journey on a motorbike ride through the Ozumba Mbadiwe Avenue, heading towards Awolowo Road in Ikoyi, one of the city's main arteries at the edge of Lagos Lagoon, it was as though I'd arrived in a new world; a world stemming of verdant lush vegetations and of fresh sea air; a world glowing in lushness, with its upscale boutiques, fancy houses, fancy cars on the driveways, posh eateries and clean roads with no noticeable potholes, league of trees, awash with colours, on the road sides – everything shinning in all its glory.

We arrived at my uncle's house. A mansion that announced its wealth. In the eyes of a ten-year-old from Ilaro, it was like a castle. The whole compound, surrounded by electric, high barbed-wire fence, had glittering lights brightly shinning from numerous florescent lamps, the generator was fully powered, two different satellite dishes on the rooftop, security men in uniform. And the outdoor shrubbery and colourful flowers were simply beautiful. I noticed a gardener too, trimming and watering plants. An idyllic place to live.

We were warmly welcomed by my cousins Rose, Damilola and Junior, and their mother, Aunty Tope, who I always respectfully called Mummy London because she had lived in London before. I wasn't the inventor of the naming ingenuity; it was a common practice. We address Aunty Ronke in Kano as Mummy Kano, Aunty Kemi in Ibadan as Mummy Ibadan. And Uncle Richmond in New York as Daddy America.

"Toyosi, you're a big boy now! Welcome to Lagos, my dear," Aunty Tope said, smiling. She spread her arms wide and hugged me tight while I quickly created a space to prostrate myself. In Yoruba culture, and many African cultures, males prostrate when greeting elders while females kneel as a sign of respect.

"My children, stand up, stand up," Mum said, as though rich kids were exempt.

The warm welcome continued for a little while and soon after we'd flipped through portraits in family albums, we were served our dinner by one of their chefs. My cousins and their mum joined us, too. My uncle had some guests, the city's pre-eminent elder statesmen it seemed, and we could hear their amusing political debates over the news on NTA Newsline.

"This place is too big, but too quiet," I whispered to Mum, as we began to eat. There were many things I could have told her. Nothing here approximated to anything I'd ever experienced; not even the commodious dining table that seated eight people. In Ilaro, our dining table was a mat. All the brands, widely advertised chocolate beverages and milks I was only ever pampered with on the verge of illness or when sickness had invaded, were set before me: Milo, Bournvita, Cowbell and Peak milk. Mum smiled and softly tapped my leg beneath the table. I got the message. Aunty Tope gave a warm smile, as if she knew what was said.

"It's OK to talk, my dear," Aunty Tope said to me. "Do you like the food?"

"Ah, like is an understatement o, Ogbono soup is my favourite," I said.

Everyone laughed. "Rich people don't talk while eating," Mum later told me.

Apart from my forgivable naivety, slurping and "slaughtering" of the chicken bone, you could hear a pin drop. The air conditioning was inaudible: no rattling, no humming. The refrigerator, next to the dining table, whirred in peaceful obedience, too. My cousins ate light; I ate heavy. Soon, a uniformed housekeeper came to tidy up after our meal.

At bed time, I thought of the differences between this place and our house in Ilaro.

We had an eight-bedroom house, each of the rooms facing one another. It was built by my grandfather in the early fifties and he lived there with his family till he passed. Four rooms, at the rear, were rented. Grandma occupied one room, Mum had one, myself and my two elder brothers shared another, and our family jointly used the remaining one as a living room. There was no TV. Pictures on the wall, of the old, dead and gone, and of the young, hale and hearty, were in a chaotic jumble. It was a mud house but neatly plastered and beautifully painted. If not for the mud-splattered house next to ours, where my childhood friends, Bose and Jacob lived, our street could have been more glorified. A big kitchen, like two king-size bedrooms, blackened by fumes was outside beautifully covered with palm fronds at the top. And it was not uncommon to hear goats bleating around the compound, all over the streets, and roosters crowning and squawking all day, sometimes the crow suggesting time of the day especially when the sun is cresting the horizon.

I marvelled at the differences, but I liked how our mango trees added beauty and greenness. And Grandma's food tasted sweeter. Sunshine in every mouthful.

———

THREE MONTHS HAD RUSHED PAST; time had hurtled forward. My holiday was over, and it was high time I returned to Ilaro.

"Oh, Toyosi, how could I have forgotten?" Mum said. "You have to do your test."

"OK, Mum, but that's not why we came to Lagos."

"Yes," she agreed. "But this is very important."

She took me to my uncle's hospital where a blood sample was taken.

"When your cousins come home for the New Year celebrations, they will bring your results; Rose may even come sooner for the yearly Orona cultural festivities," my uncle said, "or should I write you a letter?"

My mum was looking unsure of the best option.

Communication via letters was popular. My uncle had a fixed NITEL line, a cordless portable, on-hook and off-hook, analogue fixed line, of the Nigerian Telecommunications Limited, the monopoly telephone service provider of the era. We had nothing at Ilaro; no one did in our neighbourhood, not even Mr. James, the thriving cocoa trader, who had a TV. NITEL office was across the road. The only time I'd ever tried to dial the NITEL line, at least to satisfy the curiosity of my childhood sense of adventure, I could not make sense of the auto-response message, "all national trunks are busy, please try again later."

"New Year is fine, sir. *E se gan sir, ko wa* urgent at all. Thank you very much, sir. Toyosi, say thank you to Uncle," Mum responded.

"Thanks, Uncle," I said, "but can I ask you a question?"

"Yes, of course. You've always been inquisitive, right from an early age which is always good," he said, as if he knew what I wanted to ask for.

"What's sickle cell anaemia?"

"Good question. There's something in human's body called red blood cells. They are responsible for carrying oxygen around the body. Ermm, there are some abnormal forms of haemoglobin in the red blood cells. It's a condition which limits the healthy red blood cells when transmitting oxygen through the body. Are you following me? You see, normal red blood cells are flexible and round, but for those with the disease, their sickle-shaped cells are usually rigid and sticky, blocking the free flow of oxygen. Do you understand?"

"Yes, Uncle," I said, even though the medical terms sounded like the remix of a song I didn't want to know. Then, I asked, "Does it have a cure?"

"Sadly, sickle cell anaemia has no cure, but interventions."

"What about sickle cell trait? Rose told me about it. What does it mean if one has it?"

"Toyosi, for a ten-year-old, no implications but for an adult ready to settle down, yes there's a price for the wrong decision," he said, drawing me closer, "You see, arithmetic is involved. Basically, a child inherits one gene from each parent. So, if one partner has the trait, and the other doesn't, there's zero risk factor. If two potential partners have the trait, there's a twenty-five per cent chance, for each pregnancy, that their child would have the disease. If one partner has the trait and the other has the disease, the risk factor probability would increase to seventy-five per cent. If both partners are under the clutches of the deadly disease, it's a given their kids would have it. The risk, therefore, depends on whether you're AA – no trait, AS – with trait, SS – with disease or AC, and your partner's genotype."

This time, it was much clearer. "Thanks, Uncle."

"Do you have any other questions?"

"Ermm, not really. Oh, yes I have one more," I said, "which one is AC, again?"

"Those are rare cases. Still an abnormal gene. In medicine, we say, healthy carrier. The majority of people are either AA, AS or SS."

"Mama Toyosi," my uncle said, "we're just concluding a research exercise to debunk what people ignorantly called *Abiku*. Those innocent kids are dying across the country mostly due to their parents' lack of information. Ignorant decisions people make on a daily basis. It's imperative for folks to know their genotype and their partner's, to be enlightened and not blame everything on some non-existent fallacy. We'll be presenting our findings to the Federal Government in Abuja before Christmas. A swift media campaign is necessary."

"Ah, that would be great *o*, thank you, sir," Mum responded. "Those of us at the local level and down at the dispensary community centre would like to know the outcome, too."

"That's fine, Mama Toyosi," he told Mum, and added, as we began to get ready to leave, "I wish you a safe trip back home, get home safe and help me greet Mama."

We left for my uncle's house and began to get ready to travel back home.

On a notoriously traffic-heavy day, the trip could take up to three hours or more. The public transport was an old, unwashed-looking Toyota bus with patches of rust, torn seats and glued broken side mirrors, and held about thirty people, most of whom sat on each other's laps to save some money. I sat on Mum's lap, too. It was a common practice; the bus conductor decided who was old enough to pay for a seat and who enjoyed the benefits of sitting on someone's lap. As soon as that was sorted, and the driver settled the parking and loading fees and other charges levied on him, we embarked on the trip. The bus had no air conditioning to cool the searing heat. Even if it did, the window glass on the left was tampered, hard to wind up and on the right side, half-broken. Moments later, we were on our way. Fervent prayers echoed like an orchestra. You must pray to keep the devil off the road.

Mum's hands were in the air. "*Ni oroko Jesu, ni eje Jesu.* Our lives are in your hands, O'Lord. Grant us journey mercies in Jesus name." And the passengers delivered a resounding amen. Some robbed the amen on their faces, some crossed their chests three times. Mum was a prayer warrior who could go on praying for the entire duration of the trip, given the chance, not only for journey mercies but for each passenger. But that day, Mum kept it short.

Without traffic, the drive takes an hour and a half. But this was almost never the case. The roads were terrible. Some parts were narrow and unmarked, appallingly rutted. You'd have a good drive for twenty minutes and you'd start feeling like you were cruising, then the bus would get stuck in potholes, forcing the driver to step up his manoeuvring skills, negotiating the unpaved road with other drivers, kindly or rudely and then you'd hit traffic. A moment later, you'd become stuck in a bog of red mud on the express road; the wheels would have churned, the engine would struggle and lurch, and off we'd go again. Twenty minutes later, the entire cycle would repeat itself. In this part of the world, there is a popular joke: "you don't avoid potholes, you choose the ones to enter." That was how we rolled.

Soon, the road became bumpier as we ascended on a hill. By this point, we'd travelled past a few towns, knots of villages. We knew we were closer to home. Ilaro is a town on a hill.

We made it back safely. I breathed in the clean air. Our neighbours screamed my name, some cheered, hugging me so tight as if I'd returned from Olympics with gold metal. I sunk into the warmth, appreciative of being home. The lemon-scented smell in the corridor, the smell of fresh yellow-skin mangos exuding their ripe fragrance, the boundless joy of kids shouting "Up NEPA" as power came on, the love received beyond the walls of our home, the warmth of Grandma's arms as she cuddled me – everything – reminded me, I was home.

A few months after, harmattan arrived: the hot, dry and dusty winds. Clouds hung in the sky and right before our noses. New Year was approaching, and my uncle had arrived.

The door cracked open. My uncle parted the room's curtain and walked in. After exchanging greetings, he put his hand on my shoulder. "You have one sickle gene, only one abnormal gene, not a disease. It's generally called an asymptomatic carrier state," he said.

"Is the *trait* common?" I asked, with a curious mixture of happiness and fear.

"Yes, sickle cell trait is common, many many people are affected in this part of the world," he said, "and the disease, sickle cell anaemia itself, is a growing concern."

"My son, you have no disease. *Ko si Abiku ni family wa, oluwa seun.* There's no one pre-destined to die in our family, thank God," said Mum.

My uncle added, "Actually, Mama Toyosi, there's no *Abiku.* Our forefathers were ignorant. It's sickle cell anaemia."

Mum smiled, pleased to know the cause and hoping to tell

Dr. Kayode after the holiday season, to join forces and immediately start an awareness campaign within the community.

I asked in shock, "Does the *trait* cause malaria?"

"No, no, not at all," he said. "In fact, those with the *trait* are healthier. They have protection against malaria. There's nothing to worry about until you grow up and are ready to get married." Then, he paused. "That's a worry for later, not now."

Whatever that meant, for now, was insignificant.

PART 3

THREE

IT WAS NOW ALMOST three years after the heartbreak; I'd not met anyone special until I met Tamilore at Lagos airport over a month ago. I took a gap year to focus on realigning my career goal. Once I was happy with my career progression and ready for a meaningful relationship, finding someone special was harder than I thought. I was looking for a woman with mutual interests who shared the same faith, similar goals, values and purpose. It's not an unreasonable list but finding someone to fit the bill wasn't proving to be easy.

I'd tried to date Jess, but she was a chameleon.

"How's the dating business going, bro?" Matthew asked. We'd been on a call for nearly half an hour, discussing if Trump stood a better chance of winning the next US election, the current debate on my TV screen.

"I'm still on Jess's case, but she's playing the catch me if you can game."

"Toyosi, the chase is enough, let her off. What's she feeling like?"

"Persistence, bro. Persistence. Some women need time and reassurance," I told him.

"No time, man," he said. "You can't be second guessing yourself all day long. Turn the game upside down. Play her at her own game."

Mixed signals, that's what it was. One moment, Jess was excited, flirty and warm. The next, she was cold and aloof. A few days later, I'd get the flirty Jess back. Two days later, she was gone again! The hot and cold queen never stuck out her neck for me to bite.

"How old did you say she is again?" he asked.

"Twenty-nine."

"Save yourself the damn stress. She's twenty-nine, not a toddler."

"Can you recall that Congolese proverb you're always quoting: *To love someone who doesn't love you is like shaking a tree to make the dew falls.* Toyosi, please boot Jess out. OK. Remind me of your current spec," he talked as if it was a car to be changed every year.

"The spec hasn't changed, joker," I told him. "You know the *jewel* that makes you remember praising God twice every morning during your morning devotion?"

It's not too much to ask for, is it? I find intelligent women sexy. I mean *very* sexy!

"A jewel with a big *nyash, abi*?" he asked.

"Ha-ha." I put the phone on speaker and muted the TV, to silence Trump's voice. "Get out of here. *O boy*, I'll take any *nyash o*, big or small, as long as she's smart."

He burst out laughing. "*You no dey* shadow the sisters in church? That's the way, bro. Shadowing!"

The subtle weekly shadowing of sisters after church

service. The positioning in certain key spots. You know how brothers like to look around like tigers hunting for their lunch, constantly on the prowl? Bless you, sister. That's how it always starts.

"Ah! I've done everything, Matthew, still no luck. And then, the endless city meet-ups; events most folks prefer to call professional networking. Who's deserving who?"

"How about Debby? You guys are best of friends. I know she'd friend-zoned you for too long, but you can still zoom in. Try again. Things do change with ladies, you know."

I didn't say anything. I had met Debby around the same time as I had met Jess, nearly two years before. But there was a little problem I wasn't going to reveal to Matthew.

"It's game of numbers. Download Tinder, bro."

I laughed but ignored him.

A few days ago, I wrote a memo to my fictitious bride-to-be who I was yet to meet. The letter was about a page long, a summary of my meeting with Tamilore at the airport. I told the story of how I thought she was the one, but then, in the end, I realised she wasn't. I thought my future bride would want to know this, to know that I kept searching for her.

I briefly described myself as six-foot-one, with dark hair and darker skin. I said I was bearded and dimpled. I noted that I was a perfect gentleman who treated everyone respectfully. I painted my image with words, like an artist wielding his paintbrush.

It was a hilarious take on how I'd looked everywhere for her but hadn't had any luck yet. I posted the letter on XYZK, one of Nigeria's biggest blogs. I created a new email address and baptised myself with a new name. I became Ayo. I was fully masked. Although I'd left my email, I was not expecting any reply but the unexcepted had just happened.

Shortly after the letter went live, I received hundreds of

emails, one after another. Over eight hundred women emailed me from all around the world, most from Nigeria, seeking to know who the anonymous bachelor was. I was shocked. Totally stunned.

I'd scanned the emails as they rolled in, reading the playful, friendly and good-humoured remarks. There were some punchlines. Wordplay. Wisecracks. Witty one-liners. I was in stitches immediately. Even the subject of the emails was hilarious. What will I do with these bundles of joy? I was pumped up like someone who had waited all his life, obeyed all the biblical dating rules, and was ready for the *tango game* on his wedding night.

Last night, I had an idea: an adventurous, online dating competition. But I'd also doubted the idea a hundred times over, wondering if it was a gentlemanly thing to do.

I was a big fan of the American reality show *The Bachelor*. To call me a romantic guy would be akin to calling a pig greedy. When you feed pigs, you see the best side of the little gluttons: they pummel the feeder for more food. When I watch *The Bachelor*, you see me grinning like a fool and I would gladly buy you popcorn if you agree to join the party. I always enjoy the show's entertainment and its spin-offs like *The Bachelorette* and *Bachelor in Paradise*.

I wasn't looking for fairy tale love necessarily, but I wouldn't say no to it either. I was looking for real love. Sweet love. Something beautiful. I wanted to leap into a future with my arms wide open. A future not characterised with fear of sickle cell anaemia. A future unfettered by my wounds and negative experiences. I wasn't looking for Miss Perfect, nor was I looking for a whirlwind romance to boost my ego. I wanted someone special. So far, I hadn't been lucky even on first dates. Someone said my accent wasn't posh. Another said my teeth were not white enough. Someone said she wished I

THE BACHELOR'S RIDE 69

was darker, taller and hunkier. Another said if Ilaro were a borough in London, my background would have made a difference. Basically, I fell incomparably short of their dream man, Idris Elba.

And truthfully, I've turned a few ladies down, too.

So, I figured why not explore a new avenue through the invention of my own online bachelor's show. I called it *The Bachelor's Ride*.

Matthew was still on the call. "Check out Tinder, man." He sounded serious. "Dating is a game of numbers."

"I have another idea, although a little harder than swiping left or right."

"As long as it gets you the result, all roads lead to Rome, bro."

We laughed.

The Bachelor TV series placed the eligible bachelor in the advantageous position of having twenty-five to thirty single women vying for his attention and affection. He eliminates them one by one, until the last woman standing is given a final rose followed by a proposal. Each time I watched the show, I always wished I had the same privilege as the titular bachelor. Who wouldn't want that? Who wouldn't like being the man who calls the shots? The man who has the best of everything at his fingertips? What a gig! You get to laze around the place, get fed, ride in a Bentley, and get pampered night and day and at the end of it, you win love. What's better than that? It sure beats being stuck on the London Underground each day, staring at strangers, hoping one of them is a single woman who might show interest.

"So, what's your wonderful idea that's better than Tinder?" he asked.

I told him. And the full story of how I got to this point.

He burst into laughter. "What? Holy shit. Your letter went

viral? When? How? You mean you're currently trending online. Damn. Send me the link *abeg*."

I laughed.

"And to your idea. Isn't that where Prince Charming shows up in a horse and carriage, or in a Bentley or private jet?" he asked.

"Yeah, that's the show. But mine would be behind the keyboard."

"Man, I hope you find her, that's a stressful road trip you're planning."

"It's an adventure. I might get lucky. You just never know," I said.

"You should change your middle name to adventure, too," he said, laughing.

I've always loved an adventure. If I had my way, I'd swim with sea turtles. If I had the skills, I'd surf in the deepest of oceans and explore the heart of the Hawaii Pipeline, one of the heaviest waves in the world. If only I knew how, I'd indulge myself in alpine skiing at St. Anton in Austria and I'd go rock climbing in Pembrokeshire in Wales.

"Mr. Adventurer," he said. "Jokes aside man, I know you really liked Tami, and I hope someone like her comes around soon. Anyways, send the link now, bad guy!"

I paused briefly. A second thought was running through my mind.

Matthew was laughing. "I hope it's not some old grannies playing pranks on you?"

I ignored the joke. A punch of doubt had hit me again in my gut. I released a heavy sigh. "O boy, I don't think this is the right way to go about finding someone though. Truth is I don't want anything that's disrespectful to anyone. It's all fun and games and this could be my shot, but I need to have a re-think. Chances are I won't go ahead with it in the end."

"Damn. What? Why won't you go ahead? That's so dumb," he said, laughing. "This is real life, man. What you're planning to do is by no means dating. You know this, right?"

"I know. I mean the whole idea of eliminating the ladies one by one. It contradicts everything I stand for. Man, nah, I'm not doing this."

"That's nonsense talk. Forget your damn stupid principle. What do you stand for? Is that climate change or some shit." He hissed. "OK, send all the emails to me or give me your account password. Jokes aside man, why not use this as a rare opportunity to learn more about different women, how they approach relationship, how they like to be treated, what makes them happy, how to manage their mood swings, how to up your flirting game. Yeah, you know what I mean. There's always something new to learn. See it from that angle, bro."

"I hear you. But life isn't always about what we want. It shouldn't always be about our selfish interest. We ought to consider other people. How our actions may affect them. If it's insulting to them..."

"For fuck's sake," he blurted, interrupting my defence. "Please stop this your nonsense gentleman *yeye*, dating is always a number's game. Besides, this is different. Everyone knows what's up. It's not everyday you have eight hundred women wanting to know one random dude who posted some shit romance story online."

"There must be another way. A better way. How do I go about finding one special person in a flood of emails? It's probably easier to stand on London Bridge and count how many people made it to work on Monday morning."

He was laughing now. "It's a fun challenge. Don't be optimistic about finding no one. Some bored married women might have even reached out. Maybe other bunch of fake people.

Don't hang your hope on anything. Behind your keyboard, there's little you can tell."

He still missed the point. "I mean without the idea of a competition. Without weeding through any *stooopid* criteria. Without disrespecting no one."

"Ah, I know your worries. You prefer to know the women on a deeper level. And you think it's insulting to make your judgement purely based on one email. That means you're not living in a real world. Do you know how many women 'evict' guys on daily basis even before we open our mouth to say 'hello'? How about those one-liners on dating sites and SMs with no reply? This shit is real world. Start the damn *show*. You're not disrespecting no one."

After a long debate back and forth, Mr. Tender won. I decided to forge ahead.

Trump's latest tweet, which unequivocally bred a tumultuous cycle of outrageous news, continued trending on television, on virtually every station I'd tuned into in the last hour. We soon changed our conversation to the distraction – the anger-induced, unrestrained, punctuated commentary against North Korea, the concern he could launch a nuclear conflict against the country if he woke up unhappy one day – and weighed his election prospect, as if it was a subject that would light up my loveless life, before ending the call.

I crawled back into my loneliness. *Will I ever find true love?* I swallowed the thought, yet again, until loneliness feasted on my happiness and turned it to despair before bed. *How can the world be so full of people, yet finding one person becomes a struggle?*

FOUR

I SMILED all through while reading your post and I must say you are an awesome writer. I don't know if you are going to reply to this mail but if you do, then I will be elated. Looking forward to your response.

– Aretta

Read the memo to your future wife. What a beautiful piece. I pray you find that true love soon. All the best, dear, and thank you for making me smile like a little girl today.

– Samira

I found your story intriguing and got sad at the end when you did not get your happy ending. I'm not a smooth talker like you but would love hearing from you.

– Beryl

I just read your message. You sound like my perfect man, dreamy, tall and handsome! Even if I'm not your dream girl, I'd like to still be friends with you.

– Lisa

Erm, OK now I'm speechless. Just passing by, but if you reply to this we are going to make a beautiful bond. My name is Ellen. I'm the girl your mum prays you find.

– Ellen

You seem very jovial and full of life. Let's be friends.

– Jadesola

Hey, what's up. You sound like a good storyteller and I liked the flow. It's crazy I'm even writing you but then, we all do crazy once in a while. Wishing u success in ur search.

– Amy

I enjoyed the read. Please can you reply even if u have found the wife already? Hahaha.

– Vicky

I read your note with a smile. I think it was both crazy and artistic.

– Ooche

Aside from being a hopeless romantic, what else do you do for a living? Ha-ha.

– Miss K.

Saturday morning was brighter than usual. Although the weather outside was lost to haze and smog, the inside was stirring up heat and excitement like no other day. In the kitchen, sausage, bacon and tomatoes were sizzling under the grill. I kept a close eye on it while I scanned for more emails. I read the shy ones, the cute ones and the sweet queens.

"Your memo really cracked me up. The whole story (still doubting if it's real), sending a memo to an imaginary spouse. The whole post was captivating. I had to read it to the end. I hope there will be another (just kidding). I really do not have anything exciting to share about myself."

The Road Trip is on, bro. We're live. I texted Matthew.

His prompt reply was always guaranteed when it came to women. If it was business, he wouldn't have replied for at least a week.

Is there room for another bachelor in this?

Are you no longer on Tinder, Mr. Tender?

LOOL. I'm rooting for you. I pray you find this babe.

It was end of January. I was about to begin a three-week holiday in a week's time. I had time on my hands, plenty of time to reply to emails and make my adventurous show, *The Bachelor's Ride,* dream come true. At the same time, I could enjoy my trip to Cornwall.

I turned to the grill, flipped the meat and sprinkled salt, and threw some mushrooms in a pan to fry with butter. That was how I liked them. I'd peeled and removed the stalks earlier. I checked for thyme, garlic and my favourite Nigerian recipes, but I'd run out, so I reached for curry, then the sound of another incoming email distracted me.

"It's me, future wifey, but you can call me Amy as my friends call me. I'm a fashion designer from Ikorodu. It's my passion and I enjoy every bit of it. I'm petite and fair and many people call me pretty, but beauty is in the eye of the beholder. I have so much love in my heart to give you. I want you to be my best friend, my lover, my gist partner, my partner in good deeds, and partner in crime lol and I promise I'll always have your back. It's been almost 28 years, hurry, my love. Forever is not as long as they say it is."

Oh, Sweet Amy, thank you, love!

I flipped to the next email.

"I'm wife material. I'm hot and sexy. Give me a shout if you want it."

Huh! Is that some song lyric? Thank you Miss Spicy, but I'll pass.

"What a beautiful piece! I think she was just enjoying the attention and paparazzi of the airport lounge lol. Oh, when love happens (and I'm sure it would soon), it will be so unexpected; it will barge in and draw on your heart, her heart and lay beautiful claim to your souls and none of you could resist it. So, hang in there, bro! Be expectant!" That was Jami.

That was better, much better. I was a little presumptuous behind my keyboard.

Then I stumbled on another email:

"Hi, I am Sylvia. I saw your long post on TEllen. Wow! It sounded just like the movie I saw early this year *Perfect Match*. You sound great n sweet. Lemme give you a debrief about myself. Am troublesome, fun to be with, a great cook, and a great listener. Family say am smart and quick to understand. Am CHUBBY n I love myself."

Hmm. She's sweet, I thought. *Something positive about her personality. She's in.* I made a prompt decision like a deity who'd consulted the god of divination for answer.

A new email came in. I quickly opened it, while hundreds of unread emails sat in the mailbox.

"I love the way you manipulate words. I love love. Been waiting for someone who will truly understand and appreciate my philosophy about love, I don't know if you are, but your expression lures me into writing you. I'm 26 years, 5.8 ft tall, hardworking, fun to be with. I'm cute in and out. Lest I forget, if I'm late we could be pen pals."

Hmm. Miss Cute. You're not late, love.

"Hello handsome." That was a one-liner email from Hope.

"Hello Beautiful. What's up?" I started off flirty.

"Romeo, o Romeo, wherefore are thou Romeo? You've taken the internet by storm."

"Sweet Juliet, wherefore are thou?" I winked.

And the flirting went on.

This was the adventure I'd been looking for!

I glimpsed the next email:

"Call me if u need a lady who is loving, caring, smart, good cook, Godly and funny as hell. Sending u a photo of me. Plus, u can call me up on xxx."

I stretched and let out a long yawn. This wasn't the email to make me fall asleep now. I shook myself awake.

Damn. My food. I sprinted to the kitchen. *Oh, no!* There was nothing left of the mushroom, the sausage was as dark as my skin colour. The bacon was charcoal. I flipped off the frying pan. I switched off the grill, washed and dried my hands and helped myself to toasted bread and orange juice; time to focus on the important business at hand.

Thanks, Miss. But I'll pass.

Next was Isioma's:

"Your story is so hilarious. I am just wondering if such

people exist. I'm Isioma and will like to know you more. I know you have lots of msges right now, but I don't mind being a friend. I'm from a very humble background and love to meet people."

Isioma was lovely, wasn't she? This was so freaking difficult. Too many amazing people. I was indecisive, so I needed a method for this madness.

I faced an exciting challenge of filtering the emails.

The moment I read Uju's email, I knew *The Bachelor's Ride* had attracted beautiful souls.

"I don't even know what to type. All I know is that while reading your post, my heart started racing, I read hurriedly cos I wanted to know 'the end'. I realised how much I have missed being in love."

That was sweet, very sweet. I could feel her sincerity pumping beneath every word.

FIVE

OK. LET THE SELECTION BEGIN. I scrambled through the hundreds of unread emails, hoping I could find one more that exquisitely stood out. Just one more. I kept scrolling, digging for luck, swimming through the flood, reading only the subject titles. My shoulders had seized up. My eyes were exhausted. My cluttered mind was jammed with all the emails.

The phone's light peeped. It was Matthew. *Any luck yet?*

Mr. Tender, you think say nah yam, I replied. *The email floor is too high.*

Well, do you have search words?

Search words? He'd lost me. *This is so scientific.*

Hahaha. Rather than reading through hundreds, search the key words you'd like to see.

Brilliant idea. *Hmm, man of wisdom. You've cracked the code.*

And when you find that special email, pass her details to me for review.

I laughed. *Pass fire.*

The brainstorming session took over for a minute or two. I

went for "beautiful smile". A few emails popped onto my screen. I read Betty's; she'd referenced the note the flight attendant delivered on the plane. As I scrolled down, my eyes were becoming dry from staring for so long. I kept digging for gold and shortly after, my eyes caught something. I froze. Like the arrival of a moon peak in the dusk of a winter night, the unexpected had cracked through. A reply from Tamilore Talulu. A grin crept onto my face; it danced on my lips until I remembered she was not single after all. Nevertheless, I delayed opening the email, to absorb this moment. Tons of possibilities played tricks in my mind.

I never opened Tamilore's email until I'd pictured and daydreamed about the wonderful future I wished to see, then, an hour later, I got to the reality.

"I hope you're keeping well, Toyosi. I'm so sorry for keeping mute all this while. I'll explain when we see each other. Me and my younger sis, Tara, are looking forward to seeing you in London next week. Please write back. Tamilore."

Phew.

I read it a dozen time and skipped the Tara part; my head was swimming. I'd let go of her thoughts blocked in my memory. Then, I sprinted onto her Facebook page to feed my eyes. I didn't miss the updated relationship status from "In relationship" to "Complicated". It was as if I'd seen the radiance of a sunrise, the dwindled sunset of a month ago had just risen. I needed this joy, this inexplicable joy trembling inside me, this thing whirling over my head, glowing in my chest, that pumped my heart so fast: hope bursting into my lonely loveless life.

The special one slipped through, AGAIN. I texted Matthew.

Ha-ha. Na fine babe?
Must she be fine, joker?
Na correct babe?

Mr. Tender, she's all of the above. Tamilore Talulu.

What??? For real? She saw the viral memo?

I don't know. Maybe, maybe not. She replied to one of my emails.

Will get the gist when I'm in town. Please, no matter how tempted you are, don't reply her yet. Keep her guessing for a few days. You have to play a game.

Maybe I'd reply her on Thurs, in two days time. She's in London next week.

That's so dumb! LOL. Go on Tinder in the meantime. Get distracted. You MUST NOT reply her till the weekend.

LOOL. You're sooo stooopid. LOL. This girl is scattering my head.

You'll get this babe if you stick to three golden rules. Just get a beer ready for every rule. LOL. As a start, tell yourself, she's just another girl, nothing special.

LOL. Mr. Tender, is that rule number one?

Don't be stooopid. That's no rule. LOL.

Matthew was visiting London over the weekend, ahead of his training and short holiday. I delayed my reply to Tamilore. I needed his opinion before I misfired my bullet.

Let's get the road trip started.

I became a pen pal to ten women. This was the beginning of *The Bachelor's Ride*. Who knows? Maybe my future bride was among them.

In a half-humorous, half-adventurous attempt at finding true love, I wrote, "Hey lovelies, I'm super pumped to get *The Ride* started lol. I'll remain anonymous throughout and only share my pictures with one person at the end. I'd prefer if you don't share yours too, so the entire process is anonymous for everyone. Ayo." I clicked on the Send button. In no time, the reply notification drummed sounds on my phone like an orchestra.

I hoped love would unexpectedly catch up with us. Finding love should be a gradual process, like a drizzle: it comes softly, but still swells the river. I hoped no one would test the depth of a river with both feet. Anyways, after a few warm-ups, the stage was set. Red wine in hand. Ready to get cosy. I swept through and re-read Ellen's email: "If you reply to this, we're going to make a beautiful bond... I'm the girl your mum prays you find."

"Should Mama be given the credit for her prayers yet?" I replied, teasing.

She responded quickly. "Give Mama all credits already. She deserves it." She added, "I don't even know how to describe this. Before now, I was naïve and a virgin to online adventure. You, my dear, have dis-virgined me."

What a way to describe an eye-opening experience! Ellen was indeed a clown. It felt like I'd done the *thing*. Cheeky. Her light-heartedness attracted me. It was good to know I'd changed someone's perspective. I was hopeful *The Ride* was leading me down the right path.

I composed a reply. "I like the sound of that lol. So, what do you do for fun?"

"Movies. Dancing. Travelling. Watching documentaries. Should I continue? LOL. I enjoy reading gossips blogs too – about dating or relationship drama lol."

"Ah, nice lol. Have you read *how to unmask the mystery man behind the keyboard?*"

"Well, that sounds like a serial killer title, doesn't it? lol. I'd rather click on *how to know if he's the one.*" She winked. "What do you consider the sign of a great first date?"

"If it's called a date, not a hangout." I replied instantly.

"Hahaha. Sounds like one babe *don show you pepper*, LOL."

We began to exchange more emails. I learned a bit more

about Ellen, a practising lawyer who majored in maritime law and worked as an in-house lawyer for a marine firm.

Communication was easy between us and there had been no awkwardness to slough off.

It was Saturday evening, so I rushed off to Heathrow Airport to pick up Matthew. I waited for a while, watching the excited faces bouncing on their toes and the bored people dragging their feet. As he arrived at the gate, I saw him in his black slim-fit jogger, red flat hat, looking casual in his white T-shirt with the slogan: One Babe At A Time. Matthew was suave. The taxi driver standing next to me, with a tablet displaying what seemed to be a Chinese name, couldn't make sense of my giggles. My chortle had softened the driver's tired-looking face. Matthew brimmed towards me with laughter. He shook my palms, our shoulders bounced on each other, with a force of energy as if two cars collided.

"The Mayor of London. Son of a Yorubaland. Valour is a title. I hail you, bro."

"Your highness, the dreamer of French Royalty. The Igwe of Nnewi Kingdom. I accord you with a soothing crown that ascends the hills." I took a bow.

We clicked fingers as we shook hands again. "How are you doing, bro? All the babes have missed you in Lagos."

We roared with laughter.

The freestyling was the sail upon our boat. It was guaranteed anytime we reconnected. Soon, we got into the car and the real banter started.

OK, let's get to some serious gist.

"She arrives in London in two days and I'm yet to reply."

"You see, when a woman says her relationship status is

complicated, she needs another man to remove the complication. And for her bringing her sister into this, she's throwing
you a baton, to see if you're going to catch it or fling it off."

"Really?" I considered his words.

He switched to another radio station, another R & B song
resounded in the air.

"If you're a Master of Games, Mr. Tender, how come
you're still single, with your hundreds of right swipes per
week?"

"I'm not settling now, bro. Until I arrange some cash," he
said, with feigned amusement.

He didn't have any excuses. Matthew was a commodity
trader with the highest paid bank in Nigeria. He recently
bought a three-bedroom flat at Parkview Estate, a lovely, classy,
and ultra-modern estate with a rich mix of breezy neighbour-
hoods; well-off neighbours, who enjoyed luxurious lifestyles.
His side hustles, website design business at Lekki Phase II and
kids' provision dealership business at Ikeja were booming. And
he had been prudent in his lifestyle, occasionally revelled in
luxury living, but he never went on a spending splurge. I was
not surprised; Matthew hardly ever acknowledged his growing
business empire.

"I hope you're not messing around with these girls?" I asked
him with a serious face.

"No, men are on Tinder to pray for them," he said, rolling
his eyes. "Bro, I've told you, download this thing. Change your
game."

Matthew was facetious. Always a little sarcastic in his
approach. Maybe he wished to be a "bad boy", but he wasn't.
He wasn't a "good boy", either. He was perfectly in the middle.
Ladies extolled him and reviled him in equal measure.

I didn't answer him. But I was secretly considering it.

"So, how far with the road trip?"

"It's full of amazing people. These ladies are lovely. I hope love finds me this time."

"Have you seen their pictures?"

"No. I don't want to pick based on looks."

"Stop that nonsense, bro."

I laughed it off. And we bantered over and over as I powered through the highway.

An hour later, we arrived home and had dinner. My hands had been itching to scroll down my emails. I waded through the flood for Ellen's reply. *Oh no!* She'd broken the rule. Her pictures were staring at me. Then, Matthew's old joke flashed through my mind. "When a woman is picture perfect, she becomes an exception to the rule, to any rule at all."

Well, today, Ellen became an exception to the rule. I held my breath. Have you seen cherry blossom before? The gorgeous flowers with tightly curled buds, planted in pink clusters. If you have, you'd recognise the unique beauty of the blossoms; that was Ellen.

I wasn't jumping for no joy yet. Beauty is only skin deep, after all.

Matthew was on Tinder, and he'd been frozen for nearly two minutes, ready to swipe right on a topless lady, beautifully proportioned, with a classic straw hat who cupped her big breasts with both arms. Lips the colour of tangerine. "What are you looking at, Mr. I-don't-want-to-pick-based-on-looks?"

"The road trip is delivering dividends, Mr. Tender," I said, smiling, as I shrugged him off and went to bed. He laughed hysterically. He knew the score.

I sent my reply to Tamilore, as my heart continued to throb with hope.

The next morning, Matthew emerged from the guest room and flipped the light on, "O boy, *you don hit jackpot*," he said, laughing.

I fumbled about, rolling on the bed, then, stretched to read the bedside clock. It was 07:03. Too early for banter. I ignored him and rapped the duvet over my head.

He was laughing out louder this time. "If you and Tami rekindle the spark, that's a win. If I come with you for a group date and her sister finds me interesting while Tami finds the solution to her complication in your arms, then that's a double win."

"Is the app down today?"

He laughed. "I have good news for you, bro." He tossed his phone to me.

Tamilore's picture was staring at me. My heart thudded a beat. I sat upright and rested my head against the bedframe. What was Mr. Tender up to? I read the incredulous expression on his face. He had read every single article on her online, digging for her sister's name or profile or family album. Anything. I watched him, as he felt a sudden flare of joy.

He told me the outcome of his finding. "Tami is AA."

I scooted off the bed. "Matthew, please be serious. For real?"

He smiled and took his seat. "Sickle cell is off the table, bro. It all comes down to you and your weak game."

Oh, thank goodness. My heart rejoiced as if it was all I needed to know.

I'd also learned more than what her social media account could reveal. She was twenty-seven years old. I already knew that. But I didn't know she was the first daughter of a former governor during the military rule in the 80s, the old money of the Old Nigeria State.

I read the drafted notes on his phone.

Tamilore's pet peeves were lies and noisy eaters. We both detested dirty dishes in the sink. Her relationship deal breakers were cheating and abuse; mine were poor hygiene and nagging. We both cared about giving back to society, helping those in need; we were passionate about supporting charities or good causes, recognised God as the cornerstone of our lives, had similar taste in the arts and dance, and lest I forget, we're both foodies.

"Professional stalker. All this stalking for a free dinner, yeah?" I teased him.

"*O boy*, double trophy for the team isn't a bad idea, you know," he said, laughing. "OK, I know you've got games. But you need to master a few golden rules. You remember the number one dating rule, yeah? You must not let her know you're crazy about her. Women love to chase men who are not readily available; not men who are chasing them."

Hmm. Word of wisdom.

I sighed at his generalisation. "And what if she's seen the viral letter? That means she knows I'm crazy about her. I've already broken the rule, haven't I?"

"You've broken half the rule. The other half is never to be seen chasing."

"Good point, good point. OK, rule number two please."

"Nah. Not so fast. I'm in for the dinner, yeah? That's just beer equivalent, isn't it?"

I thumbed a response. He'd earned a slot to the group dinner. In his buoyancy of a character, he jumped to a dancing move. Gratitude flowed through him, as if I had the power to stitch two hearts together.

"OK, cool. Here's the thing. Make her to be doubtful of your every move. To keep second guessing if you're in or out. It's a game. Make her analyse your case with her friends. If you cross the line too quick, nothing is exciting. You will likely lose her to a bad boy."

"How's this different from *don't be crazy about her?*"

"It's not. It's rule number one, extension." He was laughing like a mad man.

"*O boy*, I'm thirty-five years old. I can't be playing dumb game at this age. I want a mature woman. No time to waste, man. Besides, at the end, she might not be interested."

"Fair enough. But you must learn to differentiate between a woman who's not interested and the one who's playing hard to get. Yes, the lines are sometimes blurred with the chameleons but that's your top job to discern. Real quick, real fast. This time, the odds are in your favour. I don't need a beer to tell you this babe is playing damn hard to get. Or at best she's indecisive. And in that case, help her decide. Help her make a good decision. On a normal day, you don't stand a chance with this babe. She's dating one hot doctor in Atlanta. So, here's rule number two. Get in her head as a good friend and tell her you have a babe."

"Mr. Tender, you're officially very *stooopid*."

He laughed. "I'll save you the last rule, the top golden rule for later."

I switched to the bulk email to fetch Ellen's out. "What's going to hurt me in all of this is I won't get to put a face to the poet who responded to my goofy ass silly mail. When all this is over, I'll beg you profusely for a picture and God will touch your heart. Amen."

I kept her in close range, and she became even sweeter.

SIX

WHILE ELLEN and I were bonding, Tinu craved for some attention. Aretta wasn't getting enough. Olamide was distressed at the slow communication pace. Queen, Peggy, and Jami were quiet. Dasola was pissed off. She didn't do competition and noted emphatically that a gorgeous queen like her should be chased by a man, and not the other way around.

I get it.

Adanna had sent plenty pictures and she wanted mine too. Mercy beaconed in the waiting game.

I rolled the dice. It was Peggy's turn.

"Your story is heart-warming. Will you be my pen pal?"

I liked the subtleness of her first email. The twenty-six-year-old hedge fund manager, a single mother of twins who worked for Bloomberg in Central London, lived within an hour's drive. Because she was closest to me, I had good reasons to stick around.

"Absolutely. We're already pen pals, let's take it to the next level, shall we? LOL. What's the most important thing you look out for in a guy?" I replied.

"I like men with good teeth. Clean teeth. You know what I mean? LOL."

"Damn. Will yellow-cheese spot in the mix make a cut?"

"You must keep hope, my friend. Nothing dentists can't fix. Are they complete?"

"Ha-ha. As at today, yesssssss."

"We thank God. That's good teeth... having them first... ha-ha."

We hit it off.

After scanning through emails like a man searching for his winning lottery ticket, I reached out to Mercy. She was the calm to my wild. What I admired most was her questioning skills. The eloquence and succinctness of her emails. "How would you describe a beautiful woman?" she asked. I smiled and composed a short reply: "A woman who is compassionate at heart, not one defined by her shining, dark complexion or lighter, brighter, and whiter skin." I clicked "send" and hit the refresh button two or three times, as if her next question would auto-display. An hour later, it did. "How proud are you of your childhood experiences?" A few hours later she asked, "How do you manage conflict resolution in relationships?" I wrote back to each question in detail, the words flowing like water.

On Monday evening, I marched into the guest room to deliver the much-awaited news to Matthew. The bookshelf was now half-empty, clothes, cushions and an unwashed plate on the floor were waiting to greet visitors, with magazines swimming on the bed. The coffee table was straining under a pack of beer; the laundry basket was pleading for help with a mountain of T-shirts, jeans and discarded wrappings. I wrinkled my nose at the smell of stale beer. Mr. Fashionista was a mess. The sound from the wireless speaker was at its loudest. His body swayed to the music. And he was drowning in the sound, pumping the music through his veins. He didn't notice me until I unplugged the iPad he was clutching.

"Tamilore and Tara have arrived in London. And a group date scheduled for Wednesday."

Smile rumbled out of his throat with expressible delight. "Yes, yes... oh... yes... yes... yes."

His happiness was so intense it scared me.

I gagged in disgust. "Clean your mess, mister. And you're coming just as a friend."

He stumbled over the cushions on the floor and picked up a pair of shoes. An exquisitely designed leather sole, with brushed calfskin, uniquely crafted. "Toyosi, check this out. I'm set for Wednesday." He chuckled, crinkling his nose and eyes. "Bro, let's do some wicked shopping tomorrow," he added.

"Dude, you're coming as a friend, remember?" I said.

"You and Tami are my number one prayer point, now. Tami is your babe, bro. Tara is mine." He sneezed and laughed at his own words, talking as if he had a magic power to make things happen.

I grabbed the iPad to reduce the volume that was blasting over our heads.

"Did you get any inclination from Tami? She is in, right?"

He looked like someone intoxicated with happiness. He seemed sincere, too. I could see how the happiness was dancing through his words. I decided right there, regardless of what happened between me and Tamilore, I'd support Matthew to find love in Tara's heart.

I watched him, as he enjoyed the soft jazz collections brightening his mood.

"I don't know," I replied, as I turned back to my online business.

"By the way, how's the road trip going?"

My expression said it all. "There is a little mystery to one of the ladies."

"Mystery?"

"Yes, but I can't place it yet."

"Lover boy," he said. "And what could that be?"

"I don't know. I'm missing the natural face to face conversation, especially the body language. And the tone of voice that can easily give a clue, whether happy, monotonous, restrained or whatever. You know what I mean. The email interaction limits this."

He paused the music, as his favourite song came on. "You feeling her?"

I let out a shrugged breath. "Well, you know... each time I reply to Mercy, I always notice a little nervousness. There's something strange about her."

I was not surprised to see the mocking laughter on his face.

Mercy lived at Anthony Village, on The Mainland in Lagos. She proved a love email is faster than a love letter. Her emails didn't leave a bad taste in my mouth. They were always beautifully written and received in good time. But there was no way to see if a single tear stained the page while she drafted them. I always sensed an emotional tone in her emails. Sometimes, she sounded scraped and bruised. Perhaps a heartbreak. She had been in a relationship with Jonny a few years back and her values of trustworthiness, honesty, transparency, loyalty and faith had been betrayed. These values defined our shared interests.

"Anyways, let's get ready for Wednesday. Remember hoodies are hot; hood up is hotter. So, top up your fashion game. This is one shot. Shoot and hit. No missing."

"Tidy up your jungle, Mr. Fashionista." I laughed as I left him in his mess.

I KEPT a close eye on another lady.

Queen Shonda. Holy cow!

She was painted in one colour, from head to toe. Her black-ness glittered so stunningly. And her skin, the dark skin that resemble night fall, appeared so soft and supple.

The twenty-five-year-old freelance journalist lived in Paris. I always wanted to see more pictures of her, so sometimes I offered to write a beautiful piece as a bribe for a picture in exchange. It worked. Queen was a lovely lady who enjoyed witty banter, sensitive gestures, and thoughtful debates. And whether she was sipping champagne or her favourite Fanta drinks; cooking a new cuisine or out for a buddy's get together party, Queen was captivated by every experience – mind, body and soul, but she held a certain mystery, too.

An hour later, Matthew strode into my room, laughing, until he noticed what seemed to be the face of a tired-looking man. "You got this, bro."

I let out a drawn-out sigh and erased whatever was on my crestfallen face. I took my eyes off the laptop, leaned back on the seat, and clasped the feeble hands, yearning so anxiously to hold someone special. He stifled a yawn like an attempt to mock me.

"Do you think I'm stupid with this whole idea?" I hadn't realised the worries clinging to my heart were transparent on my face. I'd become a shadow of my former self.

"It's an experience, mate, enjoy it. After all, you're on holiday."

I waited to hear more.

"See, life is a road trip. Sometime, the sharp bends doesn't allow you to accelerate and neither does the steep hills make it easier to climb, but soon, the road would level-up for speed and power. Well, that's my preparation speech for Tara if she comes feeling down." He laughed to his own joke. "Jokes aside man, you gonna look back and laugh at this. So, bro, keep your hands on the wheel, and you know what to do. Keep moving."

That was exactly what I needed to hear. I decided it was time to fast track the process.

He cleared his throat mockingly. "I want to ask where we're meeting Tami and Tara."

"In your messy bedroom." Laughter found its way back to my lips.

He laughed. "You scored a goal. Wait for mine." He'd unearthed a greater joy than I'd seen in him since he arrived. He ran his fingers over his untidy beard and cheeks, smiling, one hand holding up his balls in his boxer shorts, I knew a joke was coming. "Imagine all the magic that could happen if we advanced that quick. That would be the finest mess."

SEVEN

Have you ever experienced that unsettling moment when it feels like your day has fallen down a rabbit hole? Felt the feeling that originates somewhere behind your navel and steals your breath for a moment? Maybe the day started like any other, an alarm clock pulling you out of slumber's sweet embrace. And then slowly, things started to turn. Small things at first: perhaps you stubbed your foot on your bedframe or put your socks on inside out. It's funny, how a series of silly occurrences can lead to something memorable.

But I guess hindsight is always 20/20.

It was now Wednesday night. Matthew had been ironing for almost an hour, doing karaoke throughout the time, happy and humming like a bee. The T.M Lewin shirt was starkly straightened up, his new slim-fit linen jacket from Hugo Boss was perfect, and there were no creases in his chinos. I was so nervous I'd changed my clothes three times. Finally, I settled for an open-neck, fitted button-down white shirt and straight-leg cream chinos.

"Are you going to church?" he asked, crouching behind laughter.

I knew this was coming. "This is simplicity at its best, no?" I genuinely wanted support, as if my fashion sense was the cause of my loveless life.

"You look dapper, but for a church girl." He was giggling loudly this time, as he held his stomach as if his belly hurt.

Overwhelmed with the disappointment of my life, I took a second look at myself. The cotton fabric blended well, no bunching or puckering. I had ironed out every wrinkled crease. The band of rolled up sleeve was two folds below the elbow. I switched to a mirror to see my hair. Neatly cut. My dimples deflected the two pimples that sat on my cheek.

Anxiety pricked around my spine. *Do I need to brush my teeth again?* I checked the whiteness of it. Damn. I stumbled into the bathroom and gargled another mouthwash. I hated the uneven yellow spots so stubborn to wash off, no matter how hard I brushed them. Why would anyone have yellow-cheese teeth? Sometimes, I feel like punching off the two oversized 'caterpillars' in the front row that refused to form square alignment. And the gap in between, is just so cute; not alarming. If I'd been born with a silver spoon, I would have had braces as a kid. I wondered what I could ever do to make them as perfect as Tamilore's.

Maybe I should wear another perfume. It was as if worries had suddenly swallowed me. I gathered all the self-assurance in the world: *Fine boy, no pimples.* I'd no cause for alarm except for the anxiety that was grabbing my tongue and drying my mouth.

Matthew buckled his trouser as he dressed up, accentuating his features, the slimness and his sturdy physique. "You're cool, bro. I'm just messing. But leave another button open. Flex a little. Not like a bad boy, but don't be too good a guy. And if you're serious about removing her complication status tonight, change that canopy you called a shoe."

Fuck.

I took out two other loafers in different colours. "Which one, now?"

"This one, right here." He held out a pair before he gave me some shoe lectures.

Finally, we braced for the most anticipated dinner of the year. I took a pose in front of a mirror, creasing up in the little aura of hotness. A minute or two later, Matthew pushed me aside for his turn. He was ready to pull a big shot today. His beard was well-shaved. His white shirt unbuttoned at the collar. His brown starched jacket sat straight and upright, showing off his muscular forearms like a man who had been lifting Olumo rock all his life. He checked out his metallic strap watch. The Africa-map necklace on his neck, the one he took from my room, dangled beautifully, and he wore a fake ring on his wedding finger.

"You're a whole snack for Tara tonight, aren't you?" I teased him, as he carried on combing and straightening his fashionable stubble over his cheeks. "OK, serious question. Remind me of your plan again with Tara. To get down on one knee or to pop a cherry?"

"You have my word, Toyosi." His eyes promised honesty.

I trusted him.

There was only one thing left to do before stepping out. But not on my knees today, not when Mr. Tender was here. So, under my breath, I decided to say the silent words in my mind.

"Are you praying or something?" His mocking laughter was over the roof now.

Damn, this stooopid man has caught me!

I quickly rushed through my supplications. "You know, just a few carabos!"

He wouldn't stop mocking. We laughed and laughed and bantered.

In good time, we arrived at The Shard Restaurant, a contemporary cuisine with a spectacular London view. The room was vibrant and classic. The waiters were smart in their black and white uniforms. An irresistible smell of food, ambient-scenting smell, filled the space.

Twenty minutes later, the two angels walked in. At the sight of Tamilore, my heart almost collapsed with happiness. I stood up to approach her, arms spread wide, as she moved towards me. I felt every ounce as she pressed her body tighter to mine. My arms squeezed a fraction tighter. It was followed with a peck on the cheek. She smelled of fruity flavours. Sweet, creamy and soothing scent of coconuts and unguents. So light, so fresh.

Lord, let this day go in my favour. The silent prayer again. I took a deep breath, respected myself and crushed the surge of anticipation. I'll be so mad if I mess this date up.

"It's so lovely to see you," she said, in her dulcet voice. "How are you doing?"

Her words, the softness of her voice, still untied all my knots.

"I'm alive and kicking, so lovely to see you again."

I turned to the other lady in her fitted sleeveless purple dress that showed off her figure. She looked as stunning as her pictures, except for the dark little freckles. The tall frame seemed to run in the family. "You must be Tara." I stretched out my hand with a smile all over my face.

Tamilore stepped between us. "OK. Let me do the proper intro. Meet Tara, my sis."

I hugged lovely Tara who rubbed her arms warmly around my back. "Lovely to meet you, Tara. I'm Toyosi. You guys look amazing," I said, as I turned the ladies' attention to the huskiest man in the room. "Meet Matthew, my old pal from Lagos."

Matthew, who had been playing cool, nodding a cheerful hello, shuffled forward and offered a big smile. He began his charms with an handsake to the ladies and joined in the pleasantries which carried on for the next few minutes before we ordered for our drinks and starters.

"How's Houston?" I asked Tamilore.

"Houston is awesome, bright weather as always," Tamilore said. "You guys should visit sometime. I remember Toyo saying he's been a few times, how about you, Matthew?"

"I've visited Dallas, Austin and San Antonio, but not Houston. I've heard so much about its vibrant Nigerian community, can't wait to visit," Matthew said in a new, sudden rich, deep, mellow voice. Almost like a radio voice with its baritone richness. "Is Tara Houston based, too?" Mr. Tender threw his first punch to the woman of his dreams.

Tara was tickled by her own shyness. She sipped her glass of orange juice. "Yes, I'm H-Town girl." Her American accent was letter-perfect. And no slight trace of Texans drawl.

"*H-Town*," I repeated. "I like how you Americans nickname every city. *The Big Apple, Sin City, The Big Easy.*"

Matthew dropped his elbow on the table. "Hershey, Pennsylvania seems to have the coolest. *The sweetest place on earth*, they call it. I'll need to figure out what it takes to relocate there," he joked. His eyes sought out Tara, the eyes so full of longing.

Everyone laughed.

I faced Tamilore who rocked in bright apparel, in her casual staples, not a stitch of make-up. "What brought you guys to London?"

"Tara is relocating here for her PhD next month. One of

the reasons why we're here. And I'm doing some filming, to be televised next season. So, I'm here for about four weeks."

I hope one of the other reasons is to find love. That naughty feeling in my head.

We dived into the pile of food in front of us. I love shrimps, especially when they are fried to a crisp. I placed some on my plate and dished out a few for Tamilore who sat next to me. Matthew was in action mode. He took the napkin from underneath the cutlery, placed it on his knee and handed Tara hers. They both served themselves – Matthew had prawns and salmon; Tara settled for the spicy chicken wings she'd specifically requested. Matthew couldn't resist the urge to serve everyone with the mixed green salad and tomatoes, but Tara first. I helped with the glasses, as he poured some water for the ladies.

"How's your writing going?" Tamilore asked.

I nearly dropped the shrimp I was drenching in the sweet sauce. "It's going well, thanks. I'm even thinking of writing a novel," I said, smiling.

"A novel?" Tara said, matching my excitements and running her hand through her hair. "Tami did say you're a data scientist."

"I write on the side, as a hobby."

"That's so brilliant," she said. "Really, really cool. If you don't mind me asking, what are you planning to write about?"

I read Tamilore's reaction. "A love story. A beautiful love story," I said, smiling. "I'm thinking of focusing mainly on the relationship hurdles – I mean the first steps. A spin from the norm like flipping the romantic trope on its head by putting a man in the hot seat."

"Sign me up already, sounds really unique, so cool," Tara said, smiling. Her tresses tumbled, as she flicked her locks behind her shoulders, letting the hair fall freely. "Well, maybe you can me help write a story, sometime. I'd pay, if it's not too expensive."

The ladies exchanged sideways glances. Matthew took a swig of his drink.

"A romantic story?" I asked, jokingly.

Matthew cleared his throat and rested his palms on his knees. "How's the food, guys?" He pretended to ask everyone, but his first glance landed on Tara's face.

"Very nice meal," Tara answered and continued scanning through the main menu.

Damn, Mr. Tender, good luck to you.

He did a discreet throat-clearing this time, chopped and tossed the salmon, dressing it with the sauce, ready to go. "Yeah, the food is great, this is one of the best restaurants in town." He talked as if he still lived in London.

"Have you been posting on any blogs lately?" Tamilore re-directed the conversation.

Oh!

Matthew perked up and caught my glance, as if to say, "let me handle this." He quickly swallowed the smoked salmon he'd stuffed into his mouth. "Tami, your show is really amazing. I'm a fan. I'm always glued to the TV when it comes on DSTV."

I let him do the talking while I crunched another shrimp. He did well. The conversation derailed to Tamilore's TV career and took the better part of the night. Each time Tara dipped her chicken wing into her sauce before it travelled down her throat, our eyes always met. And she always held it. The seating arrangement was weird. Tara sat directly opposite me. I could read the room's temperature faster than nipples stiffen in a breeze.

The main course arrived: steak for the ladies, seafood for the men.

"Are you married?" Tamilore asked Matthew. I'd expected this earlier.

Matthew cleaned his mouth with a napkin. "I'll soon be," he said.

"You engaged?" Tara asked. Matthew was trying his hardest to hold a glance.

He cringed before fixing his gaze on Tara, hunched in confidence and delivered his next lines in his new husky timbre voice. "I've met a woman I'd like to marry but she's yet to decide what she wants. So, at the minute, I'm married to all the ladies out there."

Joker.

His first statement could have been me talking.

Tara's lips quirked in disbelief. Tamilore and I laughed. "And you?" Matthew passed the baton back to Tamilore, while his eyes heedfully tilted in the direction of his desire.

Tamilore waited for her mouthful of steak to go down. She sliced another chunk with her knife. "The steak is too thick to chew. Maybe I should have gone for medium."

Matthew allowed the question to slip off, as he steered the conversation away.

Soon, dinner was over. We headed to the observation deck on the 72nd floor to appreciate London's incredible skyline. Matthew had the chance he'd been waiting for with Tara, narrating some made-up stories about the Shakespeare's Globe Theatre, while Tamilore and I surrendered to the bliss around us. I controlled my chest shuddering at her smile.

"I'm so sorry I didn't reply to all your emails."

"No worries," I said. "I can understand. I got a reply via your Facebook page."

Her teeth were out and bright. The dimples remained as adorable as ever. "Stalker."

I loved the sound of her word, so soft on her lips. "Will I get a wedding IV, soon?"

"It's so complicated, Toyo," she said, keeping the gaze I'd recognised so well. All I needed now was a "hammer" to crush the complication. I saw the eyes of a woman who wanted something. Her footsteps were timid when she walked me to a corner. Then a little moment of hesitation. She gazed at the lights that lapped beautifully around River Thames. "I saw the viral letter, Toyo. Wow!" Her hands were now blocking her mouth. "That was the most heart-warming thing I've ever read. Thank you for being so honest about how you feel about me. And the fact that you wrote under a disguised name was so humble. Thank you."

Sigh.

I nodded. "You still haven't told me the complication."

She hunched her shoulders, gave a deep shuddering breath. The bangs fluttered a little. Her eyes were moist as she rubbed her palms down her forearms.

Where is her voice? I waited to hear what I assumed I already knew. She dug her fingers into her shoulder, stalling, contemplating, reading my eyes. I wanted her to spill it quick. She squirmed again. To throw in a joke here may not go in my favour. So, I waited. She glazed around nervously and bit the side of her thumbnail. Finally, she spoke with a light smile and stood upright as if she'd rehearsed this moment, over and again, perhaps the same way I'd rehearsed our first date, our first kiss, our future – the first of everything.

"Do you... do you like Tara?"

Damn! Oh damn! My village people, but whyyyy?

My throat instantly burned. Mouth suddenly parched. I needed water.

Are you OK? Are you freaking OK? Can't you see my blood is rising because of you?

I cautioned my spinning mind. "I mean… I mean she really likes you." Her voice was small, the quietest it had been throughout the night. She couldn't hide the quivering in her fumbling fingers, in her voice. How long has she been thinking about this?

My smile faded, but I gave the fake one I always spread on my face when the world demanded happiness from me. I'd not let anybody see my disappointment. I smiled, a stilted smile, enough to be believed. She searched my eyes for an answer, while my little hesitation wondered what her complication was. "Tara is lovely. She'd be perfect for Matthew."

"Really?" Her lips stretched wider.

I regained composure. "You're so different from anyone I've ever met, Tamilore." I paused, trying to watch her reaction. She slumped her shoulders a little and then leaned up against the wall, as if she was confused. "Will you at least tell me about the complication?"

"You're different, too, Toyo. You really are. I read every single word of your letter. That was the best thing ever. But it's so complicated. I can't talk about it now."

"OK. You mean you'd tell me tonight if I called."

She smiled and stuck her hands into her pockets. "Maybe sometime, not tonight."

Hmm. OK. I can work with that!

"OK, yep, no worries," I said, holding out my hands in a resigned gesture and played the last card for the night. "Some London arts exhibitions are coming up this weekend at The National Gallery and I got tickets for two. Wondering if you'd love to come."

Her shoulders tensed. I levelled her with a gaze. She hesitated, knitting her brow in thought for a few seconds. Her dimples were so adorable when she finally opened her mouth. "Hmm. That's so thoughtful. I'd have loved to, but this weekend is so packed. Will be with the crew for our first filming. Tara loves arts exhibitions so much, you know."

Hmm. That went so well. Second blow. OK, no worries.

I swallowed a groan and nodded without stiffening the longing expression on my face. "Alright, cool. Looking forward to seeing the production sometime. Have fun. As for Tara, I'm pretty sure Matthew's got a spare ticket for her already." I'd cracked my knuckles and smiled while talking, everything believable to hide the disappointment.

She blushed.

I wanted her smile to stay with me. But it was time to crawl back to my reality. Tara and Matthew re-joined us, giggling about how stunning Tower Bridge looked from the skyline. His flirtatious smile with her was unmistakable. We hung around a little longer as a group before Matthew and I walked them to their car, ended the night warmly, and bid our goodbyes as they drove off. Finally, I could let the smile return to its cold state; allow the façade to crumble to a grimace at the thought of my loveless life.

My whole body throbbed with tiredness as I dragged my feet towards London Bridge Station, feeling suddenly heavy, forcing one foot in front of the other. I hated this rejection (the frightening rejection that ceased to unveil itself) I'd became so familiar with, but I took consolation in my online business. And as we travelled down the train, Matthew repeated some words more than a dozen times: persistency, green lights, faith and game.

We got back home before midnight, analysed the night as if it was a football match: the smiles translated as green lights, the eye contact translated as go-harder, the flirting blush, hand and body touches that lapped on each other at the silliest of any jokes – everything suggesting the game was still on and the unspoken words with various interpretations.

I plopped down on a one-seater couch. "Why didn't you get Tara's number?"

He sank back down on the bed where he hung his head like a man without hope. He closed his eyes as if dizziness had blurred his vision, squeezing them tightly. Then, one hand was scratching on his forehead, the other picking at his thumbnail. When he finally let go of his disappointment, after he'd chewed his nails to bare skin, he sat upright, removed his fancy shoes and flipped each like baseball. "She kept asking too many questions about you. And she slipped her tongue when she asked how old you are! She's into you, bro! *Chai! How can Tami pour sand in my garri like this?*" (How can Tami have messed things up?).

I said nothing. Two minutes of silence passed between us.

Out of nowhere, he burst into a ridiculous laughter like someone intoxicated. "I don't know what else I can say to your situation, my friend. Maybe you can take some consolations from Pete Edochie who always reminds us the words of our forefathers in situations like this. Imagine yourself as a dancer and Tami as a drummer. Mr. Edochie says, and I quote: *When drummers change their beats, the dancers must learn how to change their steps.*"

Fuck off.

I left him in the guest room.

He shouted as I walked away, still laughing loud. "Not even thank you for reminding you about our forefathers. OK, don't worry bro, let's switch to rule number one extension. OK, OK, let's go for fasting and prayer. Dating requires spiritual warfare, you know."

I sank onto my bed, reclining on every side, looking at the ceiling. Isn't this all I'd wanted? To finally find love, but why has love found me the wrong person? Why is sorrow so stubborn? I lamented over and over. I rolled onto my back, then my stomach. I flumped the pillow dozens of times, but sleep faded away. I switched off the lamp, forcing my eyes shut, but restlessness refused to quit. I stood up and placed both hands at the edge of the window, opened it slightly, hoping I'd find solace in the company of the calming breeze.

The breeze drifted my way. Nature must be kind. I watched and listened to the soft whispering sound of leaves. The crunching, popping and hissing sounds calmed me like a message of reassurance, like a message of hope. *However long the moon disappears, someday it must shine again.* The words stopped whatever was brewing inside me. I kept my eyes on the leafy twigs within the eyeshot, until the breeze turned cold. The weariness that hung on my shoulder like a veil began to ease. I fell back onto the bed and slept like a baby.

EIGHT

THE NEXT MORNING, the unread emails had piled up and they kept rolling in like a river bustling its banks. How would I tackle this deluge? And given that I'd sent my email for the world to see, it was also the junkyard for shopping newsletters, and all things garbage. Everything dragged in slow motion and tiredness wore me like a jacket. My neck was stiff. My back was tight, so knotted. My body was heavy. I could hardly move a muscle.

Queen's new email came in. It led me to the others. Four breakfast pictures, already! Each one tagged with smiley faces.

I glided into the kitchen and denied the lazy feeling telling me to quit.

I had a glance of Paris through Queen's window: not anything glitzy. Still, I liked the apartments married to each other at Gare du Nord, within the hallowed precincts.

I'd become used to Queen's meals, her daily pictures. Sometimes two or three times a day. "Hey, Ayo, this is my lunch," she'd say. Or "Ayo dear, I've just finished making dinner and here's the picture." That was Queen.

Anyways, Queen's message was clear: she was a chef.

The next two days flipped passed quickly.

As I was replying to Queen's email, my phone rang. It was Mum calling.

I swiped the screen. "Hey Mum, good evening."

"My Son, *Olowoorimi* (my crown head), how are you doing? You haven't called me in a long time. Is it work keeping you busy or one of the beautiful London girls?"

I laughed. "Mum, we spoke last Sunday. Every Sunday."

"I always tell you, when you have your own kids, you will understand better. Anyway, there's a reason why I called. Are you visiting Nigeria anytime soon?"

"Anything I should be aware of, Mum? It isn't Christmas yet."

"Christmas came early, my son. I have great news. You remember Mama Tomiwa, my friend. Her beautiful daughter is in town."

Oh, I get it now.

"Well Mum, Tomiwa is like my little sister."

"No, Tomiwa is now engaged. Her sister, Ife, has returned home. She's prettier. Calmer. Friendlier. Born-again Christian. You two are perfect for each other. Her mum has already spoken to her, I sent one of your latest pictures – Ope helped me, you know I don't know how to send pictures with a phone. Anyways, she's really interested."

"Mama the mama. Well, I've got this project going on, so no travel plans now."

"Project? What type of project? But you said you were on holiday a few days ago."

Ife, my mum's friend's daughter, had just graduated from Yale and her mum was celebrating her 60th birthday soon. Mum's plan was to get me to attend the celebration so I could meet Ife. Mum and Ife's mum met ages ago through Uncle Ote at Ikoyi, and despite their different backgrounds they've kept their friendship strong for twenty-six years.

Ife's grandparents were from Ilaro and her mum visited the town regularly. Mum had been supportive in helping the family reclaim their farm products to sell every year at Ilaro. Ife's family was well-heeled while we were the opposite.

I appreciated Mum exploring available options, but I was not a big fan of matchmaking. That said, a fowl does not forget who trims his feathers during the rainy season. I must change the subject, but I bit my tongue in the process.

"Mum, any chance of visiting Buckingham Palace in the UK soon? Meanwhile, I'll have time to tell you about Queen."

"Son, I'll think about it."

"Queen is so pretty. She seems soft-hearted and calm. She has such a sweet nature, like a bunch of sweet-scented flowers."

"Son, which Queen are you talking about?"

"Ah, sorry, Mum, I mean Her Majesty the Queen of England."

"When did you start calling her Majesty sweet and pretty?"

"Erm. Mum, please can I call you back?"

"Bring her home."

Oh.

I tried to beat Mum at her game, so I responded cheekily. "You mean the stranger?"

"Yes, they are all strangers at first."

Chai, Carabos! Carabos!! All strangers? Does Mum now see visions?

We had a good laugh together.

"Take care, son, call me soon," she told me.

"Yes, sweet Mama, but do you mean the girl who emailed me recently and said that she is the girl my mum prays I find? Or do you mean Queen or one of the others?"

"What are you talking about, Toyosi?"

"Nothing, Mum, bye. I'll call you soon."

I ended the call and exhaled loudly. At least I got the job done: I distracted her from Ife.

NINE

"By now, you should have decided who you want." Matthew only ever spoke with a thin voice when he was either hungry or frustrated. This morning, it was the latter.

I was on my usual routine, so I froze the scrolling mouse. He slumped on the chair at the breakfast table in a self-afflicted despair; it was the craggiest I'd seen him in ages. Creased brow, tensed face. His shirt was rumpled. His beard was untidy. He should have left half an hour ago. But each day, before he left for his training, he always asked for an update on how close I was to finding love, as if our chances at love were mutually exclusive. Tara must have knocked out every bone in his body. He munched one or two *moimoi* with custard (I wondered why anyone would combine these), covered the hot chocolate, with the coffee cup lids, served in the steaming milky mugs in front of us. I wondered if he knew either. He hunched over, eyes glazing over, as he stretched his long neck towards my laptop screen.

"You mean between Tara and Tamilore?" I wanted to lighten his mood.

He sprawled out. That must have been a bad joke. He squeezed his eyes shut and dropped his head against the chair for what lasted close to a minute. His face becoming scruffier. When he opened them, he stuffed a slice of crisp toasted crust in his mouth. I'd never seen him eat burnt crust before. *So, he could be crushed by love!* I wondered.

His eyes settled and looked brighter. "Get serious." He said, with a slight hoarseness in his throat, before filling his mouth with the remaining chunk. Worrysome had begun to creep into his voice as he clasped his arms over his knees.

I waited for his blanched face to break, for his rigid shoulders to light up. It took longer than normal. "Tara has not slipped out of your hands, Mr. Tender." My face was mocking him. I stretched an arm high, circled my hand in the air and yawned in forced exhausted puffs.

He finally smiled and ruffled his hair, the mini afro that hasn't been shaped for days.

"I've got three potentials now: Ellen, Mercy and Queen."

"Speed the process. Pick one. Ghost the others," he said, with no blink of hesitation, as he picked up his training handbook, ready to head out. It was as if he thought the earlier I found love, the brighter his chance with Tara; he seemed worried that Tara could end up being my default option. If anything was causing him to be unsettled, it was this fact.

"I hope you find another Tara on Tinder."

The smile would put him in the perfect mood for the day.

"Go for it, man. I'm supporting you all the way. Tara is yours, bro. Just work on your extension rule or do you want me to join you in your fasting and prayer?" We laughed so hard. He rose to his six-two frame and we shook hands, as he walked out of the front door.

He'd be returning to Lagos in two days.

Hey Toyo, Tami kindly passed me your contact. I wanted to

know the best London location to rent an affordable apartment for Kings College.

Tara's text from the night before. Tamilore's agenda was clearer. If I'd met Tara under different circumstances, I'd have been on my knees thanking God.

Hey Tara, Chapter South Bank in Central London is perfect. Matthew lived there during his Bachelor's. Is it OK if I pass your mobile to him? He'll be able to advise on the student life, too.

Matthew had lived in Jericho in Oxford, the area beautifully characterised with Georgian and Victorian architecture. He would have to explain how he lived in London while he was studying at Oxford University, if he got lucky. I waited for her reply. If it was yes, Matthew would be the happiest man. But he had been too pessimistic, fearing the worst.

I resumed to my love chase business. I'd a plan to select four potentials and narrow them down to one. The email I was reading before Matthew interrupted was from Olamide. She was one of the few who had not sent her pictures. So, I loved the mystery. The night before, I'd asked if she could paint me her images in words. And this morning, she delivered.

"I'm beginning to regret not taking my comprehension classes seriously..." she wrote. "I'm 5.5ft. I like to think I'm of average height, but haters say I'm not. I won't call myself petite because I wear a UK size 8. My skin has this brownish yellow colour. I'm not a slay queen but I pay attention to what I wear and believe in looking good. I used to be all natural but, in a bid to look closer to my age, I recently joined "bad gang" and started using light make-up. It has helped a little and I don't look like a 19-year-old anymore. I have a round face, big brown eyes, a normal sized nose, soft pink lips, and a small gap between my upper incisors. People say I have a great smile. I have a healthy-looking figure, no pot belly... for now. In summary, I look like your beautiful girl next door, or so I think..."

That was four potentials. It was high time I ghosted the rest.

TEN

Edinburgh, Scotland 2008

IN AUTUMN OF 2008, I left for Edinburgh. I was twenty-six and had never been on a plane. When flying for the first time, you're as careful as a surgeon performing heart surgery; you listen to every single instruction and obey them to the letter. There is no room for error. I was that guy.

"Your passport, please," the immigration officer asked.

"Here, sir. Thank you." I handed him my passport. My answer was ready for the next question before he'd even asked it. I was *prepared*. There were so many stories of repatriation troubles at entry and I did not want to be sent back. I didn't have any issues; I made it safely onto the plane. The first leg of the trip from Lagos to London. The engines roared into life and the plane shook so much I wondered if we were all going to die.

I remembered how Mum's face stiffened, how her eyes took on the sheen of water and her teeth tugged at her lower lip, as I'd waved her goodbye at Lagos airport. "If only I'd money, if only I'd gold or silver, I'd have given you everything. How are you going to cope?"

I sensed her twitchiness and saw her anxiety beneath her words, beneath her eyes. "Fortune favours the bold, Mum," I told her. "Nothing to worry about."

"But you don't have enough money, not even enough for feeding."

"Mum, I'll be fine." I'd left her with my assurance.

I knew I was skating on thin ice.

Two hours up and high in the sky, in the middle of the night, my eyes were kept open, wide open. I'd satisfied my initial curiosity – eating on board. Although I wasn't expecting *pounded yam* and *egusi* soup, child-size portion of fried rice, tiny chicken, tiny square of cake and a plastic cup of orange juice was a complete let down. Why would anyone not treat me like a royal? Anyways, shortly after the stewards had collected their trays, I tilted my head upward, watching those whose neck had fallen sideways, and those who sat as if they were in a movie theatre. Outside in the dark skies, red and white lights continued to flash at the tail of the wings. *How stunning, oh, how beautifully stunning.* My thoughts as I savoured every moment, over and again, reminisced on my dreams before my eyes were finally put to sleep.

Touch down was smooth. And the second leg was as quick as a flash.

I made it to Edinburgh, beautiful Edinburgh, where art and architecture meet. I stopped in the city centre to familiarise myself with my new home. The twin royal burghs at the Old Town caught my attention. I turned to discover where the shrill wailing sound of Amazing Grace was coming from. I did not miss a piper nearby dressed like The Royal Scots Dragoon Guards whose parade I'd read about. His dress sat proudly on him: The tartan kilt, the brooch, and the plaid that hung in line with the spats. His headgear with red and black feather bonnet was worn with pride too and diagonal cross belt over the plaid. He played the Scottish bagpipes, blowing air through the pipes with so much patriotism. I watched the instrument being played for a few minutes before turning to the heart of the historic capital, the Royal Mile, full of buzzing restaurants, coffeeshops, pubs, cafés, museums and souvenir shops. Tourists on walking tours emerged from every corner, connecting streets and closes.

Standing on Princes Street, I watched the hills rise up to Edinburgh Castle, silhouetted against the dimming sky. I marvelled at the medieval and classic architectures of these ancient buildings, well decorated and beautified with stones; it was even better than I'd read about. A beautiful white girl with a thick Scottish accent whose gaze and mine shared mutual appreciation, pointed me to the royal residence, the Palace of Holyroodhouse resting in the midday shadow. I returned my focus to the bustling street. Traffic was moving on the wrong side of the road. *Something isn't right.* I paused for a moment. *Oh, yes. Britain drives on the left.* It looked strange, but I was enjoying the new experience. I shivered as the wind announced the coming of winter. But I was well prepared for it in my thick oversized jacket.

Looking around, I saw a garden not far off. The trees seemed to be on fire with their autumnal hues, a beacon on such a gloomy day. It was the perfect time of the year for the trees to transform with a blaze of yellow, red, and scarlet leaves. *Edinburgh is a dream.*

I bought a new sim card and called home to say I'd arrived safely. Next plan on my agenda was to google the cheapest flat share in Edinburgh. Shortly after, I made my way to the hotel a few miles from the city centre where I was booked for two nights (thank God for this gift from a well-wisher. I'd had trouble raising money in the last minutes to pre-book). The grounds were beautifully landscaped. The garden was green, well designed and well maintained, with ornamental features, trees and shrubs. *Wow, Scotland is heavenly.*

While sitting upstairs on the bus, a double decker, I wondered where the black people were. Unfazed by the change, I studied the white girls passing, their mannerisms, the warm smile on their cheeks each time our eyes met. *Is that a thing here? I'm so loving this city.* Then, a moment later, I saw one – a black man with swag. I smiled. A few minutes later I saw another – a young black woman with a backpack, holding a textbook in her hand waiting at the bus stop. As she climbed the steps, I signalled with a warm smile to the seat next to me. She smiled and joined me. Her smile was stunning, so natural and open.

I stretched my hand. "Hey, I'm Toyosi, are you a student, here?" I liked the softness of her palms when I shook them. Skin so subtle in its tan, ebony beauty.

Her smile was brighter now. "Hi-hi. I'm Bolu. Yes, here for my master's in Finance," she said, shaking my hand. Her tone was confident, not shy, not flirty. "And you?"

I shifted to accommodate her closer, kept my warm cheeks in display. "Oh, you're a Nigerian too. Superb. I'm here for my masters in Operations Research."

She reposited her legs sideways in the narrow space to face me. Great. I still remembered a thing about angle, direction and desire.

"Nice but never heard of it. What's it about?" she asked.

"It's about how two strangers can meet in a bus and fall in love on the spot."

She laughed. The bus pulled to a break. We lurched forward as the brake squeaked, both of us smiling now. "You didn't tell me you're a comedian. That's so cheesy."

"It's almost the same as Applied Mathematics, but not quite," I said.

"You must really like numbers. Tell me more about it."

"It's the application of science to solve complex problems." I paused and began gesturing with my hands excitedly, as I continued to explain. "Let me break it down: everything that happens in today's world is built on the back of Operations Research."

She nodded as I spoke. The beautiful smile was still on her face. Then she hitched her bag onto her shoulder. "I'd love to know more, but this is my stop. Our church is around the corner; it's full of amazing people. Here's a flyer for our services. Join us sometime."

"Of course, sure. Will do," I said.

She pressed the stop button. "We have an energetic Single Ministry in church as well."

"Energetic?" I echoed the word mischievously. "I'll take your word for it. See you on Sunday then."

She laughed as the bus slowed down for the next stop. "It would be good to see you either way, energetic or not energetic."

Bolu and I became acquainted and I had my first friend in Edinburgh.

A FEW DAYS LATER, I moved into my new apartment; I set free the kitchen swimming in the clutter's dust, the ancient cooker creased with grime, and steadied the wobbly three-leg dining table with a rope. I had no chair or reading table, but the bed was perfect for my needs.

My phone rang.

"Mum, how are things at home?" My eyes were misting over the Java script.

She sighed. "We're trusting God. You know, your brother's health. That's all."

I shut the book and held the phone firmer. The scold in her tone could not be mistaken for anything else but worry. My younger brother, Dede, had sickle cell anaemia. No one knew until he was ten; he hardly ever fell ill. And now, no one to pay the hospital bills except Mum.

"Everything will end in praise, Mum," I said. "I've asked my stockbroker in Lagos to sell my remaining First Bank shares. It's all I have left. But I only hear different versions of delay stories. Once it comes through, I'll send money home. How are you managing?"

"We're managing. And we're praying for you," she said. "How are you coping?"

"I'm settling in. I'll be fine," I assured her. "I've found cheap accommodation."

With two days to find low-cost accommodation, I'd been in a panic. As the pressure increased, I hurriedly settled for a reasonably priced flat share just on the outskirts of the city in the Niddrie House Park. The flat was one of the cheapest around with broken furniture and a half-broken kitchen. It was one of those unkempt apartments with many flats: no fancy garden, no views, no autumnal trees. Nothing. Just a dirty old apartment. The garden outside was covered in dog excrement and the floor was cluttered with half-empty cartons. The university prospectus must have forgotten to mention that this part of the city existed.

"Thank God," she said. "You'll find favour in that place. Men will favour you. Women will favour you. Strangers, white, black, everyone." Her endless prayers continued until she heard, "Your call credit is now exhausted, please recharge your credit."

The following Sunday, I was at Bolu's church in the nurturing dampness of autumnal colours. The building made of old stones and red bricks resembled the ancient cathedrals. The inside was modern, aesthetically pleasing with decorations – cosy wall lights, lustrous wooden floor with small rows of chairs, potted trees that flushed beautifully with leaves, ribbon with whimsical touches. And my favourite, the grand Georgian-like high ceilings.

She saw me as I walked in. "So lovely to see you, Toyo. Wasn't sure you'd come." We hugged. She'd changed her braids. Her dreadlocks were curly with noticeably tousled spikes. They cascaded beautifully. *I think someone was expecting me today.* I wondered why I liked the afro style so dearly, as if it powered my existence. I stamped my hand on hers.

"I didn't want to, but for the *energetic* Single Ministry, you know what I mean."

She laughed. "Meet Toyosi, everyone." She rubbed her palms on my hand, as she introduced me to the folks nearby. It was perfect for a freezing morning. The man wearing a full grain tailored leather jacket with ice-flake sprinkled collar, like someone from North Pole exploration, was giggling, showing his brown teeth; his eyes flicked more than necessary.

"Your boyfriend?" one of them teased.

"He's my brother in Christ," she replied.

Everyone laughed, except one person whose chin suddenly jutted out. Our friend from the North Pole. He pursed his lips and murmured something under his breath. I bet he got creative with profanities.

We soon settled in for the service. Bolu and I sat next to each other, read from the same Bible, her Bible, gossiped at the folks dozing off during the sermon, especially that man with a grain jacket, and stayed back afterwards for a free light refreshment.

"Your hair looks lovely," I told her, as we walked into the small refreshment room.

She rushed off her friend, the short man with big watchful eyes, and brown teeth, who had bid her goodbye five times already. "Take care, Fred, have a lovely week," she told him.

Fred finally left, limped and huffed. His thick jacket was unfashionably slung over his shoulder, drooping. Can sweat suddenly drench someone's body in this weather? I was sure he'd wear it outside. His frown and downcast eyes revealed what I already knew.

"Tea or coffee?" she asked, as I sat with the others.

"Hmm no sandwiches?" I teased. "Tea, please."

Her smile was infectious.

Moment later, after the tea was served, she leaned over, "accidentally" touching my hand as she passed me the NewComers Welcome Pack. *Hmm, Carabos!* I returned the smile.

I'm so looking forward to knowing you, Beautiful.

I kept that to myself. When the introductions were over, I playfully squeezed her hand just a little, our eyes exchanged something nice and promising, as we pulled into a warm embrace to bid goodbye. And for the next few months, we'd see each other every other Sunday for the same routine except the green-eyed man wasn't always there.

THREE MONTHS LATER, all I had left were coins.

I headed to a pound shop and stocked my bag with necessities – brioche, bread, some scotch rolls and biscuits. And later that day, I saw Bolu on campus, looking fresh in her new grey hoodie and black jeans. My oversized jacket remained in fashion. We hugged with a peck. Her fragrance as soothing as her hugs. "Toyo, Toyo, where have you been hiding?"

I adjusted my backpack full of goodies and smiled. "*See fine babe*. Look at you. Looking so ravishing as always. How are you doing?"

She was smiling. "I'm keeping well. What's the thing about your new afro?"

I laughed. "Afro rocks, you know."

She laughed. "*See*, Toyo, if you're not rushing, we could do lunch in the cafeteria?"

I cleared my throat, twisted my neck. "I just had a heavy lunch, you know. Maybe sometime."

Heavy lunch indeed.

She strained her eyes sideways, lifted her fingers to her lips. I allowed my open gestures to offer a promise with no words. Her smile stiffened into a rictus soon melted away. She'd regained her poise. We gisted for a few more minutes, and shortly after, parted ways.

Next morning, Edinburgh woke up to showers of rain. In my comfy closest, I wished I had pepper chicken wings to cool off the cold. Anyways, as I was helping myself to some slice of tasty brioche and elegant glass of chilled water, Bolu's text message beeped:

Kim, Tope and I are sightseeing in Prague next weekend, do you wanna come?

I flipped the phone to the corner of my tiny, lonely room.

Moments later, I placed the breakfast aside and took my thoughts on overdrive. How was I going to meet my mum's financial support at home in the interim? Since I'd moved to Edinburgh, I could no longer fulfil the financial obligations to my family. This saddened me; this was my greatest worry.

Mum had retired the year before I relocated. Her monthly pension was a meagre sum and the government was delaying prompt regular payments. Mum never complained or asked for money, but I knew her struggle. I knew the situation at home.

I scrabbled for my phone vibrating. "Mum, is everything OK?" My nerves jangled.

There was silence.

She cleared her throat. "Toyosi, how are you?" Her voice was low, so hoarse as if she had been crying, as if her throat was sore. "How are you coping?"

"Mum, what's going on? Have you been crying?"

I could hear her sobbing now. "I'm not crying. Nothing will cause me to shed tears on any of my children. My eyes will not know pain... my eyes will not know pain." Her cry burst out. "They won't treat Dede. Doctors won't treat him except we give them some deposit. Twenty thousand naira. Where on earth will I get that kind of money from? Where?"

"Where's my brother now?"

"In the hospital in Abeokuta. We left Ilaro yesterday."

"Mum, we'll get through this, please stop crying. I'll do everything I can to raise the money." I reassured her, calmed her tears, promising all will be well before the call ended.

Why does everything crumble at the same time? I clenched my fists searching for an answer. My legs twitched, and eyelids fluttered. I stifled a sob and looked up to the sky, drowning in self-pity, my mind searching desperately for solutions, to suppress the rising ocean of panic. "O'Lord, the creator of heaven and the earth, please make a way for my family. Please make a way where there's no way." On my knees, I pleaded in supplications from the deepest of my soul. A voice within slowly whispered. It told me to use the fear as a precursor to bravery. It was a voice reminding me that this storm, too, shall pass.

A week later, there was a glimmer of hope. My brother had started receiving medical treatment. Mum was smiling on the other end of the phone. All thanks to the kind-hearted doctors who'd extended the hundred-dollar payment window for a maximum of one month.

I composed a text: *I'm sorry, Bolu. Apologies I didn't reply your text the other day.*

It took hours for her to reply. *Which of them?*

Them? Oh no! I'd missed three messages on different days. They were all travel requests – Paris, Prague and Barcelona.

I'm so sorry, Bolu.

You don't have to be, she replied. *I won't be sending you another one.*

After I'd composed my next message, *Lunch?* I pondered on it for too long, wished I could send it, but couldn't afford lunch for one, let alone two. I'd been feeding on the biscuit crumbs I took during the refreshment session last Sunday. So, I deleted it.

I composed close to ten different versions and deleted them all. There was no further exchange of text messages and for the next month, I never saw her shadow.

THE DAY DRAINED INTO ANOTHER, slowed by anxiety and fear. But I held on. Biscuits again for dinner, my favourite meal option to keep body and soul together.

A month later, I met with Bolu at the library. As our eyes met, she composed her lips and cheeks to the wrinkles around her eyes, moulded them and scrunched up her face.

"Heyyy, Bolu. Is everything OK? Please smile a little." I teased as I sat next to her.

Her face remained hardened as her textbook snapped shut.

She didn't say anything at first, then she let out a quiet gasp and threw me a look, "So, you now have my time?"

I squeezed the back of her hand gently. The stillness eased a little. "I always have your time, your highness. Fancy a short walk? We could get some fresh air."

She swung her hair onto her back and locked her eyes to mine, considering my words for what lasted up to a minute, then nodded half-heartedly.

Shortly after, we went for a short walk, a stroll within the university park. She was stylish in her winter garb, scarf, blue jeans and black shoes. Her headscarf beautifully tied. I was still rocking my afro, as if the lack of cash to barb my hair had spurred a brilliant idea.

"I'm sorry about the weekend sightseeing stuff, hope you enjoyed them?"

"Was nice," she said. "Haven't seen you in church in a while."

I came up with an excuse. I couldn't afford the bus, so I'd boycotted church. We practised a Scottish accent we'd learned; sat alone on a park bench, whispering words in each other's ears, and swung on the kid's playground. Though cold had found our bodies, we were playful. Her arms flung about, sending a coded message I later understood. The smile on her face each time our eyes met, the ease of conversation, got the better of me.

The shorter day was long over as the evening got darker.

"How are your folks back home?" I asked Bolu.

"It's nice seeing this side of you," she said, mocking my face. "Everyone is cool. Dad is doing great. You missed his old-school charisma when he stopped by a few weeks ago."

I smiled. "Nice, I see why you're glowing. And your mum?"

The loud whistle of the cold was blowing our way, stirring the soft rustling of dry leaves towards us. Bolu shrivelled.

"Mum is late. We lost her a few years ago. And my elder sister. We're now family of four: myself, two younger brothers and Dad."

"Oh, no. I'm so sorry to hear this. That must have been tough times." I said, squeezing her hand. "What happened if you don't mind me asking?"

She wrapped her scarf twice around her neck. "I'll tell you more about them sometime. For now, let's get out of this cold – I'm freezing." She was laughing now.

"Sure. Whenever you're ready, your highness." I said, bracing at the winter waves.

She held herself against the wind. "We could get tea or coffee down the road," she said, raking a hand through her hair.

Damn.

I dug my hands for the coins that rattled in my pocket to check how much was left.

OK, I got this.

"Yes, we need something hot, don't we?"

On our way there, I came up with a perfect story; I was fasting. We arrived at the café. The aroma of freshly baked lasagne welcomed us, wafting along my nose – sweet smell bubbling across the open space. The wall's white and black colour design added to its atmosphere and the slow song in the background differentiated it from the park. It looked lovely, but packed. I kept wondering why the British seemed to be obsessed with coffee.

"Nice place, isn't it?" I said. We ordered for one, and I sorted the bill.

Bolu placed her coffee on the table in between us. I watched as the thick air, the scent of the latte, gushed out. My stomach growled. "When are you breaking the fast?" she asked.

I felt so dizzy and bent a little to suppress the hunger pangs. "Tonight, at six," I said, the growling was growing louder. I squirmed and, with my hand on my stomach, I tried to silence the rumbling. I'd not eaten in the past week. Just biscuits and bread.

She moved closer and rubbed my hand. "Oh no, are you ok, Toyo?"

Lightheaded, I attempted a joke. "Fasting in winter is a terrible idea, you know."

She laughed and patted me on the shoulder. "I can imagine. You're nearly there."

We talked about our courses, our lives, and people we left at home. The two-hour time off was refreshing. I felt a renewed energy coursing through me.

CHRISTMAS CAME AND WENT.

It was now mid-January. With no money to renew my accommodation, I spent half the time sleeping in the classroom, anywhere I could lay my head without being caught. For nearly a month, the cold classrooms gave me shelter, as long as the cleaners or security didn't catch me. I clung on to the ropes and continued to scoff down biscuits for dinner.

One night, in the dead winter of February – with big freeze, one of the cleaners found me. She had managed to clean a section of the classroom quietly, trying not to wake me up. Unfortunately, she did. *Oh no! Think. Pretend you've been reading.*

"Good morning, ma." I greeted her warmly.

"Morning," she responded, staring at me, a relentless stare, for clues of what was wrong. Her eyes were sober, her face consoling, as if she knew the full story.

I was cold and confused. I glanced around. Outside was sheathed in ice. The naked trees next to the classroom, beautifully hugged by the snow clinging on shrubs, were an inch taller. And there was no sign the racing snow, the clumps of wet flakes drifting down on the window was going to stop anytime soon. I returned my eyes to the woman in front of me.

"Is everything OK?" she asked.

I nodded as I stood frozen. "Everything is fine, I slept off while reading."

She sighed. "Are you sure? I've seen you a couple of times this week, sleeping on the floor. The heating is never on overnight because no student is expected to be here. So, I know everything isn't fine. You should seek some form of support or something. OK? I try to clean around you when I can, but other cleaners might not be so understanding."

"Thank you. It won't be for long. I'll sort something out as soon as I can."

After our chat, I turned to the student toilets, cleaned my face, brushed my teeth. It was Sunday morning, so I headed to church afterwards for the thanksgiving service.

The service began with worship and praise, followed by a Bible reading including words of exhortation. My spirits were lifted.

And then it was offering time. The offering baskets shuffled up and down the aisle, on every side. I looked for some coins in my pocket, searching through the wallet and took out a pound. Bolu sat next to me and noticed as I pulled out the coin. She saw me furtively wrap it up in the offering envelope. I knew she would make fun of it. Her nails dug into my hand as she blushed into her scarf discreetly. "Na only one pound una give God today."

"God will manage this, for now." I smiled back.

Soon, it was testimony time.

We expect at least four people each Sunday. That day, there were only three. Adanna's post-study visa application was approved. Tunde got cash from home. And Charlotte had a new job. The church clapped; piano and drums echoed loudly in support.

The pastor made eye contact with me. My turn. But what could I thank God for? *For your struggles.* A voice inside me said. So, without hesitating, I reached forward.

It was my turn. I held the mic, but my hands were shaking. How could I sound positive while life was overwhelming me? I attempted to quiet the doom air thickening.

Then, I completely went blank.

Seconds passed; no words came still. Tears streamed down my face, slowly easing my pain. I rubbed my eyes with the back of my left hand, held the mic with the right.

Silence.

I started wracking my brain for a positive story, anything to save face. But nothing came. A few more seconds passed. I looked embarrassed. What was I supposed to testify about now? Why was I listening to a voice? My head was spinning with questions.

I took a deep breath to stop the panic opening in my gut and whatever was suddenly eroding my confidence and then, I found my voice, one word at a time.

"I had sold my car and everything I had." I paused as I began to speak, very slowly. My fists balled tightly, eyes staring blankly.

"All my sweat, the sacrifices of years of saving, with the dream of earning a foreign degree. I left at home a pensioner mother and could no longer meet her monthly allowance. The government had delayed payment for nearly six months. Now, I'm not sure where Mum's next monthly allowance will come from. My younger brother is lying helplessly on the hospital bed again. The course posed a big hurdle for me to cross. I don't have a laptop. The one I borrowed from the library was subject to renewal. And for the past week, I've been helpless. I don't have a place to live, no money for transport, I walk miles every day from the outskirts of town to the university; I can barely afford to eat, I only feed on snacks."

I picked my words in a calm, unhurried voice. The tone walked the line between sadness and gratefulness.

I paused and took a deep breath. Shocked by the strength of my voice. My voice, like a muffled squeak, suddenly pitched clearer. "I'm thankful to God. Because I'm still here. I'm grateful for life and other things. I thank God for every pain. I thank God for every struggle."

"Yes, Lord," a member shouted.

"Thank you, Jesus," a few others said.

The congregation were on their feet clapping for God as I walked back to my seat, and those who were nearer made eye contact as if to say, "All will end well."

A member handed me cash later; it was enough for a week's lunch and dinner. Another handed me an envelope. "Please use this for transport," he said. I was blessed.

As we were leaving, Bolu apologised. Her face crumpled. "Toyosi, I'm so sorry, I didn't know you had a lot going on."

We paced our steps over the melted snow and saw our own breath through the cold. Bolu tightened her jacket and scarf and removed her hat as if she was ready for a run. I braced for position. We both kicked some ice crackle under our feets. Our spirits lifted with laughter. Then off we went. We ran for about fifty metres or so. Stopped. Ran again. Stopped again, laughing all the way. We were now at the junction where we would part ways.

"I made *efo riro* soup this morning. I have fish stew too. How about you come along. I will make rice or *eba* or yam flower, the choice is yours," she said.

"Now, you're talking. Erm, *efo rifo* and *eba* please. *Oya*, let's walk faster."

"Now I know why you only dropped one pound in the offering basket today. I'm sorry I made that joke. Please, forgive me." She looked sheepish.

"It's nothing, Joker. Let's walk faster *joor*."

We got to Bolu's flat in good time and had lunch. It was as if I had not eaten in my whole life. The *eba* was on point. The vegetable soup was delicious, prepared with stockfish and cray-fish, well marinated with pepper to make you feel alive, and some goat meat. Ah, so there's goat meat in this country! I laughed. My stabling ache of hunger was satisfied.

"Are you *still* single, Bolu?" I wasn't sure where the question came from. Maybe my full stomach prompted it. Whatever it was, I genuinely wanted to know. Her beautiful set of teeth popped out as she turned to face me. She laughed for so long. "The *eba* cleared your eyes, err." She'd repeated it like a dozen times while she tidied up.

"I was just thinking Mr. Fred may have taken the spot."

She laughed. "I think he's seeing someone now in church, I'm happy for him."

"No more competition, then," I said, laughing. She pinched me with her nails.

A few minutes later, after she'd arranged some food for me to take home, she finally answered my question. "Well, I'd like to think I am, but my father doesn't think so."

———

It had been a full one year. Two days before leaving Edinburgh, at the end of August the following year, there was a send-off party for one of the students, Danielle. She had invited everyone to an all-night party, and I tagged along with Bolu. Finally, I had a break.

"Will I see you again?" Bolu asked me, screwing up her face.

I impulsively smoothed my hand down her shoulder and said a lot with my eyes, pleasant words, pleasing words, reassurance words, before the words were finally formed. "Yes, ma'am." I then held out my hand to hold hers and held her beautiful gaze.

"Is there something you want to tell me before you travel back home?" She bit her lip and glanced away.

I rubbed a hand over my stubble. "Thank you. Thank you for the *eba*, the other day."

"Toyosi, be serious." Her face radiated with warmth, as she looked me in the eyes.

My arm curled around her waist, tugging her next to me. "You're the sweetest woman I've met on this journey." I paused. "Can we get on the dance floor?"

A smile dangled on the corner of her lips. "And?" she asked, waiting for me to spill it.

"And I'd like the journey to continue with us." I drew her closer, eyes misted beautifully over each other, as we shared our first kiss.

Afrobeat came on. The music was thunderous and made my lungs feels like mush but none of that deterred me. Bolu and I stepped on the dance floor and showed off our best African dance moves. I enjoyed my first social event in Edinburgh without any agitation.

In the morning I packed my luggage, and the next day I flew back to Nigeria.

Two weeks later, Bolu and I were on a call – gisting, flirting, anticipating her return to Nigeria in a week's time and longing for our first official date, so to speak. In the middle of it, Bolu suddenly chipped in. "Can I ask you a question?" Anxiety rose above her voice.

"Sure, shoot. Anything the matter?"

"I hope you won't think I'm being too forward."

"As long as you're not proposing, are you?" I laughed at my own joke.

She laughed. "Do you... do you know your genotype?" she asked, her words sounded shaking, little anxious, little fearful. "Please tell me you're not AS."

Damn.

"I am," I said, self-aware of the impeding repercussions, frustrated in tone like a man pleading guilty to an offence he didn't commit. I knew where the conversation was headed.

I could imagine the disappointment on her face when she said, "I am too."

We digested the new information for about an hour, rationalising it wasn't a big issue to stop us, provided we could be on the same page. Science had advanced and we had options to consider. And soon changed the subject to something exciting, swapping life stories.

It wasn't long after, I heard her sucking in breath, worrisome breath.

"You've gone quiet, Bolu. Are you worried?"

A few seconds of silence. "This AS headache, that's all."

"Babe, I'm flexible, if you are."

"My dad will not approve, Toyo. I lost my elder sister to sickle cell anaemia six years ago, it was the same shocking news that took Mum's life pre-maturely few months after."

"Oh no," I said in shock, the phone nearly fell. "I didn't know it has to do with sickle cell when you told me about them. I'm so sorry to hear this."

"I didn't want to go into details then. Besides, I wasn't sure if it was necessary. If we were ever going to date. My point is let's think things through. You know what I mean?"

"Yeah, sure." I said, then followed up with questions about her mum, her sister – the entire family – expressing my condolences again as we talked and talked for hours.

A month later, Bolu invited me to her family house at Ikoyi for a family graduation party. In the middle of the party, she beckoned to me for a chat behind the pool. I fiddled with my keys, fretfully, as if I knew what was coming. We'd pondered about the big decision and weighed the options, the pros and cons, to see if it was enough to halt our journey ahead.

"I know you know what I want to say," Bolu said, beaming with warmth.

The young chap Bolu's old man was advocating for, was AA – free of sickle cell. I'd honestly assessed my chances and accepted them. My heart no longer thudded with nerves.

My thumb stroked hers. "I think I do."

She rested her head on my chest. "I really want us, but I think it's safer if we quit now." Her conciliatory voice carried the weight of her words.

I waited for her cheeks to flush under my gaze. "I think so, too, babe," I told her.

The sparkling light streaming from the posh ceiling pendant behind the pool left a shadow, making us invisible to the rest of the world. We wanted to be there, to be invisible, as if we'd planned our last kiss. I stood tall and straightened my suit, then leaned against the wall. She trailed a finger around my shirt button, then edged closer, reaching up in her heels as my hands wrapped around her waist. It was soft, sweet and yet to leave my lips.

ELEVEN

London, March 2017

IT WAS first week of March. My holiday was over. Reality was knocking on my door. Myself and three of my London-based friends, Cliff, his wife Melanie and her twenty-eight-year-old single sister Mary, had planned a long weekend away. I'd known Cliff and his wife for six years and had met Mary about six months earlier. I wasn't quite sure if it was a matchmaking attempt when Melanie jokingly raised the idea of a weekend away the last time the family hosted me for dinner. But I agreed to the idea and the time had arrived.

I joined Cliff and his family, and we travelled to a beautiful resort in Cornwall, best known for its amazing sandy beaches and picturesque harbour villages. I knew something great would come out of my time there. I would rest. I would untie the knot of frustration hanging around my neck and find solace away from isolation, away from the email exchange.

We were welcomed to our hotel with a glass of prosecco, which we sipped gently as we sat on the edge of a glistening swimming pool, curving into the tranquil waters. Things felt different. We rested that night, had a great dinner together.

The next morning, we set out for the adventure.

"Here, you'll find one of the beautiful hidden beaches known as Leggan Cove," said one of the hotel staff who held a map, showing us the area.

So, we went there and had an amazing time exploring the stunning sandy beach.

After seeing the best of Leggan Cove, which looked like a beach that had escaped from a painting, we travelled to another nearby beach for sightseeing. We visited the snug fishing villages tucked into tiny harbours and a white sand beach for sunbathing. It was clean, fresh and different. The stress of replying to my many emails gradually eased. We ended the day by visiting the best artistic heritage places in Cornwall.

"Isn't this beautiful?" I pointed to some great painters and potters and we watched as they turned the big skies into stunningly beautiful works of art.

"Such colourful artwork plus extraordinary painters. I never knew this aspect of British life till this day." Mary's face was as bright as the light of her smoky eyes. "I've seen this type of thing in Thailand where you get lost in a tropical paradise."

Cliff and Melanie took a short stroll to see the sculptor nearby working with stainless steel and copper.

"This is a perfect time of the year to be here, isn't it?" I asked Mary who was full of the joys of spring. My smile never left my face. "Thanks for planning this; it's a well-deserved break for me."

She tilted her head to one side while listening to me talk, pulling her lips back over her teeth. "The weather is really fresh, not cold and not too warm. I'm glad you could come." A little pause, trying to hold a glance. "Many people think they must travel outside the country to enjoy a wonderful break. This one, right here, right now, is heavenly."

I couldn't agree more. From its high mountain peaks, dozens of lofty peaks cradling calmness in mountain wilderness, soothing breeze in the sun and moonlight, through its lush forests and down to its long shorelines, Cornwall is indeed heavenly. We quickly became two peas in a pod. We liked to do similar things on holiday, especially having adventures.

"Toyo, I'd like to know men's perspective to a few dating questions, you know."

I was distracted by a sporty lady with a surfboard who walked past.

"Toyosi." She called my name in a smoky voice.

I could sense that Mary fancied me. The fine line between platonic friendship and romantic feelings was becoming blurred. Dating a friend's sister-in-law can sometimes be tricky. Anyways, I threw all caution to the wind and played along.

"Are you seeing anyone?" Mary chimed in unexpectedly.

"Hmm. Not exactly. I'm dating a few women online but not seeing anyone in particular." I gestured the word "dating" using my fingers to demonstrate speech marks.

"What?" Her warm smile stilled; the air blew cold. "A few women? Why would a well-mannered chap like you do such a thing? Or you're one of *those* men now?"

"See it like a project. An adventure, nothing serious."

A wordless expression written over her face.

"Adventure? Project? Toyosi, you've lost me."

"OK, I mean—"

"You're a player?" She interjected before I'd finished my sentence, in a cold clipped tone while her eyes were unblinkingly staring for answers.

I briefly explained the story of meeting Tamilore and the subsequent viral love letter I wrote and how it led to the online dating competition. And that even though these women were fully aware it was a competition, they remained intrigued to unravel the mystery man.

She put a hand to her chest and started laughing uncontrollably. I didn't get the joke.

"What's going on?" I asked.

Mary laughed again and shoved her chest. "Oh, my goodness," she said. "It's you."

"Me?" I asked, anxiously.

"Yes. Wow," she said. "What a small world."

"Oh, oh oh, no way! Is it what I'm thinking?" I burst into peals of laughter.

As it turned out, Mary had applied for *The Bachelor's Ride*, but she hadn't been shortlisted. Her email was among those I'd never read. I was startled at her revelation. A small world indeed! We laughed as she learned that I was the anonymous bachelor, the man behind the viral love memo. Then she started pressing me for details.

"So, have you found someone?" she asked. "Please spill it all."

"Ha-ha. Mary, nah! Not so fast!" I said, shaking my head from side to side.

She was impressed, acknowledging how dedicated I'd become to the game. We had a lot to talk about and we bonded. She seemed to enjoy my company and I felt likewise.

"Cliff said you were running some campaign last weekend," she said. "What's that about?"

"It's a campaign initiative to promote awareness of sickle cell anaemia among the black community in London." I narrated my passion for it and showed her my test card.

"No! Not again," she said.

She cast her eyes sideways. The sparkle had faded. We had *that look* on each other's face to confirm it wasn't going to happen. We were, however, happy that we found out early enough, and the focus shifted to enjoying the weekend away and making good memories.

THE BEST PART of the weekend was on the Sunday when we went on a fishing adventure. It was a guided fishing experience for people like us who enjoyed dipping our toes into the wonderful world of the sea, but who were novice anglers. The trip consisted of a two-hour fishing session from the shore in the most stunning environment imaginable.

We teamed up with Cliff and Melanie on one side of the boat and Mary and I on the other side.

"So, guys, you have to master the throwing technique first," one of the fishermen said, as he gave us instructions on how to cast our nets, the basics of fishing and tricks of their trade.

Mary and I divided the task between us, coiled the net, left it to dangle as expected, held the rope and the loop. At the instruction of the boat crew, I did the throwing; Mary giggled as the net spread out over the water and sank. The instructor quickly clamped his support to close it around the bait. All we need now was to wait.

This part of the sea is home to one of the country's amazing beaches. The seashore was beautiful. Mary was born and bred in England but had never fished for fun before. She found it quite therapeutic and she seemed the happiest out of all of us.

Before too long, Mary and I were the first to pull out a fish: it was a mackerel. She hopped and screamed loudly and with so much excitement that she jumped on me and gently clutched my upper arm a little tighter and longer than necessary without realising. Our eyes met. Something else met as well. She took a deep breath and exhaled and looked in

Melanie's direction. That was the beginning of the flirting. I knew how this was going to end. She did too. We both knew it was lust, yet she encouraged it. I grasped her and gave her a bear hug. It was light and gentle, but I meant it. My hands wrapped around her waist and hers were locked around my neck as she leaned in close. It was the perfect moment for a kiss, but I behaved myself. I pretended to be distracted by the whine of a helicopter hovering across the sky, a few hundred miles above our heads. I let go of her, releasing the tension that had built up. She tied her curly hair back beautifully and we focused on our fishing adventure.

We carried on fishing, ignoring the sexual tension. Mary enjoyed my company as much as I enjoyed hers.

"Is genotype incompatibility issue a deal breaker for you?" Mary asked.

"Hmm. Sometimes I think I'm open-minded but, yes, it is. And you?"

She took a deep breath. "Same," she said, unconvincingly.

It was Cliff and Melanie's turn to celebrate a good catch. They pulled out a medium size, brightly coloured wrasse. Mary and I joined them in their celebration. We could have stayed for hours, but it was time to make our way back.

We arrived back at the shore as the evening shadows grew longer. Mary sat next to me, as we enjoyed the sound of endless waves arriving at the shore and the pure smell of nature. We prepared a fire, hunched round it to keep warm and readied the fish for cooking. They were smoked and marinated according to recipes we had bought earlier. For a lover of fresh fish, it doesn't get any better, especially when you add in the great company. After a few hours, it was time to head back to our hotel. Mary gazed at me like she wanted something, she shot me a discreet but affirmative look.

On our way back, we walked through a thicket to a lovely

secluded rocky bay. Every turn of the corner revealed another sublime scene. Mary and I talked a bit more about *The Bachelor's Ride* and life in general. When we got back to our hotel, we enjoyed a glass of wine together at the bar before calling it a night. We both seemed to be dragging our feet on our way to bed. My head knew why we did; my heart wondered why.

I got back to my room. I was half undressed and half asleep and heard someone knocking at my door. I looked through the peephole to see Mary standing there. Damn, she had hiked her skirt higher up her thighs. I opened the door a crack.

"Hey, Mary," I asked. "Is everything OK?"

"I think you took my phone," she said. "I've got yours."

"Oh, I'm sorry," I said. "Please give me a moment to get it."

"It wasn't your fault," she said, smiling. Her face swathed with impish glee.

I got Mary's phone and swapped it for mine. I didn't want her to see me in short boxers with no shirt, so I hurriedly wished her a good night. She looked like someone on a mission, hesitated, and repeated the good night wish a few times but made no move to leave. Her shirt's top buttons were undone, and she had lost the cardigan she'd worn earlier. I knew what was coming; even a blind man would know. My whole body responded to the offer at hand. Her eyes glistened, revealing what she wanted. My heart said "no" my head said "yes". I gave in, pulled her from the corridor into my room, and we met halfway with a kiss. It was rough, and my head told me I'd betrayed my heart.

I stopped. "Mary," I said, "you're beautiful but I'm sorry, I can't do this."

"You don't like me?" she asked, shy and embarrassed.

"I like you, but as a friend," I said.

Mary growled through her teeth and made to leave. Anger

was growing in her; I could sense it. I grasped her hand, attempting to ease the tension.

"You are so..."

Before I could get another word out, our lips met again. This time, it was slow. Every pretence I had fell away. She maintained eye contact and my arms encircled her waist. She reached up and clasped her arms around my neck. I pulled her closer, holding her hips closely to me. Her jaw in alignment as I used my hands to massage her body, stirring up deep emotions. Her eyes were closed. She moaned slowly, and her breathing changed. Our tongues entwined in a kiss which lasted for a minute or two. A moment so pleasurable to both. Then I pulled back and looked away, letting the expression on my face do the talking. Mary didn't say a word. Her wordless rage was defiantly profound as she reached for the door. She scowled at me, then walked out, slamming the door behind her with a bang.

For the first few minutes, a battle raged between my head and my heart. "Ah, see how you missed *hot salad*! How can you let go of a *sweet potato*?" My head sparked dirty messages. My body had responded to the stimulant; the thing between my legs was up and strong, the thought consumed my heart and jolted my body with electricity. Then, my heart restored my common sense. I was after true love. It reminded me about my commitment not to defile a woman I was not married to. It was a reminder never to sin before God.

My heart won the battle. "You did great," it said.

Our trip back to London was scheduled for Monday morning. Everyone had taken the day off. While in the car, Mary and I pretended nothing had happened the night before and somewhat surprisingly, we talked freely without any awkwardness.

"This short holiday was heavenly." Melanie started to talk.

"Sis, trust me, this place is beautiful. We have to come back," Mary said.

"Yes, I agree," I said. "It's a stunning place. For that fresh fish, I'm back already." I laughed. Everyone laughed. The growing bond among us was evident.

"Toyosi, I second that," Mary said, and excitedly kept chatting. "Those fish are, hmm, savoury. You know what I mean? The freshness: the flavour makes it mouth-watering. Next time, I'm gonna bring more recipes, from lemon juice, mayonnaise, green onions and ermm, you know, garlic and black pepper. The grill will be wicked. This was the best weekend away I've had in ages. The fish, the sea, the company, it was *almost* perfect."

"Almost?" Melanie curiously asked. "With all these descriptions?"

"I'm sure Mary meant *almost* as in," I quickly chimed in, "the stay was too short."

Everyone laughed. Mary's face with a coquettish smile. Cliff was the one at the wheel. As the rumbling of wheels eased, Cliff sampled everyone's interest for the next adventure.

"Guys, let's do this again sometime. New county, new adventure. Who's down?" Cliff asked.

Everyone echoed, "I'm down," one after another.

"Ha-ha, if there's fish there, Toyosi will come, I'm sure," Mary joked.

We enjoyed our ride back home and I bid goodbye to Cliff's family.

The short break had been worth it. I got my second wind and returned to London ready to give *The Bachelor's Ride* a final push to the finish line.

TWELVE

I OPENED my eyes to the sunrise and could hear birds chirping. "Lord, help me on this journey to finding happiness." I'd just concluded my morning devotion and let out another silent prayer to God.

I reached for my phone. "...this email business is beginning to dull my spirit, man. I feel like somehow I'm back in the medieval times and we are communicating with crows or something..." I was reading Mide's email when my phone beeped. It was Matthew. Tara had become the subject of our conversation since he arrived back in Lagos.

His laughter broke through. I could tell what he was giggling about.

"I can't wait for it to be over," I said, before he said a word.

"I know it must be stressful. Finding someone special is hard work. Knowing what you're looking for is half the battle, but you also must have the strength to find it."

I was pleased to hear his motivation.

"By the way, how's Tami? Anything new?"

I took my eyes off the email floor. "Yeah, kind of. We've met twice. The first time was a quick coffee during lunch hours. We talked about stuff, our lives, our backgrounds, our careers. We spoke mostly about her ongoing TV production. Light gist, nothing serious."

"And any green light?"

"You mean besides her showering praises about Tara?"

"Damn. OK. And the second time?"

"I went to her office to take her out for lunch. Again, nothing serious."

We'd hung out for about an hour, swapping stories of our lives over and again.

"Baddest. Nice move. And how did it go?"

"Well, I got to know some details. She's in a relationship and although she won't say the complication still, I respect that. Meanwhile, I told her I'm seeing other people online."

"You did? You played her *the never to be seen chasing* rule."

I laughed. "I played her no rule, joker."

"*Chai!*" he muttered. "So, any plan of seeing her again?"

"No. I've played all my cards. The road trip remains my priority now."

"Did *she* ever get back?"

That was why he called. To confirm Tara's interest. But sadly, I didn't have any good news for him. "No reply, mate."

His laughter sunk. Now, I became the motivator. And what better way of doing so than to play back his top dating rule. "You must not let a woman know you're crazy about her and if you break this half-rule, you must not be seen chasing her."

"How about scrapping this *stooopid* rule?"

The laughter would keep me sane for the next day or two.

*W*ILL *I be too forward if I DM her on IG?* He texted after the call.

Ha-ha. I thought you're the master, Mr. Tender?

Please help a brother. I'm drowning. LOL

Well, don't message her, I replied. *Stick to your number one rule extension.*

He called me back, almost immediately. Mr. Tell-Her-You-Have-A-Babe was clearly losing it. "Toyosi, I created the rule, I'm allowed to break it. Give me some hints *abeg*."

I laughed so hard the phone nearly fell.

"There must be something I can do to get her attention," he said.

"Sure," I answered him. "How about visiting her family in Houston or enrol for another PhD in Kings College? The options are endless, aren't they?"

He burst into laughter. "That babe is scattering my head."

Yes. For sure.

"Stick to your rules, bro, your golden dating rules," I reminded him, again.

"How's the road trip? I'm really impressed with your dedication."

That was the opportunity to table my own request. "Got two amazing ladies. I don't want to lose either of them. Maybe you can help."

"OK. Shoot."

"Mercy or Mide?"

"I remembered Mercy as the misery one. Who's Mide."

"Miss Inquisitive."

"Oh, that's a tough one," he said. "What boils one person's kettle may leave another's stone cold."

"Hmm. Man of Wisdom. Please learn to speak English next time."

He laughed. "Give me a little more info."

"Mercy appears to be more mature. Her interactions are more thought provoking than those with Mide. Her emails are always well written and well structured."

"And Mide?"

"She is a go-getter who aspires to be a doctor. She's more forward thinking than Mercy. She is more playful, witty, and cheerful than Mercy too. I think Mercy's oversea exposure gives her something that Mide doesn't have but Mide's warm personality compensates for it. I'm leaning towards Mide."

"OK. Let's cut to the chase. *Who fine pass (who's prettier)?*"

Bad boy! The grin on my face spread. "They've both played to the rule. No pictures. Hence, why I'm intrigued."

"Hmm. I see why you like them. Anything else that differentiates them?"

"Mercy appears to be spiritual. Mide seems religious. Mercy is like a therapist; Mide is like a surgeon."

"You're crazy, man." His laughter was loud. "Well, you know who to boot out."

"How do you mean?"

"A therapist is not the one with a scalpel, and your abdomen wouldn't be at risk."

Joker.

After a hard review, I'd decided whom to send off.

Sadly, Mide exited next. It's never easy to bid goodbye to anyone, but, as cliché as it may sound, you can't make an omelette without breaking some eggs.

THIRTEEN

I KNOW you're mad at me. You have every reason to be. I'm deeply sorry. The day I saw your viral letter, you put tears in my eyes, those beautiful words of yours did! Even though we can't be together, I want you to be part of my life, hence why I brought Tara into this. I saw the pain in your eyes that Weds night. And on both occasions afterwards. You still haven't let go! I thot if I allowed you to think through it, you'd change your mind. Please forgive me. If my life is not so complicated, I'd be safe and warm in your arms. Tamilore.

What could be her complication? Her text puzzled me. I would not reply to it. I'd three potentials seated beneath my keyboard. But I could not resist sneaking onto her Facebook page. This time, I saw a brighter light. Her status was now updated to single.

What? Why talk of complications again?

I composed a reply. By my calculation, she'd still be in London filming. Her TV production would be completed in two days.

Can we meet up somewhere? I replied.

OK. Please send me your address. Her reply was almost instantaneous.

I wasn't expecting to meet in my place, but I wasn't going to say no to it. Whatever knocked out her complication, and whatever it was, remained my immediate priority. I sent the address and we fixed a time for the following night. And I did what every man would do when a woman he admires is coming to visit him: I washed the flat from top to bottom.

The next day, Tamilore arrived at my door. She wore a smile different from what I'd been used to. Her hair was unkempt. Her spirit seemed sunk into nothingness. Her aura had turned monochrome. What could be wrong? I hugged her as she walked in to the living space.

"Are you OK?"

"Yes." Her face narrowed to crinkled slits. "I'll be fine."

"Let me get you a drink." I turned to the fridge.

She shook her head and held my hand. "No, Toyosi. Maybe later."

What could be eating her up?

The sparkle of her eyes from a few weeks ago had faded. No dimples on her face today; they had melted. Where is the beautiful smile? Her eyes darted across the room and ended downcast on the floor. I could understand the quiet voice when someone isn't in the mood, but I couldn't understand why she'd have visited if she was mourning.

"You have a nice place."

"Oh, thanks. Just a bachelor pad."

The splashing of the rain pattered against the window. London and rain are two words that can be used interchangeably. Until an hour ago or so, the air was not thick with any warning signs and no weather report had suggested the sea was set to unleash from the sky today. Windy light rain showers were projected. What we'd accustomed to as a trickle, that lashes the city every now and then, had heavily become a downpour in a bout of bad weather suddenly. I stood up to pull the blinds down and switched on the lights. The wall-mounted lamp added warmth and cosiness. The room was now as cosy as the nest of the bird.

She perched on the sofa, her eyes heightening with concern. "There's something I want to tell you..." She pulled a pillow and placed it comfortably to rest her back.

That was fast. I wondered why her words were slow to a crawl. I wasn't expecting bad news. There shouldn't be any that I wasn't already aware of. But I don't like being told this, at least not at the beginning of a sentence. It always pumped my blood, as if someone was about to slap my face. I sat next to her, acknowledged with a nod, face straightened up.

"But first, have you forgiven me?" Her voice was now at its lowest.

"You didn't offend me, Tamilore." I held her hand, trying to smile as I tugged her closer. "I know why you did what you did."

She raised her eyes to mine.

"You can still be safe and warm in my arms, you know."

Her dimples showed slightly, but they quickly dimmed. "But it's not going to work."

"How do you mean?"

"After seeing your letter, I searched and read every single note you wrote on that blog, under the same name, Ayo. 'Africanness goes deeper than a skin.' Oh, that was such a brilliant read. You'd have to tell me more about that sometime. Also, 'Your first loss is your best lost: dating lessons we should all learn from the ageing trading rule.' Or something along those lines. Now, to your question, I know about Silver from Edinburgh University that you couldn't end up with because of genotype issues. I read how Dami broke your heart three months before the wedding. And I saw your highest rated story: *The regrettable night but an eye-opening experience. The one-night stand that left Aisha sexually satisfied.*"

"I see you've been busy."

How does all this affect us?

I kept staring for a clue.

Emotion stung her eyes. She read my mind. "I'm not AA, Toyosi."

Was that a tear on her face?

"Sorry?"

She hurriedly scrubbed the tear off. "Yes, Toyosi."

"But you are. I even…" I swallowed the remaining words.

Her brows knitted in a frown as she wiped her face with a handkerchief. "Do you know anything about my genotype? I can't remember saying anything about this. And there's no such info on my IG page."

I cautioned my slipping tongue. "No, not at all."

She inhaled a deep breath and blew out slowly. "I did the test in Lagos ages ago and I was AA. I repeated another test in Atlanta two months ago because my fiancé asked me to re-check at the hospital where he works, and it was free test anyway, and result said AS…"

I recognised her frustrated sigh.

I rubbed the back of her shoulder. She blinked, clearing her tears. "I couldn't let go of him, because what we shared is special. I decided genotype was not strong enough to break the cord of our love. I convinced myself because I really loved him. I'd not throw away six years. If I'd known from the beginning, it would have been different. Even if I knew one year in, it would have been easier to quit. But that wasn't what he wanted. He wanted to quit on the spot. He became worried and it bothered him in a way I'd not imagined. Hence the complication. I asked if we could carry on dating, at least to figure out our options, until he... until he cheated on me... again." She stooped and bent, her hands supporting her head.

I moved closer. "Oh... no... he did?" My hand was still at her back, patting her.

Her head was now resting against her open palm. The tears rolled down her cheeks. "That was the third time. The third time in six years."

"I'm so sorry to hear this. Please be strong."

Her slumped shoulder lifted a little. I continued the patting for the next few minutes. She rested her back on the sofa while I prepared some tea for her.

"Should I add sugar?"

"No, thanks." She dried the remaining salty water off her eyes. "My cousin is pregnant by him now and she's planning an abortion. I never knew until two weeks ago." Her head fell against the cushion cradling her back with both hands in a supporting position.

"Your cousin? That's too bad. What kind of a man does that?"

She used her handkerchief again. "I know you only write about real-life stories. Is Dami story true? And are you Ayo?"

I placed the tea on the coffee table in front of her. "Yes."

"That is wickedness."

I squeezed her hand and offered a soft smile. "For now, I need you to be strong."

Her lower lip quivered slightly as her next words were about to come forth. "Why did you go ahead with Dami when you knew the genotype issue from the onset?"

"Her name is Sisi. We were both in agreement and loved each other."

"I'd never do such. If I knew from the onset, it's definitely no, no. I mean hundred per cent no. My ex..." She narrowed her eyes as she bowed her head. The sobs again. "I can't believe

I'm even calling him ex already. We've been engaged for four years."

I held her closer. "I'm so sorry. You'll be fine, OK." I gently rubbed the pad of my thumb at her shoulder, then my arms were wrapped around her, patting consolingly.

She trailed her hands through her hair that bounced and coiled around her face. "How can men be so wicked?" She made no attempt to wipe off her tears.

This wasn't the time to correct the generalisation. "Everything will be OK. Time heals all wounds." I kept rocking her, like a mother would rock her crying baby.

Her hand rested on my knee. Her warm body kept mine warmer. "Why my cousin, of all the women in Atlanta?" The searing pain of her voice was easing.

I hugged her tighter. "Time heals. Just give it some time. Maybe three months. Maybe six months. Maybe a little longer. Time always heals."

She rested her head on my shoulder, then it slid to my chest. I cradled her head in my arms. The tears flowed through. I kept wiping them until she was no longer crying.

I took a deep breath to allow the silence to crack a little.

Then, her lips covered mine, as she stretched.

Oh, no, I wasn't expecting that.

I slightly pushed back and rubbed her hand. I would not do this at her weakest point. "No, Tamilore. You're vulnerable right now. It won't be right on my part."

She said nothing at first, then she spoke, shy and timid. "No, I'm not. Don't you like me anymore?" She looked into my eyes, "At least kiss me. Show me you still want me."

I rubbed her palms and let my hands, my eyes, my whole body, revealed I wanted her today, tomorrow and forever. Then, I pulled a step back, trying to diffuse the tensity that had filled the air. "You're not thinking straight now, Tamilore. Of course, I want you. I want us, but only when I'm sure that's what you want. Let me go make some food for us."

She pressed her palm tighter to mine, stopping me from standing up. "I'm not hungry, Toyosi." Then, she let go of my hand and swiped at her eyes.

Oh no, a single drop of water had touched her eyes.

I moved closer, placed my hand on her shoulder, "Tamilore..."

She turned, looked up and stretched.

I'd lost my words. Because our lips were now intertwined.

The bulge in my trouser became victorious. In a matter of seconds, we had hovered into each other's presence and space, exploring, probing, appreciative. Our lips rewarded each other; our tongues curled up from corner to corner. Her eyes were clenching shut already, in a light trance, mine were still opened. While we were busy, my hands had gained independence under the hem of her dress. In no time, her clothes began to roll onto the sofa, while mine, to the floor. Oh, things were moving too fast. This wasn't how I'd imagined our first time. I quickly ignored the stupid French kiss idea I'd once premeditated and put my hands to good use. To everything beautifully and wonderfully perfected. Oh, yes! She arched with a moan, a whimpering moan. She'd grabbed me at the scruff of my neck in my seating position where I leaned against the sofa. I controlled the pace and went for her rib cage, letting my mouth be of blessing, too. I smelled her, blessed her, appreciated her. She lost composure. I held on, remained to the course, the oral expedition. She gripped my shoulders as she fought for air. I wrapped my arms around her and guided her hips to the right position.

Oh, my goodness. Something had blazed fully to life.

Dear Jesus, allow me this moment. We'll talk about this later.

She rewarded me. Tamilore rewarded me. She took doubt out of my mouth, every apprehension that ever existed, every uneasiness, every senseless anxiety ever hung to my throat – everything, as if it was therapy I needed to cure whatever was plaguing my mind. As we continued swapping saliva, inch by inch, she slided, and grinded and rocked on my hardness. Sweet Jesus. We were now speaking in heavenly tongues. Two breaths synchronised in gasping pants. That was all I could remember before I took charge, turned her around, stretched her, blessed her, again and again, as we rode to a bliss.

Time stood still. Half an hour should have been defined as a flash.

That was my first time in eleven years. I hated myself for 'cheating' on the innocent people behind my keyboard; and above all else, for failing God.

She rammed her foot into her underwear. "We shouldn't have done this."

I couldn't have agreed more. I snapped out of my guilt and excused the senseless remaining part of my brain. I'd deal with my foolishness later, the self-loathing suddenly hardening to my throat. I reached for my scattered clothes and began covering my nakedness. Someone was already boiling with raging eyes. She angrily grasped her handbag and yanked her phone charger off the socket, before I experienced the hottest cry of a woman. It started with silent tears as she held the bead that threatened her eyes, before the fresh bawl burst forth – raw, uncontrolled tears. I began another round of consolation. The cry surging with every spoken word; the surges grasping for every breath, intensifying in peaks.

Against the edge of the sofa, she rumbled and clumsily maintained her balance as she stepped into her shoes in a flash. "Let me go. Toyosi, let me go." She pushed my hand off, exploded out of the chair, and marched towards the front door, smouldering; her handbag caught the edge of the staircase, the items therein flung all over the floor.

I bent to help.

She screamed. "Just keep your hands off." Her eyes were no longer tear-soaked; they were furious, lighted with slits of emotions, innumerable emotions – of hatred, of self-blame, of anger, of disappointment. "How can we do this? Is this how people start a relationship?"

"I'm sorry." I looked like an idiot.

"Sorry for what, precisely?"

"Tamilore, you kissed me. I tried stopping you."

Her face was scrunched in pain. She surged forward, almost like shaking. She'd picked her items off the floor. The strap of her purse seemed broken. She snatched the tissues and hand sanitiser off me and headed for the door, twisting the doorknob. "Leave my hand."

I read the pained sneer on her face. I watched her heels slapping the floor.

Goodness me. Have I ruined my chance? Have I freaking ruined my chance at love?

She sucked in a loud breath, then scrabbled for the door handle. My eyes were doing the pleading. She wheezed with what sounded like the last of her air.

My heart thudded warnings, so I slowly removed my hand over her chipped nails. "Tamilore, please take it easy. Please don't leave with anger."

She looked away, cupped her hand around her mouth, then rocked back and forth on her heels. Her fingers tugging closely to her mouth now as though she was chewing her teeth.

I slumped against the door. "OK. Let me get you an umbrella. I'm so sorry." The rain was pelting outside the window, ranging and screaming like a tantrum, as London continued dancing in a waterfall. The thrumming on the roof swallowed my voice. "I'm really sorry."

What was I sorry for? What the hell was my sorry ass for!

She swung her clenched fingers that covered her mouth, before she began drowning in her sobs and sputtering through her tears. Like someone growling in self-inflicted frustration.

I watched to see if my words had calmed her. She sat at the dining table, relocated to the armchair, the sofa, rocking back and forth. She finally settled on the snuggler chair, but the balls of her feet were still bouncing on the floor. Hot tears welling up in her eyes, dripping and trickling down the bridge of her nose to her top.

I crouched down in front of her. "Tamilore, I'm so sorry, you mean the world to me. Can we please talk about this?" The tears rolled more and stung her lip. I reached for her hand and pressed my lips to her palm so tightly. Her eyes never met my gaze.

Almost an hour of pleading went by. She was still blinking wetness from her eyes. As if the world had fallen through my feet, I kept pleading, rocking, entreating and hoping to mend it; to save my world. I wished I'd mastered this moment; I wished I knew how to calm a broken woman. Because everything I knew about persuasive words had failed me. I held her on the sofa; she seemed so fragile.

Lots of coaxing and sweet words followed. I gently cleared the teardrop on her cheek with my handkerchief and stroked her shoulders. Moments later, my words, in tender tone of voice, began to ease her tears. My hands were, thankfully, no longer shoved away.

She banged her hands on my chest. "We shouldn't have!" The banging was no rage.

"Yes, we shouldn't have!" I agreed and let a soft smile plead my course.

My body remained the punching bag as she was repeating her words, the furrows from her brow were clearing, the tears soothing, the anger calming, until we were hugging. It is indeed one of the best feelings in the world when you hug someone you admire and they hug you back, even tighter. Thank goodness. Thank freaking goodness.

Half an hour of cuddle time eased pass.

Oh, no, not again! Master Jesus, I promise I'll debrief with you tomorrow morning.

Like two spoons nested together in a drawer, we were back to where it started, right there on the couch. This time, it was the most pleasurable life experience yet. No grief, no guilt, no sobbing. I'd take care of the global map drawn on my skin with her crawling nails.

FOURTEEN

I'D TITLED my next story that I was never going to post *Dating and Other Forms of Insanity*. I should have written this before now, at least attempted to solve one of the world's underrated problems. Shouldn't dating be classified as insanity on a global stage? Anyways, I dished out all my stupidity. Writing real tales was the best therapy to ease my pain. So, I used it.

Tamilore had not replied to my messages or calls for three days. I knew she'd have travelled back to Houston, but I visited her hotel to double check. My shame worsened as each day passed by. It was Saturday morning, and Matthew had been on a video call for nearly ten minutes, persuading me to continue with *The Bachelor's Ride*. I lied about an argument that broke out between Tamilore and me when she visited. I would not kiss and tell.

"I can't," I kept repeating.

"The show must go on," he kept shouting.

"But I can't! Besides, I'm tired of this online dating."

"What you are doing online is no dating. Only a fool would call that dating. I know you've never dated two people at the same time in your life. And now, you still haven't! You don't even know the ladies. They don't know you. You're all testing the waters. OK, consider this. What about people you make happy? The business advice you're giving Angel. The mentoring for Tola or whatever her name is. Have you thought about Mercy, how she is always excited to read from you? How about Ellen who is hopeful? And all the others. Do you even know if one of them is your bride and you're here killing yourself on self-blame?"

"And Tamilore?"

"Give me a break. The calories between you two is too strong. You've burnt it a little with your... your argument. Move on. She may come around later. She may not. But for now, cast your net wider." He'd shouted each word, blended in between a scream and a laugh.

Calories? Burnt it a little? And the stammering! Fuck! He knows, doesn't he?

"What nonsense are you saying? What do you mean move on?"

The shouting subdued. He dragged a hand over his head with a wry amusement as if he was saying, "I get it. You're stupidly in love. And when people are stupid in love, they do stupid things, they act irrational," as if he was fighting the words worming from his mouth. Then, he cocked a half-smile, "Tami is not in a place for relationship now, Toyo."

"Then, I'll wait."

"Nah, you're jumping the gun. Remind me who's left on the road trip."

"Queen, Mercy and Ellen."

"You see? Your finest selection. They are all AA. You can't afford to quit."

I said nothing. I couldn't shake off the feeling of guilt.

"Move on. Besides she's AS."

"And so?"

He smacked the back of his head this time. "Move on. Finish the road trip. Whatever happens, that's destiny. And when you get to the river, you can figure out how to cross it."

I finally gave up and pondered on his words.

"We've had a false start, haven't we?" I said in the quietest voice.

"Speak English. You say?"

"I mean... I mean arguing with high intensity."

He took a deep breath. "That's from a place of love."

"OK." I muttered, as I agreed to continue with the show.

Whether he'd figured it out or not, he was the calming breeze to my head's storm that morning. He doffed his hat. "Take it easy, bro. All will end well."

I buried my pride, asked God for forgiveness and continued with the road trip.

FIFTEEN

I T WAS S UNDAY AFTERNOON . I'd invited a few friends over for
dinner including Cliff and Melanie.

Onions half chopped and diced and thyme ready. Garlic
minced. Maggi lined up. Fresh tomatoes boiled with scotch
pepper and steamed. Lamb slowly cooked to tender. I was now
in the kitchen thick with spices, making Afang soup made of
spinach, simmered vegetables, with lamb and a separate beef
option, when Kunle arrived. He was recently engaged and
planning his wedding in a few months. So, we had good reason
to be jolly together.

Kunle knew how to cook with his mouth. "You put in
groundnut oil first, add pepper, chicken, some water, squeeze
together, boil for a few minutes. Done," he'd say.

"*Otunba*, the chef." We laughed, as I welcomed him.
"Lamb on the menu, bro."

He wafted up his nose. "*Correct. Your wife go dey enjoy o.*"
"If I find her."

"When, bro. When you find her. Stop using if."

I always pondered on the difference between "if" and

"when", wondering which day I'd also share in the indescribable joy of loving someone and being genuinely loved in return. I dwelled on the weak smile I gave each time, pretending to believe it would happen despite fear looping my thoughts and wrapping itself around my neck with anxiety that refused to quit.

I snapped out of my thoughts. "Make yourself comfortable, bro." I told him.

As the host, I wanted to cook two dishes. Since I'd moved into my newly rented apartment, I had yet to invite friends over for a housewarming. So, it was good timing for a get together dinner before I resumed my work in the world of financial crime detection.

Before too long, Cliff and Melanie arrived. To my surprise, Mary had joined them. We hugged each other. "Thank you for not inviting me." Her smile spread widely all over her face. We hadn't spoken since our weekend away.

Finally, Debby walked in and lit up the place. Everyone pulled her in for a hug.

Debby Oyedepo Ojo was born and bred in Bristol, a city in the county of southwest England. She was very proud of this compass city. Until four years ago when she relocated to London for a new job, she'd lived her life admiring the River Avon that straddled across the city. Twenty-six-year-old Debby was single but she'd friend-zoned me for nearly two years. I'd tried to get out of the friend-zone to no avail. Even though Boris Kodjor, the tall, dapper Hollywood star, was already taken, he was the man of her dreams. I was not her cup of tea as far as relationships were concerned. That was fine because I knew I was one fine pineapple juice. She set up a torrent of defence mechanisms to keep me off the chase, so we'd settled for friendship. And if I could say I'd a best female friend, that would be Debby Oyedepo Ojo.

My final guests of the night, John and his wife Christina, couldn't make it. In total, I had five guests to cater for. Everyone knew each other besides Mary and Debby who were meeting for the first time. It was a good gathering of folks who liked to have fun.

Ayamase stew with white rice and plantains on one side, pounded yam with Afang soup, drizzling in the roasted lamb sauce, was nicely on the other. Two dishes stretched on the dining table, begging to be savoured. And two bottles of wine, orange juice, apple juice and still water. And with that, dinner was served.

"Thanks for having us, Toyo. This is amazing," Melanie said, as she handed me a bottle of Chardonnay. She looked around the dining table, the open space of the living area, the Africa collections of paintings on the wall and walked towards the vintage, country-farmhouse vase that collected coins. "Toyo, this is really a beautiful flat."

"Thanks a lot, dear." I placed the wine on the table, asked Melanie for advice on the best plants, something suitable that can survive outdoors in the winter for the flat. She was going to help figure something out. Kunle leaned forward to examine the wine.

As we were having dinner and making small talk, Mary asked, "So, Toyo, have you made your final choice on *The Bachelor's Ride?*"

I foresaw this happening but not in front of everyone.

"*The Bachelor's Ride?*" Melanie asked. "What's that? A movie? What do you mean if he's made his final choice? Don't keep me in the dark, guys."

Kunle busted into laughter. "Toyo is running some project, I believe." He'd said this while uncorking the wine bottle.

"Project?" Melanie asked, searching my face for answers.

Mary laughed. "Toyosi is a player," she loudly told everyone, as though making an announcement. "His love letter went viral and he capitalised on his internet fame and started dating multiple women online in a game show he invented called *The Bachelor's Ride*." Mary gave a chuckle and stared at me for reaction.

I ignored her tongue that was sticking out.

Melanie rolled her eyes. "Wow, for real? Toyo, is it true? What love letter? Can I see it? Who are these women? Tell me, tell me, please spill it." Melanie asked several questions and just before she finished, Cliff became inquisitive, too. "*My guy, when you turn baddo?*"

"Nah, Toyosi can never be a player. I can bet my life on it." Debby, whose face suddenly became tired looking, something close to sadness, finally said something.

My guests, except Debby, were so hyped up to get the full gist that they left me with no choice but to spill the hilarious accounts of the past few weeks.

Kunle poured the wine into six glasses and raised his over-full glass, for a loud toast. Seconds ago, he was swivelling his tongue, savouring the lamb down his throat. "To the lover boy, may *The Bachelor's Ride* ride you to a happy ending," he said, and everyone clinked their glasses and giggled and chorused, "Cheers." Cliff shouted, "Amen to that, boy!"

"So, who are these last three ladies?" Mary and Melanie asked, after one another.

Great. This was perfectly suited for a hometown visit. I felt that I'd somehow mirrored *The Bachelor*. I had my close-knit friends, who were family to me, round the table for dinner to discuss who was best suited and deserving of the final rose. My potential bride.

I brought out my phone. "Here are Ellen's pictures."

Kunle took the phone, licked his lips, and grabbed a

handful of pounded yam before he passed his judgement. "Oh, my goodness. You've been scammed. Is she a model?"

"These pictures are not real. They can't be!" Mary echoed Kunle's thoughts as he tilted the screen for her to see. Mary tipped her wine glass with Kunle whose mocking laughter had been the loudest and she kept raging about common online scams.

Kunle nodded with his mouth still full and gave Mary a thumbs-up. Cliff who sat next to him on the right, saw as he flipped through the pictures. He held the meat that slid off the bone, ready to be swallowed. "Before I say anything, let's see the other two."

I skipped Queen. "I don't have any for Mercy. She stuck to the rule."

Kunle and Cliff exchanged glances.

"What rule?" Melanie again, blushing this time.

I reached for my glass of wine. "I wanted to pick based on everything but looks, so it's anonymous show."

Melanie placed both of her hands to her chest and displayed her affectionate smile. "For real? Oh, that's so sweet. I really pray you find love, Toyo."

So, Ellen became the subject of discussion for the first half of the night.

"First thing first, you need to get on a video call to authenticate her identity," Kunle said and trailed on, after he had unashamedly licked the salt and lamb sauce from his fingers and let the wine down his throat. "Too many scammers online these days, wise up bro."

"Toyo dear, you have to be careful. I agree with Kunle," Melanie said.

Debby said nothing. Her hands were either limped in her lap or cupped around the Kopparberg cider. I noticed she wasn't as loud as she had been when she'd arrived. *What could it be? Pang of envy?* Ellen was prettier than Debby, although not as intelligent.

Debby cleared her throat and sat up straight. "Sorry guys, please excuse me. I need to check for some sparkling water, I normally don't drink still water." Her voice sounded detached.

She was up before finishing her sentence.

"Oh, my bad. Let me get that for you." I told her, rising to my feet.

She patted my shoulder, (almost like saying, "sit your ass") and smiled, a forced smile. "I'm not a stranger here, mister," she said, walking towards the kitchen.

I took my seat. Everyone continued eating. It took longer than normal for Debby to return. Between five to ten minutes. I excused the group and headed to the kitchen.

Oh, no, what's eating her up?

Clenched teeth, furrowed brows, she was hovering back and forth like a hummingbird in a confined kitchen space. In fact, Debby was like the bird's iridescent plumage: unique. But, as fierce as a hummingbird is, so was Debby, ready to drive intruders away.

I closed the gap between us. "Hey Debs, everything OK?"

The pressure had built. The bubble had burst.

She took a breath and hugged her elbows, allowing her eyes to talk harsh words, angry words, disappointing words, perhaps the tendrils of her mind were causing her muscle churning, before she opened her mouth. "Sure, yeah... yes, everything is fine, I just got off a call." She then avoided the eye contact, brushed past me and rushed back to the dining table.

Cliff turned to face Debby as she took her seat and took a sip of his wine. "Any thoughts on Ellen and online dating in general?" Judging from Cliff's mischievous look, there was a good chance he knew what was going on and had intentionally poured kerosene on a burning fire. And there was the flirting Mary with disapproving click of her tongue.

Debby grinned and wiped something off her forehead. Then she reached for her water. You should have seen her eyes; they were filled with sadness and anger. Her hands moved, and her upper body quivered slightly. Her face was tight, and her lips revealed disgust. Have you ever tasted a Nigerian cuisine called "bitter leaf soup" when the bitterness isn't properly washed off? How about grapefruits, lemons, or limes? Do you remember the expression on your face when you did? That was Debby's facial expression.

"She's fake." Her voice was the coldest in the room.

I levelled her eyes with a gaze. "You mean the pictures couldn't be real?"

"I can tell you a hundred per cent. Yes."

"OK. Maybe I'll arrange the video call this week."

"You don't have to. Drop her and stop the whole show or whatever you are calling it."

"You don't believe in finding love online?"

She sputtered into her sparkling water at first, her cheeks flaming then snuck a sideways glance at me. "Toyosi, there are plenty of interesting single women in London."

To Debby, a man who lives on the bank of a river does not use spittle to wash his hands. "How can you be in London with so many single ladies and go after some random, unknown, fake people online?" Her tone was firm. I ignored it. I checked her facial expression, discreetly. The over-confident Debby Oyedepo Ojo had suddenly become subtle.

Mary, whose hands were now folded between her thighs, glanced at the door. Her arched eyebrow returned and mirrored mine, then she glanced again at the door and mouthed something.

OK, it's time to put the past where it belonged.

"Toyo, can you please show me the restroom?"

I figured it was a good time to apologise for the kiss. So, I walked her out of the dining room, stepped out of the living room, and pointed to the restroom.

"Mary, I know you want to talk."

"I really feel sorry about last time. It was my fault." Her tone was low, but uncertain.

"I was just about to say the same thing," I said. "My apologies. I don't want to blur the lines."

"I don't feel a twinge of regret, though," she said. "Do you?"

"You feel sorry, but no regret? I don't understand you," I said.

Her eyes pinched at the corners. "Yeah."

"Erm. OK. Thanks," I stuttered.

Mary peered at me with suspicious eyes. "You haven't answered my question."

"Mary, I don't want to break anyone's heart, not a beautiful one like yours." I smiled.

"Hmm. OK. Is she your girlfriend?" Mary asked, like a sharp-witted observer.

Someone's in an investigative mood today. Has she noticed Debby's jealousy? Maybe she wanted to understand the backstory. Maybe she hasn't yet given up herself.

"You mean Debby?"

"Yes, she seems to be into you."

"No, she's not. We're just friends. Old friends."

"Toyo, I'm a woman," she said, with half-rising of an eyebrow. "I'm telling you she's into you."

Mary slowly opened the restroom door and gave me a funny look with a playful protusion of her lips while I re-joined the other guests.

"Toyo, please tell me a little about Queen," Melanie asked.

I'd introduced Queen without revealing her pictures. I already knew what the sentiment would be.

"Queen *nah* babe," I laughed. "She is adorable. Nice lady. She's a journalist. She comes across calm. Based in Paris. And she loves old fashion romance. My type."

"I think you should drop her," Kunle chimed in.

"Why?" The couple asked, almost at the same time.

"I'd say keep your options open to the UK. It's hard to let go of your dreams to chase after love in another country, especially when you have an established career."

"I'm happy to relocate to Paris if she's The One," I said. "But I want someone flexible to locate here."

Mary overheard the conversation as she walked in. "Drop Ellen, she's..." She clasped her hand, as she was talking.

"Keep her," Cliff interrupted.

"Drop her, and now."

"Keep her."

And the argument went on for nearly half an hour until a loud ringtone, PSquare's latest song, started pouring from Kunle's iPhone, a perfect distraction to quit the debate.

I re-introduced the third lady, Mercy. At this point, dinner was nearly over. So little had been said about Mercy. Mary picked Queen as her favourite. It was unclear if she meant it. Melanie picked Ellen. Debby picked none of them. Kunle and Cliff endorsed them all.

It was ten o'clock and dinner was over. I had just finished scraping the plates and stacking them in the dishwasher. My guests made their way out as we called it a night. Mary hugged me tighter than the others. "I pray you find the true love you seek soon."

SIXTEEN

Two days later, Debby called. We engaged in some light banter. We mocked Kunle who'd licked his fingers more than necessary during dinner. I'd defended him and blamed it on the delicious soup. She called him a "bush man". "How can someone, in a setting like that, always place his palm underneath every swallow, dramatically oh, as if the soup was going to drop on his lap. And as if that wasn't embarrassing enough, he shamelessly digs hand on the soup like a shovel," she'd said, mocking him. We switched to the trending online gossip on Instagram with hashtag #whyimsingle. Laughter had returned to her lips and it kept us bound.

"I'd like to help with your plants. Maybe over the weekend, I'll get you some fresh plants for the balcony." She sounded a bit warmer and friendlier than usual.

I was touched when Debby volunteered to help. I hadn't seen this side of her in a while. And more so, the sound of her voice, the warmth and sudden richness beneath her British accent, signalled a clue of what I was thinking about.

"Oh, that's so kind of you. I really appreciate it, Debs."

"I'll send you some samples I already checked online. Let's think about reflecting sunlight, sun scorch, and plants that can thrive in blustery garden, winter or summer."

Hmm. OK.

Debby turned up at my flat on Wednesday evening, seeming quite relaxed; she wasn't in a hurry to leave. We were sitting on the sofa having fried rice and chicken. Debby had prepared the dinner for us. She's done this before, but it had been over a year ago.

She leaned forward to pick up the remote control, *accidentally* snuggling into my warm body. Her button-up tea dress hugged her tightly, enough for her heart-shaped hips to show. Her pink heels remained as fashionable as ever. "There's this TV series I'd like you to see." Her hand landed softly on my shoulder.

"Hmm. Nice. What's it about?"

She searched the YouTube videos for the newest Nigerian TV productions about a young couple, love and marriage. "Wait a sec." The grin on her face was bright and beautiful.

"OK." I waited.

Her eyes were half on me and half on the loading video. "This Is It."

"You say?"

She laughed. I noticed her dress had peeled up a few inches. Her look was soft, pleasant, and unlike in recent times, undisguised and frankly, it was beautiful to see. Her arms pressed on mine, lightly. "That's the title. *This Is It.* It's such a beautiful love story. Let's watch from the beginning," she said, as she searched for season one.

We were wrapped under a warm blanket and watched the sitcom together.

Someone was letting a brother off the hook for sure.

Finally, I was going to be out of the friend-zone. It should have brought me joy. I could end the road trip. I would be the happiest man. Love would have gradually found me. Yes, I would have simply said: THIS IS IT. But no, it was too late. I was no longer interested.

About six months earlier, I'd submitted a short story to one of London's storytelling gigs, a night of open mic, spoken word, myths, riddles and poetry.

Debby had been sitting next to me reading the latest issue of *Wedding Planner* magazine when I was brainstorming new ideas. I was thinking out loud when she interrupted me.

"I have an idea of what you can write for your next story," Debby told me.

I should have said, "Thank you, but no thanks." Maybe love would have found me in her arms. Maybe the sitcom would have been our story.

Instead, I looked up and caught her brimming smile, face lightened with an unusual surprise. I was pleased to hear her suggest something on my writing for the first time. She knew it had to be a true story. That was what I'd been known for, telling real-life tales.

"Oh, awesome. Let's hear it. Hopefully it's interesting."

She held her breath, shut her eyes, as if she was counting seconds to let out a bomb, as if she was giving it one final thought. Then, she opened her eyes and smiled half-heartedly. "But you'd have to sign non-disclosure agreement."

"What?" My grin spread out.

"I'm kidding. It's Tutu's story. Promise me this would remain with us for eternity."

"Sounds like something dangerous. Please don't reveal it, if it's too personal."

She twisted her neck, in thoughtful consideration it seemed, before placing her hand on mine. "It will boost your writing career. Just promise me, it stays between us."

"You got it. You have my word."

Unknowingly to me, it was her story. She'd, understand-ably, avoided self-abasement. In the piece, I had written a sex scene with a character grossly described by Debby. The woman character named Aisha had a one-night stand with a character named Andrew. I later found out that Andrew was Ade, a friend of a friend, and Aisha was Debby.

I had sent the links of the short story gigs to my contacts, and asked them to forward it on, for voting support and reviews. Debby's friend, Tutu, who she claimed was the char-acter in the story noted with a comment on the posted piece, how she was sure the story was Debby's, as it was exactly the same as the best sexual experience ever that Debby had shared with her closest female friends. An unexpected fling, so good, so satisfying good, that left her sexually fulfilled. A tape to replay on a rainy day, on a lonely day. I read the comment and screen copied it before it was deleted by Tutu, about thirty minutes later.

Ade attended the same church as me and each time I saw him as an usher welcoming me on Sunday, I always remem-bered the graphic scene I'd written.

One Sunday, as the service was going on, Ade stood in the front row of the church walkway, ushering energetically, flowing in self-acclaimed salvation's glow. The pastor was just a few yards behind him.

"You're welcome to church, this way ma/sir." That was Ade. The popular Adeoba Adepekun Thomas.

He was muscular, tall and dapper. Demon casting, prayer warrior, tongue speaking, Ade. Everyone liked him. He was as quiet as a mouse, but I knew he was a crook. He was the fake *holy as thou.* "God bless you, sister" was his favourite line to the ladies. Mr. Crook.

In the middle of the sermon, I saw the flaky usher in my

mind. *Why is he opening his belt and pulling off his trouser in a rush? Oh no! no! no! Are they fighting? Why are they bumping themselves against the wall?* His tongue was now busy sweeping between her lips.

The loudspeaker hummed in my ears, from the prolonged shriek of the microphone. I stretched my neck, for this Isaiah's message to sink, the hot prophecy from the altar.

Now, nobody dares distract me!

A few minutes later, his scent sent her into a heady trance. He placed his fingers in the right places. And used them gracefully. His arms had guided her body to pleasure. His heart fluttered when he drew her to his lips. She sizzled on the tip of his tongue; he trembled. The flames of torches ignited again; her spark got fire. "Oh... oh... yes... yes... yes."

In no time, Ade had pulled down his shorts and stripped her to her underwear. The trembling breath got louder at his exploration, and the stupid man wasn't going to stop now, not when he had taken control of her nipples and breasts with the flicks of his tongue.

The pastor's microphone was at his loudest. "Children of God, Isaiah prophesied again..." The word of fire landed on my face, but I was cold with anger at the sight of Ade.

My eyes blinked. I cleared the blurred vision. The lady next to me had a pen and notebook, writing. The moans and sounds at every touch played repeatedly in my head. Mr-God-Bless-You-Sister was pressing something hard against her bare skin, still busy sliding his tongue to hers. Even if it is one word, Isaiah or Isaac, I wanted to write something, too. I heeded to catch the prophecy, but Ade beat me to it again; this time, he was moving too fast.

He held something in his mouth like an apple, caressed it, licked honey from her nipples, and used his hands slowly on every part, relishing in her body softness, from her cheekbones, lips, to caressing her breasts, and slowly down to her stomach, to her hips, and down to the lower part, teasing her, thrusting her, experimenting her – with his mouth – like a drummer stepping on his base drum. She longed and begged for air, settling her hands on his busy head between her legs, pleading in some foreign languages, before she began scratching her fingers against the bedsheet turning to rags. When her scream for pleasure subsided, he turned to strokes and kisses before he got down to the main business that lasted a lifetime. Dipping and climbing and turning and bending. Damn, that foolish man was a devil.

"Hi. What's the verse again? Isaiah 54: verse what?" The lady snapped me out of my wonderland, just when he'd sparked her and sprinkled his juices.

"Erm, ah, erm. Is that not from verse... ah, I didn't hear. Sorry." I spluttered words like the confused man, I clearly was.

"OK. Bless you," she whispered. Her knitted brow passed the scoffing message.

Debby had no clue I knew what had happened. If only I could erase the gross graphics I'd created with my own bare hand, this disturbing flash that got stuck in my mind! If only!

SEVENTEEN

Hey Toyosi, yes, it's OK. Please pass my mobile to him.

Matthew had struck gold. Tara finally replied. She'd arrived in London for her studies and all my attempts to reach Tamilore had remained abortive. Through her Instagram page, I learned she had been in Cape Town with her girlfriends on holiday. The captions of her pictures had been positive: *the sliding through of the dancing shoes; the spinning groove in the township; born for the outdoors.* So, I knew she was having a blast.

My phone beeped. It was Ellen's email. I'd sent an email last night asking for her opinion on long-distance relationships.

She wrote, "...it completely suits my personality. Besides, I'm not the most romantic person on earth, so I won't be crying and cuddling my pillow because bae is far away..."

"LOL. Superb. How long have you been single for?" I replied instantly.

"I'm in an open relationship actually."

What? Is that the same as being single? Damn.

"How's it going? Is the open relationship a mutual decision?" I replied.

She wrote, "The open relationship is going alright, amazing actually. Well was it really a mutual decision? I wanted it open on the basis that once we find someone else, then we call it quits. I didn't want to leave such a good man and be single for nothing or start getting to know someone else. I'm really lazy about the whole process of getting to know someone new. He's widowed, his wife passed on a few years after they got married while trying to have their third baby. They had twins already. So right now, I have three amazing stepchildren and I love them shitless. My mum doesn't know I'm playing stepmother at my age. The whole marriage is dead on arrival. So, my relationship is literally leading nowhere."

Within the blink of an eye, the "beautiful bond" was sadly dissolved.

I got on a call to deliver the great news to Matthew. He was ripped with joy. If you asked me when Tara and Matthew started dating, I'd have told you it was that day.

Pleased to have crossed the most important hurdle, he texted after our long call.

Happy for you, bro, I replied, *you won't have to do another PhD in Kings College.*

LOOOL. How do you sum up your long exhausting road trip in one word?

Adventurous.

LOL. Hit the babe up and let's pop some champagne, it's double win for the team.

Ha-ha. I know there's more to finding love than having the same musical tastes. However, I'm hopeful that time will tell. I can't wait to meet HER.

You didn't say how Queen was booted out at the drop of a hat.

LOL. Queen Shonda! I'll let you figure that out.

Ha-ha. No time for sloppy romance. Oh, shit, wait, she kicked you out?

LOOOOL. Yes, she did!!!

I guess Queen could not deal with my major weakness of being over analytical. I was glad someone pointed to my own flaws too.

I CALLED Mum to confirm my Lagos trip, as Ife's mum's sixtieth birthday celebrations drew nearer. "Mama the mama, good evening Mum."

"Hmmm Toyosi. You sound very happy. I suspect there's good news?"

"Nothing new, Mum, besides finding Mercy and knowing God's mercies follow me."

"Praise God. I'm happy you're growing in faith."

"Hmm. I'll be visiting home sometime before Christmas; most likely the weekend before Ife's mum's sixtieth."

"That's great news. You mean to meet Ife?"

"Erm. Erm, Mum." The stutter again.

"I'm so happy. What food should I prepare? I'll make your favourite. Should I hint to my friend, I mean Ife's mum? You can even marry her in six months. These days, nobody does long courting anymore. You find the right girl, you marry her." She laughed, sounding like she was already planning the wedding.

"Mum, that's like two to three months away."

"I'm sorry, son. I'm just so happy."

"I'm coming to see if I can possibly give a distance relationship a chance."

"Yes, you can. Ife is a beautiful young lady. Twenty-five.

Top university graduate. A promising lawyer. You two will get along well. What more can you probably ask for?"

"Hmm, what a coincidence! I've to go now, Mum. I'll call you sometime soon."

"What coincidence, son?"

"Nah, never mind, Mama."

"OK, my dear, remember to always pray *o*, especially for God's mercy."

"I agree, Mum, Mercy is my priority for now."

"When God shows you His mercy, you find love."

"Thanks, Mum. You couldn't have said it better. And bye for now."

I stood on the balcony staring at the wisps of evening clouds, looking out for God's mercy that someday I would find love, tell a beautiful story, and stop confusing my sweet mother. I could hear a solo sound, a lovely melody from afar. Michael Bublé's magic voice. The airy breeze waved the sound my way. It was a beautiful melody, perfect for the moment. I kept my gaze on the beautiful clouds and listened on till the song ended.

Who will save me the last dance?

EIGHTEEN

"Good evening your highness, the beautiful Mercy Jones Spinach, it's Toyosi Isola from London."

"Oh... oh... oh... my goodness, it's you," she screamed. "Finally, I get to know your full name and hear your voice. I'm happy you called. You're so full of surprises. Aren't you?"

"Don't mind me, you sound really amazing," I said.

"And you too," she gushed. "You have plenty questions to answer, you know."

"I know, right." The grin on my face was brighter.

Finally, we could hear each other's voices after nearly two months.

"I'm glad you proved me wrong about meeting people online," she said with an overbright voice that sounded nervous.

"That's great to hear. I'll be working in our local office in Lagos for two months, so we can get to know each other better. I can't wait to see you and enjoy Lagos with you. Is that OK? Are you happy to have me visit?"

"You're coming to stay in Lagos," she asked in shock, "because of me?"

"Yes."

"Oh, thank you so much. Toyosi, believe me, that's the sweetest thing ever. I can't wait to... see... you... but, erm, erm," she started to mumble.

Mercy seemed like she didn't know how to handle the news of my visit. She sounded like she wanted to smile and jump for excitement, but something grasped her heart tight, crushed it, and made it less joyful. It was an inner cry. The joy consumed by sadness.

"Any problem?"

"No, not really." Something stinging the corners of her eyes.

I wondered why the air between us suddenly became still, so hazed in gloom.

I remained calm until she was comfortable enough to share. And after I'd hung up the call, I pondered on the journey, yet again, as the evening leached quietly into midnight.

I was on a video call with Mercy two days later when she dropped a bombshell.

"Toyosi, I'm sorry. I'm... on... a... *home lockdown*." She sounded like someone who was traumatised, disturbed, bitter and frightened. It was no different from someone who was filled with smoke and desperate for air, brimming with spirits and fighting loneliness.

"Are you OK?" I asked. "Home lockdown? What does that mean?"

Tears stung her eyes. "House... arrest. House arrest." Her chin trembled.

I looked at the corner of the room, as far as I could to see if there were any clues. I tried to make sense of the long curls of hair on the floor, the clothes stacked on the falling wardrobe, the piled nylon bags next to it, the socks, the empty pizza boxes. I turned my attention to her. She was pale, pale and queasy; her hair was gone. "Are you in trouble of some kind?"

She was gasping and wheezing now. "No, I'm grounded." The tears spilled uncontrollably down her innocent face. "Due... to... health... related...issue."

"Oh, I'm so sorry to hear, dear. What health issue?"

Her cry punched through again. Her eyes were red already. She turned the camera away from her face. Her cry became louder. I could hear the drips, the pain in her voice, the sobs, the gasps. When the camera came on about ten minutes later, her chest was soaked. She was a picture of devastation. The tears had torn her apart. She cast her head down, pressed her hand to it, wiping off the tears with the back of her hand and her nose. Her voice split with a groan of misery. "It's no different... than... being... in prison."

I drew in a lungful of air. How could I soothe her sobs painfully wracked against her chest? "I'm so sorry to hear this. So sorry you're going through a lot. What happened?"

She dropped her head to the side and used her drenched shirt to wipe her face, but her chin remained wet. "I feel empty. I feel pain and misery." Her voice was cold, like her words.

I waited for a moment. "I'm so sorry. Have you seen a therapist?"

A little moment of silence. "My... uncle... promised... me... one." The tears flushed through, as if the pain was rolling in waves, and this time it consumed her. Her howls of depression and misery escalated. Her pain surging in stammering groans. She took short pauses to clear her nose, wiping off the snot, streaking from her nose to her trembling lips.

"I'm so sorry, dear. I really am. All will be well," I kept repeating as she recovered her breath. She changed her seating position. I could now see the remaining section of the room. Dark and dirty, the crumpled white tissues scattered around and piled up in a corner like mountain ranges. At the point where the trail of tissues ended, the trail of clothes began, strewn all over on the floor. Natural lights streamed in through the panels of the dusty window, revealing the dust motes floating about. I watched, with horrifying pictures of neglect – the reflection of a small broken mirror, with smudges all over it which was placed next to the bedside – what seemed to be piles of empty skin care products, creams, lotion, blob of toothpaste, toothbrushes – everything in a film of grease. And the combs dressed and clogged with hair. "Hiding behind my keyboard is all that gives me a breath of fresh air. You have given me a meaning to life when I'd thought of killing myself many times. Not once, not twice. Many times." Her words awoke a sense of urgent responsibility in me.

Oh, my goodness!

"Mercy, please. I want you to hold on tight. Please I beg of you, don't do anything."

"OK."

I came off the video and put Matthew on speed dial. He didn't pick up. I called my doctor in Lagos. He didn't pick up, either. I sent both the same text. "Urgent. Please. Help. Suicidal." In a blink of an eye, the doctor's mobile call overrode Matthew's call on WhatsApp.

I screamed for help. "Someone in 306, Anthony Block Street needs our help. She is drowning." The doctor kept asking dozens of questions at the same time. "Who's she? How did you know her? Is she on TV? Are you related?" I gave him her name.

"Please act fast. Please." I screamed.

He could feel the pain, the pleading of my words. Otherwise, Dr Agbo would never act.

Within an hour, Mercy was safely placed in his hospital at the Anthony Village. A suicide note was found in her bedroom, dated the day before *The Bachelor's Ride* began. Matthew later visited her in hospital with the roses I'd asked him to buy.

I stood by her throughout the difficult time. After a few weeks, she gradually began to halt her drowning and overcome adversity. It was a remarkable turning point and an important journey that she had to make on her own, so I slowed down frequent contact as time went by. I remained in touch with Mercy, but we began to drift apart. Maybe there was something there, but sadly, it never sparked. And circumstances never allowed it!

PART 4

NINETEEN

It's been three months since *The Bachelor's Ride* ended. Tamilore never replied to my calls, text messages or emails. Instagram has been kind to tell me her whereabouts. She'd spent the summer break in Dubai and Abu Dhabi with her co-TV presenter, the popular Mr. Dalasi who aired love shows. Although her pictures from Abuja parties to New York trips had no traces of Dalasi, her latest update, "Greetings from Wayag Islands," did, with captions of the two adults *seemingly* flirting in the centre of a romantic-looking wedge-shaped island. Matthew and Tara had been to the US for their third vacation together. They cruised along the popular Route 66, drove along the iconic American hotspots and roads of faded glory, from Chicago through St Louis to Oklahoma City, all the way to Las Vegas. Heart-warming experiences were told through their pictures and short Instagram videos especially the stopovers at different spots they described as "small-town America, the best of America." You can't blame me for being jealous. That would have been horrendous for a solo traveller, wouldn't it?

In the last three years, I'd visited romantic destinations around the globe, ideally meant for two; from the humbling, effortlessly beautiful Hawaii to artistic, pure-bliss Venice; from the fascinating, soul-stirring Bangkok to breath-taking, paradise-found Bali. I took myself to lunch and dinner. "A table for one, please," I'd say every time.

I'll have to hold the paddles tight, as the dating boat rocks from left to right. Some folks had started advising me to try *anointing* oil on my forehead.

It was Saturday morning. Debby was coming to see me later in the day. We had planned a group hangout with three of our mutual friends. During the week, on Monday 19th June, this year's World Sickle Cell Day, we'd joined forces with NGUK Warriors, a local non-governmental agency promoting awareness of sickle cell anaemia both in Nigeria and the UK. "Shine the light on Sickle Cell" was the year's theme. We distributed T-shirts and flyers at a street rally. We campaigned, demystifying several myths about the disease, pain, cure and lifespan and shared the facts. The most important being not everyone living with sickle cell would experience intermittent pain, constant illness or die early in life. We raised awareness on common pain triggers such as stress, extreme temperatures, dehydration, overexertion and for women, menstrual cycle. We sang. We danced. We celebrated. We shined the light. Throughout the week, we'd been busy creating a range of graphics for social media posts and campaign. Twitter and Instagram had been buzzing with the help of social media bloggers posting with trending hashtags: #SickleCellMatters #ConquerSCD #SCDSCTMatters. So, today, we planned to grab a beer or two after a hockey game.

Mum had been on a call for about ten minutes. We spoke

about Ife, briefly. We already did. "You'll meet the bone of your bone, and the flesh of your flesh," she said. It always ends with a prayer point about me finding a wife. And her favourite line. Every call. Every Sunday.

"Amen. Amen. Amen," I said and swallowed the saliva.

Until next week, I'd worry less on what I needed to do differently; maybe shout a resounding and bigger amen to shut the devil's ears and bash the evil spirit out of my space once and for all, or maybe shout a seven-fold amen. There must be something to fast track answers to prayer requests other than swallowing my saliva and drying my throat.

———

A MONTH EARLIER, I had met Oma at a station in London on my way to work. Odaoma Nwachukwu. I was in a hurry to get to a meeting and it wasn't a good time to socialise. But as I was getting off the escalator, I saw the lady making her way in the same direction. Her long hair caught my attention. I quickly orchestrated a "coincidence". We walked through the barrier at nearly the same time, in such a way that eye contact was inevitable.

She wore an air of confidence. Her eyes caught mine. It was an over the shoulder glance, but she didn't say a word. She seemed focused and kept walking. There was no time to be smooth; I needed to act fast and be sharp.

I walked a bit faster, matching her stride and said, "Hello."

I had about five minutes to make it count.

"Hi," she said, then paused for a moment. "Sorry, do I know you?" Her surprised look almost threw me off.

I regained my composure. "Err. Not really. Your hair looks amazing. I'm Toyo by the way."

She gave a half-suppressed laugh, as if I had said

something funny. I later understood she was amused and mocked the way I pronounced my name. To her, a Yoruba name for someone she'd assumed was born in Nigeria should be correctly pronounced with a Nigerian accent. I was unaware, thinking of the next line I'd use to make this first impression count. Then she smiled and introduced herself. "Oh, thanks Toyo. Lovely meeting you. I'm Oma."

She spoke with a Nigerian accent and I quickly changed the phonetic and relaxed my tone. I extended my hand. "It's lovely meeting you, Oma. And my apologies, it seems like I'm walking a bit fast. I'm running for a meeting, so I don't get sacked today."

She smiled. "Then, don't get sacked." She seemed like the typical girl next door.

"Are you London based?" I asked Oma.

"I live in Surrey, not too far off," she said.

"I guess you work in London, right?"

"Not exactly. I visit London every Friday for a *routine*."

"Oh, a *routine*? That's nice." I was clearly confused but there was no time to clarify what she meant.

"Yeah, it's nice meeting you, Toyo." She smiled.

"And you too, Oma. Have you finished your routine for the day yet?" I tried to make a joke.

"Yes, thanks, but I've got to return a dress at the mall nearby. I must go now. It's nice meeting you."

She seemed like a lovely lady. She appeared decent, warm and friendly so I thought that perhaps it would be a good idea to get her mobile number. A three-minute conversation was too short to ask for her number without seeming creepy. But sometimes, a man's got to do what he's got to do. You don't want to miss a chance you may never have again.

"Erm, I appreciate we've just met," I said, keeping a smiley face as I inched closer, "if you don't mind, may I please have your mobile?"

"I'm sorry but I don't give my mobile to strangers," she said, shaking her head.

"I promise I'm a good stranger." My teeth spread out like that of the white shark.

She tucked her hands in her waistcoat and smiled. "Is it written somewhere on the face where I can see it?"

I laughed.

I tried one last attempt; added a bit of salt and pepper to the rhymes before I gave up. Most Nigerian women like to test a man's persistency and intention on the spot.

"Giving my mobile out comes with a condition." Her furrowed brow gave the clue I needed. The tone was warmer too, and her face, as bright as her smile.

I nodded and listened.

She put a fist under her chin which lasted for a few seconds. "There will be no disturbance calls." She appeared to have feigned the reluctance.

Standard play hard to get. OK!

"Yes, of course. Totally." I nodded in agreement.

A week later, Oma and I had had a few telephone conversations. Someone had breached the "no disturbance call" rule and someone was so happy to get the "disturbance call". She later confessed that she was secretly waiting for me to ring. We connected naturally, and soon became well acquainted. Gradually, we began to talk every day.

After two weeks, we met up for early dinner at a local bar. It was full of British couples, the majority of whom were in their late fifties. We were the only blacks. And the only people with no glasses of wine on our table. That was intentional, to keep the date low-key. My eyes scanned the faces at each table, searching the room for love, I saw too many. I loved the couple next to us, giggling over their tea, in white teapots, joking and teasing each other and the old man next to them, singing out of tune for his old wife. Another couple greeted me with nods and smiles. Their smiles tickled my heart and extended to our table.

Salt and Sugar Bar is best known for its romantic connections, for the young and old alike. It had been repeatedly featured in the popular *First Dates* series on one of the TV channels. The love images pinned to the wall, colourfully designed, caught our attention. She sipped her coffee gently, after blowing off its steaming hot cream. "You still haven't told me why you randomly approached me with cute hair bla bla," Oma said. That was probably the hundredth time she'd asked this funny question within two weeks.

I laughed. "Your hair makes you look too young." Her thirtieth birthday was in two months. She looked half a decade younger.

She flashed a grin. It was as though we'd known each other forever. It was effortless to engage. The genuineness and softness of her words was slowly warming my heart.

After our meal, we held hands, enjoyed some sightseeing nearby, hugged tightly, cuddled, and took some lovely pictures together.

We sat at a park bench in front of a watercourse stream, enjoying the fresh weather and the beautiful view: the sunlight had splintered out between the clouds. Oma placed her hand to her forehead and leaned her hip to the edge of her seat. "I have something important to tell you," she said in a hushed voice with tone of concern, tearing grass into little pieces. She paused for a little moment, keeping a gaze, then staring at the kids running around the water fountains in the opposite direction, as the calming breeze rustled the leaves towards us.

I squeezed her hand gently. "Hmm. Let me take a guess. Like winning a lottery?"

She smiled, elbowed me. "It's about me. But I'll only tell you when I'm comfortable."

OK. I'll keep that in mind.

The sunset had painted the sky pink. Shortly after, the skies dimmed. Yet the night wasn't over without a piggyback ride. I gave Oma a piggyback as we walked towards Blackheath station. She grinned in excitement. The pathway looked serene with colourful streetlights, a pleasantly windy night for a new friendship to blossom.

It was one of the best first dates I'd ever had. I finally had something different from "you're a great guy, bla bla bla" dates, the typical ending speech of my recent first dates. After that, I kept in touch with Oma and we discussed plans to meet up for a second date.

"I remember you wanted to tell me how to share your winning lottery. Are you now comfortable to share half of it with me?" I asked over the phone, gleefully.

"Oh, *that*?" She laughed. "OK..." She paused for about a minute.

"When you're comfortable, dear. Take your time." I interrupted the hesitation.

She inhaled a deep breath. "OK. Let me let it all out! I'm an illegal immigrant and I'm under border control monitoring. The day we met, I told you about a *routine*, right? I was returning from a police station where I go for my weekly sign in. I had recently made a new appeal application to the Home Office but it's pending approval."

"That must be hard," I said, in shock. "How long is the approval process for?"

"I'm expecting to know the outcome within the next month."

"OK. That sounds good. And how many appeal applications can you make?"

"If the application is not approved this time, which is most likely, I'll have no option but to relocate back home to Nigeria. My case is so complicated."

"Oh, I'm so sorry to hear, Oma." I said, as we began analysing the issue.

I appreciated Oma's honesty and openness. It was clear at that moment that we needed to slow down and understand the dynamics of our friendship and the effect of her uncertain immigration status. Nevertheless, we felt it was a good idea to meet up for a second date but delayed it a bit. We clung to the slim hope that all would be well.

———————

WHILE I WAS REMINISCING about the potential complications of dating Oma, my phone rang. It was Debby; she was already outside.

I opened the door, hugged her. She held two turquoise plant pots, beautiful artworks.

"Oh, Debs, are those for me?" I teased.

"Yes. They are nicer for your plants. I saw them while shopping earlier today."

"Wow." I was pleasantly surprised. "Very thoughtful of you. Thanks a lot." I gave her another hug, as I collected both pots, and the grey pebbles, and led her to the balcony. The plants were branching out gleefully, growing into a tall profusion of floppy leaves and becoming greener as each day passed by. The top forming new leaves, the bottom tumbling down faster than expected. Debby was staring at the stems that sprouted around the edges, then moved closer to touch the leaves, observing the greenness peeking through the bulbs, as if she was scrutinising their lives. It was as though she had imagined besides these plants, and me, there was no other living thing in this flat. If that was true, she was indeed right.

Debby gasped in awe. "I really like how the stems are growing and they're so tightly budded," she said.

They were so tightly budded indeed except for the bifurcate stems splitting in opposite direction. I wondered if the characteristic plants had a message for our lives.

"Many thanks, Debby. I owe you, you know. Maybe some groundnuts or your favourite plantain chips from Nigeria," I said, smiling.

She pinched my hand. "Well, I'm glad you know you're owing me something." She over-enunciated each word slowly.

"I made your favourite, I'm sure you can't wait."

She smiled and rolled her eyes playfully.

I'd not taken my gaze off her yet. She looked livelier and gorgeous in her chunky light-green cardigan. And I noticed she was wearing the layered necklace I'd given her two years prior.

She walked to the fridge, twirling a strand of her hair. "I like how you always stock non-alcoholic Kopparberg in your fridge. Now, you've made it my favourite drink."

"Have I?" I smiled, as I took out the freshly prepared meal. "I'm glad you like it."

"Have you seen the new season of *This Is It*?" she asked.

"I'd love to, you know. I really enjoyed the last one we saw together. The couple are really in love. But I'm pretty much overwhelmed with many commitments now."

We talked while I prepared rice and microwaved the freshly prepared seabass stew for lunch. I thought about how much warmer, refreshingly kind and different Debby had become. This had been going on for a while. Besides, she'd been asking the right questions.

"Toyo, who's the lucky girl now?"

I smiled. "No one yet. I'm single and searching."

I checked the bowl of seabass stew revolving under the microwave light. In a few minutes, lunch would be ready to be served.

"You make that sound like lyrics to a song. Why? What are you waiting for? You want to grow old before finding a wife?"

"Debby, I want something special. You already know that."

"What if you've already met her but you can't see?"

I suck in a lungful of air. "You may be right. I met someone but there's a problem."

She tilted her head with narrowed eyes. "And who could that be?"

"No one you know." My eyes repeated the same thing as I walked towards the dining.

She squelched on her seat. "Talk, please. Who's she? And what's the problem?"

I placed the food at the dining table and turned to face her. "Her name is Oma."

"Oma?" Her eyes disapproved. "She's a Nigerian, isn't she?"

"Yes," I said. I resisted the urge for lectures today. She could be an Aborigine for all I cared.

"And do you really like her like that?"

"My heart skips a beat for her."

Debby understood what I meant. Anyone who was close to me knew what that meant. She knew Oma must be special and whatever I had for her was real.

I explained the circumstances.

She kept her gaze on me, soft gaze, as if she was assessing how deep I was into Oma. In an unsettled moment, she folded her hands in between her thighs and leaned backward. "You *can't* go on the second date. People like this are desperate, always looking for a guy with papers. Toyosi, please don't make that mistake. Let her go!"

I smiled. "Can't, or shouldn't?"

Faint smile on her lips. "You know what I mean. Don't go! Free the girl."

I served her favourite seabass and prawns. "I like her, you know. And even if her application is rejected, we can always work something out, provided we get along well." I paused, looking into her eyes, as if I needed her approval. "Trust me, I'd know if she's playing games. Those that play games wouldn't reveal such a complication so soon."

She leaned into the table now. "You cannot be too sure. Scammers are smart. OK, there's this documentary that aired on BBC One last summer, about the life of illegal immigrants in the UK, or 'life without papers' as they called it. You should see this documentary and see what I'm saying. They are mostly scammers and fraudsters who played the system to get ahead. Sadly, some people fall into those traps. They become blinded by fake love and get used and dumped. Don't let any girl blindfold you into this."

I watched as she hunched her shoulders. "Debs, I can understand the challenges of those without papers. Against all odds, they settled for no welfare, no benefits, no decent jobs, living on relatives' support, constantly on police watch, running from one city to another, and living a low-key life. I appreciate your caution but some of them keep their dignity, they don't become involved in scams or fraud, they're just normal people."

"How do you explain what happened to Yetunde in church? And did you hear the testimony of Stephanie, Kellie and brother Roy? The list goes on. It's a common pattern."

"The second date will help me figure things out. You don't think so?"

"OK. If you say so." Her smile was gone.

As we were having lunch, I noticed she wasn't as playful as

she normally was. Our group hangout was scheduled for the next hour.

"Toyo, I'm not sure I'll be coming to this hockey game. I've just remembered Mum is expecting me to pick her up from a party at Peckham. That's like half an hour's drive away, so I'll need to leave in a few minutes." She'd said this with the bored tilt in her voice, an ounce of suppressed anger it seemed, as she buried her face in her hands.

I knew exactly what was going on. Hardly ever would you find a Nigerian party that ended around 3.p.m. In fact, the party wouldn't have started, if there was one.

"Please, stay. The guys will be excited to see us, you know. Please? OK, maybe we can watch *This Is It* briefly before we step out." My words lightened her mood.

She gazed at me and her look said it all. There was some-thing on her mind, but she was fighting the urge to say it.

"Debby, are you OK?" I asked.

"Yeah, I'm fine. Why do you ask?"

"I think there's something on your mind."

"Nothing, except work stuff. You know."

"If you say so."

"OK." She relented. "Maybe there is. Why do you always find love with complications?" She looked like she was still fighting to say something.

"How do you mean?" I asked. "You don't find love; love finds you. And sometimes it is complicated."

Following what appeared to be a resigned sign on her face, she gave a mocking one-shouldered shrug. "Toyosi, you have ladies who like you. British born. No immigration issues. No genotype issues. No complications of any sort."

"But Debby," I said, "you know none of those things are criteria for love. Those aren't the main factors."

"I know, but I'm just saying."

"OK?" I asked, wanting her to continue.

"Could it be that you can't see a lady with no complications who really likes you?"

I did not miss the switch from "ladies" to "lady".

"Debby, everyone has complications of some sort. And besides, who's this beautiful lady?"

"I disagree," Debby said, ignoring my question.

"If you say so," I said, content to let it go.

Debby gave me a funny look. If you knew Debby, you'd know she's a confident woman. But on this day, she seemed meek and timid. Her eyes looked dry; she kept blinking, as if her eyes were moistened. "And what do you mean everyone has complications?"

I talked about human imperfections to illustrate my point.

I pretended as if I knew of nothing major that would bother me. How could I tell her that I knew about her graphic one-night stand with Ade and that I still remembered every detail? How could I tell her to her face that she was a liar? Or would it be easier if I revealed I had been diagnosed for an eidetic memory; and that once images aree stuck in my head, neither a surgeon nor a seven-fold hallelujah could scrape them off?

In my head, the graphic nature of her encounter with Ade was as real as a sex tape. And worse, the way she described it was as if it was the best thing to ever happen to her. It was a mistake but ironically, it was also the best sexual experience of her life.

Ade and Debby were prayer partners who met up occasionally to pray. They had never dated and somehow, one thing led to another on the day and their clothes began to fly off. According to Debby's story, it was not premeditated. But how could I erase the images from my mind? I hated that it was my highest rated online story. How do I forget this? My mind was in shreds. I've tried therapeutic measures to remove the tapes clogged into my memory, but I was drowning more and more, each time I tried.

"Toyo, did I do anything wrong to you?"

"How do you mean?" I asked.

"You looked slightly worried just now."

"No, Debby," I said. "I'm just thinking about Oma's little complications. That's all." This was a big fat lie of course.

"And do I have one, too?" Debby asked finally.

"Yes," I told her honestly.

"What? What did you say?" She was curious and looked bewildered.

"I mean everyone does," I said. "Including me."

"Toyo, be more specific," Debby asked, clearly agitated.

"Do you remember, *A regrettable night but an eye-opening experience*, the piece I submitted for the London gig?" I asked her. "Who's the real character called Aisha?"

The air suddenly became still and stale.

"You have me confused," Debby said. "Aisha?"

"I mean the story you told me," I said. "You remember I named the lady character Aisha."

She scratched her nose. Shoulders tightened with eyes shifted back and forth. "I told you it was the story of a friend. I told you it was Tutu. But remember, that's confidential."

"Yes, of course."

Debby hesitated and knitted her brow. "Why are you asking me this, Toyo?"

"Nothing," I said, waving it off. "Let's get ready to meet the guys. I don't want us to be late."

I attempted to divert the conversation, but Debby wasn't having it.

She flinched and stood up to block my direction. "No, we're not moving an inch until you tell me why you've asked *that* question," she said, crossing her arms.

"Debby, let's get going."

"Toyosi, don't make me regret telling you a confidential story." Her voice seemed louder than thunder.

"I don't want you to regret it either. Can we go now?"

"Toyo, let's talk about this. What's going on?"

"Let's have this conversation later," I said. "We're late already."

"Toyo, please talk to me. Please," she insisted.

"You lied to me, Debby. It was your story."

"How? That's not true. It was Tutu's."

"OK." I shrugged. "If you insist."

Her pulse seemed quickened. "How could you possibly make such assumptions?" Her arms waggled. Jaw churned. Accusatory eyes dissolved. She gasped and balled up fistfuls of her top. It was as though she'd swallowed her remaining words nervously. I tried not to drag out the conversation any longer, paused for a moment, and began tidying up after our meal.

"Toyo, I'm sorry I lied to you," she said quietly.

"OK," I said, waiting for more.

She blinked a few times. Her face was still creased with concern. "It wasn't premeditated. It was a mistake. You're the only male friend I shared it with because I wanted you to write a true heart-warming story. How could I tell you it was mine?"

"What's heart-warming about this?"

"You know what I mean."

"No, Debby," I said. "You'd been bragging about the night and how satisfying it was to your female friends. You wanted it written down, graphically, so you could read it as a reminder. You used me to achieve that, to put it down on paper. You've not only committed a sin, you wanted to nurture it."

"I'm sorry I lied. But you and I never dated. Is this the complication you've been hinting about?"

I exhaled in thoughts. "Please understand I don't have

issues with what happened. I'm not a saint either. Sometimes, we make mistakes, and that's fine. The flaky usher I see every Sunday makes it a complication," I said. "And I can't get the images out of my head."

Oh no! There was a shift in her contenance, sudden unpleasant shift. Her top bunched, her viens bulged. Anger on her face. "How do you know him?" she asked. "Who's been feeding you this information?"

I went quiet in thought for a few seconds and resolved any potential consequences before delivering what I knew. "Debby, please don't get defensive. I know it was Ade. And it really hurts. It's not about my ego. It's as if you've brought me your sex tape to watch."

I'd hit the nail on the head.

It was a heavy punchline that evoked silence. Debby was lost for words, rubbing her thumb over her hand, nervously, as if her skin was suddenly prickled in defensiveness. She knew I'd either seen Tutu's comment before it was deleted or assumed one of her closest female friends was a traitor. At this point, there were no more cover up stories.

Debby felt terrible, that much was clear to see. Her shoulders were slumped, and her eyes were cast down, as she wrapped her arms. I hadn't seen Debby this sad in a long time; sadness nestled in the creases of her palms, her face and her body. I saw a woman in love.

Oh, no! I messed up.

Something was suddenly suffocating her face. I walked closer and rested a gentle hand on her shoulder, striking it softly. "I'm so sorry, Debby. I didn't mean to hurt you."

She quietly picked up her bag and put on her jacket, shoved her hands deep into her pockets, avoiding eye contact and made her way to the front door.

I felt sad. I'd ruined the afternoon. I reached for my jacket too, slipped it on, hoping we could leave together, as we had planned. Debby insisted that she was going home instead and no matter how hard I tried to persuade her, she wouldn't change her mind.

"Thanks for the lunch, Toyosi," Debby said, looking defeated.

I shouldn't have landed a terrible punch today. "I'm sorry I've ruined the afternoon. I'm really sorry," I told her with a wince.

I watched as Debby drove off. She waved half-heartedly. I was no longer in the mood to join our friends, Melissa, Dave, and Kwame, but I did nevertheless. They were shocked not to see Debby who was usually up for anything, but I made up an excuse for her and the four of us went to see an indoor ice hockey game, followed by dinner.

Later that evening, just before bedtime, I had some more time to think about the two ladies: Oma and Debby, and their complications. Oma's stumbling block could be overcome. In the event of worst-case scenario, I would eventually bring her back to the UK.

However, Debby's complication was more difficult to overcome. I wished I'd never written the story. I wished I had no eidetic memory or something of that sort. Debby was truly a phenomenal woman. She was a beauty, inside and out. A definition of sweet. She was compassionate and had a heart of gold. She loved God, was career driven, a wonderful future beckoned, and she was passionate about helping others succeed. What more could a man possibly ask for? And there was the bonus that we were already good friends. I assessed the two ladies, weighed my options, and before bedtime, said my prayers to God.

TWENTY

THE FOLLOWING day was a Sunday and the church service had just ended. I walked towards Debby. The moment she saw me, she began walking faster and took a different exit, the one specially reserved for kids and their parents. A few moments later, I caught up with her. "Good morning, Debs. I'm so sorry about last night. Hope you are well rested."

"Fine," she said, avoiding the usual warm greetings and eye contact.

She had turned sideways. I touched her hand briefly, teasing, and turned to match her body angle. "Your dress is lovely. White always looks good on you!"

She sidestepped and raised her eyes. The determined frown on her face remained unbroken. The cool air of annoyance remained undissolved between us. "Thanks."

"Mel and the guys really missed you yesterday. I made up good reasons."

She pursed her lips. "Thanks."

She continued to answer me in monosyllables when we talked, spoken with cold formality. Her arms were crossed, and she'd suddenly become red-faced. I tried to chat briefly with her, but she dashed off in long strides, without a backward glance. I understood. I knew she was still upset and that eventually she would come around. I composed a short message. *Have a lovely week.* And pressed *send* as she walked off around a corner in a huff.

Later in the day, after I'd finished sorting the laundry, I texted Oma.

Hey, nice dp. Colourful weekend, yeah?

Yeah. My niece's birthday. She replied. *What are your plans for next weekend?*

I'm off to Cambridge for sightseeing.

Oma called me.

"You know, I've always liked the idea of getting lost in the beauty of sightseeing in nearby cities and towns."

"That's great, you should do it," I told her.

"I've never liked exploring alone," she said.

"Yeah, I know what you mean about solo trips. But it's great sometimes, too."

On an impulse, I thought it would be a good idea to ask Oma to come with me but we both knew a weekend away wasn't ideal for a second date; it was too quick. While I was thinking about the right time to make our second date, Oma interjected.

"Can I ask you something?" she said.

"Of course, please shoot!"

"I'm thinking we could go to Cambridge together but on the condition that I would stay at a different hotel. How does that sound?"

"That sounds great," I told her. "How about staying in the same hotel but in different rooms to make travel easier."

"No," she said. "That's a no, no! It's not appropriate." She explained her rationale.

I obliged.

The plan was to meet at the station on Friday evening around 4 p.m., board the train together, and have a chat over coffee in Cambridge in the evening before going to our respective hotels. On Saturday, we planned activities like punting, sightseeing around Cambridge University and other great landmarks during the day, and a dinner at night. And for Sunday, we planned to attend a local church before making our way back to London. Oma's task was to arrange the activities (because she preferred to), schedule the timing, and manage the logistics between events, while I planned for the Saturday's dinner date.

"Please, don't forget to bring a dress for dinner," I reminded her, as we ended the long call. I wanted to be more formal for dinner than we would be during the day.

I booked my hotel and sent Oma the details, so she could book hers.

A few days later, Oma confirmed. *I've booked my hotel. It's a twenty-five-minute walk from yours.*

I didn't have the details, but it sounded like a reasonable walking distance.

Awesome. Train departs at 16:14pm. Let's meet 30 mins before. Yeah?

Yes. 30 mins before sounds great! I don't have any fine dress, though LOL.

LOL. Any will do. OK?

Superb. See you on Friday.

Our second date was set.

Finally, I'd not be travelling alone, even though Cambridge is only a forty-five-minute train trip from London. During the week, Oma sent me pictures of activities and events to assess my interest while I kept the dinner a surprise. I'd made a reservation for two at a lovely French restaurant near the town's centre.

I called Oma on Wednesday night but there was no response. We didn't get to speak the following day either. She was always busy, so it didn't register as an issue. She worked for a family member in the house and looked after their kids, which could be very demanding sometimes. It was a temporary job before her visa issue was sorted.

On Friday morning just before ten o'clock, I called her but got no response. I assumed she was busy and would return the call at her earliest convenience. I called again around lunch time and sent a text twice before three.

I waited for Oma's reply but got no response. I waited a little longer. Still, I got nothing. I became slightly worried and wanted to make sure that she was OK. I called again. By this time, I'd arrived at the station and was waiting at our meeting point. The phone rang but she neither answered nor called back.

I'd been calling her for two days with no response. I paused to think logically; something was wrong. Several possibilities flashed through my mind. Even if Oma was busy, I expected at least a text message in two days.

As our departure time drew nearer, I walked up and down the platforms, looking for Oma but she was nowhere to be found.

At 16:08, I rummaged in my pocket for my phone and watched the minutes tick past. I thought perhaps her phone battery was dead and it was a good idea to stay at the meeting point. My priority was no longer the weekend; I wanted to be sure she was OK. Everything else could wait. I sent her another text message but, again, got no reply.

It was less than six minutes to our departure time.

I hurried towards the platform but wasn't sure whether to

go or stay. I hesitated, trying to figure out the right thing to do. I'd had calls from a few friends earlier, but ignored them, as I anxiously waited for Oma. As if by magic, a call finally came through. Oh, no! Not now! It was Debby. I ignored it.

At 16:10, I got a call from an unknown number. I don't answer unknown calls unless I'm expecting one. Since I'd met Oma, she had never called me from an unknown number, so I thought it was OK to ignore this one too.

It was 16:14. I stood close to the train door, which was nearly closed. Should I jump in or wait? A guard bounded towards me, signalling departure. I had to make a decision in a split second. I jumped on. The train was moving, but I really needed to know if she was OK; it remained my priority. While on the train, I analysed the top three worse case scenarios. The greatest likelihood was that she'd lost her phone. Maybe she'd changed her mind and stood me up. Maybe Oma was in trouble of some kind. She could have been arrested because of her immigration status or, more unlikely, she was dead.

Fuck off; I don't want her dead.

I swallowed my own thought, the string of profanities.

At 17.02, the screeching of the train stopped. I arrived in Cambridge. I waited at the station, looked around and hoped that Oma had been on the same train with me. I sat there and waited for the next two trains to arrive from London. If Oma had lost her phone, which was the most likely possibility, or if she had missed the train, chances were likely that I would see her at Cambridge station. At this point, I was convinced there was nothing else I could have done. I'd called several times, sent text messages, WhatsApp messages, and left voicemails but had got no response for two days. I made my way to the hotel and tried to justify Oma's behaviour.

Without being silly, I narrowed down what could have happened to two options: Oma either lost her phone or stood me up. Either way, I just wanted her to be OK. I dropped my bag at the hotel and reflected on the different dating roller-coasters I'd been on in recent years.

Ah, I've suffered.

At 18.36, I finally heard from Oma. *Oh, thank goodness!* I thought. She's alive and well. She pinged me on WhatsApp. *Hi. I called you back.*

It was a big relief. At least I knew she was OK. I couldn't care less about anything else. However, my ego was becoming an issue. I was stunned that despite my many calls and texts, her response didn't give any additional information. I waited for more responses.

That was where things fell apart. My ego became a problem.

An hour or two later, I got another call from an unknown number. I was not in the mood, so I ignored it. There was no voicemail.

As I sat there, rolling up the sleeves of my shirt, I looked at the surprise gift I'd bought for Oma and remembered all the rigmarole I'd gone through to buy it. I'd contacted a friend, Bisola, the same day Oma joked that she didn't have any suitable dresses for dinner. Bisola was fashion savvy, so I'd asked her for help. She got Oma a lovely red dress. Oma had returned a red dress the day I met her, and I wanted the same colour for her. I'd no idea what her size was but Bisola figured it out from her pictures. I had arrived in Cambridge with both the red dress and flowers I had intended to give her at the station in London.

At 20:45, I came to the sad conclusion that Oma had stood me up and she probably didn't know how to say it. My ego wouldn't allow me to attempt another call. I was sorry for myself. How could something so beautifully planned go so wrong?

At 21:00, I felt that it was high time to move past the idea of a weekend away with Oma and focus on my original plan to visit Cambridge alone. After all, it was probably a bad idea to have planned a weekend trip for a second date, even if it was only forty-five minutes from home. It was frustrating that I hadn't seen this coming. Our first date was heaven on earth and the second was turning into a disaster. My heart sank, and my temper flared as I tried to replay events. I angrily threw the flowers into the bin. I couldn't have treated anyone this way. Never. I thought that if Oma respected me, she should have done something different, she should have reached out to me, even if she had changed her mind.

My time in Cambridge was a sober experience: a time to reflect on a few dating rollercoasters, circles of hope and disappointment, and learn some new lessons. I went out briefly, enjoyed some sightseeing, and took some pictures. I took myself to lunch and then dinner. Sadly, I didn't have any of the activities or schedules with me, or the tickets Oma had purchased. We'd paid for all the events – attractions, punting, and historic buildings to see, and Oma had the details. I knew only the French restaurant I'd scheduled for dinner, so I went there around the same time to apologise in person and cancel the reservation. I never heard back from Oma throughout the weekend, either by text, call, or on social media.

I arrived back in London on Sunday afternoon. On the train back, my muddled expression (seen through the window's seat reflection) revealed my heart-rending weekend. I thumbed the pages of a free newspaper next to my seat, the *Evening Standard*, but I was staring rather than reading, so I flipped it off. As much as I tried to rationalise Oma's behaviour and put the weekend drama behind me, my mind wouldn't stop evaluating events. Maybe I was wrong. Maybe I should have conquered my ego and replied to the chat. I sat there, quiet, feeling profound sadness, like a soul reflecting the aching hollowness of self-blame. Then, my logical sense was restored, and I was reminded that there was obviously no justification for Oma's behaviour. I got back home safely and put the weekend behind me.

Later that evening, I got a call from Oma. It was her normal number, not an unknown caller. Unbelievable. Something told me to simply ignore it, but I didn't. I answered.

"Why didn't you show up in Cambridge?" she asked.

"Huh?" I mumbled in shock but shielded it. "Oma, sorry what did you say?"

"Don't play that game. Why didn't you show up? Why did you decided to ruin the experience?" Anger crept into her voice.

"What! Wait. What are you saying? I was in Cambridge. What happened?"

My mind spun with many questions at once.

"I was in Cambridge for the entire weekend of course," she said.

I was stunned, dumbfounded and upset but I kept my cool. "Why didn't you answer my call or text or call me back or something?" I asked.

She said nothing. I could only hear the clattering of plates.

"What happened? Did I miss you at the station? Say something." I asked questions, but she didn't answer. She was disappointed. I understood, but it didn't make sense.

"I was there, Oma."

The conversation quickly turned into an argument. "Tell that to your brain-drain girlfriends. You think I'm a fool."

"Oma, come on, why are you talking like this? I was in the freaking Cambridge."

The argument got really heated.

"You liar!" she said.

She was shouting at the top of her voice. I was confused.

"What kind of a man are you? I thought you were different. You were playing games with me." She was boiling hot.

"Which game? Oma, I was there. I was in Cambridge."

"Hold it right there. You bloody liar."

"No matter what you say, please don't call me names. Why didn't you pick up my calls or text me back? Drop me a voicemail or something?"

"This is just a mess. I can't stand you." A storm was raging.

"Oma, what happened?"

"I can't stand you," she yelled.

Anger heightening. A cloudburst of anger. It would have been childish to begin trading insults, so I hung up. That wasn't right either, but the blazing heat had hit the roof.

The rest of our conversation took place over email that night.

She wrote, "My brother-in-law said he'd drop me off (bad idea) I couldn't call with my number because I didn't have a top up. I showed up for all we had planned at the time we had planned with the hope that you might just show up with an explanation and we'd push past it. This whole time I wasn't sure what to think but I decided to keep an open mind and live my life. I went punting according to the schedule. I was there hoping I wouldn't have missed you if you had showed up. Went to the botanical garden again with high hopes, no Toyo but it was fine too, I was insistent on living my life.

"On Sunday, I was sure I wasn't going to see you. I thought you got angry but for how long though. I went back home which was why I hadn't seen you anywhere around this city I had toured alone on foot. I went to church, went past your hotel and was wondering... what if you were there? Going in to find out would have been going overboard, I didn't nurse the idea." Oma explained.

I saw many lapses in Oma's accounts that couldn't be justified. I was surprised Oma didn't use free text messages to communicate. I was surprised Oma waited until just about departure time before she called me back from an unknown number, which I'd ignored. I had a lot of questions, but I knew she was upset too, so I replied politely, explained my position, and noted how sorry I was to learn that she had been in Cambridge.

Following my reply, Oma was still feeling hurt even after reading my account of what had happened. "I haven't had a change of heart, even after reading your account. Was I hurt? Yes. Was I disappointed? Yes. Would I have thrown out what would turn out to be a good experience? No. Would it have been better with a friend? Yes," she wrote.

"Oma, I'm so sorry about how things turned out. I share in the blame. Please, let's put this behind us. I'll keep the surprise dress I got for you till we see each other again," I wrote.

That was where we drew the line for the night. What an awful weekend.

The next day, she became even-tempered. She wrote, "Thank you for responding very politely. Thank you for showing up. It was also very nice and thoughtful of you to buy me a dress and flowers, thank you. I apologise for not communicating effectively and I apologise for how it has adversely affected our plans for the weekend. I apologise for taking this long to empathise and apologise; I haven't handled this in the best way possible. I hope you are able to leave all the hurt the weekend has caused and move on with your life."

And that was the beginning of the end.

The next day I called Oma to apologise for the way the weekend had turned out. She was calmer and willing to talk. But the episode had a knock-on effect on our communication. We kept our distance for about a week. It was good for both of us to clear our heads, think and reflect. Thankfully, we got past it and were both willing to rekindle our connection.

The third date, a week later, restored our friendship. The fourth date restored the faith. And the fifth date re-confirmed the natural connection we had established. We were good again. But there was a problem; Oma had just received bad news. Her visa application had been denied and she had been asked to leave the country.

I read Oma's text a few times, hoping for the day love would happen.

On the bright side, this setback is a good opportunity to regain lost years. As a trained Nutritionist, I see the repatriation as a blessing, a great opportunity to relocate back home, start a career, and grow a business I've always dreamt of. This brings me joy. I'm already fed up with my stagnant life, earning a meagre income babysitting for my aunt.

There were many uncertainties surrounding her case and it was not in our best interest to begin building castles in the air. Having broken a few immigration laws, Oma was at a disadvantage to renew her visa for the foreseeable future. Although I was keen to follow up and see where this could lead, Oma insisted it was better to quit.

A week later, Oma called to say her goodbyes as she prepared to leave the UK. We reminisced about our few good memories and made fun of the dispiriting Cambridge trip that shoved confusion down our throats. And that was the end of Oma and me.

TWENTY-ONE

"Ermm, erm please don't be offended, what's the visa situation?" Christina asked, in a frankly unpleasant demeanour, adjusting her seating position and chewing gum.

We'd met earlier during the week at a friend's birthday party in Blackheath, a stone's throw from where I lived. We were now sat in Cappuccino Best in Central London for coffee.

She popped the bubbles, monotonously shaking her head at the same time, while staring for an answer with keen assessing eyes. I smiled and did not show any repulsion at this or her off-the-shoulder shirt with the top two buttons undone revealing her two precious gifts nor at her cream-bleached skin. I tried to breathe fresh air away from the smell of cigarette smoke. How come I didn't know she smoked?

"You mean what's my immigration status?" I asked.

She nodded, as she stirred her vodka cocktail.

I doodled on my phone screen and tapped the air with my foot. "All cleared," I said, uncomfortably. I didn't want to get into the details even though I was a British citizen.

She swigged her remaining vodka in one gulp. "Great," she said, japing her arms excitedly. "Do you drive?"

"Not at the minute!" I responded.

"Hmm. OK. Are you renting or own your apartment?"

"Renting."

"It can be quite expensive to buy in London, isn't it? I hope you don't think I'm rude with my questions, but I like to ask these things. What do your parents do for a living?"

"Dad is late. Mum is a retired nurse living in a small town in Nigeria."

Shortly after she completed her checklist, we shook hands – firm palm to palm, no hugging, as we fleetingly bid other each goodbye. It was a *business* meeting, not a date.

TWENTY-TWO

London, July 2017

She said yessssssssssssss!

As my eyes creaked opened, I peered at the text message flashing light on my phone. *Whaaaat.* My reply was instantaneous. *Congratulations Mr. Tender. Calling you noooow.*

We're in Budapest, in the middle of SOMETHING now. Let me holla you in the morning.

LOOOL. Damn you LOL. I replied. *Many congratulations, bro. I can't wait to hear the gist.*

And yours is on the way, soon by God's grace.

Abeg, if you're still on your knees, pray for me! Abeeeeg!

Ha-ha. There's something new about Tami. Holla you in the morning!

Matthew's amazing news brightened my rather exhausting day. I mean the news about his engagement with Tara, not the stale disappointment hoofing over my head from hearing Tamilore's name. Truthfully, I wanted to hear *her* name, but after I'd conquered my weakness from stalking her on Instagram, a reminder of her was no good for me.

It was past midnight, I jumped off the bed like something had hit me. I was very happy for Matthew. I knew he was the luckiest man on the planet right now. We'd only spoken twice since he returned from his US tour; Tara had occupied his world. The last time I spoke to him, Matthew had successfully processed a relocation to his bank headquarters in London, but he was yet to move. A perfect opportunity to be closer to Tara who was barely a few months into her three years PhD programme. Matthew never played a waiting game.

I sat up in bed and wondered why my heart was pounding against my ribcage, as if it was going to rip me apart. For three months, I'd not visited Tamilore's Instagram page, and that was the biggest battle I'd won internally. I'd deleted the app from my phone, too. And now, I wished I could sprint onto her page for a clue of what was "new". But no, I didn't. My fingers tightly pressed to my forearms, as I tossed for sleep. I'd not expected my sleep to be disturbed by some thick spirals of growing hope and anxiousness of something "new".

I got out of bed in my pyjamas, stretched my limbs and went into the bathroom to splash some water on my face. Then, I returned to the room, got down on my knees for a silent prayer. Followed by moments of reflection, anticipation, hope, dreams and wishes.

The next day, I celebrated with the newly engaged couple via a video call. You should have seen the wide smile spread over Matthew's cheerful face. He was brighter than I'd seen him in years. We'd joked for nearly half an hour about how he proposed. "I had both knees on the floor, bro, like I was begging," he said. I overheard Tara laughing and water running. I guessed she was in the bathroom. "Don't mind him, Toyo, he's exaggerating."

I hoped someday, I'd know such happiness.

"There's a video on YouTube I want you to see," he said eagerly.

I reared back from where I stood and plunged on the sofa. "What video?"

He sent me a link. "Tami was recently interviewed by one of the entertainment TV stations, and the short video clip was uploaded on YouTube."

A few possibilities flashed my mind. Perhaps she was ready to settle down. Perhaps her TV production in London that called out prominent issues such as African brain drain was trending. Perhaps she'd won another TV personality of the year award. None was promising. Uneasiness had settled in as I tilted my head back to the sofa and dropped the phone. "Matthew, I don't have time to watch half an hour clip. What's the point anyway?"

He sensed the frustration in my voice. "Chill, bro. You don't have to watch everything. The last five minutes will do."

I fast-forwarded the video.

Beautiful lighting kits sparked the studio. Two people were on camera, Tamilore and the popular Ayo Jones who anchored *This Wedding Rocks* on Africa WR Channels. It was a beautiful studio with marble floors, gleaming in a colourful rose pattern.

"I bet all the guys are vying for your heart. Who wouldn't? You're a woman of class, drive, decency and simplicity." Ayo's smile was bright, as she bent forward and swung her arms towards Tamilore, as if a life-important question was about to be asked next. "So, who's the lucky one now? Everyone says Dalasi. Is that true?"

She blushed. "Of course, not. He's a colleague and a friend. He's helped me through a difficult time when I was heartbroken and someone I can confide in. Our friendship extends beyond being in the studio recording TV productions."

"Rumour has it that you two go on holidays together. We saw your pictures in Dubai. He always captures and tags you on his Instagram page. The sexy pic at Jumeirah Beach got everyone's attention. Is there something we should know?" Ayo asked, trying to maintain a neutral tone.

Tamilore tightly held the cushion draped over the sofa. "*Amebo* (gossiper)!" she said, laughing, then smoothed creases out of her dress, "No, the Dubai trip was with the whole TV production crew. Maybe Dalasi fancies me, but we're not dating. He's a good friend."

Ayo gave a gleeful chuckle. "So, is the lucky guy in the entertainment industry?"

"Well, I'm not seeing anyone at the minute. I need more time to myself."

Ayo flipped her Brazilian hair backward, smiling, as if she was about to hit the nail on the head. "Are you in love?" she asked, "I mean are you crushing on anyone?"

Tamilore didn't answer. She pressed her lips together, then crossed her legs, with a warm smile on her face.

"Hmm, it's what I'm thinking. Isn't it?" Ayo was a joker.

"I don't want to answer this question, if that's OK," she said hesitantly.

"Hmm. You're in love, Tami. This is so beautiful. You don't have to tell us who *he* is. Is *he* in the entertainment industry? Give us something. Radio? TV?"

Tamilore smiled and held her forehead like someone who needed a head massage. Seconds later, she was rubbling her eyes with balled fists as if she was getting emotional. "No, he's not in the limelight, Ayo. It's so complicated." Her tone was soft and pleasing.

I turned to Matthew who was holding a handcrafted piece,

something like the Hungarian traditional porcelain. "She's talking about her ex. Nothing here is new."

He patted the table in front of him with pile of souvenirs. "*My friend*, listen *joor*. Or do you want me to slap your head from here?" Mr. Tender refocused my attention.

I enlarged the video to full screen. She seemed to have lost a bit of weight. She looked happier, with her sunburned face, covered with light sprinkling of freckles. The glow on her cheekbones was dazzling. She must have been on one holiday after the next. I watched her body in a simple, figure-hugging yellow dress that stretched against her curves. Her diamond hoop earrings dangled beautifully. I couldn't help but notice the casual open-toe velvet heels she rocked in. It looked exactly like the pair she wore the day we met at Lagos airport.

"Is *he* a celebrity?" Ayo leaned forward, perching at the edge of her seat as she patted her hair extension over her shoulder.

Tamilore wiggled her eyebrows. I could see her cute smile coming. "Ayo, you never give up. Do you?" she asked, laughing, and adjusted comfortably. "*He*'s not. *He*'s a writer. We're not dating and, sadly, won't be dating. And please don't ask me anything more." The tenderness in her eyes at the mentioning of the word *writer* was so soft and beautiful.

"A writer? You're crushing on him?"

"I said no more questions," she said, smiling broadly.

"Why won't you be dating?"

"No more questions." Her dimples flashed over my screen.

And that was the end of the video clip.

The short clip lightened my mood strangely, even though I had no outlet for it. The situation was still deadlocked, obviously. I was about to ask Matthew what exactly he considered "new" in this video. I'd imagined he must have thought if Tamilore still nurtured an interest, regardless, there was at least a chance she might eventually change her mind. But before I opened my mouth, Tara interrupted the video call, flashing me the glittering diamond rock on her wedding finger while dancing to the latest Davido's song *FIA*.

"*See correct ring!*" I muttered, high-spiritedly, looking at the diamond beautifully encapsulated to match Tara's style and taste. "Many, many, many congratulations, dear."

She smiled and dried her slightly wet hair. "Thanks a lot, Toyo. Your friend caught me unprepared. Who proposes in the midst of strangers enjoying their peaceful evening cruise on Danube River?"

He toyed with the hem of her cloth playfully and swung his arm around her waist in admiration. "So that if you say 'no', I can beg the Hungarians and tourists to help me plead my case, and you know, there's no way of escaping on a river." His laughter was loud. Tara could not hold her laughter too. Matthew leaned closer and kissed the nape of her neck. "I chose the perfect place, babe. You were stuck with me to say yes."

She played with his beard fondly, gently stroking and smoothing, before feeling the oily curve of his scalp, her eyes glinting with excitement. Love is, indeed, sweet. "It was an awesome night, Toyo." Tara said, smiling. She murmured something, affectionately, against his lips, draped her hair over her shoulder, as she continued to speak. "We'd past the Buda Castle district. One of those heritage, historic sites and quite a romantic attraction with all the beautiful lights and were close to taking a view of the stunning Royal Palace when he silenced the audience so he could make a speech. I didn't know he'd got rhythms."

"Mr. Tender is got more than rhythms, for sure. That's so lovely. Congratulations. You two look amazing together," I told her, as she leaned over Matthew's back.

"Toyo, I want you to know that Tami really loves you. She told me several times how she feels about you. Take it from me, Tami is in love with you. I can see it too."

"Tara, how? She never replied to any of my texts or answer my calls."

"She's fighting to let go of her feelings for you. She was crying the last time we spoke about you. Her heart is soft. Believe me, she wants you. It's a shame genotype is causing the problem. She won't date anyone with AS because we lost Dad's younger brother to sickle cell anaemia. Tami was the closest to him. I'll share the story sometime," Tara explained. "I think you should re-test. Remember Tami re-confirmed hers at Atlanta, maybe you can re-check yours too in London. You just never can tell. You may have a different result."

"No worries. Thanks Tara," I said. "I hope you enjoy the rest of your vacation in the Pearl of the Danube and I can't wait to be at your service when jollof is ready."

She laughed. "We're leaving Budapest for Zurich this evening. Matthew says Switzerland is your favourite country on the planet, is that true?"

"Absolutely," I affirmed. "If you had to choose the country with the most show-stopping scenery, Switzerland would be a very good bet."

We laughed, as we closed the call.

I returned to the YouTube video and humbled myself. I watched the full clip from start to end. Later that day, I booked an appointment to re-test for sickle cell trait. And each day, anticipation robbed me of sleep. When the result came back two weeks later, I'd not expected my tea mug to be smashed into pieces.

TWENTY-THREE

London, October 2017

THREE MONTHS HAD HUSTLED FORWARD QUICKER than I'd thought.

"Why go to Amsterdam for the bachelor's night?" I asked Matthew.

Tara and Matthew's wedding was drawing closer each day. He'd arrived in London a week ago and we'd been busy planning the big day. We had been shopping for the past two hours and were now on the fourth floor at John Lewis in Oxford Street. The store glittered beautifully, the air smelled of freshness, as if it was perfumed. Moderate crowds, tripping in and out. Music playing softly and special sales deals staring at us at every corner.

"Toyosi, it's fifty minutes on a plane. It's quicker than going to Aberdeen, after all. And that's if anyone travels there for anything funky," Matthew said, laughing. The white lady next to him in a cute tartan skirt and a tartan shawl, face flushing with Scottish accent, who was perusing the cabinets crammed full of latest range of merchandise, smiled before giving him a perfect look. "Leave all the planning of the bachelor's party to me," I told him.

"Oh, yeah, definitely. As the best man, I'm leaving everything to you, bro."

"Just drop me your credit card and you can go home."

He laughed. "You have to coordinate the groomsmen's dance rehearsal. I'm not even sure if the lads have the time to practise. But I'll leave that to you."

"No worries. I've made a list of activities before the task of offering the first toast, cracking a few jokes and getting the crowd to the dance floor."

"I trust you," he said. "And the shopping spree?"

"The shopping spree? Don't worry about that either. I'll break the bank for you." We laughed, as we descended on the escalators to the third floor where we made our payment.

Afterwards, we toured a few flagship stores, like lost men trampling the streets of London. We got black shoes, grey suits and ties for the groom and groomsmen at John Lewis, nice crisp white shirts at Zara, and all the whistles and bells at Selfridges.

"Anything else we've forgotten?" Matthew asked, as we were heading towards Bond Street underground station.

"Oh, that reminds me. Your wedding gift for your bride," I reminded him.

He shrugged. "*Chai.* This prep is hard. Another gift after all the ones I've been giving?" The cheeky smile on his face revealed exactly what he meant.

I sighed and wrinkled my face. "You say?"

He shrugged me off. "Accessories would be perfect for her. Right?"

"Accessories?" I had no clue. "You mean like jewellery or fragrance?"

"You're asking the wrong person, bro."

"OK. I know the right person to help us."

"Tami?"

"Joker, it's Debby. As a side hustle, she's a wedding planner, you know."

"Get her involved, please. I think you should give Debby a chance anyway. You still haven't told me what the problem is. Or, tell me, is Jess giving you enough green lights now?"

As for Jess and me, we continued to meet at some Black Professional networking events and mutual friends' birthday parties, usually in a group, and we were always comfortable with each other. Social events were our meeting point, it seemed.

"Debby is truly amazing, but the image refuses to go," I slipped.

He looked confused. "What image?"

"Ah... erm." I stuttered. "I mean the image of Tamilore."

"Tami is in the past, bro. Yes, I want you guys to be together but she's not responsive. *You don over try man.* Erase her image from your mind. I know you have an eidetic memory, or whatever the doctors have called it, but you have to try harder and erase registered images from your mind. You've done everything. You've re-tested for genotype, nothing changed. She's never replied to any of your calls, messages or voicemails. Move on, bro. Right now, if I were you, I'd play Debby and Jess at the same time. Yes. I'm not saying you should sleep with them but play a game. It's a shame you will never do that. *See*, dating is always a game and until you see it that way, you're not playing according to the rule."

At least I got away with my slipping tongue. "Another stupid rule, eh? How come you didn't play this stupid game with Tara?"

He laughed. "I'm just looking out for you, bro. Anyhow, if all else fails, you can always count on the dance floor in Lagos."

"We better arrange correct DJ, no dull moment," I said, laughing.

We were now seated on the Tube.

"Anyways, I've wanted to ask about Mercy, I'm really pleased with how you've kept in touch with her all this while. How's she holding up now?"

"Oh, lovely Mercy. She's fine, fully recovered now. We talked last week."

"Holla. Baddest. Anything new I should know?" He rolled his funny eyes. "Jokes aside man, do you think she may possibly be ready for dating anytime soon?"

"*Nah.* We're staying in touch as friends. She acknowledges she needs time. She went through a lot, man. Got heartbroken. Lost her job. Lost her mind. Everything due to her health crisis. She wrote me a letter a month ago. The most emotional letter I've ever read in my life. I'm so glad God used what was supposed to be a mere adventure to save her life."

"I'm so glad you did not ignore eight hundred people behind their keyboards."

We laughed before starting our real banter.

LATER THAT NIGHT, I called Debby.

"You remember me today?" she asked in a bored tone.

"I always remember you, Debs. I sent you couples of messages in the past weeks. But I never got a reply to any of them."

She didn't respond.

I broke the silence. "My apologies for not calling as often as I used to. It's been busy lately. I can understand you must have been busy, too."

"Yes."

"And how was the last wedding party you guys pulled off at Coventry? I saw the amazing pictures on Facebook. You really did an excellent job."

"Fine."

Hmm.

"And I guess you probably planning another one soon?"

"Yes." She kept to her one-word response.

"Debby, I'm sorry. You seem offended about something. Can we talk about it?"

"I'm not offended. You called me for something, right?" A hint of warmth in her tone.

"OK. You remember Tara? You guys met once when I invited her to the last Total Worship Experience in church."

"The fair complexion lady with an American accent who is doing her PhD at Kings?" Her voice was monotonous but at least there was no resigned tone to it anymore.

"Yes. That's right. She's getting married to Matthew and their wedding is coming soon in Lagos. I've recommended you as a co-wedding planner. I was thinking maybe we can meet up for dinner sometime during the week to discuss the specifics?"

"*Dinner?*" she said, excitedly.

"I mean *catch* up, you know."

"OK," she said. "*Dinner* sounds great."

"Erm. Alright, we'll *catch* up. I'll fix something and let you know," I told her.

We'd never had a special outing like a one-on-one dinner before. We would normally meet indoors, eat, play games, watch TV, hang out, and meet mutual friends, but we'd never dined together at a restaurant before.

We met few days later. It was a Thursday night. I was the first to arrive at the Eko Bar near Rathbone Square, off the bustling Oxford Street in Central London, a cosy West African-inspired restaurant. I waited for a few minutes, then

Debby arrived. When I saw her walk in, it took me a few seconds to realise who she was. She wore a gorgeous purple dress with frayed lace at the hem, a perfect-fit split neck, beautifully paired with gold high heels, leg-lengthening heels. She looked well toned, like a golden goddess. The glossed lustre lips finely applied and in colour matched. I hadn't seen her made up for ages. She had concealed the little dark spots on her face and her eyeshadow was bright, giving her a smoky eye effect and a smouldering stare, as if she was up for a modelling assignment. Her manicure matched her purple dress. Yes, she looked very beautiful. I clenched my jaw at her sight.

At this point, I didn't know if starting a conversation about wedding planning or gift ideas would be any good. The setting was nothing short of a date, so I played along.

"You look stunning," I told her, as we hugged. "Please make yourself comfortable."

A waiter, a lady in her early twenties with red bounteous hair, and pierced nose with pins, approached us to take our order. Eko Bar was next to Debby's office, she'd been there countless times. "The grilled tilapia for me, please," she said, without checking the menu.

I scanned through the starters list and pointed to the top item: chicken wings.

Her body stiffened, as she glanced across the table. "You think the dress is nice?" she asked, sheepishly.

"Sure. Very lovely," I said, sincerely.

"Thanks. We had a client in for lunch today for one of the new workspace products we're rolling out, so I had to spice up, that's all."

"Yeah, I know. How was your day?" I quickly changed the subject so as not to make her feel uncomfortable. I knew no one wore glam to work, hardly ever at a Facebook office.

"It was great. I had good news today."

"Really? I'm all ears. Please tell me."

"I'm one step up my career ladder. I got promoted."

"Wow, Debby, are you serious? Congratulations, dear."

"Thanks a lot. It could only be God."

"Yes, indeed."

I signalled to the waiter to come over. "Can we kindly have two glasses of wine to celebrate, please? Laurent-Perrier Cuvee Rose Champagne is my friend's fave." I had ordered orange juice before, but this was not the time to be conservative.

"Of course," the waiter said, smiling.

"Hmm. You still remember my fave?"

I nodded. "I still remember the oldest rose champagne remains one of the best."

Her smile was beautiful. "Still in touch with Oma?" Debby asked, even-voiced.

"Nah," I said, as I regaled her with tales of my dating roller-coasters.

Two glasses of wine had been served as we were talking. She smelled the wine, before swirling the bubbles that danced gracefully in her glass. "I'd love to come with you for the wedding in Lagos. This is my opportunity to step foot on the African continent. I can't wait to see where my mum and dad were born and raised," Debby said, excitedly.

"That would be awesome. It's a good opportunity to see the motherland, isn't it?"

Her breath was light. "Promise me you'll be my tour guide while in Lagos."

"Of course. At your service, anytime, ma."

She pinched my hand. "I'll take you up on that. How's your chicken? You should try some of these. The tilapia will get your taste buds racing."

I smiled. "Thanks Debs. Great food. To your promotion." I

raised my glass of wine, as we toasted and shared a drink to celebrate her new milestone.

We spent the next two hours talking about the wedding bits, dating, relationships and everything in between. We wrapped up the night on a high note, hugged as we normally would do, and bid each other goodnight as I walked her out and saw her off.

Thankfully, the image I'd concealed in my mind did not ruin the night. No voice of doubt. No unwanted spirals of memory. None of that. Nevertheless, I was sure, to a certain degree, that there was no future between Debby and me. I was sure the image would come back, like a trip down memory lane, in my unhappiest moments.

TWENTY-FOUR

Truth be told, Jess was out of my league. It would take a miracle for her to be interested in a guy like me. But as a man, I'd to put it together as if I had any control.

Jess was a warm, sweet, beautiful soul who loved God genuinely and possessed lovely traits for a bride to behold. She was driven, smart, God-fearing and fun. She was a sunbeam to warm my heart. It had been a hard decision to move past Tamilore, but I was glad I got past the stalking on social media. Now, when I think of marriage and I envision a beautiful future, a future where the sunset would not frighten me as a sign of darkness to come, I see Jessica Adebayo and no one else. Not even Tamilore Talulu.

But I knew she was tough and would continue to play hard to get. If I thought I'd pegged her as bold, she'd turn bashful. During a group hangout, she'd noted the best approach for a man to win her heart was never to skip the friendship hurdle. That was exactly what I was looking for: friendship. But I don't do dumb chases. When I was in my late twenties, chasing a girl was fun, and girls playing hard to get was a boost to my ego.

However, in my mid-thirties, my tolerance level has waned. I was now playing the friendship card to assess if she was in or out, so I didn't misfire my shot. I'd made some efforts in the past few months to increase my visibility, but I was not sure where it would lead.

I tried my luck again and invited Jess for lunch at work recently, but she invited her friend along to the party meant for two. After nearly two years, not much had changed. It was hard to fast track the friendship. It was annoying. But for Jess, I would have to take a chill pill and dance to her tune as she continued to play the "catch me if you can" game.

I was determined to get a one-on-one date with Jess again, to tell her how I felt. If I missed the shot, I'd re-fire or shoot a missile.

TWENTY-FIVE

It was a week before the Lagos trip and I couldn't wait to experience the glamour and style of the city's epic wedding. Everything is on a different level in Lagos. If you've heard of the party-hard revellers, then welcome to Lagos. Most Nigerian parties are loud and flamboyant, regardless of location but in Lagos, there's a little something extra. Some folks are out to outperform each other, whether it's the star-studded parties or normal people's *Parole*, the vibe is the same. The City of Excellence never disappoints.

I hadn't attended a wedding in Lagos in years, so I was looking forward to a great time. The story of Tara and Matthew mirrored the popular saying, "money meets money". I had been a bit nervous as the fear of ruining the day sometimes overwhelmed me. This was my first time playing such a role and I was not really in their social class or league. I didn't belong to the old money cliques or the upper-class royalty.

Jess and I had been communicating better than before. I had briefed her about the trip, hoping I could arrange a date before travelling and *shoot the shot* (go for it!). I made an evening call, just before the late hours, speaking in a hushed voice and revealing what the heart wants, but discreetly. We talked about everything, shared goals that we had never achieved, and disappointments life threw at us as well as our hopes for the future.

"Any plans for next weekend?" I asked Jess.

"The usual weekend routine: fix my hair, laundry, the weekly shopping. That's it. And besides my usual gym, dance classes and swimming lessons, I'm free."

I picked up on some clues and had an idea for a date plan. "It would be lovely to learn some dance routines with you next weekend," I told her.

"Hmm. Are you asking me out?" She laughed. "As long as it's not a date."

Whatever it's called, does it really matter? I wondered.

"Is that a yes?" I smiled to the phone.

"If it's a *hangout*, yes," she said.

"Sweet."

"Why did you choose a dance class? I'm just intrigued."

"Hmm. Great question. I've seen *Strictly Come Dancing* too many times and I know a man can get lucky if he's got his salsa moves right."

She laughed. "Dancing is one of my best hobbies, for sure. The truth is, when I was heartbroken, I had used dancing as a recovery therapy. So, it's great choice for a *hangout*."

I arranged a three-hour amateur dance class for next Saturday afternoon. The bachelor party planned to Amsterdam was scheduled for the evening on the same day.

The excitement built up just a little. I'd prayed about this the whole week, binding the spirit of "you're a great guy but the problem is me" talk. *Carabos! Carabos!* I knew it was a golden moment that could either fan the flames or snuff out the spark.

We arrived on our date at Clerkenwell Road, in Central

London. A fit-looking instructor led us through the building doors, down a corridor, then up the staircase to the upper dancing floors where we joined the newbie dancing class. A large room with glass walls. "This is where all the action take place, guys," the instructor said, smiling.

Jess clamped her fingers into my hand and led me on the dance floor. Unknowingly to me, she was a pirouetting pro. Her moves were classic and on point, like a professional dancer. "This is called Samba, the Brazilian dance," she said, after a short dance.

"Hmm. Nice."

She slowed down and danced towards me. "So, what do you prefer? Zumba, Mambo, Rumba. Reggaetón. American Rhythm. Tango. What's your thing?"

"Afrobeat," I said.

She laughed.

As a beginner, I was taught the basics beforehand, until half an hour later when I began to master the correct posture. Jess and I joined other dancers in a formation routine, ready to show off our moves and have a good time. We were at ease. The music came on. It was a beautiful love song – *Perfect* by Ed Sheeran. Although I had hinted to the instructor that we were on a date and asked if it was OK to play Jess's favourite love songs, I didn't know if the request would be granted since there were other dancers present. Luckily, we got a good song. Jess was excited and grinned. I stepped up to the challenge on the dance floor. The song was the perfect moment for a slow dance. The lyrics hit the shot on my behalf.

I whispered a few words to Jess on the dance floor.

"Mr. Sheeran is genius with his words, you know," I said, staring at her and hoping she'd get the message.

A smile dangled on the corner of her lips. "Hmm. You think so?"

"Yeah," I assured her.

"Hmm. You're not a bad dancer, after all."

"Ha-ha, so I'm scoring above average points?" I asked.

"You're better than average," she told me.

"That's kind of you to say. You're way ahead. You're amazing."

"Thanks. Be honest, did you ask them to play the song?" she asked.

"Nah, it's a *hangout*, isn't it?" I teased.

I got distracted and missed the steps. We had a good laugh as I made a fool of myself around the dance floor. At the mention of an angel, I locked eyes with Jess. Our glances held a beautiful message and without saying a word, I let my heart do the talking. The dancing continued. We looked at each other the way we hadn't in over two years. Jess wasn't saying much but her body was. A smile radiated on her face. It was innocent and beautiful to see. We connected, danced, laughed and enjoyed the evening. The three-hour session went by so quickly. It was a great first date or hangout depending on who you ask. We then took a long walk over London Bridge, ambled along overjoyed, arm in arm and talked a bit more before we parted ways. Afterwards, I hurried up to join the boys for our flight to Amsterdam.

TWENTY-SIX

Amsterdam, October 2017

"MATTHEW, did you notice something different about Toyosi? Who's the babe?" Dayo asked while fastening his seat belt, as the British Airways cabin crew were preparing us for landing at Schiphol airport.

"Dayo, trust me, I was about to say the same thing," Brownson said, laughing as he buckled up his seat belt.

I smiled. "So, guys, once we're on the ground, top of the agenda is to hop on a bike." I'd refused to take the spotlight throughout the short flight.

"You're trying to change the subject, er." Dayo groaned. "You should have consulted me for a grand plan. Top of the agenda should be the Red Light District."

"We're not here for no Red Light District, fellas," Matthew cautioned, smiling.

Everyone laughed.

On leaving the airport, we travelled to Dam Square, the city centre, and began a little tour. We walked the well-trodden tourist path of the city and enjoyed the best of Amsterdam's attractions, from a canal cruise to having beers and soft drinks under the windmill, and a visit to Vondelpark where we joined the crowd to enjoy a live concert. There were artists from around the globe and we got a taste of some African Afropop and jazz, too.

"Guys, thanks a lot for making this moment memorable, this woman is a purist, glad we ran into this concert," Matthew said, rubbing his hands in excitement. We were watching Angelique Kidjo, one of Africa's most iconic singers, who was lighting the crowd with fire.

Soon after the concert, we left and wandered around this city full of bicycles and canals. We had a brief stopover at some of the antique shops to window shop and saw the Hermitage's beautiful courtyard gardens, the largest in the city, afterwards. Against Dayo's wishes, we were nowhere near the pleasure district laced by lasciviousness.

It was all going well until a revelation ruined the day. At this point, we were sitting outdoors at a French restaurant, De Belhamel, lounging on the terrace and watching the tourists puttering in boats along the canals. Breeze skimmed the canals, footsteps echoed back and forth in large crowds. Everyone hunched in autumn jackets, on boats, on countless bicycles, and through their gentility and shining teeth, I saw a city full of warmth. And there we were. Five single men and several beers. Today, the weather played along, late autumn sun glowing on the horizon, even though winter was already announcing its arrival.

"Reformed bad boy." The boys had been teasing Matthew all day. We'd had a few jokes about pretty women in slender skirts in Matthew's life from his advanced degree on Tinder before he met Tara, debated a few social issues from corruption in Nigeria politics to police brutality in America and switched to Matthew's favourite subject after Tinder: music. From music, the conversation switched back to women. Brownson was resting his arms on a wooden deck, drinking beer when he began to raise his voice, grumbling under his breath. "Tiana is a hedger, a gamer." His face grimaced. "She's a stupid girl."

"How long have you been dating her?" Ifeanyi asked, facing Brownson, seeming astounded at the sudden outburst, his taunting tone could be felt beneath the words.

Brownson stared at him in exasperation. Seconds ago, his eyes were clamped shut. "We've been dating for six months. And you?"

"A year, next month." Ifeanyi said, rising to his feet. I doubted if he knew his left hand was on his head. He began to shake his head, looking lost and confused.

"Who's this Tiana girl, for goodness sake?" I asked. The text message from Jess had distracted me from the cause of the argument. She'd requested the hospital details where I did my genotype test, so she could book appointment for hers. It became a priority to find out before we began to invest any emotions in our relationship.

Matthew barked out a laugh as he rested his elbow on the bar and raised his voice a little. "Tiana Bakare. The spa therapist. The giver of all good things. You know her, *nah*. That light-skinned babe I met while in Dulwich College."

I pressed one finger to my forehead, then gave a nod the moment I recollected the discreditable story behind. "The giver of all good things."

"Toyosi, the lads have been victims," Matthew said, laughing, pressing his palm against his stomach, as if the laughter hurts. "Tiana is using Ifeanyi for shoes and bags, and for her travel upgrades. Dude has been her credit card, and Brownson for free dinner dates."

"Matthew, stop. This is not a joking matter," I said.

Unbeknownst to Ifeanyi and Brownson, they had been dating the same girl, Tiana.

Brownson suddenly lighted his eyes with a whoop of victory, bouncing with his beer, as if he'd great news to deliver. He turned to face Matthew who was struggling to stifle his laughter. "As for me, it's Tiana's loss, not mine. If you guys must know the truth, she was paying her part in kind for cash. Yes. And to top that, I have been double dating too, squeezing some juice from her and her best friend, Anna. *So, two ge four!* (equal game!)." Brownson revealed his antics. Yet, he was hypo-critical. "That girl is a bitch," he shouted.

Huh! What? You mean you're a he-goat?

But I stomached it. Talk about the pot calling the kettle black.

Ifeanyi darted an angry look at Brownson, who had shown no remorse, ready to punch him in the face. He moved away from him and plunged back to the nearest armchair, next to Matthew's, scrunching the city's map in his hand into a ball. His fingers were clenched. And side of his jaw pulsed with glut of muscles. He continued to bite the corner of his lower lip.

Seconds later, Ifeanyi nestled his head between his knees, then sat up, releasing the words burning on his lips. "Shame on you. Big shame on you," he yelled, boiling hot, as he faced Brownson. Matthew stepped in and wrapped his arms around Ifeanyi, trying to hold him back. He yanked Mathew's hands away. "Tiana is the choir lead in church. I wonder why you people are so fake, the so-called Christian brothers and sisters. You sleep around, play the field, and yet behave like innocents in church, living lives of hypocrisy, lifting holy hands, week in, week out, and praising God. You're such a horrible disgrace. And you are the first to come for mid-week prayer meetings and daily morning devotion. Shame. Big shame."

Brownson walked a step closer to him, keeping a straight

face, stern and freckled. "You should direct the shame to Tiana, not me. Learn to play the game, boy, and stop being childish." He was four beers deep already. He sniggered, pumping his fist in the air.

Ifeanyi swivelled his chair and scooted up on his seat, a wan sadness written all over his face. He held his arms up behind his head as he walked restlessly around the same spot with short quick steps. You could see his veins as they stood out. He turned and wagged his pointer finger aggressively towards Brownson, tucking his lips against the teeth. "How dare you call me childish. How dare you! You fucking hypocrite. If you want to be a player, a bad guy, keep a straight line. If you want to serve God and you claim to be a Christian, stay as one. Stop being in the middle, one leg in, one leg out." His words may have hit everyone.

Ifeanyi was right. You can't run with the hare and hunt with the hounds. "Ifeanyi, please calm down. And guys, I beg of you. We came here for fun. Let's not ruin it for Matthew. Look at the way the tourists are staring at us. Let's reduce the volume, please." I mediated and walked Ifeanyi to a corner. "I'm sorry this is happening, take it easy. OK. I know you're hurt. Let Brownson be. And let Tiana be. I know how you feel about some of the folks in church. We sometimes fail God. Always remember there are some genuine Christian folks who always keep the faith. You'll find someone new. Someone better."

Ifeanyi nodded. Gloom etched on his face and the veins protruding from his hands were still visible to see. "Thanks, ToyoToyosi," he said, as we hugged, shoulder to shoulder. Whatever was dripping down his nose must have been sweat, not tears. He'd already got an engagement ring, ready to propose in a month's time on their one-year anniversary.

Brownson set his empty beer bottle on the table and

signalled the bartender for more. Then, he turned around, a taunt in his eyes. "Two can play the game," he said, nodding at Ifeanyi. He always had the last word.

Dayo shrugged and tapped his collarbone as his face was mocking Ifeanyi. All this while, he never said a word. The man who'd flown on the same wind as Brownson and swum on the same tides. Then, he began to talk. "Brownson did the right thing. Yes, that's how you play the game. Smart move, bro. You spread their legs quick and fast," Dayo said, laughing. He stood from his fancy lounge chair and walked towards Ifeanyi, threw his arm around his shoulder. "Bro, I'm sorry this one hit you. But you've got to play the game next time."

Ifeanyi's face was expressionless. A blank stare was all he could muster.

Tall, dark, handsome and honey-mouthed, Dayo was a player, a bad guy. Mr. Casanova of London. Even among his "squad", he was accorded as a master of players. Dayo Olulade Martins. An unrelenting sex-hungry hawk. He was thirty-three and had no plans to settle down. He was well known for his line: "Get in, get out, and move on." He never hid his behaviour. "Eat the damn cookies and clean mouth." That was his second favourite line. He'd been telling me to loosen up and be a bad guy for one day. Of course, that was never going to happen. "Chill out mate, chop these chicks," he always said. He'd been a bad influence. I'd met Dayo a few years back through Matthew and we'd stayed friends ever since.

Matthew read my mind. He grasped Dayo's shoulder, laughing. "Just say ladies."

Dayo bared his teeth before choking with laughter. "What the hell is the difference?"

"Women don't like to be called chicks. It's kinda rude," Matthew lectured him.

"Actually, it is," I chipped in.

Everyone exchanged glances. No argument, no debates. That must have hit home.

Dayo took another sip of his beer, threw his dismissive eyes and continued to utter rubbish. "See, guys, the game is simple with the chicks... the ladies, whatever. You scratch my back, I'll scratch yours. And I'll scratch it even harder. It's transactional. No woman is worth love because when the hands of time turn, they usually leave you cold and in pain."

Everyone steered in the bartender's direction, at the other end of the bar, who seemed to have overheard the conversation and still, disguisedly listening. I frowned at Dayo's flippant remarks, lowered my voice as I lectured him a little. "Dayo, we've been through these many times. Stop generalising. And besides, there's no need to pick up bad lessons from our bad experiences. Men break women's hearts and vice versa. It has always been that way."

Matthew laced his fingers and tapped his lips. His face disapproved of Dayo's excesses too, as if he was saying, "you can't stop a pig from wallowing in the mud."

Brownson's leering eyes were on me. "I know why this news hit Ifeanyi so badly."

Dayo removed his hands thrusted deep in his pocket and boasted an authoritative composure. "That's obvious, *nah*. If Ifeanyi is allowed a chance to see her *temple*, we won't be here shouting at each other. In fact, he'd never kissed a woman in his life. That itself is a problem," Dayo said in a contemptuous tone and turned to face Ifeanyi. "Bro, *chop* these girls. Wake up. And stop dating only one babe. You need a few in your backlog."

Backlog? What a jerk!

Ifeanyi shot him a dark stare. Even though he said nothing and had remained in his sudden frozen silence, I caught the unspoken words floating angrily through his mouth.

Dayo reached for another beer, held the bottle edge to a table with his left hand and slammed down the cover with his right, in a flash. "*Chop* them," Dayo repeated, nodding his head and began to mouth some afrobeat lyrics to fortify his point. Everyone rolled their heads toward him. He took a swig of his beer. "Yes, *chop them wella.*"

A vein bulged in Ifeanyi's jaw.

"Enough, guys. Enough." I faced Dayo. "I need to talk to you."

Away from the beer-scented heat, I pulled Dayo to a corner, shutting out the sun that was glittering into our eyes. We took a few steps along the canal, away from the group. It was time for a serious talk. It had been overdue. "Be sensitive to other people's feelings, Dayo. And please, take your faith seriously," I told him, without any righteous emphasis.

He shook his head in disbelief and spoke with a softer voice but without hiding the scorn. "Just bang the girls and let's worry about faith or your shit talk later. Toyo, how did you deal with your heartbreak? I really want to know. I witnessed how your heart was brutally broken, man. And yet, you don't play the field. Is that being smart or foolish?"

I recognised the voice of a frustrated man.

I smiled. "Of course, that's smart, Dayo. No matter how badly others have treated us, we are expected to suck it up, put our trust in God, act in love, dust off the bad experiences, and focus on the bigger picture," I reminded him. "God's got our back."

He looked stunned. He always does each time I have the honour to chastise him.

"Toyosi, you're missing the point. Women like bad boys. Men who can spread their legs and do the job, so hard, so bad. Men who can bang them like no other. Men with no emotions.

And guest what, I love them back when they are in my bed." He cocked a smile.

I scrubbled a hand over my head, furiously. Will he ever learn? "Stop generalising, please." I moderated my voice. "And for how long, Mr. Casanova?"

"For as long as necessary," he said, frankly. "Imagine what that girl did to you. That stupid girl. The girl you did so much for. How could someone be so heartless? And you are here talking about love. That's foolishness if you ask me. Wake up, man. Wake up."

"No need for name calling." I cautioned him. "Besides, break-ups happen."

He shook his head. "Break-ups happen, sure, but if someone breaks you and watch you bleed, that's evil."

"Well, forget about Sisi. Like I said, let's focus on the bigger picture."

Dayo squinted. His face creased in puzzlement. "Are you kidding me?" he asked, bitterness laced every word. "Say it as it is, man. Hold no emotion for no girl, man. She is a coward. A coward who stood tall in gleaming armour. A black hole, a dark queen. *You dey feel me so?* Yeah, you *sabi* the shitty names for shitty girls. She's nothing but shit." He poured heavy contempt into his voice as he rambled his last sentences in pidgin English.

I sensed, underneath his supposedly happy Casanova's life, some cobwebs, some unhealed pains, deep hurt and bruises only he could understand, were dwelling in every corner of his heart. Nothing gorges the soul more than the pain everyone has forgotten but you.

"Dayo, you need to heal from your heartbreak. I'll recommend a therapist who can help. I think you're talking from the unhealed wound of your *own* experience, *not* mine."

Even though I truly felt Sisi was a coward, I never wanted anyone to call her names.

He was muted for a few seconds, scratching his beard and raking his fingers over his head. Pain written all over his face, as though he was blanketed with hurt from the past.

"I know betrayal creates a thirst for revenge," I said. "But regardless of how others treat us, we must not retaliate evil for evil, or transfer aggression or bad experiences to other innocent people. Dayo, we can't take our revenge out on innocent people. It's not fair."

He poured the remaining beer down his throat, then held up a pointer finger, the way he often did when he had something important to deliver in defence. "Life isn't fair, Toyosi. If you'd *chopped* that girl, *knack am well* and spread her legs between the north and the south each time you had the chance, even if she wants to break up, *she go behave.*"

I shook my head. "And despite you turning Sarah's legs between the east and the west, didn't she leave? Huh? Take it easy, Dayo. I know you're still hurting. But a year is a good time to heal."

"Never mention her name again. I beg of you." Dayo scowled defensively.

Alright. OK. I finally confirmed the cause of his anger.

If you have the habit of spiting in the sky, then you shouldn't be so angered when it comes back hitting you in the eye. I could have told him and be very blurt. Rather, I adapted my Grandma's style of persuasiveness. "Let me ask you something, if you continue to throw an arrow in the air carelessly, do you know where it could land someday?"

His dismissive eyes were on. "That's bullshit talk. Complete bullshit. I don't care where it lands or who it lands on. Wake up Mr. Lover Boy and stop talking bullshit."

I paused to process his defence. Sometimes, I wanted to live Dayo's life for one day, play the field and damn the consequences, and watch to see if heaven would collapse on the earth. But each time I took the left turn, I always missed the road and returned home.

"Heartbreak is an experience that makes us better and stronger, not bitter and weaker. You sound bitter, Dayo," I told him frankly.

And the conversation dragged on for another half an hour.

In the end, we shook hands and he gave me a look, defining look that resembled "stop wasting your time, dude," before he said, "I realise I'm talking from my own unhealed pain. I'm giving you my word. No more getting into ladies' pants. You have my word!"

We left it there and walked away from the men and women between cigarettes puffs.

Anytime I shared words of wisdom with Dayo after his ex-girlfriend, Sarah, cheated on him with his married best friend, he was always receptive but somehow, in the end, he still couldn't take his eyes off those ladies' lingerie. He continued sleeping around, dumping the girls, one after another. I was hopeful Dayo would turn over a new leaf and discontinue trampling and scoffing the Word. I hoped I had not cast the pearls before swine.

"Man, they are plenty babes everywhere. Take your time and take it easy. You deserve someone better," I heard Matthew telling Ifeanyi, as Dayo and I re-joined the group who were now stood in a huddle. The anger and fury strewn over his face had smoothened. No more grumping from anyone either. Brownson shoved a can of beer in everyone's direction, laughing. "Fellas, let's drink our sorrow away. At least one of us got lucky."

Matthew looked distracted. Everyone followed his eyes to an adorable couple, in their seventies, who sat by a window on a canal cruise in front of us, brushing their lips together. "How romantic. Oh, beautiful. Gentlemen, more than one of us got lucky." He laughed.

Ifeanyi lighted up better. Dayo embraced him. "I'm sorry, mate," he said, but judging from his mocking face, the way he cast a wary glance at him, at everyone, and his tettering laughter, I could tell his words, like his voice tinged with doubt, were clotted with insincerity.

We'd managed to help the grown adults who were behaving like kids.

What a day.

In the end, the boys got over it and we enjoyed our stay in Amsterdam. It was a struggle for Ifeanyi, but he managed to get past it, at least for the weekend.

TWENTY-SEVEN

London, October 2017

WE GOT BACK to London safely on Sunday evening. My flight to Lagos was scheduled for Thursday. Jess and I had kept in touch and our communication got better each day. She had booked an appointment for the genotype test, but she wouldn't know the result until I returned from Lagos. We didn't want to rush anything, but the sooner, the better.

On Wednesday, the day before the Lagos trip, Jess and I met for dinner. Jess turned up looking lovely, wearing a beautiful orange dress, a nice pair of heels, with light make-up, and a sweet perfume. I wasn't badly dressed either. I had on casual blue jeans, a grey slim-fit suitcoat to match, and I smelled good. We went to a lovely Mexican restaurant with a great view of the city. The place had been newly deco-rated. It offered the finest of charms, with romantic lighting and there was a rose candle on the table. The food was amazing and so was my date. There was no pressure of any kind. We had a lot to talk about including family, background, career, hobbies, travelling adventures, and a host of other fun stuff.

We'd been served a bottle of non-vintage red wine earlier. I refilled our glasses and Jess braced into some wine commentary. I remembered she did the same during the group hangout. "Oh, Cabernet Sauvignon! Wine of flavour. Smell so good. With smooth vanilla. The rich cherry, the plum, the dryness of tannis, the hints of spice. You know what I mean."

I smiled. My knowledge of wine was rather too little to start a debate. "Wine expert, yes, I know what you mean," I joked and let a dip touched the back of my throat.

She sipped a little and leaned forward as she placed the glass between her hands on the table. Her fingers formed wall around the glass. "Why are you single, Toyosi?"

"There are no single ladies on the London's Jubilee Line. I tried my luck a couple of times," I quipped.

She laughed into her wine and the chocolate mousse. "You should have tried the Northern Line or Victoria. Please be serious *joor*."

"I like to think I've not met the right person for me."

"How will you know the right person?"

"When they dance with me on a hangout night rather than a date."

She smiled broadly. "You're such a clown. Will you ever get serious?"

"I like a woman with a kind heart. A woman with similarity in faith, values, life goals and visions."

"Hmm. Are you not a Nigerian guy? I'm sure you're into fine girls too, with *figure eight* like a Coca-Cola bottle shape."

I laughed. "This is not about being Nigerian, though. Every man is attracted to a beautiful woman and from my personal experience I've found that women are as visual as men."

"So, you like pretty women?"

The laughter wouldn't leave my lips. "Who doesn't? But jokes apart, beauty isn't the main criteria. You know, the truth is beauty fades and passion dims. Over time, the beautiful face and tender soft skin will become wrinkled. I want a kind-hearted woman. And if beauty comes into the equation, it would be an added advantage," I explained, making a funny face.

"But how come you haven't picked one? There are many kind-hearted and pretty ladies in London."

"I've met different types that fit that description, with personalities to match, but they either say I'm not as tall as Usain Bolt, or I don't speak impeccable Queen's English like Prince Harry."

She laughed. Her wine tastebuds savoured the last drop of its rich cherry. "Joker."

"I'm just waiting to find true love. Until we find a place where the sea and the sky meet, for co-habitation, a bird and a fish can fall in love but where would they live?" I said, using words of wisdom to reveal my thoughts on finding the right person.

"Hmm. I see. Indeed. Birds marry birds," she said.

We talked the whole evening and had a great time like two love birds. One joke after the next. I could feel the warmth in her heart, the smile on her face, and the gleam in her eyes. It was a beautiful evening. I was hoping for a kiss at the end of the night, something to seal the deal, but I wanted it to be natural and real. That's not what most people do on the second date. Throughout the evening, my head and heart had been debating if it was a good time. As always, my head told me the smart move. My heart did the soft whispering, *shoot the shot only when the timing is right*. That sounded more like it. Either way, I knew I had a shot to shoot and wanted some sort of extra connection before the Lagos trip.

Luckily, the opportunity presented itself. We left the restaurant, held hands, and took a short walk along the River Thames. The autumnal wind turned warmer, so it seemed. I could smell winter already, in the warmth of my jacket. No rain, no misty weather. Fallen dried leaves, trailed colourfully along the Southbank. We could see the beautiful London Eye with it's colourful lights, not far off. I've seen it a million times but not when holding the hand of someone who means the world to me.

I looked through her eyes,and saw the world spinning and the earth shuddered. As if she knew I was waiting for a kiss or the right moment, Jess glanced at me in a way that suggested, "here's your chance." Oops, I took it. Our lips touched, and then the kiss, the butterfly kiss like a smile in the wind. It was a magical moment that made my heart race. I could tell we both knew that it was the beginning of great things to come.

"You're sweet," I said.

The taste of her lips was much sweeter than the sweetest of wines.

"Hmm. Thanks. You're different," she said, with a beautiful stare.

"Oh, really? Thanks. I have a surprise for you."

"A surprise? How? What is it?"

Jess lived in Canterbury, just over an hour by train from London. I'd considered the inconveniences and knew she would have to walk for an extra fifteen minutes from the station to her house. So, I'd pre-arranged a taxi to take her home; the driver arrived with a flower I had bought earlier. I collected the flower from the driver and handed it to her. We hugged each other as I opened the door of the car for her. She kept looking at me, stretched out her hands, her eyes almost brimming with tears of joy.

"Thank you, Toyosi. I really appreciate it."

"Jess, I should be the one to say thanks."

"Have a safe trip and be careful in Lagos," she told me.

"Sure. Will do. Speak later. And bye for now."

An hour later, I called her. It was supposed to be a few minutes call. We spoke for nearly an hour before calling it a night. And still, we couldn't stop behaving like love birds. We sealed the night before holding our pillows tight. "I think it went well," I mumbled to myself. Then I refocused. I began to pack my bags for the following day. Debby was on the same flight with me and Dayo. I caught up with them and we planned to meet up at Heathrow the next day.

Dayo sent me a text message that night. *Get ready, buddy, Lagos awaits us.*

Yes. Indeed. I replied. *I'm sure we'll make Matthew proud. Get your dance swag ready, no dull on the dance floor.*

Toyo, who's talking about dance?

Ha, baba. Please remind me. What else awaits us?

The chicks, of course.

Dayo, after all we've talked about? I ended the chat.

I'd kept my distance from Dayo for nearly a year because of his bad behaviour and disrespect for women. I'd seen him date three women at a time: using Uju for his sexual breakfast, Bimpe for lunch, and Hamza for his dinner and dessert. And lest I forget, the list of white, Asian and Chinese girls on his sexual timetable! Despite his bad behaviour, women hung around him. We hadn't been close until lately. Matthew's wedding brought us closer.

I sometimes wondered why some women preferred bad boys. The last time I asked for Clare's opinion, a friend, she blamed it on her ovaries that never stopped ogling at the sight of a bad boy. "Toyo, let me keep it real. Bad boys make me cling," she said, gesturing with her hands and cuddling up. She liked the mesmerising first impression of a bad guy.

When I asked Ibidun, another female friend, she admitted the boy's swag and rule-breaking attitude is sexy. "I like men who break all rules," she said. For Genevieve, a colleague, her preference was bad boys who turned into good guys. "Experience is gold," she said. And the last time Tinu, Aretta and Queen shared their views on the subject, during the road trip, I was made to understand that women love the unpredictable behaviour of bad boys and their intense fiery passion that comes with hot sensual kisses and secret trysts.

No wonder Dayo gets them whenever he wants. He was the most selfish, arrogant, vain person you'd find, yet he got the babes.

Minutes later, Dayo sent me another text: *I'm so sorry, Toyo. I've given you my word and I promise you before God and man, I'll stick to it. Promise!*

Apparently, my question had struck a chord with him.

I arrived at Heathrow the next morning and met Debby at check-in. We'd spoken earlier on the phone while I was on the Uber ride to the airport. "I'm so excited visiting Lagos for the first time," Debby told me, looking lovely in her holiday kaftan.

Her luggage had been passed through the conveyer and I was next in line. "Trust me, you'll have an awesome time. Lagos is beyond fun," I said and turned back to carry my luggage. Then, I noticed Dayo was right behind me. "Hey, big man..."

"My chairman," Dayo interjected, laughing. "Toyo, I owe you a big thanks for the words of wisdom last night." He sounded sincere with determination in his gesture. I passed my passport to the check-in assistant with a cheery smile. "No worries, bro, let sleeping dogs lie," I said and turned to introduce Debby. "Debs, meet Dayo. Dayo, Debby."

Dayo cleared his throat. "Debby, your closest female friend?"

They shook hands.

Debby squeaked and hugged her elbows tight. "Hmm. Closest female friend?" she repeated slowly, searching my eyes, as she peered straight through them.

We laughed.

Soon after, we checked in and took the escalator to the British Airways lounge where we had breakfast, talked about our expectations and activities, and an hour later, lined up to board our flight.

Six hours later, we arrived in Lagos safely.

Later that evening, I called Jess.

"Thank God for journey mercies. Guess what? I was just about to text you. My day was superb in the company of Netflix," she said, laughing.

I smiled. "Netflix, that's lovely."

"I envy you now, you know. In that lovely weather."

"So glad to be here, again. The feeling here is unexplainable. Lagos has a way to make you happy besides the heatwave that welcomes you," I said, without making no reference to the dry air that assaulted me as I came off the arrival point.

"Please savour the sunny weather. London is not smiling now. I can't wait for the summer already," she said, the fresh air between us, miles away, was warm.

TWENTY-EIGHT

Lagos, November 2017

Two days later, it was the wedding day of Tara Talulu and Matthew Obialom.

The church service lasted for about two hours.

We were now at the wedding reception, a state of gloriousness, tastefully colourful with jaw-dropping decorations. Fresh flower topiaries, floral centrepiece, candelabras, glass vase tables, exotic potted palms, lush fairy tale lightings – everything – were brought to the forefront of contemporary decor. The gold theme tied perfectly. The ambience oozed elegance. Timeless elegance. The hall was a five-star hotel gallery at Victoria Island; the best one that befit royalty. Love was indeed in the air. And you bet at a Nigerian party, the guests were dressed to impress; the majority wore the latest fabrics, the latest traditional attire mixed with contemporary cutting-edge designs. There were beautiful and colourful wax-print fabrics in champagne gold. While gold was the colour of the day, some guests rocked their styles with shades of plum, charcoal grey and inky blue – rich assortment of colours glamorously calling for attention. Everyone was on top of their fashion game.

The DJ dropped a danceable afrobeat song, as the bride and groom danced in through the grand foyer. Their dance steps flowed effortlessly with a dazzling grace and swag. Tara was on fire, swinging her body, swaying her hips. Matthew came well prepared, too. He matched her at every step, teasing the crowd, hands aloft. Afrobeat makers must be genius. The guests and family gave a standing ovation, as we watched the couple. Some were cheering loudly, others whistling. The room was buzzling. The MC kept shouting, "Please move back. Allow the photographers do their job." The chattering, the noise, the music, almost swallowed the man with a microphone. Their joy ripped through the bridal train who had swarmed the aisle, competing for the best dancer and extended to the crowd. Shortly after, the couple made their way to the beautifully decorated head seats reserved for two.

Tamilore was the chief bridesmaid. She was glowing in simple sophistication. A gold, body-fitted, floor-length, off-the-shoulder gown. The intricate designed lace, the embellished style, so elegantly stunning. We'd been running into each other throughout the church service. And more so at the reception since we arrived an hour ago. As the couple sat comfortably, Tamilore looked at me, tenderly, before signalling me for a talk.

We headed to one of the less crowded exits where the throng wasn't in our faces and sat on a couch in the hallway. We could see the couple from our seating position. She sucked in a breath and reached for a pillow. Then hesitated for a moment. She appeared to swallow. Her face twisted. Maybe agitation, maybe regret, maybe guilt, maybe nothing. I had no clue. "I want to tell you something, but I don't know where to start from or the best time really. I didn't have a chance to tell you last night. But I want you to know that I'm deeply sorry for ignoring your many text messages, emails and voicemails. And your handwritten letter. I know Tara gave you all the details. I'm so proud of this moment and I have you to thank for it," she said, tensing, then nibbling on the end of her hair, tumbling in glowing curls.

"Tamilore, God made this happen, you know," I said, graciously and smiling. "And you played the major role. And as for the apology, it was accepted before you said it."

"Thank you, Toyosi. And to be candid, it was you who played the major role. When they fought and wouldn't talk to each other for two weeks, regardless of how much I intervened, you stepped in, met with Tara, and made the tension go away. And above all else, thank you for handling things well *that Wednesday* night." Her cheeks dimpled, as she spoke.

I smiled. "I'm happy none of us missed today's jollof. That would have been more painful."

She laughed, nervously. "How's Jess? You should have invited her," she said, but her gaze, the unspoken words in her beautiful baby brown eyes, said otherwise. Something close to jealousy clawed deep and drawn thick on her stunning face.

"I did," I joked. "We're taking things slow. And you? How's the dating—"

She ran off, leaving me with her fresh, light, earthy fragrant scent, and the smell of her body, the orange blossoms mustered my senses, put a smile on my face. The bride had beckoned her. Last night at the wedding rehearsal in church was no different.

I breathed in her scent and resumed best man duties shortly after.

The highlife music performer, Juju music icon, King Sunny Ade, was on top of his game, with praise-singing, under the synthesise sounds of strumming guitar chords and band drumming, as food was being served. His current perfor- mance was for the parents; the couple would have to wait for their turn. The couple knew this; it is ingrained in our culture.

There was less drama in the crowd and no unnecessary delay waiting for food to be served. The couple had engaged the services of professional caterers and everything was perfectly put together, not the folks who always forget to show up on time, those that blame everything on Lagos traffic. No overcooked or burnt jollof rice. No under-cooked *moimoi*. The unripe plantain porridge was at its best. Yam pottage and stew were not in short supply. The "small chops", meat pie, and pepper soup were more than enough. And did I mention chin-chin? You know, the crunchy chin-chin to keep the stomach together before jollof is served? And then, the traditional meal options from the best of Yoruba to Igbo and all the tribes in between, the best of Nigerian cuisines were in excess supply.

Unlike the last wedding I attended, there was no dramatic ex-girlfriend who showed up to ruin the happy day or hit on the groom, no overbearing ex-boyfriend who gatecrashed to have the last word, and no strange drama on the dance floor or in-laws throwing tantrums. The air was pungent with love. No resentment, no petty jealousy.

"This is how you get married. If you must do it, do it in style." Dayo was too loud. "Guys, this traditional meal is everything you need in life, not some dose of mayonnaise."

The groomsmen laughed. Ifeanyi wasn't in the mood for Dayo's joke.

Tamilore approached me, *seemingly* breathing the air of a woman looking for something. "Toyo, I need you to give me a hand. Let's help the groom's family and their guests arrange some food." The crowd was gradually becoming uncontrollable. Folks moving up and down, engaging by familiarity with their large smiles, hugs and kisses, backslaps and the never-stopping vigorous handshakes. The Nigerianness of greetings and over-greetings.

"Of course," I replied, heartily.

Tamilore steered me away from the big men with protuberant stomachs, the beer belly men and city women of high calibre, who were blocking the aisle, exchanging business cards and greetings, towards the food table where the tasty treats were lined up like a market square. We worked as a team and with the help of the hired uniformed food vendors, in white coats and toques, English lamb shanks, banga, efo riro, egusi soup with pounded yam, semo, fried rice and the much spoken jollof rice, began flying over people's head, on trays.

The guests who sat at Table 201 were not served on time, only the crate of Coke and stout. "Are you not going to serve us food or is it because we're not wearing *Aso ebi?*" a lady asked, letting out a loud hiss of breath as though she'd not eaten in a lifetime. In the background, the MC's voice was humming the speakers, as he repeatedly announced some ancient Volkswagen and Toyota models and their old registration numbers for re-parking.

"I suspect they are looking at faces before they serve food. Are we not well dressed?" another woman responded, holding two toddlers shuffled closely to her, one emitting baby sounds playfully, the other looking tired. The annoyed look on the woman's face resembled an angry frustrated passenger, a non-Lagosian, stuck on Third Mainland Bridge at rush hour.

The whole table echoed the same.

"Don't mind them," a man retorted.

I remembered there was no Table 201 on the plan. We'd seated six people per table, numbered from one to two hundred. It looked like one of the impromptu tables someone created to accommodate more guests. In the same corner, there were a few people standing. There were no chairs or a table on which to place their food. Some folks managed the situation, held their plates, and put their drinks on the ground. The bottles of Star, Extra Stout, and Gulder – top favourite local beers – and empty Malta Guinness bottles were piling up on the floor. And some spilled drinks and broken glass. That's what happened when there are more gatecrashers, uninvited guests, than expected. Tamilore and I closed the gap and ensured new emerging tables were served on time. Despite the little hitches, the wedding was perfectly executed. Debby and her team deserved applause for doing a great job.

Dayo and Brownson had been discussing the women all day, straining their necks and peering, scoring the best dressed and the hottest lady among the bridesmaids and strategising the move to *hit a shot* after the party. They were commanding the groomsmen table's attention.

"This is a place to count your luck. *See wetin that babe carry (Look at the big boobs).*" I heard Dayo whisper to his fellow lady-hunter while sipping on his beer, leaving his moustache decorated with white foam. "Brown, look, I like my women to make-up a bit, you know what I mean? Light powder or something but does this obscure manicure match up?"

Brownson was laughing hysterically as he munched on another round of jollof. "You better clean your mouth before your face resembles the same obscurity you are describing."

Dayo laughed, sipped the layer of his beer before wiping off the frothy foam.

"Check this out." Brownson tapped Dayo on the shoulder, helpless with laughter, and pointed to a lady with thick eyelashes, blusher on her cheeks like apple-red complexion, overly exposed pink gunk eyeliner beneath the eyes, calling for attention. Slim and slender, her furrowed face and mottled skin, bleached skin, were noticeable from afar. She was wearing a dauntingly monstrous pink dress, ankle-length satin robe that

THE BACHELOR'S RIDE   269

magnified her breakable beauty, oversized earrings, baggy neck-lace, glitters of metal rings on the fingers painted in rainbows, rings that resembled the ones from Tejuosho markets. Her big breasts were unbound, dancing as she walked along. Her Brazilian hair, in its voluptuous weaves, trailed heavily down her back. "There's always one person who over do this thing. Look at that babe in front of Titi, Tara's cousin. Over-dressed is a sign of desperation. Isn't it?"

Dayo's eyes travelled the length of her. Swearing under his breath, he snapped his eyes away, then lowered his head closer to Brownson looking around like a fugitive. "First, I can recog-nise *fake* hips when I see one. Plastic things, you know." He laughed so loud before he controlled his voice. "Second, she's too ripe for plucking. You know what I mean? Besides, all I see is bones. If she falls, *walahi*, she *go* break. One time, she *go* drop a bone."

Brownson laughed like a mad man before he pointed to another woman, this time a stately looking, curvy woman with a luxurious figure, blessed in weight and height.

"Mate, I've got my eyes on the target. Check this out. Finest. This Titi babe is damn sweet: tall, full-lipped and the curves, *chai*. See how she's flaunting it. And no marriage ring on her finger. You dey feel me? Even if there's one, I swear, I'll remove it." Dayo moistened his lips, giggling as he adjusted his tie that flung upward. "Boy, it's time to zoom in."

Almost every lady within their eyeshot was analysed.

The MC began to speak. "All single ladies, can you please step forward majestically, just as elegant as you are. This includes all categories of singleness: single and searching, all complicated status, in relationship but confused, God is in control, dating more than ten years, no ring, engaged more than three years, no marriage. Please step forward."

The crowd shrieked with laughter. Tamilore, standing in

the small circle of the bridal train who had already braced up for the moment, chuckled through her nose with her hand covering her mouth. My eyes had caught her direction unintentionally and I watched to see if she was joining the group. Our eyes levelled a glance at each other over her shoulder, followed with a soft smile. She smoothed her dress before she lined up behind her sister.

One after another, about thirty ladies quickly stepped forward, looking lovely in their colourful *Aso ebi*, different versions of African headgear and pumps-heel shoes and stilettos. Doses of glamour, shades of beauty, so spotless and faultless, everywhere you turned.

One of the women on the table next to ours leaned her ear to her reluctant daughter who seemed to be in two minds. "Go try your luck, Abike," the woman said in a panic tone, as the bride walked forward, getting ready to throw her bouquet. "The bachelors are looking now. This is your year to find a husband. Smile, Abike, my daughter," she continued.

Dayo and Brownson caught the drama from the corner of their eyes and whispered into each other's ears. Abike fanned herself nervously, then shifted under Dayo's gaze who wiped one hand over his mouth, striking his stripes of goatee beard at her. His big watchful eyes had dropped to the centre of her mouth and soon flickering over her chest. Abike sat cross-legged and changed direction. After what seemed to be a thoughtful consideration, she yielded to the call. The woman's eyes were filled with hope.

Some ladies were pushing past each other for the perfect location to catch the bouquet. I recognised Oyindamola and Titilayo, Matthew's cousins, very well.

Oyindamola and Titilayo catch bouquets at every wedding, four in a row the previous year. After the last one, which got them featured under the headline *Wedding Guest*, a local nationwide entertainment newspaper, they became popular across the country. Why hasn't luck come their way after so many desperate attempts to catch wedding bouquets? While some people know this is truly not a sign of luck, catching a bouquet is a competition for single ladies, especially at a Nigerian wedding reception. Even the uninvited folks who gatecrash the wedding participate. Whoever invented this stupid superstition must be genius. Anyways, the ladies exchanged air kisses on the cheeks and confidently braced for position.

Ready for the time-honoured tradition, the bride, in her stunning embellished pearl Monsoon Helena wedding dress, was shaking her body with a big grin spread all over her face, teasing the crowd, as the flowers entwined in her hands. She sneaked a look back at the line-up, as if she had a target. Her fingers curled around the bouquet, as she continued teasing the ladies. And on the count of three by the MC, she threw the bouquet over her shoulder.

As the bouquet was tossed, the ladies shouted and pushed each other. As it descended, Debby jumped from behind, navigated the single crowd and shoved past them. Boom. She caught it. She screamed and spun on her heel. "Yes," she said, chuckling, truly overwhelmed with excitement. The crowd greeted her with loud cheers. Someone puffed out a loud breath.

Some balloon decorations bobbling against the walls busted coincidentally as the crowd shouted. "Congratulations," the MC said, walking towards Debby. "Ma, please, which sport do you play? Because your speed... your gymnastic jump is out of this world."

Debby squealed with delight, sounding out of breath as she gave the MC a side hug. Her face brightened with laughter, soaking up the spotlight, as if to say, "Do you think I've come all the way from London for jokes?" Every eye was now on her, women and men, old and young alike, seemingly dissecting every inch of her gymnastic jump; the perfection of it.

Some of the ladies walked back to their seats, disappoint-ment on their faces, while others hugged Debby with exagger-ated courtesy who was beaming in triumph. They congratulated her as she joined the bride for a photograph. Oyindamola and Titilayo were not in the latter group. Their faces flared, fizzled and flickered before their heels clicked in frustration and barged past. I was not the only one who saw their beautiful eyes filled with sadness of defeat. The MC was in stiches already, wiping the corners of his eyes from mocking laughter. Abike squeaked out a laugh too, then pulled her chin into her neck and lurched forward in their direction before she, too, was greeted with disdainful eyes.

And then it was the groom's turn.

The MC walked towards the groomsmen's corner. "Can all single men step forward please?" he said, resting his hand on Dayo's shoulder. "You have to represent, fellas."

Dayo raised and waggled his index finger. He turned and faced me, laughing. "You know the man who catches the garter is supposedly the next in line to get married. Right?"

Brownson echoed him. "And you're the oldest. You get the drift?"

"Guys, this is not about who's the oldest o. Dayo, I'd say it's your shot; it's time to start giving marriage a chance. And guess what guys? I'm not even participating."

"You have to," Brownson and Dayo said, almost at the same time, looking at each other mischievously, as if they had some-thing fishy rapped up under their noses.

"I really don't like the garter part," I said.

Matthew cracked, as he'd overheard the conversation.

"Toyosi, please join the lads. I know it's not your thing, but I need you today."

"OK, boss." I laughed.

A slow love song came on. *Let's Get It On* by Marvin Gaye. The boys dragged their feet forward, as the MC continued shouting, "You must represent, fellas." The line-up was about twenty gentlemen, including the eight groomsmen, who were in a circle formation.

The crowd began cheering the groom, as he went for the garter in the hidden spot, showing off his muscles. All his charismatic personality in action – the flirtation in his smile, strength of his biceps. The bride chuckling with a broad smile all over her face. The groom found it on his new wife's leg in a dramatic, sexy display. Laughter overtook the crowd at his exaggerated gesture. The DJ dropped another hit to match the crowd's excitement.

He threw the bride's garter to the assembled single men, in my direction precisely, in the middle of the circle, as the groomsmen cleared the way for me.

My breath stalled for a moment before I picked it up. "Oh yeah, I see. This is your game plan, yeah?" I laughed as I faced the groomsmen. Dayo and Brownson were in stitches.

After slumbering on my feet, the MC pulled me to his left. "Traditionally, the single man who catches the garter must pass it on to his future bride. You know this, right?"

"Yeah. I guess so," I said, looking confused.

"But today, there's a twist from the norm." The MC collected the garter from me and replaced it with a new bouquet. "You have to pick your future bride, pass on the bouquet, and share some danceable moments. So, pick wisely. This could be the future."

Plenty heads swivelled in my direction. Some plucked eyebrows too.

At this point, I wished Jess was in the crowd. But since she wasn't, I had to play along and pick a "future bride" from the bunch of strangers lined up before me.

Whatever happen here is only a drama; Jess remains my goal, I reminded myself.

My eyes darted sideways and searched the line-up. My mind leaped in different directions. I quickly narrowed my options to two people: Debby and a lady in a patterned gold dress and bangles: dark skin, average height, easy smile and effortlessly charming. She looked familiar. She had winked at me twice. Tamilore had remained seated since I caught the garter. I wondered why her eyebrows were now frowning. I'd imagined her cooling off the heat of jealousy, perhaps anticipating her next move, pulling her knees to her chest.

"You can only pick from the line-up," the MC said and interrupted my gaze.

I breathed.

Dayo and Brownson discreetly pointed to the corner with the ladies in fancy dresses with colourful heels, twirling their thumbs towards targets. "Shoot your shot, bro," Dayo whispered. "This is Lagos. I told you, the babes were waiting for us."

Ifeanyi plonked his elbows on the table and cautioned him with a tinge of grief in his voice, a tinge of uneasiness, gentle but unforgiving. He was yet to crack a big smile today. "A love to his heart is never to be found in the pants. Let the man be," he said, not maintaining eye contact with Dayo. He buried his head on his plate of Ayamase rice.

Dayo stirred at his voice and sipped his drink. "Bro, leave poetic talk," he snapped jovially at him, with a mocking frown.

"Please make a choice," the MC said, hurrying me up, as he checked his wristwatch.

I nodded in slow dips. "Give me two seconds. Please." My eyes swung from left to right, tossing between Debby and this calm-looking lady with the wink, projecting her warmness and freshness like a daisy. Then, unexpectedly, Tamilore appeared in the line-up.

No! What's she doing? My eyes widened in astonishment.

I began to laugh, studying her in silence. She wasn't rolling her eyes; she kept them glued to mine, as if she was saying something I needed to hear. Jealousy had surged clearer. I saw a woman with a memory in her eyes. Her dimples had faded into smooth cheeks. If I'd magic eyes to see through clothes and flesh, I'd most likely be looking at a pumping heart, beating too fast, perhaps in the brink of collapse. I had enough reasons to think so. Why was she scratching the back of her hand, compulsively? Why the sudden inscrutable face? Oh, wait. Did she just heave a shuddery sigh like someone harbouring heat under her skin? Was her heart hammering and thudding in her chest or was it blunting the edges of her memories?

Whatever it was, it was already late.

Debby interrupted the gaze. Her brow tinged with a sense of apprehension, it seemed. She muttered something under her breath and tugged her two plaits. I returned the smile.

"See babes everywhere. Why are you confused, mister?" The MC interrupted my thoughts. Some ladies nodded in agreement, squealing with laughter while others were talking in hushed voices. Someone's head was nodding up and down on its own. Someone else was standing on shaky legs. I tore the gaze and refocused. *Oh, no!* My eyes were in a wrong direction again. I looked away from the over-dressed lady with the pink glossed lips running her tongue over her teeth. I wondered why she planted her hands on her hips.

Debby cleared her throat, forced a gulp. A little louder than normal. Neck twisted and turned, not once, not twice. I did not miss her fingers twining and untwining. Tamilore kept her eyes glued to mine, crossing and uncrossing her arms. I turned to the calm-looking lady with the wink, now talking gently with the toe of her heels. Eyes beautifully fixed on me.

Jess, you should have been here. OK, let me get this done with. Whoever I pick does not matter. Drama, it is and drama it shall be. I reminded myself again.

OK, I've decided.

Seconds later, I took a slight breath, then a bold step, walking towards the ladies. "You are all beautiful tonight," I said, and stood in front of *her*. I saw her heart in her eyes as she closed her eyes for a second and joyfully breathed out relief. "You look stunning."

She displayed her best accessory as we hugged: her smile. I gave her a cheek kiss, nuzzled her cheek. She pressed her mouth to my shoulder and held the hug a little tighter.

Clouded and sober, someone else's glaze held a reproach. *She* shot me an angry side glance, before she picked me up with her eyes, rolled me over and smashed me on the floor.

Debs, I'm so sorry! You're absolutely stunning in every way. I was worried you'd most likely take it the wrong way and I don't want to hurt your feelings. My face did the pleading.

I heard Matthew shouting. "Yes, yes, yesssssss. Made in heaven!" He gave me a supporting thumbs-up. The bride was in awe, holding her hands close to her mouth, as the groom tugged her closer. And the couple grinned into warm cuddle.

"Thanks for waiting for me," Tamilore said, in a voice of self-consciousness, each word deliberately pronounced slowly, as if she wanted me to ponder on them.

I handed her the flowers. "Would you like to dance?"

"Yes." Her expression was priceless. And the satisfied smile was beautiful to see.

The crowd shouted, with an exultant cheer, as if it was a proposal.

"Ready for our first dance?"

She banged my chest, playfully. With her dimpled cheeks, biggest smile radiating on her lips. "It's just a dance. We are not the couple, after all."

I smiled. "Thanks for reminding me."

We allowed the photographers do their job as I slipped my arm around her waist. Shortly after, we turned away from the cameras, getting ready to shake our legs.

"You like afrobeat?" Tamilore asked, slightly entwining her fingers with mine.

I did what I needed to do for the moment, just for the moment. "Afrobeat is always irresistible, you know. Even if the lyrics make no sense, the dance does. The vibe does."

She dusted something off my suit, on the shoulder blade and flicked out her tongue playfully. "Let's see your dance steps then," she said, smiling, twirling her hair with her fingers, smoothing them gently, as we stepped onto the dance floor, ready to groove.

The DJ dropped an afrobeat song for the three-minute dance and we bounced to the music. Just as her audience does when watching her show, the crowd erupted in applause, almost everyone on their feet, cameras snapping our faces. We were shoulder-length apart. I held her left hand, as the loud music was twirling. She swayed her body around me, showcasing the latest dance moves in an epic sexy move. Unrestrained joy took over us. Like the makers of the lyrics who invented the moves, I beckoned to her style, flickering. Then, Tamilore stole the show when she rolled, whined and twisted her waist, letting loose her hair that flowed flawlessly. The MC screamed, pushing the excited crowd back who circled us, with their phone camera lights that were flashing and twinkling at every dance step.

"This is amazing. This is incredible. This is how you do it!" The MC's scream became louder, as he analysed every move, every vibe, every wicked lyric, as if he was a referee. "We're witnessing something here, folks. Can you all see what I'm seeing? Dads and mums, please close your eyes!" Laughter erupted; the crowd was swooning with delight.

As we continued dancing, the "wink" lady flashed me a big grin.

Who is she? I kept wondering, a little intrigued.

Shortly after the dance, I saw Debby. She still looked confused, hazy and quiet. Debby didn't know anyone at the wedding except the couple. So, I went to her table for a little chat. "Hey, Debs, you OK? Congrats on the bouquet. That was an excellent catch."

Her body stiffened. "Hmm, thanks. Can I ask you a question?"

"Of course, please go ahead."

Her face came into curiosity, an unease settling over her. "The bride's sis you picked, do you already know her? Erm... I mean is she... anyways don't worry," she trailed off.

I smiled, fully aware of what was going on, and leaned closer to squeeze her soft hand. "Debs, Debs, smile small *nah*. Please ask your question, what about her?"

She sighed, her eyes softening, mood lifting. "Hmm. Erm. Maybe later," Debby said, letting go of my hand. She crossed her arms over her chest. Her smile seemed forced.

I halted her retreat with a smile. I felt a bit guilty not to have picked her, but I believed I did the right thing. When her expressive eyes pinched at the corners, I got the message. I gave her shoulder a nudge. Her face stayed the same, then I attempted a playful hi-five and this time, she responded. She wiped cleaned her phone screen and I leaned closer for a selfie. Our teeth were bright and white as we winced at the camera. I was pleased to see her genuine smile. "OK. I've got to go now. The groom is waiting for me," I told her.

It was time for a toast. I hurried up for the two-minute speech. I rolled the tape of the moments I'd rehearsed countless times in my lonely room. I held my wine glass, rapping it with the teaspoon, as I signalled the guests to silence. "Ladies and gentlemen, I give you the bride and groom. What a wonderful and awesome day, it is. Please allow me to tell you a little story about the groom's number one dating rule and its extension." The words were refreshing, and the crowd roared in excitement and support. I kept it brief, as I shared stories of how they met, joked about Matthew's dating rules and ended with best wishes. "And to you two, may love comfort you like sunshine after rain. And may your marriage be so sweet and filled with love. To a beautiful happy ending. Congratulations! Folks, let's drink to love."

The guests clapped. Miss Beautiful wouldn't take her twin-kling eyes off me. She sat, legs draped elegantly, looking relaxed, seemed entranced by everything happening. She had clapped and smiled through the whole toast. I'd caught her gaze many times in mid-laughter and looked away. And each time, I'd wondered if I'd seen her pleasant broad-featured face before. As I re-grouped with the groomsmen, I saw her making her way out of the hall.

Dayo seemed to know everything that was going on. He'd been hovering about like a bird of prey. "Hey, Toyo, cough-cough. Don't miss your shot. She's leaving."

"Who's leaving?" I asked curiously.

He patted the back of his head, one hand stuck into his pocket. "You think I don't know? I know your taste. You two have been staring at each other all day. This is a match made in heaven. Go shoot your shot, bro. And now, please."

I followed his gaze towards the exit door where Miss Beau-tiful swung a little girl up onto her hip. She brushed the girl's hair, held her cheekbones playfully and tickled her head. A moment later, she released the girl back to her mother and waved the family. Her heels clicked elegantly as she left the hall. "Nah, I already told you, Jess and I have started something. But I'm curious to know who she is though. I think she knows me."

He choked out a laugh and tipped his head back, mocking. "Two dates or three. Is that something?"

"I mean Jess is a potential. And yes, it's something," I told him.

"This babe is hot, Toyo. Forget potential, this is the real deal. Good luck."

"She's hot for real but Jess remains the target."

He flicked his palm upward to dismiss my point. "Why are you two staring at each other all day, if you had a potential? *Leave potential, see clean babe.*"

I followed the lead and saw Miss Beautiful as she approached her car. I had a feeling we'd met before and wanted to find out. She noticed I was right behind her.

The cultural troupe, popularly known as The Talking Drum performers, who speak to people with songs, cut in as if they had been waiting. We respected the two-minute interruption. They were about eight drummers in their grey, wide-sleeved Ankara gown called *agbada*. Half of the group held the leather cords of their drums in similar display (the percussion instrument called "Gangan" which help to upshot the tone and prosody of performance) and took to action with their drumsticks, squeezing the cords between their arms and ribs, increasing the warbling notes collectively. The others braced into the recitals with their hands, the drumhead at both ends echoed louder with "talking" voice and synthesises as they imitated rhythms, songs and prayers of good wishes. Miss Beautiful reached for her purse. I reached for my wallet and we did what was expected of us. The performers bowed their heads in appreciation of our little gesture and left joyfully afterwards.

"Hi. I'm Toyosi. I thought I should pop out to say hello before you leave. By the way, your dress is lovely."

She beamed. "Thanks, Toyosi. That's thoughtful, Mr. Joker. I'm Ife."

"Joker?" I said, smiling but waiting for clarification.

"Your pick was heart-warming. You took your time. And you two danced well."

"Oh, *that*? Thanks. Have we met before?"

There was a knowing glint in her eyes. She nodded before removing her black-framed eyeglasses and wiped clean the lenses with her handkerchief. "Yes, indeed. But I'll let you figure it out," she said.

"Hmm. Really?" I began to wrack my brain.

She curled her hair at her shoulders and smiled. "Your toast was lovely, too, by the way. Excellent speech. Short and sweet. Are you a poet?"

Her American accent gave her away. Some words pronounced tensely, highly strung; others pronounced laxly. I didn't miss the high vowel, voiceless consonant intonation. The American twang. Like the quintessential accent of the southern and northeastern American folks. The blurring of the lettered "t" and rhoticity of "r" sound. It clicked instantly. "Oh, wait. Wow! You're Ifedamola. Ifedamola Jacob. Aren't you? Mummy Tomiwa's last daughter from Ikoyi. The beautiful lawyer, who made a First, alumni from Yale."

"Yes. I'm Ife. I wasn't quite sure if it was you or not," she said.

"Wow. What a small world! That's over eighteen years. It's so lovely seeing you again. You look very stunning."

"Thanks, Toyosi. It's lovely seeing you too. You're not looking bad either," she said.

"Oh, thanks. It's the Vaseline, you know."

She laughed. "I think I need some Vaseline if it makes you look this fresh."

We both smiled and hugged each other.

"I actually have a plan to visit your family residence before I return to base, and my apologies, I couldn't attend your mum's sixtieth birthday celebration."

"No worries, Toyo. You can still bring the gift."

I laughed. We talked a bit, shared a few jokes, and exchanged mobile numbers.

"I'll call you to arrange a coffee and catch up properly," I told her, as I dashed off.

The groomsmen and bridesmaids had been called to the dance floor to join the couple who had changed to their traditional attire. The bride looking stunning in her embroidered *buba* gold fabrics, with the chunky pink coral necklace, bracelets and mint green head wrap to match. And the groom matching his bride, rocking joyfully in his trendy *agbada* gliding down his arms, his outer robe nicely studded with tiny, embroidered beads at the centrepiece.

The DJ turned up the music hits, family and friends roared at the couple's sexy, sweet-synchronised dance, dollars began to fly in the air, multiple one-dollar bill bundles raining on their forehead, spray of a thousand-naira wad of cash flaunting and floating mid-air from left, right and centre. The dance floor was flooded in cash. Dayo, who had been peering around at the ladies, skulking on the edges of the crowd, furtively took a phone number from a bridesmaid as she was sweeping the money off the floor, the third lady I'd noted so far. Brownson exerted himself, sneered and flicked lint off his grey suit, giving his first attempt at the best shot. Ifeanyi had loosened up and was now fully absorbed in the party mood. Another groomsman, tall and lanky, staggered unsteadily then keeled over to

Debby who looked discreetly in my direction. I glided towards her. Her face softened with a smile, at first briefly, then broadly as we began to dance the night away. As the reception lights were dimmed, and the DJ's grooving beats began to hit the high note, everyone knew it was the beginning of the party. Here, you were meant to go home only when your legs hurt.

Tara and Matthew's wedding was a fabulous success. I had a wonderful time. I caught up with Jess on the phone later that evening and she was excited to hear from me.

TWENTY-NINE

"I can't wait to savour the Lekki Market, it has the best arts and crafts, and enjoy the outdoor peppersoup experience," Debby had said, a week before our Lagos trip. Musical theatre shows at Terra Kulture in Victoria Island topped her list.

She was also looking forward to relishing the awesomeness of Nike Art Gallery, one of the largest in West Africa, with its rich embroidery arts, enjoying some live music at Bogobiri in Ikoyi (a hotbed and hub of musical and artistic talents) and losing herself to beach parties especially at the La Campagne Tropicana. Those were her priorities.

Debs dear, are you OK? Please text me when you see this. I sent Debby a text message after she'd missed about four calls from me, without returning any of them.

Two days after the wedding, Debby finally reached out. She sounded lighter. We met for lunch at Hard Rock café in Victoria Island where warm ambience met with great cuisine, the restaurant I'd imagined would get Debby raving but she could barely look me in the eye. Her eyes, her face, her whole body reeked with nervousness. Heavy with worry.

"There's something I want to tell you," she began, looking intently. "I want you to hear it from me directly." Her hand trembled a little, as she jammed her fist together.

I nodded curtly, a slow nod. "OK," I said. "I'm all ears, Debby."

She swatted a mosquito. I welcomed the distraction, but I didn't blink.

Her seat squeaked beneath her as she sat upright, then rested her left hand on her head. She took her time as she fumbled about. For a moment, her eyes were half-shut while her lips were pressed together, as if she was fighting to let the words out. When she began to bite the side of her nail, I knew something terrible had happened. I waited. And when she was ready to speak, she raised her eyes to mirror mine. "I made another terrible mistake on the wedding night." Her face twisted into a grimace, as the words came out slowly.

"Which wedding night? What mistake? You mean two days ago?"

"I want you to hear it from me because I know that stupid friend of yours will eventually tell you or brag about it." Frustration crinkled her eyes.

"You mean Dayo?" I asked, cradling the curve of my jaw.

"Yes. He's a fool."

"Debby, what happened?" I was already processing the worst-case scenario.

Her face curved down and she was muted for about a minute. "I was drunk. He sweet-talked me into drinking, and I don't know when we ended up at his hotel. Nothing happened o! But getting conned by him was a mistake. We live and learn, don't we?"

Damn it.

The thick silence melted instantly. "What? Did I hear you

right? You slept with Dayo?" I bristled at her bombshell, with curiosity, not with judgement as if I was her lover.

Her eyes swivelled over mine. "No, no. I didn't. But kind of." Her voice was quiet, her words slurred and lisping. Her shoulders slumped with irritability.

I leaned forward and controlled my rising voice. I didn't want the expression of disgust to show on my face either. "Debby, kind of? What does that mean?"

Something wedged inside her, it seemed, as she defensively put her phone away. Embarrassment perhaps. She sat upright again, letting her cheeks and her unblushed face flushed it off in a disguise. "I don't have to be descriptive, Toyosi. It was just a little... erm. Err, we didn't have sex. I couldn't bring myself that low. You know what I mean. That's all. I slapped him and left afterwards. I don't want the bastard to brag about it." She reclined her head, wiped her forearm across her eyes. Something had melted into her eyes already.

"Oh, no! Debs, please cheer up." I held her hand and handed her a handkerchief.

I wondered why Debby was telling me this. I'd imagined whatever transpired indoor between two adults should have remained between them. I looked into her eyes, the lids of her eyes, for the words unsaid and I knew instantly that the horse had bolted, and Debby was acting rather late, trying to close the stable door. I gasped. *Dayo is such a jerk.*

She fluffed her hair, tensing, really unsettled, then removed a tissue from her bag and sniffed into it. I tried rubbing the pad of my thumb on her finger, to ease the unpleasantness. "I know I've failed God for walking that path. It's not like anything happened like I said but I feel so ashamed. I was lonely that night and kind of sad, and he took advantage."

I felt a wince of empathy for her. *Sad? Why sad though, Debs? How can you be sad on a beautiful wedding day?* I did not let the words out. I could really understand. I inched closer to hold her hand again. "Please cheer up, Debs. Everything will be fine. Please cheer up."

There was silence. Companionable silence.

She let go of my hand, slipped her phone into her bag and threw me a worrisome look. The awkward moment became heavy as she stood up and hung her bag onto her shoulder. "I just wanted to let you know... erm." She talked in a lower mumble. Words took long to form. "I've re-scheduled my flight and I'm going back to London tonight."

A glint of pride that was always present in Debby's eyes had been replaced by something close to defeat. I closed the gap between us instantly and gave her a big hug. She burst into tears as I pressed my body tighter to hers. And soon after, she left for her hotel.

I was not surprised that Dayo, as cunning as a fox, could play such a foul game with his cheap, fake, sweet talk, despite all my sermons before the trip.

I saw Debby off to the airport that night. "Please don't be too hard on yourself," I told her, as we arrived at the Muritala Airport. "Everyone makes mistakes at some point. I did, too. I want you to know you're an amazing person and nothing will ever change between us."

"I'll be fine, Toyo," she said, as we hugged tightly and said our goodbyes with amiable smile.

She knew the news had already broken the camel's back. However, regardless of whatever happened, our friendship remained unwavering. I knew that for sure.

THE SECOND I returned from the airport, I called Dayo, my voice catching in my throat. "Dayo, what happened on the wedding night?"

"*O boy*, we need to catch up. I'll give you the *download*."

"I'm not in the mood for such nonsense. What did you do to Debby?"

"Eh, chill bro. Take it easy. You're not dating the babe, no need to be jealous."

"What did you do to her?" I raised my voice in anger.

He was laughing, mocking. "Nothing."

"She already told me. Don't even lie. How could you get her drunk and then take advantage of her? You're such a huge disappointment. How dare you? Dayo, how dare you?"

"What? She wanted it. We got on. I didn't rape her. That's the line I had never crossed in my life and will never cross. That would be senseless and foolish. I may be a player, but I don't have sex without consent."

I lowered my voice. "How do you mean she wanted it?"

"We had a fling, there was mutual consent."

"A fling? Mutual consent? After getting her drunk? How can that be mutual consent?"

"It was. She was flirting with me, even before we started to drink."

"She did? How?"

"Of course. She gave a green light and I didn't miss it. Mate, I know when a woman wants you to give her a few strokes. Why price the milk when you can get it for free? Eh. Dude, this babe is so sweet. Ah, her hips, the way she moves and rides it, hitting me hard from left to right and divinely at the centre. She's a Master Grinder. The groove was awesome bro. The moan, the yell, the breathing. Goodness me. All natural, no fake orgasms. The slap I got in the end was worth it. And those intensely light bite. Sweet. She's a—"

I hung up.

I nibbled my thumb in anger and tried so hard to suppress the sudden gritted teeth. *No! No, no, no! Oh, no, no!* Both hands were now stacked on my head before I punched the wall, before I punched it so hard with a thud in my gut. It was as if I'd been played another of Debby's sex tapes. My mind speedily flashed back. A replay of the old and the new events interplayed, simultaneously. It was vividly clearer than ever before, as if I was right there, watching. I staggered clumsily, my throat suddenly became dry and tight; the reflection in the mirror in front of me showed a man whose face was flushed and ghoulish; whose eyes were bulged and enraged. My mouth was twisted to one side with a crease on the cheek.

I moved away from the mirror, as if I hated the reflection of the man, flipped my phone on the bed next to the mirror and did not realise I'd slammed my fist on a table until it hurt. It was sad to learn about Debby's vulnerability and that Dayo remained a disgrace. All my advice to him went in one ear and out the other. I doubted he would ever change.

Frustration made its presence felt. It was high time to cut off all ties with Dayo.

———

Fresh air breezed in the following morning, cleared the burdened air of previous night, as I looked out of my hotel window and glanced at Victoria Beach, not far off. A gentle wind blew calmness; waves rippled on the swimming pool nearby. Exactly what I needed this morning. Peace. Then, I messaged Debby to make sure she had arrived in London safely.

Her reply came minutes later. *I got home half an hour ago. Thank you and I'm sorry for everything. I'm truly sorry.*

I'm happy you're home safe, dear. Let's catch up when I'm back in town. Do take care. I replied, as I cleared my head with the fresh, calm-relieving whiff of breeze. The aura between us which can be perceived miles away was, however, stiff.

A text message peeped. It was Jess. *Heyyy Toyo, make sure you visit Mum as planned and remember to hint her that her daughter in London says hello.*

LOL. I'll surely do. Be rest assure she'd pick a wedding date asap LOL.

LOOOOL. She replied. *That's even better. Speak later, dear! xoxo.*

I reached for Chapman, the local cocktail drink served earlier with breakfast, and slowly let the fruity flavour – every sweet drop of its cherry – bless my soul.

THIRTY

THE NEXT DAY, Tuesday morning, I woke up to Tamilore's text. *Heyy Toyo, hope you're well rested. I was thinking I could show you a good restaurant today either for lunch or dinner?*

After I was done speaking to Jess, I replied to her. *Sounds great, Tamilore. But I'm sorry I'd have to say no. I'm meeting up with a friend later. And boys get together in the evening.*

What about tomorrow? She replied instantly.

I'm off to Ilaro to see Mum.

And on Thursday?

I'm back to London.

Hmm. And you can't squeeze in any time for us to see? You avoiding me?

I took gasps and flung the phone away. I headed to the kitchen to fix breakfast. By the time I returned, I'd missed a call from Tamilore and had another text.

I'm sorry about keeping mute for so long. All I ask for is lunch!

I hurriedly typed a reply. *I'm done with you, Tamilore Talulu. I'm so done with you.*

But I couldn't click *send*.

About five minutes later, the phone light peeped, vibrating again and again and again. There had been five missed calls from Tamilore. On the sixth, I answered the call.

"Heyy hey, whatzup. How are you doing?"

That wasn't so unfriendly, was it?

I imagined something had caught her throat. Something capable of causing agonising gasps. She waited for a few seconds. "Hmm. Why do I have a feeling you're avoiding me?"

"No, not at all." I sounded convincing.

"Hmm. You sure? Messaged you on Sunday morning. Till now, no reply." A tinge of tenderness in her voice, a soft tone of apology it seemed.

"Ah, did I miss your text? Sorry about that, it wasn't intentional. I've been resting. Massive congratulations on the wedding. That was a big success. Really amazing."

"Toyo. I'm sorry. Don't change the subject. Please let's talk about it."

"Sorry for what, Tamilore?"

She sounded as if she'd forced breath from her lungs. "We had a great time at the wedding. A beautiful time we both treasured so much. Why tension between us now?"

"There's no tension between us. I just want you to know that whatever happened at the wedding was only a drama. You aren't reading any meaning to that, are you?"

The words landed well. Evoked silence. Hurting silence, I'd imagined.

I could hear voices in the background fizzling into whispering. She fought for her breath. I swallowed and fought for mine.

"We were supposed to talk about *this*, but you told me at the wedding you've forgiven me. Your actions said so too." Whatever *this* means was obviously disguised.

"I don't have anything against you, Tamilore. We'll always be cool as friends."

Silence.

I wondered if someone's throat was blocked with a cheese grater.

"Friends? OK. That's fine." Tone of anger or frustration was rising above her words. You had so many options of who you could have picked and danced with. Why did you pick me, Toyosi? Don't even lie. Why did you pick me?"

"Two people we care a lot about were getting married. That's why."

"That's a lie, Toyosi. Yes, you are dating Jess. But you can't lie that what we shared on that stage, what we'd always shared, was a drama. I know how you feel about me. I know it's still there. I know why you picked me and deep down in your heart, you know too."

"Tamilore, whatever has happened in the past is now left in the past. You can't zoom in and zoom out whenever you like. I'm done with you, Tamilore. I'm so freaking done with you." I'd said this in a borrowed South African accent. I wondered where that came from.

The words must have been sharpened like arrows, like the stabling spears of Zulu warriors. They must have hit her and crushed her defence, humbled her pride, humbled her ego. Silence took hold of us, drenched us, waited for us to mend or break. The thought of hanging up the phone crossed my mind. But I kept the line open. I must remain a gentleman.

All I could hear was her breath, startled breath, sharp breath, shrivelling inhaled, like someone sucking in lungfuls of air as though spasms of shock had rocketed through her.

Seconds later, she broke the dreadful silence with a soft tone. "I'm so sorry, Toyosi."

"For what, precisely?" I asked. Our lungs were still heated, as if someone had a confession of love to make and the other had a confession of someone else's love to profess.

"So sorry for everything. For ignoring you after Lagos Airport. For trying to make you date my sister. For not looking back after I left London. For ignoring all your attempts to reach me. For everything I must have done wrong, knowingly or unknowingly."

I controlled my tongue not to let out the blunt words I'd reserved for her. I waited to hear more. "When I left London, I was broken. Totally broken from the six years wasted relationship. I needed to heal. I'm sorry I took my anger on you. Deep down in my heart, you're the only person I wanted to reach out to. Only person I wanted to be with. I ended up fighting the urge everyday, to let go of my thoughts of you because of our incompatibility genotype news. I hated the feeling. Two months ago, as the wedding prep started, I wanted to call you, to explain, to apologise, but I thought it would be easier if I did in person."

"That's OK, Tamilore. Apology accepted. I'm glad you realise something wasn't cool about how you handled things. And that you could have done better, at least reach out once. Let's move past it. You're a lovely person and it would be great to stay in touch as friends."

That silence again.

"OK," she said, unconvincingly. "OK, if that's what you want, that's fine."

We soon ended the call after we'd *amicably* decided to honour friendship.

It wasn't long after the call, I received Tamilore's text message. *Love doesn't vanish, love doesn't! It may be quenched, maybe quiet for eight months, but it doesn't vanish.*

Thanks for the poetic line, friend. I should have clicked *send.*

I MET up with Ife later in the day at an African themed bar and restaurant on The Island. The live jazz was on. The vibe was good. She looked even more beautiful than she had on the wedding day. She wore a brown casual lace dress, which was well suited for an evening rendezvous. Simple but classic and sexy. I was well dressed too. Dark-coloured chinos with a white shirt and a navy slim-fit blazer. I looked smart and sharp.

A server approached us, and we placed our orders for the cocktail of the day.

"I really like how our mums' relationship has lasted for many years. That's not so common these days," she said as we took our seat with a beautiful ocean view.

"That's true. So hard to come by these days."

I sensed a woman with a beautiful soul.

"What's been going on after Yale?" I asked.

She took her elbows off the table and sat comfortably. "Hmm. Nothing much. I did an internship with a law firm in New York and was offered a job afterwards." She locked eye contact and tucked her hair beautifully behind her ears.

"Oh, great. Congratulations, dear. New York is a great city."

"It is," she said. "I've got a lot of friends there and nearby in Connecticut and New Haven, so my social life was balanced. But I had to relocate home to start a project here."

"A project?" I said. "I heard about NG Girls, Voice for Voiceless through Mum. How's that going?"

"God has been faithful. It was initially a slow start, but it's picking up. We got funding."

Our mix of gin, lemon and soda was served. We clicked glasses and toasted.

"Wow, I'm so proud of you. Congratulations. So, what's next? The *brothers* must be trailing now *o*?"

She laughed and took a sip of her drink. "The *brothers* are fine, I suppose. Why are you still single, Toyosi?"

"Ah, I get this question every time. The simple answer is that I'm yet to meet HER."

"With all those London babes," she said. "Genotype issues are the major constraint for me."

"Oh, no. Same," I said in shock.

She sat upright. "I have a sickle cell anaemia (SS) and as a result, I had to reject bunch of suitors with the sickle cell traits. It's been an exhausting experience."

I learned forward in surprise. "Oh, no. How have you been coping?"

"It's been tough. It's been overwhelming," she said, and then shared her journey of the occasional crisis over the years. Somehow, many of the gents she liked were usually sickle cell carriers. This made the combination riskier and, hence, she got picky.

"I can imagine how difficult it must have been."

"It is. I wish more people knew about the challenge. Since I returned to Nigeria from the US, I've devoted my time to the sickle cell anaemia campaign, creating awareness. Not just in cities like Lagos but in small, rural communities with limited access to information."

"That's impressive. Really really impressive. I'm very pleased to hear this. Guess what, I do the same in London," I told her. "So, how's that going?"

"The campaign has really snowballed. We debunk lots of myths. Can you believe some parents don't feel comfortable telling their kids they have sickle cell after diagnosis? Because they ignorantly assume it's a death sentence. Sometimes telling the kids it's nothing but bone pain or rheumatism or something else. So, we're changing that. Our enlightenment programme isn't limited to those who have it but also the general populace. We encourage early detection too. We provide information on how to manage the crisis. A lot is going on in the space and I'm glad more people are getting involve supporting the campaign. What's the situation like in the UK? Are more black people encouraged to register and donate blood?"

"Yeah, pretty much. It remains the fastest growing genetic disorder in the UK. I'm working with my local community to create awareness. We encourage folks to support those who need blood transfusion and to sign up to become stem cell donors. And in some cases, we follow up with guidelines on how they can complete the "cheek swab kit" after signing up, so it doesn't end up in a bin bag. We should really join forces to do more in Nigeria."

She laughed. "That's so cool. We really should work together."

The discussion about sickle cell campaign, our hope and dreams, took the rest of the evening. The dinner went well. We had a good time and promised to stay in touch as friends.

Later that evening, as I returned to the hotel, I stood at the terrain looking over the Lagos skyline, staring straight into the spectrum of colours, spread over the coastline along the Victoria Beach. My mind troubling with history of events. Why is it that the ones I genuinely admire were those who were either sickle cell carriers or who had the disease? I reflected on the ladies I'd met in the past few years. Bimbo did. Rene did too. Isabella, Sophia, Hannah, Ada, and Zara. And now Ife. I cannot rule out the fact that I hadn't set out to date Ife, but she could have been a great potential, should my prospect with Jess go downhill.

I prayed it wouldn't.

Cloud slided past the crystal sky, breeze filling the night air. I stood there, with layers of thoughts on my mind. My puzzlement ripening to more worries like no time in the past.

THIRTY-ONE

London, December 2017

I ENJOYED my remaining few days in Lagos and flew back to London afterwards. Jess and I met up a few days later at the beautifully decorated Hope Café near Elephant and Castle in south London. It was one of the city's oldest cafés. I liked the quietness, the warm interiors and the colourful walls. And the best part, the messages of hope printed on the wall, from Barrack Obama's favourite lines to Nelson Mandela's powerful speeches. And all the great leaders and influencers around the globe. Jess was quite excited to see me, as I was to see her. She still had not received her test results and seemed curious and a bit nervous.

"Toyo, what are your preferences?" Jess asked, after we'd placed our orders. Our plan was to grab a quick coffee and Jess's favourite Greek yogurt here before heading out for a proper meal next door.

"Preferences? I'm sorry I'm not following, dear."

She playfully hit my hand. "I mean suppose I am AS."

My eyes caught the framed print screaming "hope" in front of me. "Hmm, I'm open-minded provided you are too. But it is subject to hearing God's mind about it," I said.

"Does that mean you're willing to compromise?"

"Yes and no."

"You're such a typical Nigerian man. Take a position," she joked.

"The last time I was open-minded, I got my hands burnt. One who has been bitten by a snake lives in fear of worms. *No be so?*" I said, laughing.

"You mean, once bitten, twice shy?"

My thumb up was in the air. "Yes. And that's a big yes if God approves of the relationship, especially with someone as special as you. And no if we cannot agree on any of the options science provides to get around it. Did I clear the ambiguity, your highness?"

She smiled. Her spark grew a little brighter. "You did, Mr. Isola. Hmm, genotype is a *witch*."

"I know, right. It ruins relationship potentials for many couples. A lot of people who genuinely love each other have had to walk away from their love. Yeah, you're right. *Na witch.*"

Jess and I discussed the subject in a relaxed manner, having fun educating each other on the options science provides without any pressure. It was more like we were enlightening ourselves rather than working out a solution that didn't yet have a problem.

"Let's talk about the hard choices," Jess said, blowing out a breath.

I sat upright. "First, there is pre-natal diagnosis. The option of pre-natal diagnosis is becoming increasingly popular. This involves testing the foetus before birth and provides a chance to determine the possibility of sickle cell disease or any other genetic disorders. In the event of a worst-case scenario, the couple has the option to terminate the pregnancy. For each pregnancy, there's a twenty-five per cent probability of having a child with sickle cell anaemia if both parents are AS. The downside of pre-natal diagnosis is that in the event of repeated bad luck, couples will have the hard choice of potentially terminating every pregnancy."

"Nah, nah. It's a no-no," she said, clucking her tongue.

"Yeah, I'm not surprised. It's perhaps one of the hardest decisions to make. OK, can I ride on?"

"Shoot." Jess listened carefully like it meant a great deal to her.

"Secondly, the Pre-Implantation Genetic Diagnosis (PGD) option. This is like the pre-natal diagnosis. The option offers the advantage that it avoids pregnancy termination. The PGD is a genetic profiling that tests for specific genetic conditions. It provides an opportunity for embryos to be tested and screened and those free of sickle cell disease, or any diseases, can be implanted into a woman's uterus. Like most fertility treatments, it can be expensive, and success is not completely guaranteed. It can take a few trials."

She placed her glass on the table between us. "Ah, Toyo. This is hard, too. From my research on it, I hate that the unused embryos will be discarded. That's not what I pray for. It's a no for me," Jess explained.

"There are quite a few options to keep the embryos frozen or donate to other people with fertility problems. People in this situation have options to consider."

"You mean like donate the diseased embryos to innocent people? Nah, that's not fair. Why would anyone do that? And I can't stand it being discarded either. The dilemma of what to do with the remaining embryos is my major concern with this option."

"I mean the *unused healthy embryos* can be frozen for

future pregnancies or for donation while the *unused unhealthy embryos* are discarded," I explained.

"I can't imagine any being discarded, regardless of its healthiness."

"OK, I get your point but for folks in such a situation, it's probably not quite as hard as you've imagined it."

"Toyosi, I honestly feel bad for people facing a dilemma like this."

"Well, this is one of the options science provides," I told her.

She removed her neck scarf and swayed it on her lap. "At what stage does life begin? At the embryonic stage or when the embryos are implanted into the womb or later, when a heart beats or when a foetus can survive outside the womb on its own?"

I pondered on it for a few seconds. "Hmm. Excellent question. I think I know your rationale. But I'm not sure I know the answer."

"I want to know if discarding the embryos is killing innocent children. Anyways, what are the other options?" Jess said, looking concerned.

I bent my elbows unto the coffee table. "Stem cell treatment offers some hope, too, in case a kid has the disease. Basically, a bone marrow transplant is carried out from a donor. There must be a donor with a hundred per cent match though. Downside is that there's a minor risk of death or the child later becoming infertile. And it isn't cheap," I explained.

Something close to fear unveiled on her face. She drank some water, then squirmed in her seat. The air smelled of worry.

I stroked her wrist gently with my right thumb. "You OK?"

"Not a fan of transplant," she told me. Her voice was muffled.

"Let's go for pizza, dear," I said. "Maybe we can continue later."

She dug into her handbag and took out a pen and a notebook. "No, not yet. I'm enjoying it. It's very educational. Tell me more, please," she insisted.

"Another hard choice is marriage without kids," I said.

"Hmm. Nah," she dismissed that quickly.

"Adoption is another option for couples in this situation."

She twitched a shrug. "Adoption is great, but I would like to have my own babies."

"Those are the few options I'm aware of," I told her.

"These are all hard choices. Is there no easy option?"

"Gambling. Close your eyes. Damn the consequences. Throw your dice and hope for the best?"

She laughed. "It sounds like hoping for a winning number to come up in a lottery."

"Oh, yeah. But better than the lottery though. I think seventy-five per cent is a good probability to gamble with but the consequences of the odds for an innocent child can be eternally painful."

"Tough choices indeed. Are those all the options?"

"The safest option is the toughest. To take a walk. Quench the feeling. And hope for the best."

"Thanks, Toyosi. It's so enlightening. My mum says I'm likely AA, so fingers crossed."

"You're welcome, your highness. Pizza now?"

"Yes, please. And a sparkling cold water too. It's hot in here." Jess breathed a sigh of relief.

It's weird discussing babies after a few dates but that's what genotype issues call for, the earlier, the better. We changed topics and enjoyed the rest of the evening, from dinner to the movies.

A WEEK LATER, Jess received her genotype report in the form of a Haemoglobinopathy card. The card report is the size of normal credit card. She took the picture of the front page and sent it to me with a caption: *My test result says Sickle Cell Carrier (HbAS). I've never been this devastated at news of anything.*

Something spun in my head as if I'd been hit with a ton of bricks. Something else rot in my stomach. Like pain, like stabbing. It crushed through and arched inside me.

Oh, no. Not again.

I kept staring at the report, as if it was going to change. I ran my forefinger over the screen, under the letter "S", as if the word "Carrier" wasn't specific enough. The room turned airless. A bright day brusquely became a cheerless winter afternoon. I remembered this junction I'd become so familiar with. This time, it caused me more pain. Reading the message felt heavy beyond measure. It was like grabbing onto a handful of sand that represented hope and then gradually watching as it fell through my tightly clenched fingers.

MOMENT LATER, I rose to my feet. Enough was enough. *To hell with genotype.* I smashed the sinking feeling. I was determined not to allow the news to devour the rays of light that were already shining brightly. A drowning man will clutch at a straw, for sure.

If Jess is in, I'm in, I murmured to myself.

My whole body stilled. I knew I could not allow emotion to dictate what I should do. It requires a lot of care to kill the fly that perches on the scrotum. I must pray about it. And I aimed to encourage Jess to do likewise. But deep down in my heart, I knew it was all over. That was not the outcome I wanted but I was familiar with the rollercoaster. Nevertheless, I buckled my seatbelt, hung on, and waited to see how it would unfold this time.

I called Jess later. We talked about the report; it was light.

"What does this mean for us?" she asked, anxiously.

"We'll be fine, dear. Let's pray in the meantime," I told her. I didn't let it weigh down the conversation.

"You're my breath of fresh air, Toyo. If you feel the same, let's make it work," she said, her voice chimed with real warmth and emotion.

"Thanks, dear, I do. You're everything I want in a woman and more. So, yeah, I'm open-minded to make it work. Let's pray in the meantime."

We agreed to meet up for dinner the following Saturday to talk face to face.

In the end, we reviewed the options again. This time, we talked about it seriously, went over the pros and cons. We continued to see each other for about a month while waiting to hear God's mind on the matter. Finally, we opted for one of the options.

I'm so sorry, Toyo. I find all the options very hard and my parents are not helping matters, advising me to let go. This is the safest but also the hardest. Let's summon courage for the toughest decision now; let's take a walk. It hurt so badly, I can tell you. Jess texted.

Reality had unleashed its ugly head again.

Have you ever been to a wedding reception and you only managed tasting the wedding cake, not the happy meal? And it wasn't like you arrived late. Everyone enjoyed a three-course meal but you. Yet you were starving. That was the best way to sum it up.

THIRTY-TWO

Accra, Ghana, January 2018

I KNELT NEXT to the bed in my hotel room, drained of energy, overwhelmed with epitome of exhaustion as I said my prayers quietly. My throat was clogged with words as I wished for luck in this new city. I had arrived in Accra two days ago. My current client was based in Ghana with operations across the sub-Saharan Africa where international businesses had profilerated in the last few years and I would be working here for the next six months. Moments later, I dragged myself off the floor and headed to the shower, ready to start afresh.

I needed to get away from London and the opportunity came at the right time. Lagos is less than an hour by flight. I was pleased to be closer to home. Also, in my local church in London, I had become the longest member in the Single Ministry. Leaving that, too, behind for someone else to take the spot counted for something.

At the press of a tap button, the water flowed, my toes

flinching in the bathtub, my mouth shouting songs of new beginnings. I poured the lemon verbena shampoo on my head, bathing, washing off all bad luck, if I had any, beseeching God for my genotype to change. The water poured down on my body softly, massaging pain out of my muscles, refreshing my thoughts, and its steamy sensation began to calm me, slowly, in steamy rivulets.

I regulated the hot water halfway to make it colder, and controlled the shower heads, the massage options that produced a spa-like effect, as the water circulated all over my body. I reached for the calming scents and poured all the lavender oil on my head, shutting out whatever upthrusted in my eyes – tear or water. I began to scrub, harsh and in pain, every part of my skin, from head to toe, as though I was desperate to rip the skin off. I questioned God in silence. *Why?* The wailing continued until the bitterness of the silence spilled on my tongue. I did not realise the moment when I'd shouted the word so loud, so intense, at the highest pitch of my voice, like a violence in the air, that the force could have broken the wall of a prison, any prison. One word. One thunderous shout. And I was calmed. The breathing eased and soothed. The shower took the pain out of my head and left it on my feet. I wailed in sorrow as the shower's steaminess released the oil all over my body.

Maybe if I stayed long enough in the shower, pouring my heart out to God in my nakedness, maybe He would answer. Maybe He would hear my inner cry. I crouched down in the tub, sliding as the water cascaded on my head, easing and softening my worries, my pains, my anger. My phone had beeped thrice in the last hour. I kept staring at the white-panelled wall, the mosaic tiles, then my mind swirled, rescuing the shredded thoughts; it flashed back and painted me the pictures of my struggles at Edinburgh, reminding me of how God came through for me. Each time this happened, the flashback of Edinburgh days, I always returned to my knees in gratitude. Half an hour later, something brought a chill to my skin at the thought of counting my blessings. As if by magic, I snapped out of my worries and allowed songs of thanksgiving to fill my mouth, as I came out of the shower and dressed. I put on joggers with a tight-fitting T-shirt, ready to hit the streets of Accra to socialise.

I scanned through my text messages. I got one each from Mum, Tamilore and Matthew. I hurriedly opened Mum's. She'd never sent me a text before. *I hope you're enjoying Accra. It's well with you, son. Always remember God answers prayers. Soon, you will find the bone of your bone and the flesh of your flesh.*

I smiled and then sighed deeply after I'd read it in her soothing tone. *Amen, amen, amen,* I replied, the same way I would have answered on the phone.

I turned to Matthew's. *In life, there can be no sunshine without a little rain. Without the rain, we may never feel thankful for the warmth of the sun. Stay strong, bro. Love will find you someday soon.* The couple had just returned from their honeymoon at a luxurious safari camp in Nairobi.

Then, I breathed deeply, multiple scenarios running over my head as I slowly opened Tamilore's message. *HNY, Toyo! I'll be at yours by weekend. PLEASE don't say no!*

I sighed. *Hell no! I'm already done with you.* That would have been a perfect reply, but I politely composed a message, *Happy New Year, Tamilore. It's lovely hearing from you. No need coming to Accra though. Maybe I'd see you sometime when in Lagos.*

Air was forced out from my lungs as I clicked *send.* I was ready to head out, determined to start afresh. Seconds later, my phone started vibrating. I ignored the call. The vibration again. I didn't have to check the caller; I knew who was calling. I waited for the call to ring out while I processed my thoughts, set my clogged mind free. I'd made up my mind.

After five missed calls, I got a text message. *Everyday, I wished I'd done things differently. I really want you to know that I LOVE YOU WITH MY WHOLE HEART.*

I did not bat an eye. I headed to the city of Accra for my first beer. Alone.

———

Two LONG DAYS passed without communication. Fresh air had cleared my head. I'd composed many versions of "Yes, you're right!" but I deleted them all. I knew she'd decided on something, perhaps one of the options. Perhaps more than one of the options. Who knows?

My anxiety, my worries, my fear – everything – bled into resolve. Half expected, half hoped, I called Matthew, wanting to know if he knew anything to warrant Tamilore's message. He answered after the first ring. "Mr. Tender. Latest hubby in town. What's good, bro?"

"The Mayor of London. The Son of Egbaland..." His laughter interrupted the flow.

I laughed. "How was your trip, man?"

"Ah, man, we'd a superb time. Perhaps the best holiday ever. We need to catch up. Kenya is truly amazing, bro. Definitely more than a safari destination."

I smiled. "Indeed. You couldn't have said it better. How's Tara doing?"

"Toyosi, you won't believe this. Tami was constantly texting Tara during our honeymoon, asking if you were really into Jess.

She's even been stalking you on blogs to see if you've posted anything about your relationship. I slipped about what happened. I asked Tara not to tell her sister, but I baited too late. Tami's crazily in love with you, bro. Thank your stars you picked her at the wedding, otherwise you'd have killed someone by now."

I laughed. "But there's no outlet for it, still. She's coming to Accra next weekend, she says. She's not shooting any film here, I believe. Anything new? Has she changed her mind?"

"I need to keep you up to date on what's going on. You know Tara specialises in Genetic Complexity. Tami's been asking her lot of questions; she's considering settling for one of the options. It's been very tough on her. Really, really tough. Now, she doesn't know if you guys would sync on the *only* option she preferred. Tara won't tell me."

"You mean one of the options to avoid having a child with sickle cell?"

"Yes," he said, lowering his voice, more like whispering. "A day before the wedding, Tara told me Tami couldn't sleep because of you; because you told her at the church rehearsal how happy and in love you were dating Jess. That triggered jealousy. I think it was such a memorable night that she forgot about her uncle who was dead and gone, allowing the living to live. Your *argument* in London couldn't make her forget, your romance with Jess did."

I laughed. "OK, I give up. There was no *argument*, you *stooopid* man."

He laughed. "I'm super proud of you. Now, you've won halfway, if she comes to Accra, make sure you have another *argument*. That's the freaking third golden rule. I know you gonna say nah and some shit, but you need *the stamp*. The combination of the romance plus *argument* will seal the deal. It always does. It's never a false start. You hear me?"

We laughed, so loudly.

With no response, he knew where I stood. He knew under no circumstances would I intentionally take his preposterous suggestion seriously. The laughter must have woken Tara up. "Speak later, bro," he said, as he hung up the phone.

Meanwhile, last night, I saw Tamilore in my dream. It was blurring, I had not given it much thought, but now, I rolled onto the bed, eyes facing the ceiling, both hands supporting my head, scratching it to roll back the tapes. Moment later, the short images came back, crystal clear. Tamilore and I were on a boat, painted in stripes of blue, on a lake. I could not tell which city it was, but the white cross in the centre of the square red flag, flying beautifully, suggested we were somewhere in Switzerland. Maybe Lake Zurich. We wore life jackets, held hands and were staring at the beautiful lights sparkling and dancing on the lake front. The boat was yet to leave the shore. Then, it suddenly began drifting away and tumbling. Tamilore recoiled in fright, as I struggled to control the boat against the howling wind and tried refocusing my mind, choking fearfully with mud. Her arms were paddling while my heart was pounding. Then, as if by divine intervention, Dayo ran towards us from a dirty puddle nearby and swam through the waves, helping to guide the boat to safety.

While in the shower, I remembered a voice kept banging in my head, telling me to reconcile with Dayo; that the prayers were already answered. This was no ordinary voice. If I remember correctly, this was the second time I'd ever experienced it. The last time a voice spoke to me this clearly, was at the Niddrie House Park in Edinburgh during the church service when I had testified against all odds. I knew better; there was no need for further hesitation.

I hurriedly reached for my phone and began scrolling through the contacts. I shouldn't have deleted Dayo's number. I checked call logs and text messages and dialled him, looking anxiously on the phone, as if my life depended on the call. He picked up after the first ring.

"Toyo Toyo! For you to have called me today, I bet God is at work," he said, laughing.

Literarily.

"God is truly at work," I replied, laughing. "Happy New Year."

His laughter was consumed by the loud noise of what sounded like a train wheeling on the tracks. "Same here, bro. I'm so happy to hear from you. Where are you? Brown was saying you were considering a relocation to somewhere in Africa."

"I'm on assignment in Ghana now. I needed to escape London's flurry of snow and cold this year. How are you holding up?" I asked light-heartedly.

"Toyosi, I know I messed up. Big time. Please forgive. I've texted Debby, asking for forgiveness, too. You won't believe this; I attended the Holy Ghost Congress last weekend, and I've turned a new leaf. It's the hundredth time, I know. But I'll hold firmly this time." I hoped he did but from his over paced tone, I could tell insincerity lurked beneath his words.

I could hear the train chugging; the whistling sound echoed loudly in my phone. "I'm pleased to hear, Dayo. *See*, I don't mean all the ranting messages I sent you after the wedding. Let's put the past where it belongs. My apologies if I crossed the line."

"No, no. You didn't," he said. "Congratulations on your new assignment. Make the best of Accra. I heard it's a lovely city. My last girlfriend was from Kumasi. She's the babe that arrested my heart to Christ. I felt terribly guilty after what I did to her."

"Oh, really? How? What did you do?" I asked.

He sounded like he breathed in, then out, as if what was to be said needed his stuttered breath. "Toyo, the babe is AS. She gave me the hardest time. Three months chase, no *cookies*. Oh... pardon me for using that word. It takes some time, isn't it? I'm really getting better. She'd some strange ninety days rule. You know one of those babes who had read too much of Steve Harvey's book? Anyway, I played the *old* game to fast track the process."

"The *old* game? What's that?"

"Bro, *chai*. You haven't heard the coded *old* game? You're too soft. Yes, I claimed AA. And played every card right. Got her a promise ring. Wedding talk was smooth. When I pulled out after I got what I wanted, I told her I was AS. Some testing error shit talk."

"Ah, Dayo..."

He interrupted my rising voice. "*See*, I wasn't the one who invented the best way to break up with babes without drama. Some guys have been using this method since the Stone Age. And I kid you not, I've seen women use genotype as a falsehood weapon, too."

"Dayo! You're so heartless, *sha*..." I quickly cautioned my tongue, remembering it was a reconciliation call. "Did you then apologise, and are you guys together now?"

"It's all in the past. At least she led me to Christ in the end. I'll do the genotype test soon. Never done it before. My train heading underground now, losing signal..."

"OK, thanks Dayo. We'll speak sometime. Cheers, bro."

"Cheers brother," he said, as we lost signal.

The old game. I moved to the balcony, open-mouthed, as I stared across the shore of the private hotel lodge. I stood a little longer, in the company of the fresh blowing breeze, surrounded by stunning architectural buildings. I'd been told Trasacco Valley was a spinner on Accra's hallmark of affluence. It was indeed. I dug deeper into my thoughts as I stared across the green neighbourhood. It was quiet except for the sound and whisper of the moving trees, the rustle and shuffle of the leaves. *Testing error?* I relived my thought yet again, as if I was testing the importance of the words. *What if Tamilore's ex had played the same game? What if he doesn't even know his genotype? Tamilore is AS, after all.*

I pondered on it.

No, no, he never gave her such excuse as Dayo's. I relented. Besides, what did I stand to gain from knowing why her ex pulled the trigger? So, I dropped the thoughts.

Moment later, *oh... oh... oh... hang on.* I pressed my palm tightly to my forehead.

A player could manipulate *his own* genotype report, if any, as a weapon to quit. What if the reverse was the case? What if a player twists the game to achieve the same outcome, the same incompatibility result? What if a player manipulates *not his own* report, but *hers?*

Damn. It was as if I'd stumbled on gold, something that would pave way for a future without fear. I scratched my head, left the balcony and sat in the living room. I began to analyse many possible scenarios, trying to solve this puzzle and understand the connection, if any. Has Dayo given me a clue to solve a misery? My eyes darted across the room. They caught the painting on the wall, a good resemblance to the one in my living space, in the empty flat I left behind in London. An extraordinary painting of an African couple, young and fragile, in the conquest of life. Classic, heart-warming vignette of a beautiful love story. It soothed my soul. I looked from the painting to the TV screen mounted on the wall. My eyes wandered around the floor, the contemporary parquet floor that lightened the space like an autumn garden. Everything was new and fresh, except there were no plants, no bookshelf.

Two hours later, I dialled Tamilore to a video call on WhatsApp. Time to let go of my ego!

She picked after the first ring. "Heyy, hey. See who's calling." She poked her tongue out. "I thought you wouldn't reply, let alone call." She was smiling now, as she walked into another room. Her floral jumpsuit matched the shades of the morning sunlight streaming through my window. "Just two seconds, I'm trying to find a quiet place. How are you?"

"Tamilore, I'm sorry I..."

"Shhhhh. We're both sorry." She interrupted me.

Our giggles dissolved the tension. Then, we exchanged new year greetings.

"OK, cool. You're looking lovely by the way." I teased, "How's Lag?"

The door was shut behind her. Then, she sat on a bed, rested her back comfortably against the wall, well supported by some comfy pillows and positioned the camera better. "Lag is nice. You came home for New Year celebrations and couldn't say hello. I'll let you explain yourself later," she said, with a smile on her face. "How are you finding Accra?"

I smiled and skipped the first part of the question. "Lovely city, you know. The people are warm and welcoming, just like back home. I arrived here from Lagos two days ago. Work begins next week, so I'll be using this weekend to get familiar with the new city."

She held her pillowcase tighter, snuggling up under the duvet. It appears she knew I'd called for a reason, an important reason, so she waited for me to talk.

I got straight into it. "Tamilore, if you don't mind, can I ask you a question about your ex? I hope it won't upset you bringing him up."

"Are you working for the FBI, now?" she asked, smiling broadly. "Yes, go ahead."

"You told me he worked in a hospital, right?"

"Yes." She nodded. "Maybe he still does, who cares?"

"And when you re-tested for the sickle cell trait in Atlanta, it was at his hospital?"

"Yes. Any problem? Toyosi, you're speaking in parables."

"There's no issue at all. Please remind me how you got your test result?"

She pressed her fingers to her head for a moment. "He gave me the result. He brought it to the house."

I adjusted my seating position better. "And did you confirm the result? I mean did you call the centre to verify. Did you receive the testing card?"

The camera spinned. "Toyosi, you're freaking me out. Why all these questions?"

I sighed. "I'll tell you my thought process in a sec. There's a game some of these bad players play and I just wanted to be sure."

"Sure, of what? And why?" she asked. Her face stamped with a mixture of curiosity and fear. "I'm not answering any more questions unless you tell me what's going on."

I gulped. "Tamilore. There's a chance he may not be AS, as he claimed."

She sat upright. "He's in the past. How does this matter anyway? Even if he is AA, how does this matter? I don't understand your logic," she said, panic in her voice.

I let out a drawn-out sign to relieve the doubts spinning over my head. I sat there silent, thinking maybe I'd been over analytical; maybe none of this mattered. Maybe the dream held no significance after all. Maybe Dayo had no freaking role in any of this.

"Toyosi, he showed me *his* test report and card. He's definitely AS."

Her softer voice was helpful, so I cracked on. "In that case, there's also a chance *you may not* be AS. I'm not saying you're not, but there's a chance." I told her, and to unravel the misery, I re-paraphrased my previous question. "Did he show you *your* test card?"

"No. There was no card. Just a printed test report."

"Did you call the hospital to confirm?" I asked again.

She shook her head and whimpered. "No."

"You said he wanted to quit on the spot when he brought you the test result, right?" I asked, anxiously. "It raises some suspicion, you know. And you had previously tested AA in Lagos. What if he fabricated the test report to create a legitimate scenario to quit?"

"What's your rationale for this theory, Toyosi? And why are you asking now? Yes, it bothered him seriously, in a way I'd not imagined. He wanted to end the relationship the same night. I was so bothered. But wait. Fabricated the report? How?"

"I had a dream last night. And somehow, I'm learning a little more about players. I'm trying to connect the dots. Maybe there's a dot to connect, maybe not. Maybe none of this makes sense. Just following a lead in my spirit. There's nothing to lose by finding out."

"A dream? About me and my ex?" Tamilore pressed on for clarity.

"I'll tell you all about it, I promise. But please, do me a huge favour. Please re-test."

"Toyosi, I've tested twice already, I don't think I need another one. I know you really want this to work. I do, too. And I'm not even going to pretend. I'm tired of pretending. This is a New Year; I want to get things straight and right. I'm so sorry for how I've handled things in the past. Please forgive me. I should have done better. Taken a firmer decision. At least I should have returned your calls and messages prior to the wedding. But I needed that phase of my life, to heal from all the pains of the past. We're both AS. Let's just deal with it."

She paused. For the few seconds, a hush fell over us. I stared, processing the words she'd said wistfully. She brushed her double-twisted ponytail. "I've now made up my mind on *one* of the options. But I wanted us to discuss it, face to face, that's why I was thinking of coming over to Accra. It's a serious conversation and I don't want to have it on the phone."

"OK, I can understand," I said, with a half-smile.

She paused again, staring, moving her lips with no sound, as if she was considering what to say next. Her ponytail swung. "If we can agree on this *one option*, the rest is history."

My eyes widened with anxiety, fear ruffling my stomach in tense cramps. I narrowed my eyes to ease the consternation, but the fright persisted. I was flexible with *all the options but one.* For now, like Tamilore, I would keep that to myself. "OK," I muttered courageously, with a smile, the slanted smile, projecting my face, arms, body – everything – calmly, silencing every tingling that wasn't mine to keep. I broke the long pause and swallowed the anxiety. "Let's talk about it when you're comfortable," I said, trying to hide my anticipation.

"I think I'll call the hospital in Atlanta directly first thing on Monday to confirm."

"Perfect. That's even better."

Sudden wave of happiness pelted my soul, but in brief flashes.

She pulled the duvet on her lap. "Hmm. Is this why you called?"

I smiled, took a deep breath before answering. "Nah, just to see your dimples."

"Joker."

I ran my palm over my hair, "See you next weekend, yeah?"

As I had expected, her trademark dimples were flashed over the camera, as she held it closer to her face, speaking in her soft voice. "No, I'm not moving an inch, until you tell me when you started working for the FBI. Start speaking, I want to hear all about the dream."

THIRTY-THREE

THE PAST WEEK was the longest in history; each day crawled like a snail living its shell. It was Saturday morning and Tamilore would be flying into Accra that evening. We'd spoken each day since last week, kept sleep at bay, burnt call credits at midnight hours, flirting. We'd also discussed important issues, the beginning of our future if we had one. She'd not told me the outcome of her enquiry from the hospital and for once, the suspense was very comforting.

"My flight arrives at 6.p.m local time," Tamilore said, blushing. We'd been on video call for about two minutes. "Anything in particular you'd like me to bring from Lagos?"

With so much air of eagerness, I smiled, a smile that lit my eyes and spread happiness all over my body. "Just bring the good news. I'll be at the airport waiting to receive it."

She laughed, leaning against the back of a brownish sofa, adjusting her grey oversized T-shirt and cycling shorts. "You still won't believe me. The hospital is yet to tell me anything. You know the confidentiality stuff, especially on health-related matters. I've asked the letter to be sent to my Houston home address and Mum is keeping an eye open for it." Her mouth twitched as she spoke; her body language had failed her as she tried too hard not to smile.

"OK, no worries." I said, smiling, as I waved it off with high hopes. "Anyway, I got us tickets to experience part of the Akwasidae Cultural festival."

"Brilliant. That's so cool. They do it every six weeks, don't they?"

"Yes, they do. The next one is this Sunday. I've been told we're in for a special treat. I heard Kente dance groups in their cultural gold trinkets are intriguing."

"I'm looking forward to it. That should be lot of fun. We've showcased Akwasidae on our show before. Also, the traditional festivals like Homowo, the colourful harvest of food."

"Awesome." I said, with a warm smile, keeping the other itinerary a suspense.

"See you in a few hours," she said, soothingly.

"Have a safe flight," I told her, as we hung up the call.

I walked to the balcony, hands shoved in my pocket, looking across the city of Accra as far as my eyes could see, relishing in the thought of hope that tonight could be the beginning of great things to come. All tension coiling around my lungs lost in the fresh air blowing my way. No nerves shredded me from the inside. No black placard of fear planted in my heart. No anxiety in my blood either, I was as calm as a millpond. A flock of birds, lemon doves, screeched and took off from the treetops nearby, swooping. I watched and listened to the soft ringdoves, the cooing sounds they make in their triumphant sync-flying display, as if nature had a blossom message to deliver, a message of peace, the deepest kind, and of love. The silver-white sky was domed and dapped by the cloud; everything promised a great day.

Half an hour later, Matthew dialled me on a video call.

Melodious afrobeat blasting in the background. "Mate, how do you prefer to receive the news: over the phone or in person?"

"Mr. Tender, you better spill whatever you know now before I break your head."

"Congratulations bro. Your babe is AA."

I got up from my seat, like something shook me and screamed from the depth of my belly. "Yessssssssssssssssssss. Yessss. Oh yesssssssssssss. I suspected it. When did you get the gist? Please spill the full story." The same way sunrise heralds the beginning of a new day, happiness began overflowing inside me, shining brightly, soaking right into my bones.

"Tami got the news from her mum on Wednesday. I overheard the conversation with Tara. Tami was telling Tara about a letter their mum opened from a hospital in Atlanta. I know Tara is trying to keep the secret because she's not saying anything. What's going on? She couldn't have possibly re-tested in Atlanta while in Lagos."

"It's a long story, bro. You're not up to date. The bottom line is that she called the hospital to verify the result of her previous test. Apparently, her ex had played her a game. That's a gist for later, not now. I'll give you the details. So, what happened next?"

"Wow. They were giggling like folks in a celebratory mood. Since I didn't hear anything from you, I guessed you've been in the dark."

"We spoke longer that Wednesday night. Same thing on Thursday and last night. I suspected the great news, but she was keeping the suspense till she gets here, I believe."

"I hope I didn't spoil the suspense game. Tami is the happiest woman in the world right now. So, you've got to be at the airport, waiting for her as the happiest man."

I smiled and clasped my arms in appreciation. "No, you did well. She arrives in a few hours. Can't wait."

"Well, you know how we do. You don't know anything until she tells you."

"Sure," I said. "Mr. Tender, I owe you a beer for stretching your long ears."

His face brightened with laughter. "Get out of here. I'm so happy for you, bro. Let me know how it goes. This deserves a big celebration, you know."

"Big one indeed." I grinned.

"Maybe a group holiday. Let's figure something out. Congrats, bro."

"Holla you later. Thanks, bro," I said, as I ended the call.

This latest news of genotype was the springboard upon my life; I felt something new. Joy flowed through my veins like living waters. I sat on the sofa in the living space, happiness shimmering inside me. When my eyes caught the expressionist painting again, the stunning Gouache painting of the African couple, I relished in the timeline story told, steered across the forty inches rectangular art, slowly from the left, the portraits of the couple's early days' struggles, to the far right under coconut trees where the couple kissed at sunset.

Oluwatamilore! (*God's gift to me!*)

Thank you, Lord, I murmured in silent appreciation, blinked a tear, before I got on my knees and said a few carabos. Then, I turned to YouTube and let Frank Edwards latest hit, *Under the Canopy* take hold of my brain. I danced and danced and danced.

Soon after, I began scrubbing the hotel room especially the muck on the kitchenette floor. Standard, isn't it? As happy as a rabbit in the carrot field, I spent the next hour in the shower, grabbed the shower head like a microphone, and sang so badly doing karaoke like a man who's hit the jackpot. "Ain't no stopping us now." Thanks to McFadden and Whitehead.

By 5.p.m, I'd arrived at Accra's Kotoka International

Airport in my white smoothly ironed, camp-collar T-shirt and blue jeans. The cloth sat flat against my skin. My Nike Jordan Jumpman shoes gave me double inches to the tall frame. The new bold fragrance smelled just right; not the barbecue scent I had worn throughout the week that cuddled me like a cloud. The terminal was under major re-construction, to mirror airport hubs around the globe. Still, the air conditioner blasted the heatwave off the tarmac. I walked towards the Arrivals pick-up point where the crowds were building up in their colourful rainbows. I stood at the centre, not to be missed, longing like a man waiting for his bride to walk down the aisle.

Oh, what a feeling of bliss!

It wasn't so long before the magic happened. I turned around and saw people coming from the arrival exit with their suitcases as the hinges creaked and the wheels rattled, not letting the overzealous folks driving luggage carts like motorcade distracted me. My eyes caught Tamilore in her stylish casual outfit and matching heels: black jeans, cute white top. The scene became as serene as ever, as if this moment was destined to happen again in an airport. Unlike that moment when our eyes first met at the Muritala International Airport nearly thirteen months ago, my heart was pumping with laughter today, not flinching in trepidation, as I watched her approach the waiting crowd from about forty metres away.

Her big smile grew so beautifully, as she saw me at twenty metres or so. I could not tell who closed the gap quicker, as we walked hurriedly and scampered through the crowd towards each other. I stretched my arms wide as she wrapped herself around me and clenched her arms around my neck, warmly and tightly. We held on to the hug. And held it a little longer as if she was saying I'd never let you go again. Her body melting to mine, as the crowd stared in our direction. The fast thud of her heart was beating drums to mine.

She adjusted her long alluring hair, loose in ringlets. "Too many eyes on us, Toyosi," she said, smiling, trying to walk me away from the centre of attention.

"I know you're shy, aren't you?" I whispered, laughing.

"No, I'm not," she said, laughing, as her hand glided down my arm.

I reached for her luggage and we began walking towards the exit. "You smell so lovely," I told her.

"Thanks." She wrapped her arm closely over my hand. "Hmm. I can see someone has been going to the gym," she said, mocking my eyes.

"In the last two hours, yes."

She laughed, using one hand to dress her natural hair that looked more stunning than ever.

"How was your flight?"

"It was great. Good to be back in Accra. It's been three years. The airport is changing."

"This airport will be one of the flagships in West Africa when it's completed."

The sunset had tinted the sky a rose hue as we stepped outside the gate. Nature delivered on its promises. She held onto my hand as the Uber driver approached to help with the luggage. I recognised her mischievous smile when she locked her eyes to mine. "Hmm. Toyosi, tell me, you already know something, don't you?" she asked with a smirk.

I opened the door for her. And took my seat next to her on the other side. The car prepared to drive forward. It felt like a great journey was about to begin. The journey of our lives, of discovery, of dreams, of hope, of fulfilment and many more. She kept searching my eyes for clues. Our dimples synchronised and revealed what we already knew. I rubbed my palms warmly on hers ready to tease again. "You mean about you coming over to Accra?"

She pinched me before she laced her fingers with mine, smiling, as she rested her head to my chest. "Plenty gist to tell you, babe," she said.

Lord is Listening To Ya, Hallelujah by Carla Bley was the soft jazz oozing from the driver's playlist. He switched to a beautiful old classic jazz by Kenny G – *Forever in Love.* Oh! The flawless rhymes of the baritone saxophonist, the perfection of it, dazzled me.

She was ticklish in my arms. She banged my chest gently, and this time, when our lips met and covered each other, it was predated with smiles, not tears. And the man at the wheel giggled, as if to say, "Congratulations, bro."

ACKNOWLEDGMENTS

Mama doesn't read big grammar, so I'll keep it simple. Thank you, Mum, for all your sacrifices, your love. From the beautiful hills of Ilaro, I'm so proud of how far we've come.

To my US editor, Kristen Weber of Kevin Anderson & Associates, and UK editor, Debbie A, I'm thankful to you both.

Lezanne Clannachan of Cornerstone Literacy Consultancy, thank you for the mentoring hours. Natalie Young, Cate Hogan, Femi Adedoyin, Abi Dare, Gale Winskill, Jane Ighalo, your suggestions - even with sample read - were so valuable.

To my beta readers, Joan Embola, Kristyn Fortner, Ljubica Stamenkovska, Serena Kohar, Beatrix Sasvari, Lwandlekazi Masule, Kat Pierce – thank you so much for reading the manuscript in full and for your feedback. Lucy Raposo, Graydon House Books, thank you for the kind words.

To friends, family and colleagues always longing to see what I've been cooking, all the cheerleaders, you guys are amazing.

Omowumi, my precious wife, thank you for our happy ending babe. Looking forward to telling our kids our own beautiful love story - how one of us boldly shot a shoot at first glance and how the other discreetly shot a missile at second glance.

All thanks to God for helping me through this journey of turning a nightly hobby into a printed debut.

ABOUT THE AUTHOR

Kolapo Akinola is a data scientist, working for a global technology consulting firm in London. He writes leisurely at night. Born and bred in Ilaro, a small town in Western Nigeria, Kolapo enjoys chasing sunrise and sunset around the globe and while at it, he collaborates with NGOs to promote awareness of sickle cell in the UK and West Africa. The Bachelor's Ride is his first novel.

instagram.com/letsgiveloveachance